PRAISE FOR JENNIFER CRUSIE AND HER NOVELS

Fast Women

"Sheer reading enjoyment . . . hilariously funny."
—*Library Journal*

"A fast and funny read!"
—*Woman's Own*

"Move over, Susan Isaacs. Crusie is just as smart and sassy about the things a woman has to do to make love work, and a lot funnier to boot."
—*Kirkus Reviews*

"A detective agency may be a sure setting for mystery and adventure, but in Crusie's latest, a likable cast of characters also finds sex, love, and empowerment. . . . The novel's provocative title says too little about this entertaining romantic caper which will satisfy fans and new readers alike."
—*Publishers Weekly*

"Hilarious . . . Crusie's great gift is her ability to make readers laugh at the inanities of life with her spunky women and strong yet compassionate men: imagine a combination of Nick Charles from *The Thin Man* and the women of *The First Wives Club*."
—*Booklist*

"With humor, irony, and a whole lot of wit, Jennifer Crusie straps in her readers and takes them on a memorable ride . . . a masterful storyteller."
—*Romantic Times*

Turn the page for more acclaim . . .

"*Fast Women* is her best work to date . . . a spectacular read you will no doubt savor more than once."

— newandusedbooks.com

"An extraordinary romantic comedy . . . fascinating . . . hilarious situations, strong characters, and a powerful message." —*The Belles and Beaux of Romance*

"Wise and witty." —theromancereader.com

"Absolutely hilarious . . . dialogue is witty and fast-paced . . . one of those stories you can read over and over without it getting stale." —*Affaire de Coeur*

"Perfect entertainment for a lazy summer afternoon."

—modemag.com

Welcome to Temptation

"Crusie charms with her brisk, edgy style . . . a romantic comedy that adds luster to the genre, this effervescent tale will please readers." —*Publishers Weekly* (starred review)

"Bright, funny, sexy, and wise."

—*Kirkus Reviews*

"Crusie blends a combination of likeable characters, gossipy small-town life, and a plot spiced with some steamy sexual situations into a highly entertaining read."

—*Library Journal*

"Funny and inventive, this is sure to please Crusie's enthusiastic fans and attract new converts."

—*Booklist*

"An updated, rollicking version of *Peyton Place* . . . Crusie infuses a great deal of humor about human nature into this contemporary romance, deploying as well an engaging cast of characters."
—*Publishers Weekly*

"A sexy, humorous romp with complex relationships and entertaining characters."
—*Rendezvous*

"Funny and entertaining, Crusie's novel presents a lively cast and an exciting conclusion."
—*Booklist*

"Romance has a new star in Crusie . . . one of the few in the genre who can make you laugh out loud."
—*Kirkus Reviews*

"Hold onto your seat for a hysterical look at relationships . . . Crusie has you laughing and crying as these special people struggle to find that elusive something within themselves."
—*Old Book Barn Gazette*

Tell Me Lies

"Jennifer Crusie presents a humorous mixture of romance, mystery, and mayhem. A winner!"
—Susan Elizabeth Phillips

"A ferociously funny, sexy read."
—*Redbook*

"Smart, sexy, romantic suspense."
—*Minneapolis Star Tribune*

"Lovers of Susan Isaacs' mysteries take heart: there's a new author on the block!"
—*Woman's Own*

Fast Women

Jennifer Crusie

St. Martin's Paperbacks

This is a work of fiction. All of the characters, organizations, and events portrayed in this novel are either products of the author's imagination or are used fictitiously.

FAST WOMEN

Copyright © 2001 by Jennifer Crusie Smith.
Excerpt from *Bet Me* copyright © 2004 by Jennifer Crusie Smith.

For information address St. Martin's Press, 175 Fifth Avenue, New York, NY 10010.

ISBN: 0-312-35709-5
EAN: 80312-35709-2

Printed in the United States of America

St. Martin's Press hardcover edition / May 2001
St. Martin's Paperbacks edition / April 2002

St. Martin's Paperbacks are published by St. Martin's Press, 175 Fifth Avenue, New York, NY 10010.

20   19   18   17   16   15   14   13

My Thanks To

Clarice Cliff, Susie Cooper, and the *Walking Ware Designers*
for designing pottery that amazes
and delights me every time I see it.

eBay
for having everything in the universe for sale sooner or later,
thereby making research much more fun than it used to be.

Abigail Trafford
for writing *Crazy Time,*
her brilliant, compassionate study of divorce and recovery.

*Jennifer Greene, Cathie Linz, Lindsay Longford,
Susan Elizabeth Phillips,* and *Suzette Vann*
for listening to me plot my books every spring without
snickering and for being the only reason to ever fly into
O'Hare.

Patricia Gaffney and *Judith Ivory*
for perfecting the art of friendship and the craft of
unconditional cheerleading, and for putting up with an
inordinate amount of e-whining and cyber-moaning.

Jen Enderlin
for being once again an editor whose intelligence, insight,
empathy, enthusiasm, and saint-like patience
make it possible for me to write without drink or drugs,
although not without chocolate and french fries with vinegar.

And *Meg Ruley*
for protecting me from everything, including myself, and for
negotiating a damn fine contract while she's at it.

Without the help of these fine people,
I couldn't have written this book, nor would I have wanted to.

Chapter One

The man behind the cluttered desk looked like the devil, and Nell Dysart figured that was par for her course since she'd been going to hell for a year and a half anyway. Meeting Gabriel McKenna just meant she'd arrived.

"Yes, I think you better to look into that," he said into the phone with barely disguised impatience, his sharp eyes telegraphing his annoyance.

It was rude to talk on the phone in front of her, but he didn't have a secretary to answer the phone for him, and she was a job applicant not a client, and he was a detective not an insurance salesman, so maybe the regular rules of social intercourse didn't apply.

"I'll come up on Monday," he said. "No, Trevor, waiting would not be better. I'll talk to all of you at eleven."

He sounded as if he were talking to a fractious uncle, not a client. The detective business must be a lot better than this place looked if he could dictate to clients like that, especially clients named Trevor. The only Trevor Nell knew was her sister-in-law's father, and he was richer than God, so maybe Gabe McKenna was really powerful and successful and just needed somebody to manage his office back into shape. She could do that.

Nell looked around the shabby room and tried to be positive, but the place was gloomy in the September afternoon light, even gloomier because the ancient blinds on the equally ancient big windows were pulled down. The McKenna Building stood on the corner of two of the city's prettier thoroughfares in German Village, a district where people paid big bucks to look out their windows at historic Ohio brick streets and architecture, but Gabriel McKenna pulled his blinds, probably so he couldn't see the mess inside. The walls were covered with dusty framed black- and-white photos, the furniture needed to be cleaned and waxed, and his desk needed to be plowed. She'd never seen so much garbage on one surface in her life, the Styrofoam cups alone would—

"Yes," he said, his voice low and sure. The light from his green-shaded desk lamp threw shadows on his face, but with those dark eyes closed now, he didn't look nearly as satanic. More like your average, dark-haired, fortysomething businessman in a striped shirt and loosened tie. Like Tim.

Nell stood up abruptly and dropped her purse on the chair. She went to the big window to open the blinds and let in a little light. If she cleaned the place up, he could leave the blinds open to make a better impression. Clients liked doing business in the light, not in the pit of hell. She tugged once on the cord and it stuck, so she tugged again, harder, and this time it came off in her hand.

Oh, great. She looked back, but he was still on the phone, his broad shoulders hunched, so she shoved the cord onto the windowsill. It fell off onto the hardwood floor, the plastic end making a sharp, hollow sound as it hit, and she leaned into the blind-covered window to get it from behind the chair that was in the way. It was just out of her fingers' reach, another damn thing out of her reach, so she pressed harder against the blinds, stretching to touch it with her fingertips.

The window cracked under her shoulder.

"I'll see you on Monday," he said into the phone, and she kicked the cord behind the radiator and went back to sit down before he could notice that she was destroying his office around him.

Now she had to get the job so she could cover the tracks

of her vandalism. And besides, there was that desk; somebody needed to save this guy. And then there was her need for money to pay for rent and other luxuries. *Somebody needs to save me*, she thought.

He hung up the phone and turned to her, looking tired. "I apologize, Mrs. Dysart. You can see how much we need a secretary."

Nell looked at his desk and thought, *You need more than a secretary, buddy*, but she said, "Perfectly all right." She was going to be cheerful and helpful if it killed her.

He picked up her résumé. "Why did you leave your last position?"

"My boss divorced me."

"That would be a reason," he said, and began to read.

His people skills needed work, she thought as she stared down at her sensible black pumps, planted firmly on the ancient Oriental rug where they couldn't walk her into trouble again. Now if he'd been Tim, he'd have offered her sympathy, a Kleenex, a shoulder to cry on. He would have followed that up by suggesting the purchase of some insurance, but he would have been sympathetic.

There was a spot on the carpet, and she rubbed at it with the toe of her shoe, trying to blend it in. Spots made a place look unsuccessful; it was the details that counted in an office environment. She rubbed harder, and the carpet threads parted, and the spot got bigger; it wasn't a spot, she'd found a hole and had managed to shred it to double its size in under fifteen seconds. She put her foot over the hole and thought, *Take me, Jesus, take me now*.

"Why do you want to work for us?" he said, and she smiled at him, trying to look bright and eager, plus the aforementioned cheerful and helpful, which was hard since she was middle-aged and cranky.

"I think it would be interesting to work for a detective agency." *I think I need a job so I can hold onto my divorce settlement for my old age.*

"You'd be amazed how boring it is," he said. "You'll be

doing mostly typing and filing and answering phones. You're overqualified for this job."

I'm also forty-two and unemployed, she thought, but she said brightly, "I'm ready for a change."

He nodded, looking as though he wasn't buying any of it, and she wondered if he was enough like Tim that he'd recycle her in twenty years, if after the passage of time he would look at her and say, "We've grown apart. I swear I haven't been interviewing other secretaries on the side, but now I need somebody new. Somebody with real typing skills. Somebody—"

The arm of the chair wobbled under her hand, and she realized she'd been pulling up on it. *Relax*. She shoved it back down again, clamping her elbow to her side to stop the chair arm from moving any more, keeping her foot on the spot on the rug. *Just sit still*, she told herself.

Behind her, the blind rustled as it slipped a little.

"You certainly have the skills we need," McKenna said, and she forced a smile. "However, our work here is highly confidential. We have a rule: We never talk about business outside this office. Can you be discreet?"

"Certainly," Nell said, pressing harder on the chair arm as she tried to radiate discretion.

"You do understand that this is a temporary position?"

"Uh, yes," Nell lied, feeling suddenly colder. Here was her new life, just like her old life. She heard a faint *crack* from the direction of the chair arm and loosened her grip a little.

"Our receptionist is recovering from an accident and should be back in six weeks," he was saying. "So October thirteenth—"

"I'm history," Nell finished. At least he was letting her know ahead of time that the end was coming. She wouldn't get attached. She wouldn't have a son with him. She wouldn't—

The chair arm wobbled again, much looser this time, and he nodded. "If you want the job, it's yours."

The blind slipped again, a rusty, sliding sound.

"I want the job," Nell said.

He fished in his center desk drawer and handed her a key. "This will get you into the outer office on the days my partner, Riley, or I haven't opened before you get here." He stood and offered her his hand. "Welcome to McKenna Investigations, Mrs. Dysart. We'll see you Monday at nine."

Nell stood, too, releasing the chair arm gingerly in the hope that it wouldn't fall to the floor. She reached for his hand, sticking hers out forcefully to show confidence and strength, and hit one of the Styrofoam cups. Coffee spread over his papers while they both watched, their hands clasped over the carnage.

"My fault," he said, letting go of her to grab the cup. "I never remember to throw these out."

"Well, that's *my* job for the next six weeks," she said, perky as all hell. "Thank you so much, Mr. McKenna."

She gave him one last insanely positive smile and left the office before anything else could happen.

The last thing she saw as she closed the heavy door behind her was the blind slipping once, bouncing, and then crashing down, exposing the star-cracked window, brilliant in the late afternoon light.

When Eleanor Dysart was gone, Gabe looked at the broken window and sighed. He found a bottle of Bayer in his middle drawer and took two of the aspirin, washing them down with hours-old coffee that had been awful when it was hot, grimacing as somebody knocked on his office door.

His cousin Riley loomed blondly in the doorway, doing his usual impression of a half-bright halfback. "Who was the skinny redhead who just left? Cute, but if we take her case, we should feed her."

"Eleanor Dysart," Gabe said. "She's filling in for Lynnie. And she's stronger than she looks."

Riley frowned at the window as he sat down in the chair Eleanor Dysart had just vacated. "When'd the window get broken?"

"About five minutes ago. And we're hiring her, even though she's a window breaker, because she's qualified and because Jack Dysart asked us to."

Riley looked disgusted. "One of his ex-wives we don't know about?" He leaned on the chair arm, and it cracked and broke so that he had to catch himself to keep from falling through it. "What the hell?"

"Sister-in-law," Gabe said, staring sadly at the chair. "Divorced from his brother."

"Those Dysart boys are hell on wives," Riley said, picking up the chair arm from the floor.

"I mentioned to Jack that we needed a temp and he sent her over. Be nice to her. Other people haven't been." Gabe stashed his aspirin back in the drawer and picked up a coffee-soaked paper. He used another paper to blot the coffee off and held it out to Riley. "You've got the Hot Lunch on Monday."

Riley gave up on the chair arm and dropped it on the floor to take the paper. "I hate chasing cheaters."

Gabe's headache fought back against the aspirin. "If relationship investigation bothers you, you might want to rethink your career choice."

"It's the people, not the job. Like Jack Dysart. A lawyer who thinks adultery is a hobby, there's the bottom of the food chain for you. What a loser."

That's not why you hate him, Gabe thought, but it was late on Friday afternoon, and he had no interest in pursuing his cousin's old grudges. "I have to see him and Trevor Ogilvie on Monday. Both senior partners at once."

"Good for you. I hope Jack's in trouble up to his neck."

"They're being blackmailed."

"Blackmail?" Riley said, his voice full of disbelief. "Jack?

There's stuff out there that's even worse than the stuff everybody knows about him?"

"Possibly," Gabe said, thinking about Jack and his total disregard for the consequences of his actions. It was amazing what a handsome, charming, selfish, wealthy lawyer could get away with. At least, it was amazing what Jack got away with. "Jack thinks it's just a disgruntled employee trying to scare them. Trevor thinks it's a prank and if they wait a few weeks—"

Riley snorted. "There's Trevor for you. A lawyer who's made a fortune *delaying* the other side to death. Which is still better than Jack, the devious son of a bitch."

Gabe felt a spurt of irritation. "Oh, hell, Riley, give the man some credit, it's been fourteen years and he's still married to her. She cracked thirty a while back and he stuck. He may even be faithful for all we know."

Riley scowled at him. "I have no idea what you're talking about—"

"Susannah Campbell Dysart, the defining moment of your youth."

"—but if my choice is between the Hot Lunch and Jack Dysart," Riley went on, "I'll take the Hot Lunch. I was going to campus on Monday anyway; it'll be on my way."

Gabe frowned at him. "I thought you were working a background check on Monday. What are you doing on campus?"

"Having lunch," Riley said, looking innocent.

Gabe's irritation grew. Riley was thirty-four. Maturity was long overdue. "You're dating a grad student now?"

"Junior," Riley said, without guilt. "Horticulture major. Knows everything about plants. Did you realize that the coneflower—"

"So she's what, fifteen years younger than you are?"

"Thirteen," Riley said. "I'm broadening my horizons by learning about the plant world. You, on the other hand, are in such a deep rut you can't even see your horizons. Come out with us, get hooked up—"

"With an undergraduate." Gabe shook his head, disgusted. "No. I'm calling Chloe for dinner tonight. I will be hooked up."

Riley shook his head, equally disgusted. "Much as I like Chloe, sleeping with your ex-wife is not going to get you out of your rut."

"Much as sleeping with a college junior will not help you achieve adulthood," Gabe said.

"Fine, be that way." Riley stood up, affable as ever. "Give my best to Jack and the boys on Monday." He picked up the broken chair and switched it with the one by the window and then left, and Gabe began to sort through the rest of the splattered papers on his desk. As an afterthought, he picked up the phone and hit the speed dial for The Star-Struck Cup, his ex-wife's teashop. He could have walked through the door that connected the agency reception room to The Cup's storeroom and talked to his ex in the flesh, but he didn't want Chloe in the flesh at that moment, he just wanted to make sure he had access to her flesh later.

When Chloe answered, her voice bubbling over the phone, he said, "It's me."

"Good," she said, some of the bubble gone. "Listen, a woman was just in here buying almond cookies. Tall and thin. Faded red hair. Pretty eyes. Did she come from you?"

"Yes, but she's not a client so you can skip the pep talk about how I have to save her. She's Lynnie's temp replacement."

"She has an interesting look to her," Chloe said. "I bet she's a Virgo. Give me her birth date."

"No. Dinner at eight?"

"Yes, please. We need to talk. Lu thinks maybe she'd rather backpack through Europe this fall."

"Not a chance. I paid her first-quarter tuition."

"This is your daughter's life, Gabe."

"No. She's only eighteen. That's too young for Europe by herself."

"She's the same age I was when I married you," Chloe pointed out.

And look at the lousy decision you made. "Chloe, she's going to college. If she hates it after the first quarter, we'll talk."

Chloe sighed. "All right. Now about this Virgo—"

"No," Gabe said and hung up, thinking about his lovely blonde daughter making plans to backpack through faraway countries filled with predatory men while his lovely blonde ex-wife consulted the same stars that had told her to divorce him.

He reached for the aspirin again and this time he washed it down with the Glenlivet he kept stashed in his bottom drawer, just as his dad had before him. He was going to have to do something about Chloe and Lu, not to mention Jack Dysart and Trevor Ogilvie and whatever mess they'd gotten themselves and their law firm into this time. The only cheerful thing in his future was that he'd be sleeping with Chloe later. That was always nice.

Nice? He stopped. Christ, what had happened to "hot"? It couldn't be Chloe, she was the same as she'd always been.

So it's me, he thought, looking at the scotch bottle in one hand and the aspirin bottle on the desk. *I'm played out, relying on booze and drugs to get me through the day.*

Of course, it was Glenlivet and Bayer he was abusing, not Ripple and crack. His eye fell on the photograph on the wall across from him: his dad and Trevor Ogilvie, forty years before, hands clasped on each other's pinstriped shoulders, grinning at the camera, which they toasted with glasses of scotch. *A fine old tradition,* he thought and remembered his dad saying, "Trevor's a great guy, but without me, he'd ignore his problems until they blew up in his face."

You left me more than half the agency, Pop.

Not cheered by this, Gabe stashed both bottles in the desk and began to sort through the mess on his desk to find his notes. Damn good thing they had a secretary coming in on Monday. He needed somebody who would follow orders and make his life easier, the way Chloe had when she'd been his secretary. He shot an uneasy glance at the broken window. He was pretty sure Eleanor Dysart was going to make his life easier.

And if she didn't, he'd just fire her, even if she was the ex-sister-in-law of their biggest client. If there was one thing he didn't need in his life, it was more people making him crazy.

He was full up on those already.

On the other side of the village park, Nell sat at her large dining room table in her very small apartment and said, "And then as I left, the blind fell down with this *huge* crash and there was the broken window." She watched straight-faced as her sister-in-law Suze Dysart hiccuped with laughter, platinum beautiful even while gasping.

"Maybe he'll think it was somebody outside who broke it," Nell's other sister-in-law, Margie, said from beside her, her plain little face as hopeful as always over the cup of coffee Nell had just poured for her. "If you never tell him, maybe he'll never know." She took a small silver thermos out of her bag as she spoke and topped up her cup with the soy milk she carried with her.

"He's a detective," Nell said. "I hope to God he knows, or I'm working for Elmer Fudd."

"Oh, God, it's been too long since I laughed like that." Suze took a deep breath. "What are you going to do about the rug?"

"Maybe you can stick the holey part under his desk." Margie reached for an almond cookie. "If he never sees it, maybe he'll never know." She bit into the cookie and said, "I love these, but the woman who makes them is very stingy with the recipe."

"If you could make the cookies, would you buy them from her?" Suze said, and when Margie shook her head, she said, "Well, there you are." She turned back to Nell and pushed the cookie plate toward her. "Eat and tell us about it. What's the place like? What's your new *boss* like?"

"He's a slob," Nell said. "It's going to take me the entire six weeks just to clean off his desk." That was a good thought, organizing somebody's life, getting back in charge of things. *Time to get moving again*, she thought and sat still.

"Ouch." Margie looked under the table. "What did I just kick? Why are there boxes under here?"

"My china," Nell said.

"You haven't unpacked your china yet?" Margie sounded scandalized.

"She'll *get to it*." Suze sent an unmistakable *shut-up* glare Margie's way.

Margie, of course, missed it. "If she had her china out, she could look at it, and it would make her feel more set-tled."

"No, it wouldn't," Suze said, still staring at her with intent. "Mine's out and it makes me want to throw up, although that may be because I'm stuck with the butt-ugly Dysart Spode."

"I love looking at my dishes," Margie said sadly over her coffee, which was not news to the rest of the table. Margie had more Franciscan Desert Rose earthenware than any other woman on the planet.

Suze finally caught Margie's eye, and Margie straight-ened, smiling. Nell wanted to say, "Look, guys, it's all right," but then she'd just have to cope with both of them reassuring her again.

"Well, I think it's wonderful," Margie said, faux chipper. "This new job and all. You've always liked working." She sounded slightly bemused by that, as if it were a mystery to her.

"I didn't like working," Nell said. "I liked running my own business."

"Tim's business," Margie said.

"We built it together."

"Then why does he have it now?" Margie said, and Nell wished Suze would glare at Margie again.

"Well, *I'd* like working," Suze rushed in. "I don't know what I want to do, but after fourteen years of college, I must be qualified to do *something*."

Then get a job, Nell thought, impatient at hearing Suze's lament again, and then felt guilty. Suze talked about work and didn't do anything about it, but Nell hadn't done anything, either, until Jack had called about the McKennas.

Margie was still obsessing about Tim. "Tell me you at least got half of those ugly glass awards he was so proud of."

Nell kept her temper. Snarling at Margie was like kicking a puppy. "The Icicles? No. I left them with the agency. It wouldn't have been fair—"

"Don't you ever get tired of being fair?" Suze said.

Yes, Nell thought. "No," she said. "And as for the new job, all I'm going to do is answer phones and type for six weeks. It's not a career. It's like practice, just to get me started again."

"It's a detective agency," Suze said. "I thought that would be exciting. Sam Spade and Effie Perine." She sounded wistful.

"Who?" Margie said.

"A famous detective and his secretary," Suze said. "I studied them in my film noir course. I thought Sam and Effie had the best jobs. The clothes were good, too." She pushed the plate toward Nell. "Have a cookie."

Margie refocused on Nell. "Is your boss cute?"

"No." Nell stirred her coffee and thought about Gabe McKenna. It was his eyes that had made her nervous, she decided. That and the sheer weight of his presence, the threat of potential temper there. Not a man to mess with. "He's tall and solid-looking, and he frowns a lot, and his eyes are dark so it's hard to read him. He looks . . . I don't know. Annoyed. Sarcastic." She remembered him sitting behind his desk, ignoring her. "Actually, he looks like Tim."

"That doesn't sound like Tim," Margie said. "Tim's always smiling and saying nice things."

"Tim's always trying to sell insurance," Suze said. "But you're right, that doesn't sound like Tim. Don't get them confused. Tim is a loser. The new guy might be good. Anybody but Tim might be good."

Nell sighed. "Look, he was very polite, but that was it."

"Maybe he was fighting his attraction to you," Suze said. "Maybe he was distant because he didn't want to come on too strong but his heart beat faster when he saw you."

Margie shook her head. "I don't think so. Nell isn't the type to drive men crazy on first sight. Men do that for you because you're young and beautiful, so you think it's that way for everybody."

"I'm not that young," Suze said.

"He was not attracted to me," Nell said firmly. "This is a job only."

"All right," Margie said. "But you do have to start dating now. You should be married again."

Yeah, because that worked out so well the last time.

"She's right," Suze said. "You don't want to be *alone*." She said it as if it were a fate worse than death.

"Although maybe not," Margie said, staring off into space. "Come to think of it, it's the men who always want to get married. Look at Tim, marrying Whitney so soon."

Ouch, Nell thought and saw Suze swing toward Margie, ready to snarl.

"And Budge can't wait, he's driving me crazy about setting a date." Margie bit into her cookie and chewed, deep in thought. "You know, he moved in a month after Stewart left, so I never had much of a chance to look around. There might be somebody better."

Nell was so surprised she almost dropped her coffee cup.

Suze put hers down in her saucer with a loud clink.

"Marjorie Ogilvie Dysart, I am astonished at you. That man's lived with you for seven years and you're thinking about leaving him?"

"Well," Margie began.

"Go for it," Suze said. "Don't think twice. If you need help moving, I'm there."

"Or maybe I'll get a job," Margie went on. "If you like your job, Nell, maybe I'll get one. Not at the agency, though. Budge says the McKennas deal with too many low people."

"Really?" Nell said, not caring. Margie's Budge looked like the Sta-Puf Marshmallow Man and talked like a Moral Majority leader. "I'm amazed Budge lets you hang out with me, then."

Margie blinked at her. "You're not low. You're just depressed."

Suze shoved the cookie plate toward her to distract her. "Nell is not depressed. And speaking of Budge, if you're going to stay with him, would you please tell him again not to call me 'Suzie.' I've reminded him over and over and he still does it. One more time and I swear to God, I'm going to break his glasses."

"I just wonder sometimes," Margie said, not paying attention. "You know. Is this all there is?"

Nell nodded. "I used to wonder, too. Sometimes I'd look around the insurance agency and think, 'This is *the rest of my life*?' Then it turned out it wasn't. Trust me, Margie, don't push your luck."

"You didn't push your luck," Suze said. "You married the wrong guy."

"No, I didn't," Nell said. "He was the right guy for twenty-two years." She stared into her coffee cup. "It's not like he cheated—"

"Oh, for heaven's sake," Suze said. "If I hear one more time about how it's not Tim's fault because he didn't cheat before he left you, I'm going to throw something. He left you alone and hurt you so much you don't even eat anymore." She stared at the cookie plate, visibly upset. "He's scum. I hate him. Find somebody new and start a new life."

I liked my old life. Nell took a deep breath. "Look, can we wait to see if I survive working for Gabriel McKenna for six weeks before I deal with other men?"

"Okay, six weeks, but then you date," Suze said. "And you eat *now*."

"I think we should unpack your china," Margie said.

God, preserve me from those who love me, Nell thought and drank the rest of her coffee.

Five hours later, in his third-floor apartment above the agency, Gabe would have thought much the same thing if he'd been thinking at all. After the day he'd had, all he'd wanted was sex and silence, and now he was halfway there, making only a vague pretense of listening to Chloe in bed beside him.

"I liked the way she looked." Chloe was saying. "And I checked her birth date on the application, and she is a Virgo, just like I thought. She's going to be an excellent secretary."

"Hmmm."

"So I think you should fire Lynnie and make this Eleanor permanent," Chloe said, her usual delicately suggestive voice blunt, and Gabe woke up a little. "Even before I knew Lynnie was a Scorpio, I didn't trust her. I know she's efficient, but she doesn't take care of anybody but herself. That dark hair. Eleanor will be perfect for you."

Gabe ignored the dark hair bit—tracking down Chloe's free associations could take hours—to concentrate on the important point. "Chloe, I don't tell you how to run your business, so butt out of mine." Another thought intruded. "How did you see that application?"

"It was on your desk. I looked·after you left. She has a Cancer moon."

"If that means she has a nice ass, you're right. Stay out

of my office." Gabe rolled away in the forlorn hope she'd shut up.

"I bet she was a real redhead once," Chloe said. "There was fire there, I'd bet anything. But she's all faded out now." She nudged him with her elbow. "You could do something about that, put some of the fire back into her."

"She's going to answer the phone," Gabe said into his pillow. "Unless AT&T inflames her, she's out of luck."

Chloe sat up and leaned over his shoulder, and he closed his eyes in pleasure at all that warm softness pressed against his back. Then she said, "Gabe, I don't think we should see each other anymore."

Gabe turned his head to look up at her. The moon came through the skylight and backlit Chloe's short blonde curls, making her look angelically lovely. Too bad she was insane. "You live next door. You work in the same building I do. You sleep with me several times a week. What's your plan, blindfolds?"

"I'm serious, Gabe. I think it's time we broke up."

Gabe turned his back on her again. "We did that already. It was a success. Go to sleep."

"You never listen," Chloe said, and Gabe could feel the bed bounce as she rolled out of it.

"Where are you going?" he said to her, exasperated, as she struggled into her clothes.

"Home," Chloe said, and since that was just next door, Gabe said, "Fine. See you tomorrow."

"Gabe," Chloe said a minute later, and Gabe rolled over to see her standing at the foot of his bed, braless in her moons-and-stars T-shirt, her hands on her hips like a particularly demanding child. When she didn't say anything, he propped himself up on his elbows and said with exaggerated patience, *"What?"*

Chloe nodded. "Good, you're awake. You and I have stayed together partly because of Lu but mostly because there wasn't anybody else we liked better. You're a very nice man, but we're not right for each other, and we owe it to ourselves to find our soul mates."

"I love you," Gabe said. "If you weren't such a fucking wacko, I'd still be married to you."

"I love you, too, but this is not the great love we both deserve. And someday you're going to look at me and say, 'Chloe, you were right.'"

"I'll say it now if you'll shut up and come back to bed."

"I think this Eleanor could be the one for you. I spent two hours on her horoscope, and I can't tell for sure without getting her time of birth for her rising sign, but I really think she might be your match."

Gabe felt suddenly cold. "Tell me you didn't tell her that."

"Well, of course not." Chloe sounded exasperated. "Look, I know how you hate change, so I'm setting us both free so you can start over with Eleanor and I can find the man I was meant to be with."

Gabe sat up straighter. "You're not serious about this."

"Very," Chloe said and blew him a kiss. "Good-bye, Gabriel. I'll always love you."

"*Wait a minute*." Gabe rolled toward the foot of the bed to reach for her, but she faded away into the dark, and a moment later he heard the door to his apartment close with a finality that was rare for Chloe.

Ninety-nine times out of a hundred, Chloe did exactly what he told her to do. This was clearly the hundredth. He fell back into bed and stared up at the skylight, depressed by the realization that his ex-wife had just dumped him again.

A shooting star traced its way above the skylight, and he watched it fade. Weren't those supposed to be good luck? Chloe would know, but she'd walked out. His future now consisted of an endless string of days spent coping with clients like Jack Dysart, keeping his daughter in college, chasing down a series of cheating mates, and watching his temp secretary destroy his office, all as a celibate. "I want my old life back," he said and rolled over, pulling his pillow over his head to block out the stars that were responsible for his latest disaster.

Chapter Two

When Gabe came downstairs at nine on Monday, the outer office was empty. Not impressive. He was in a bad mood, and now his new secretary was not there with a cup of coffee. Her ass was fired in six weeks, that was for sure. He turned toward the coffeemaker to make his own, and it wasn't there, either. In fact the entire top of the old oak bookcase was empty—no dented coffee can, no stack of Styrofoam cups, no little red stirrers, nothing.

"We've been robbed," he told Riley who came down from his second-floor apartment a moment later. "Some caffeine addict has wiped us out."

"It's not like it was good coffee," Riley said. "Want me to go out—"

He stopped as Eleanor Dysart walked by the big window at the front of the office, carrying a cardboard box that looked too heavy for her thin arms.

"I'm sorry," she said as she came in and set the box on her desk, her brown eyes opened wide in apology. "You were missing a few things, so I went to get them."

"Like a coffeemaker?" Gabe said.

"That was not a coffeemaker. That was an antique that should have been put down long ago." She unpacked the box as she spoke, putting paper towels and spray cleaner on the desk before lifting out a gleaming white coffeemaker.

"You bought a coffeemaker?" Gabe said'

"No, this is mine. I brought my coffee, too." She tore a paper towel off the roll, picked up the cleanser, sprayed the coffee shelf, and wiped it clean with one ruthless swipe, her hand a pale blur against the dark wood. "I'm going to be drinking it here for the next six weeks anyway." She set up the coffeemaker and added, "Also, your coffee was terrible."

"Thank you," Riley said, clearly fascinated by the whole process, which Gabe could understand. He'd never seen anybody as gracefully efficient as this woman. She'd pulled out a small white coffee grinder, plugged it in, and poured beans into it from a shiny brown bag, and now she flipped the switch and went back to unpacking as the heavy, sweet smell of the beans filled the room.

"God, that smells good," Riley said.

She was setting out china cups in their saucers, her long pale hands almost the same color as the cream china. "How do you take yours?"

"Four creams, two sugars," Riley said, still mesmerized by her.

She stopped with a small waxed carton in her hand. "Really?"

"He's very young," Gabe said. "I take mine black."

"He's very boring," Riley said. "Is that real cream?"

"Yes," she said.

Riley peered into the box and pulled out a bottle of glass cleaner. "What's all this cleaning stuff for?"

"The office. You really should hire a cleaning service."

Gabe frowned at her. "We have a cleaning service. They come once a week. Wednesday nights."

She shook her head. "This place hasn't been cleaned in at least a month. Look how thick the dust is on the windowsill."

There was a faint coating on everything, Gabe noticed. Except for the bookcase where the new coffeemaker perked cheerfully, the whole office was full of dust and gloom.

"The number for the cleaning service is in the Rolodex." Gabe opened the door to his office, escaping before

he went headfirst into the coffeepot. He'd forgotten anything could smell that good. "Hausfrau Help."

"You're kidding," she said, and he closed the door behind him to shut her out. Thank God he had an office to
escape into.

An office that looked like hell, he realized when he was
sitting at his desk in the unblinded light from the broken
window. The room was littered with papers, Styrofoam
cups, books he'd pulled off the shelf, and the other general
rubble of his daily work. When had this place been cleaned
last? Some of the mess looked like it dated back to his dad's
day. His keyboard was buried under more paper, and there
was dust on everything, and suddenly it mattered.

It was Eleanor Dysart's fault. He hadn't noticed any of
this until she'd come in with her coffee and her china and
her Windex and torn down his blinds.

He picked the Styrofoam cups out of the mess and
threw them away and went through the papers, pitching
notes he'd already dealt with and putting letters that the
Dysart woman would have to file in a separate stack. That
would slow her down. He'd just turned on the computer
when she came in, bearing a china cup and saucer and a
determined expression that sat strangely on her finely
drawn face. Gabe thought of his father, three sheets to the
wind, reciting Roethke to placate his furious mother: *I
knew a woman, lovely in her bones.* Eleanor Dysart was too
thin and too pale, but she was lovely in her bones.

"I called your cleaners," she said, setting the cup down.
"They haven't been here in six weeks because they haven't
been paid."

Gabe frowned at her and forgot his father. "Of course
they have. I signed the checks."

"Not for July and August, according to their book-
keeper. If you'll tell me where you keep the canceled
checks, I'll fax them over."

"Reception desk, bottom right-hand drawer," Gabe said
automatically as he hit the keyboard to open the office

bookkeeping program. He did a search for "Hausfrau."
Eight entries came up for 2000, including two for July and
August. "There," he told her, and she came around behind
him.

"That's Quicken, right?" she said. "Is that on the computer on my desk? Good, I'll take care of it. Thanks."

"For what?" Gabe said, but she was heading for the
door, a woman on a mission.

When she was gone, he sat back and picked up the coffee cup. It was a sturdy but graceful piece of china, cream
colored with a blue handle, and it felt good in his hand, a
luxury after the flyweight Styrofoam he'd been drinking
from for years. He took a sip and closed his eyes because
it was so rich, speeding caffeine into his system while as-
saulting every sense he had. When he looked again, there
were blue dots on the inside, appearing as the coffee level
dropped. It was absurd and charming and completely un-
like the tense woman vibrating outside his door.

Maybe he'd misjudged her. Maybe she was nervous because it was her first day. He didn't care, as long as she
kept the coffee coming.

Fifteen minutes later, he went out to the reception room
for a refill and found her with a frown on her face.

He picked up the coffee carafe and said, "You okay?"
as he poured.

"I'm fine," she said. "You have a problem. Look at this."

She had eight checks spread out before her. "These are
all from Hausfrau," she told him. "Here are the endorsements from January through June."

Gabe shrugged as he looked as six smudged stamped
endorsements. "Okay."

She pointed to the last two checks. "These are the endorsements from July and August."

The checks were endorsed in blue, loopy handwriting.
"That's Lynnie's writing."

"It appears she turned to embezzlement in her last two
months with you."

"She was only with us for six weeks," Gabe said and thought, *Damn good thing, too.* "Give Hausfrau some story about administrative screwups. I'll handle the rest." He took his coffee back to his office, thinking of Lynnie, black-haired and lovely, making lousy coffee and embezzling the cleaning money, and now sitting at home recovering from her sprained back with a thousand dollars and, he hoped, a sense of impending doom.

He took another sip of coffee and felt slightly better until another thought hit.

He was going to have to hire Eleanor Dysart permanently. For a moment, he thought about keeping Lynnie— so she stole money, she was cheerful and pretty and relaxed and efficient—and then he gave up and resigned himself to a tense reception room filled with the smell of great coffee.

An hour later, Riley knocked on Gabe's heavy office door and came in. "I finished most of the background check," he said as he lounged into the chair across from Gabe's desk. "I'll go see the last guy and then I'll ruin the rest of my day with the Hot Lunch." He ducked his blond head to look at Gabe. "What are you pissed about?"

"Many things," Gabe said.

"Nell?"

"Who?"

"Our secretary," Riley said. "I said, 'I'm Riley.' She said, 'I'm Nell.' I think she's doing a pretty good job."

"She seduced you with her coffee," Gabe said. "And you have no idea what a good job she's doing. She was only here an hour before she nailed Lynnie for embezzling the cleaning money."

"You're kidding." Riley laughed out loud. "Well, that's Lynnie all over."

"Since when?" Gabe scowled at his partner. "If you knew she was bent—"

"Oh, hell, Gabe, it was in her eyes. Not that she'd embezzle," he added hastily as Gabe's scowl deepened. "That she'd cheat. Lynnie was not a woman you'd leave alone for a weekend."

"Or with a checkbook, evidently," Gabe said.

"Well, that part I didn't realize," Riley said. "Although she was into luxury. Her furniture was all rented, but everything else in her duplex was first class with a label on it, right down to the sheets . . ." His voice trailed off as Gabe shook his head.

"We have three rules at McKenna Investigations," he said, reciting his father's words. "We don't talk about the clients. We don't break the law. And—"

"We don't fuck the help," Riley finished. "It was just once. We were doing a decoy job, and I took her home, and she invited me in and jumped me. I got the distinct impression she was just doing it for practice."

"Does it ever occur to you *not* to sleep with women?"

"No," Riley said.

"Well, try to restrain yourself around the new secretary. She has enough problems." Gabe thought about her tight, frowning face. "And now she's sharing them with me."

"If you're that unhappy, fire her, but do *not* get my mother back from Florida."

"God, no." Gabe said, picturing his aunt behind the reception desk again. He loved her dutifully, but duty only went so far. She'd been a lousy secretary for ten years, and a worse mother for longer.

"Get Chloe back. She's tired of selling tea, anyway. She asked me if I knew anybody who'd like to run The Cup for her."

"Great." Chloe and the stars. "I married an idiot."

"No, you didn't," Riley said. "She's just wired different from most. What's going on?"

"She dumped me," Gabe said, and decided not to mention that she'd done it in favor of Eleanor Dysart. Riley would have a field day with that one.

"Now see, that's what I hate about women," Riley said. "They divorce you, and then ten years later, right out of nowhere, they stop having sex with you. She have a reason?"

"The stars told her to."

"Well, then, you're screwed," Riley said cheerfully. "Or in this case, not."

"Thank you," Gabe said. "Go away."

His new secretary knocked on the door and came in.

"I fixed it with the cleaners," she said.

"Thank you."

"Now, about your business cards. There's a note in the file from Lynnie that says it's time to reorder." She was frowning, as if this were a major problem.

Gabe shrugged. "Reorder."

"The same cards?"

"Yes, the same cards."

"Because, while they are lovely, of course, they could be better—"

"The same cards, Mrs. Dysart," Gabe said.

She looked as if she wanted to say something else, then she lifted her pointed chin, took a deep breath and said, "Fine," and went out, wincing as the office door creaked behind her. It had probably creaked for years, but Gabe hadn't noticed until Eleanor Dysart showed up and started wincing.

"I don't think she likes our business cards," Riley said.

"I don't care," Gabe said. "I have to go see her brother-in-law and then deal with Lynnie. I am not screwing with perfectly good business cards on top of that. And you've got the Hot Lunch. Go act like a detective so I can get some work done."

"Maybe Nell could do it," Riley said. "You were training Lynnie. Nell—"

"She'd stick out a mile. People would stop by, trying to feed her."

"Just because you like your women upholstered doesn't mean everybody does. You have to broaden your tastes. Which in your case would mean anybody besides Chloe.

You know, she did you a favor by dumping you—"

"And God knows I'm grateful," Gabe said. "Now I have to work, and so do you. Go away."

"Fine," Riley said. "Resist change. It'll get you anyway."

Five minutes after Riley had gone, Eleanor Dysart knocked and came in, creaking the door again, and Gabe closed his eyes and thought, *The hell with her bones. She's going to drive me crazy.* "Yes?"

"About these business cards—"

"No." Gabe shoved himself back from his desk. "We're not changing the business cards. My father picked those out." He shrugged his suit jacket on. "I am now leaving. I will be at Ogilvie and Dysart and I won't be back until well after lunch." He detoured around her to the door, adding, "Just answer the phone, Mrs. Dysart. Don't change anything. Don't cause trouble."

"Yes, Mr. McKenna," she said, and he looked back to see if she was mocking him.

She was standing in the doorway, looking down at his business card with a potent mixture of displeasure and frustration on her face. He didn't care. His business card was staying the way it was.

She looked up and caught him watching her. "Anything else?" she asked him, her voice polite and professional.

At least she was obedient. That was something.

"Good coffee," Gabe said and closed the street door behind him.

Nell went back to her desk and sat down, disliking Gabe McKenna intensely. She watched him through the big plate-glass window as he put on sunglasses and got into a vintage black sports car. He looked the epitome of retro cool—big guy, sharp suit, dark glasses, snazzy car—as he pulled out into the street and drove away.

Well, looks could be deceiving. After all, he'd hired a secretary who'd embezzled a thousand dollars and left the place looking like a hellhole. How smart could he be? And then he'd dismissed her with those dark eyes as if she were just . . . a secretary. *Well, the hell with you, Mr. McKenna.* Frustrated beyond measure, Nell picked up her paper towels and spray cleaner and attacked the reception room, grateful that his good-looking younger partner wasn't as annoying as he was. She wasn't impressed with Riley's intellect or energy so far, but he was big, blond, and blue-eyed, so at least he was fun to look at.

An hour later, the phone still hadn't rung, but the room was clean, right down to the big window in front that said in ancient, worn gold lettering, MCKENNA INVESTIGATIONS: DISCREET ANSWERS TO DIFFICULT QUESTIONS. Nell had scrubbed it with enthusiasm until she realized that she was taking some of the flaking paint off and slowed down. Not that it would have hurt if she'd taken it all off; the lettering must have been on there for fifty years or at least as long as they'd had those ugly business cards.

When she went back inside, the window let in enough light that the deficiencies in the rest of the decor were plain. Nell's desk was a scarred mess, the couch where clients presumably waited was a brown plastic-upholstered nightmare on its last spindly motel-Mediterranean legs, and the Oriental rug on the floor was so threadbare it was transparent in places. The bookcases and wood filing cabinets were good quality and had probably been original to the office, but the middle cabinet had an unfortunate black statuette of a bird perched on it, brooding over the place like something out of Poe. She gave one despairing thought to the office she'd lost in the divorce—the pale gold walls and gold-framed prints, the light wood desks and soft gray couches—and then she sank back into the battered wood swivel chair—her chair at the insurance agency had been ergonomic—and thought, *At least it's only for six weeks.*

Except maybe it wasn't. She straightened slowly. He was going to have to fire Lynnie. Which meant she might end up permanently employed here. She looked around the office again. If she were permanent, she could make some changes. Like get the place painted. And lose the couch and the bird. And—

Her eyes fell on the business card on her desk. "McKenna Investigations" it read in plain black sans-serif type on plain white card. It looked like something somebody had done with a kid's printing set. But the boss didn't want them changed. He didn't want anything changed, the dummy.

She went back to the computer, wondering if he was going to do anything about Lynnie or if that would be too much change, too. He hadn't even told her to check the rest of the finances. Nell stopped typing and opened the drawer that held the canceled checks. There was a gray metal box tucked in behind the check folders, and she pulled it out and opened it to find a stack of papers, each marked "Petty Cash" followed by a dollar amount. They were all signed "Riley McKenna" in writing that wanted to be spiky but kept rounding off at the end.

Nell leafed through the reports she was typing until she found one Riley had signed in a strong, dark, jagged scrawl. Nothing round anywhere, much like Riley. She went back to the petty cash slips and totaled them: $1,675. You had to admire Lynnie; the woman was thorough.

She spent the next hour compiling a stack of forged checks. The breadth of Lynnie's perfidy was astounding; she'd managed to cheat the McKennas and their creditors out of almost five thousand dollars. Just making good on the forged endorsement checks was going to cost the agency over three thousand. If Gabe McKenna didn't go after this woman—

Somebody tried to open the heavy street door, and the glass in it rattled. Nell jammed the slips back into the cash box as a sharp-faced redhead popped the door open and came in frowning, dressed in a good business suit and wearing even better shoes. *Money*, Nell thought, shoving everything back in the bottom drawer. "Can I help you?" she said, smiling her best we're-the-people-you-need smile.

"I want to see somebody who can handle a sensitive matter," the woman said.

"I can make an appointment for you," Nell said brightly. "Unfortunately both our—" Our what? What the hell did they call themselves? Detectives? Operatives? "—partners are out. They could see you on—" She turned to the antique computer on her desk as she spoke and opened the file labeled "Appointments." It was blank. They were both out on jobs right now and the damn page was blank. Who ran this place, anyway? "If I could have your number," Nell finished, even more brightly, "I'll call you when they get in and set up an appointment."

"It's sort of an emergency." The woman looked doubtfully at the couch and then sat gingerly on the edge of it. "I'm getting a divorce, and my husband is mistreating my dog."

"What?" Nell leaned forward, propelled by outrage. "That's *terrible*. Call Animal Control and get—"

"It's not like that." The woman leaned forward, too, and Nell held her breath that the couch wouldn't tip or break or just give up and fold. "He yells at her all the time and she's very nervous anyway, she's a dachshund, a longhair, and I'm afraid she's going to have a nervous breakdown."

Nell pictured a longhaired dachshund having a psychotic episode. Just like a man to pick on something that couldn't fight back. "Have you tried Animal Control—"

"He's not hitting her. There aren't any marks. He just yells all the time, and she's a mess." The woman leaned closer. "Her eyes are just *tortured*, she's so unhappy. So I want you to rescue her. Get her away from that bastard before he kills her. He lets her out every night at eleven. Somebody could take her then. It would be easy in the dark."

Nell tried to imagine Gabriel McKenna rescuing a

dachshund. Not likely. Riley might, though. He looked as though he'd be up for anything.

"Let me take your name and number," she told the woman. "One of our partners might be able to help."

And if they wouldn't, maybe she would. Maybe she'd just go out there and rescue the poor trapped dog from the man who'd promised to take care of it and then just *changed his mind*. She tried to picture herself creeping into somebody's backyard to steal a dog. It didn't seem like something she'd do.

"I'll have Riley call you," she said when she'd taken down the woman's name—Deborah Farnsworth—her expensive Dublin address, and her dog-abusing husband's even more expensive New Albany address.

"Thank you," Deborah Farnsworth said, casting one last dubious glance around the office before she left. "You've been very helpful."

Gotta get this office fixed. Nell found 3-in-1 oil in the bathroom and oiled the front door, hoping to stop it from sticking, and then did the partners' office doors, too, because the creaks were driving her crazy. Then to distract herself from the neglect and the dog, she went into Gabe McKenna's office and began to clean, dusting off the black-and-white photos on the walls and wiping down dark wood and old leather until the place gleamed from the power of her frustration. She noticed an odd striped pattern to the dust on the bookcases, as if somebody had pulled books off some of the shelves and then shoved them back again. Maybe Gabe McKenna had lost something and had gone looking for it behind his books. God knew, he could have lost damn near anything in that mess.

Near the wall on the last bookcase, she found an old cassette player and punched Play to hear what he listened to. Bouncy horns blared out followed by an easy, deep voice singing, "You're *no*body till *some*body *loves* you." She hit Stop and popped the cassette out. Dean Martin. That figured. That might also explain why his office looked like a set for the Rat Pack. There was even a blue pinstriped jacket hanging on a brass coatrack that also held a slouch hat covered in dust. She dusted off the hat and shook out the coat with an angry snap and then put them both back where they'd been.

She heard somebody call out, "Hello?" and went back to her desk to find the little blonde from the teashop standing there.

"I'm sorry," Nell said. "I didn't hear you come in. The door usually rattles—"

"Different door." The blonde jerked her thumb over her shoulder. "That door leads into my storeroom. I'm Chloe. I run The Star-Struck Cup. So I was wondering. You seem very efficient."

"Thank you," Nell said, not quite following.

"Do you know anybody who'd like to run The Cup for a while? Until Christmas? We're only open in the afternoons, so it's not hard."

"Oh," Nell said, taken aback. "Well . . ." Suze wanted a job, but Jack would talk her out of it the way he had a hundred times before. And Margie . . . "Would the person who ran the shop for you get your cookie recipe, too?"

Chloe looked surprised. "She'd have to, wouldn't she? To make the cookies?"

"I might know somebody," Nell said. "She's not really the business type, but she'd probably love to run a teashop in the afternoons. You sure about this?"

"I just decided today," Chloe said. "Really, when all the signs say it's time for a change, there's no point in waiting, is there?"

"Uh, no," Nell said.

"Do you know what time of day you were born?"

"No," Nell said.

"It doesn't really matter. Virgos handle everything beautifully." Chloe smiled. "What sign is your friend?"

"My friend? Oh, Margie. Uh, February 27. I don't know—"

"Pisces. Not as good." She frowned. "Of course, I'm a Pisces and I'm doing okay. Have her call me."

"Right," Nell said. "What—"

The doorbell clinked from the depths of the teashop, signaling a customer, and Chloe turned back to the storeroom door.

"Chloe?" Nell said, on an impulse. "Is there a reason everything here looks like something from a Dean Martin movie?"

"Gabe's dad," Chloe said from the doorway. "Patrick raised both Gabe and Riley. They have father issues. Unresolved."

"It's a little . . . outdated."

Chloe snorted. "Are you kidding? Gabe's still driving his dad's *car*."

"That car's from the *fifties*?" Nell said, dumbfounded.

"No, from the seventies. Of course, it's a Porsche, but still."

"Somebody needs to bring this guy into the twenty-first century," Nell said, and Chloe beamed at her.

"The stars never lie," she said and went back into the storeroom.

"Oh-kay," Nell said, not following, and called Margie, getting her machine. "I think I can get you that cookie recipe," she told the machine, "but you're going to have to work for it. Give me a call." Then she hung up and went to finish her cleaning.

Riley's much smaller office had the same leather furniture, but the resemblance stopped there. His desk was empty except for his computer and a plastic Wile E. Coyote mug full of pens, his bookshelf held computer manuals and detective novels next to the same directories she'd found in the big office, and his wall had two huge framed movie posters featuring a scowling Humphrey Bogart in *The Maltese Falcon* and a sultry Marlene Dietrich in *The Blue Angel*. That was like Riley, romantic and bigger than life. Gabe McKenna obviously ran a business while his partner played the game.

She cleaned Riley's office, noticing the same dust patterns on his bookcases, and then she went into the grimy green bathroom to wash the coffee cups and saucers she'd collected, hating the cracked linoleum and dingy plaster. A good coat of paint would do wonders, but Gabe McKenna's father had probably picked out the color while listening to "In the Misty Moonlight" in 1955. *Honestly*. She washed the cups and then, with a last impromptu swipe at the age-speckled mirror, she caught a glimpse of herself that froze her in place.

She looked like death.

Her hair was dull and so was her skin, but more than that, *she* was dull, her cheekbones protruding like elbows, her mouth tight and thin. She dropped the paper towel in the sink and leaned closer, horrified at herself. How had this happened, how could she look this bad? It must be the light, horrible fluorescent light bouncing off ugly green walls, nobody could look good in this light . . .

It wasn't the light.

She realized now why her son Jase was so sad and careful when he hugged her good-bye, and why Suze and Margie kept doing their cheerleading routine. She must have looked like a corpse for the past year and a half, must have sat like a ghost in other people's lives. She'd looked in the familiar mirrors in her apartment a million times since the divorce to comb her hair and brush her teeth, but she hadn't looked at herself once until now.

I have to eat, she thought. *I have to get some weight back on. And do something about my skin. And my hair. And—*

She heard the front door rattle and thought, *Later. I'll do all of that later. My God.*

Driving a vintage sports car through a beautiful city on a September morning would cheer anybody up, and Gabe was no exception. Unfortunately, fifteen minutes of listening to Trevor Ogilvie, Jack Dysart, and the head of their accounting department, Budge Jenkins, pretty much took him back to ground zero.

"She called, she accused you of adultery and embezzlement, you refused to pay, and nothing's happened," he summed up for them. "What exactly is it you want me to do?"

"*Catch her*," Budge said, looking like the Pillsbury Doughboy on a hot plate as he cast a sidelong glance at Jack.

"Well, let's not be hasty," Trevor said, looking like an expensive liquor ad in *Modern Maturity*.

"If this were your problem, what would you do?" Jack said, looking like a very wealthy Marlboro Man who'd just gotten his first subscription to *Modern Maturity*.

"Hit star sixty-nine," Gabe said. "Failing that, I'd try to think who disliked me enough to blackmail me."

"Every business has disgruntled employees," Trevor said.

"Anybody recognize the voice?" Gabe said.

"No," Trevor said before anyone else could answer. "We have *many* disgruntled employees."

"You might want to work on that," Gabe said. "Has anything happened lately that might lead to a *newly* disgruntled employee?"

"What are you talking about?" Budge said.

"He wants to know if we've pissed off anybody in particular lately," Jack said. "No. We've won cases, of course, which always leaves some people unhappy, but nothing stands out. We haven't fired anybody."

"How about the accusations she made?" Gabe said.

"I'm insisting on an outside audit," Budge said, expanding with outrage.

"We're not going to pay for an audit," Jack said tiredly. "Nobody thinks you're embezzling. I'm not cheating on

Suze. Trevor says he's not cheating on Audrey. It's a nuisance scam."

"It's outrageous," Trevor said automatically. "But she hasn't called back. I think if we wait—"

Jack closed his eyes.

"Where did she want you to leave the money?" Gabe said.

"She said she'd call back and tell me," Trevor said quickly. "In a day, when I had it."

Jack shot Trevor a glance and said, "That's right."

No, it isn't, Gabe thought. "What about you, Budge?"

"I hung up on her before she got that far," Budge said. "She accused me of *stealing.*"

"That's what blackmailers do," Gabe said. "Accuse people. Okay, as this stands, there's not much I can do. If you want to bring in the police, they can check the phone records, but I'm guessing she called from a public phone and not her living room."

"No police," Jack said. "This is a joke."

"I don't think it's a joke," Budge said. "I think—"

"Budge," Jack said. "We all think it's a joke." He said it with enough intent that Budge shut up. "Thanks for coming out, Gabe. Sorry we wasted your time."

"Always a pleasure," Gabe said, which wasn't true. O&D was rarely a pleasure, but it was always profitable. He stood and said, "Let me know if anything else happens."

"Certainly," Trevor said, but his face said, *Absolutely not.*

"Wonderful seeing you all again," Gabe said and left, wondering what the hell was going on but not caring much.

Back at the agency, Riley slammed the door, threw a file folder on Nell's desk, and said, "I do not *like* that woman."

"What woman?" Nell pulled the file over and sat down

at her desk to read the label, trying to get her balance back after the mirror. "The Hot Lunch," she read. "What is this?"

"One of our regulars." Riley dropped onto the couch and made it creak in anguish. "The client has a wife who takes a new lover a couple of times a year. She always meets him at the Hyatt on Mondays and Wednesdays at noon, so we call her the Hot Lunch."

Nell looked at the folder, confused. "And she's been doing this how long?"

"About five years." Riley stretched his legs out and put his hands behind his head, still scowling. "And I'm sick of it."

"*You're* sick of it?" Nell opened the folder. "How's the *client* feel about it?"

"All he wants is the reports." Riley closed his eyes. "It's a farce. She knows both of us, so it's not exactly a covert operation. Today she waved at me on her way to the elevator."

"At least she has a sense of humor." Nell scanned the report and shrugged. "So you did the job. What's the problem?"

"I feel like a marital aid." Riley shifted on the couch, and it creaked again. "My guess is, we deliver the report to the client, he shows it to her, they fight, and they have hot make-up sex for a while. Then it starts to taper off, and he calls us and says, 'I think my wife is having an affair.' No shit, Sherlock." He sighed. "That is not a marriage."

"Are you married?" Nell asked, surprised.

"No," Riley said. "But I know what a marriage is."

"And that would be . . ."

"Commitment for life with no whining," Riley said. "Which is why I'm not married. I'm more of a live-in-the-moment kind of guy. Can you type that report for me?"

"Sure," Nell said. "Can I have your datebook so I can log your appointments into the computer?" When Riley nodded, she said, "Okay, then, one more thing. When was the last time you took money from the petty cash?"

Riley shrugged. "Whenever it says I did. Last month sometime. Why?"

Nell took out the cash box and handed him the slips.

He shuffled through them, frowning. "These aren't mine."

"I know. My theory is that Lynnie signed them for you."

Riley whistled. "How much did she get?"

"With the other checks, over five thousand dollars."

"And Gabe says to forget it and swallow the loss." Riley tossed the slips back in the box. "You know, once he'd have gone after her just for the exercise. Now he's practical."

"What happened that he changed?"

"His dad died, we inherited the agency, and he got way too serious. He'd already started to slow down because of Chloe and Lu, and because Patrick was the world's worst manager, but that was the last straw."

Nell frowned, trying to keep up. "Chloe and Lu?"

"Wife and daughter. He was really something once. He was like Nick Charles."

"Who's Nick Charles?"

"Nobody reads anymore." Riley pointed at the black bird on the bookcase. "Do you know what that is?"

"Poe's raven," Nell guessed. " 'Nevermore.' "

"And you work in a detective office." Riley sighed and slouched toward his own office. "You don't know literature, and Gabe's given up the chase. All I can say is, I hope I never get that old."

"We're not that old," Nell said to his back, but he shut his office door behind him before she could finish the sentence. "Hey!" she said, and when he didn't open the door again, she buzzed his office and told him about the Farnsworth case, omitting the part about stealing the dog. Let the client tell him.

Then she sat back and processed the new information.

So Gabe McKenna was married to Chloe. She tried to imagine them together, but it was too absurd, like Satan with a Powerpuff Girl. And they had a daughter. How could you mix those two sets of DNA? She and Tim had been perfect for each other, had made a perfect son, and their marriage was over; McKenna and Chloe were at opposite ends of the human spectrum and they were still together. Marriage was a mystery, that was all there was to it.

She picked up the Hot Lunch notes that Riley had written about a woman named Gina Taggart who got away with adultery on a regular basis. That was the problem with the world. People did stuff they knew was wrong because they knew they could get away with it and other people didn't stop them. The Hot Lunch cheated, and Lynnie stole, and that guy in New Albany tormented a dog, and Tim dumped her and left her looking like she was a million years old—her heart clutched at the memory of the mirror—and nobody paid. Except she couldn't be mad at Tim, he'd played fair, it was her fault she looked like hell, she couldn't be mad.

Sitting there in the dim office, she realized that she wanted to be mad, wanted to say, "No, you can't just change your mind after twenty-two years of marriage, you spaghetti-spined weasel." But that wouldn't have been productive, it would make things more difficult for everybody, it would do nobody any good at all. Imagine if she'd screamed at Tim when he'd said he was leaving; their divorce would have been hell instead of civilized and fair. Imagine if she'd screamed and thrown things; they'd never have been able to maintain the friendly relationship they had now. Imagine if she'd screamed and thrown things and grabbed him by the—

"*Nell!*" Riley said and she swung around in her chair to face his office doorway.

"Yes. What?" She frowned at him. "Don't yell. Why didn't you buzz me?"

"I did. I'm leaving. Back around five."

"Okay," Nell said, and then she frowned, transferring her frustration with Tim and Lynnie to him. "Explain this to me. You guys do background checks all the time. Why didn't you do one on Lynnie?"

"We did, or at least my mother did when she hired her. She had great references." Riley dropped his datebook on her desk. "Ogilvie and Dysart, same as you. She was only supposed to be here for a month until Mom got back. That's why the appointments have never been in the computer. My mother doesn't like computers."

"That explains a lot," Nell said. "So your mother quit?"

"She decided to take a two-week trip to Florida in the middle of July, hired Lynnie, and then when she got down there, decided to stay. That's when we made Lynnie permanent. There wasn't any reason not to trust her."

"I suppose," Nell said. "It just makes me mad that she got in here."

"Yeah, I can see you're frothing," Riley said.

"I'm a quiet kind of person," Nell said. "I do a subtle mad."

"Kind of takes the fun out of it, doesn't it?" He headed for the door, and then stopped. "Did you get lunch? I can cover the phones for a while if you want to go out."

"I'm not hungry," Nell said.

"Okay. If Gabe asks, I'm out working on the Quarterly Report."

"The what?"

"Trevor Ogilvie," Riley said, from the doorway. "Of the infamous Ogilvie and Dysart, Attorneys at Law. He hires us to check on his daughter every three months to see what she's doing."

Nell gaped at him. "He hires you to check on *Margie*?"

"No, we check on Olivia, the twenty-one-year-old. Margie is the older daughter, right? By the first wife? Margie evidently makes no waves."

"I forgot about Olivia," Nell said, remembering Margie's spoiled little stepsister. "I don't think she and Margie talk much." She sat back. "So Trevor hires you to follow Olivia?"

Riley nodded. "It's his idea of parenting, and it's a miracle he survives the reports. Olivia has a very good time. Oh, and before I forget, we are not rescuing SugarPie."

"Who?"

"SugarPie, your abused dog," Riley turned back to the doorway. "Rule number two: We do not break the law."

"There are two rules?" Nell asked, but the office door slammed before she finished her sentence. "You know, it's *rude* to do that," she said and then picked up Riley's datebook to enter it into the computer, trying not to think about the dog and the Hot Lunch and everything else that needed to be fixed in the world.

Chapter Three

"You've got to admit, the place is cleaner," Riley said when he came into Gabe's office the next morning to find him scowling at his desk.

"So clean I can't find anything." Gabe shuffled through the papers on his desk. "She *stacked* things."

"That's a woman for you." Riley sat down across from him and stretched out his legs. "Look on the bright side. She's concentrating on the bathroom now. That can only be good."

"She'll find some way to make it ruin my day."

"You know, we're going to have to make her permanent."

"Oh, God." Gabe knew he was right, but he didn't want to dwell on it. "So what happened yesterday?"

"I did the Hot Lunch. Gina's cheating. What a surprise."

"Anybody we know?"

Riley shook his head. "Never saw him before. He was wearing a really ugly tie and looking at Gina like she was the best thing that ever happened to him. If only he knew. She waved and said to give you her best."

Gabe shook his head. "And people think detective work is exciting."

"What happened at O&D?"

Gabe told him.

"Jack's cheating again?" Riley said. "He never learns."

"That's it, keep an open mind." Gabe sighed. "I don't

think any of them are guilty. But I do think Trevor lied about the accusations she made. I find it hard to believe that he's playing around."

"True," Riley said. "It's not like Trevor to work with his hands."

"And I know he lied to me about how she wanted him to get the money to her." Gabe leaned back. "I think he went to meet her."

"And Jack knows?"

"Maybe. Budge Jenkins called me first. Then I got a follow-up call from Jack that played down the whole thing, told me not to start investigating until we'd talked. And then I got a call from Trevor trying to cancel the meeting." He shook his head. "You have to wonder what would happen if Budge met a problem he couldn't tattle on, Jack met one he couldn't solve with fast talk and charm, and Trevor met one he couldn't delay out of existence."

"So Trevor and Jack are hiding something and they haven't clued Budge in." Riley thought about it and grinned. "I'd hate to be Budge right about now."

Gabe nodded. "I have this ugly feeling that the way to find out who's blackmailing the clients is to investigate the clients."

"Let me do the easy one," Riley said, standing up. "I'll find out if Jack's cheating."

Gabe shook his head. "We're not going to investigate it. They don't want us to, and we don't have the time."

"I might do it just for the hell of it," Riley said.

"It wouldn't be just for the hell of it," Gabe said. "It'd be to nail Jack Dysart. I can't believe you're still hostile about that woman after fourteen years."

"What woman?" Riley said and went out, passing Nell on her way in.

"I need your appointment book," she said to Gabe briskly.

"Why?" he said, feeling the need to annoy her.

"Because your appointments are not in the computer, and I need to put them in."

"Fine." Gabe handed over his datebook.

"Thank you." She took it and turned back to the door.

"Mrs. Dysart," he said, hating what he had to say next.

"Yes?" she said, patiently.

"Would you like a permanent job?"

She surprised him by pausing for a minute. "Would I get to fix your business cards?"

"No."

She sighed. "Yes, I'd like a permanent job."

"You're hired," he said. "Don't change anything."

She shot him a look that was completely unreadable and left.

"Yes, she's going to be a great help," he said to the empty room and turned back to his neatly stacked desk to get some work done.

An hour later, with both partners gone and the bathroom still to be cleaned, Nell began to enter Gabe's appointments into the agency's antique computer system. After typing in his future workload, Nell went back through the book for the past year and realized she'd misjudged him. He might be a controlling fiend, but he was a hardworking controlling fiend. No wonder he hadn't caught Lynnie embezzling; he'd barely had time to catch his breath. A significant amount of the work he'd done was background checks for Ogilvie and Dysart, and Nell stopped long enough to flip through Riley's past appointments, too. Even more O&D, close to a quarter of their business.

The door rattled, and she looked up from her computer screen to see her handsome son come in with a paper bag in one hand and a drink in the other.

"Lunch," Jase said, hitting her with the irresistible smile that had been getting him out of trouble for twenty-one years. "Also I wanted to check out your new salt mine."

Nell smiled back in spite of herself. He was such an all-American boy, tall and sturdy and open. "You look wonderful."

"You have to say that, you're my mother." He put the bag and the drink on the desk and kissed her cheek. "Aunt Suze says you're supposed to eat, so eat. I don't want her on my case."

Nell ignored the bag and picked up the drink. "What's in here?"

"Chocolate milkshake. She said to get high-calorie." He looked around the reception room. "So you've been here a day and a half and it still looks like this? What have you been doing with your time?"

"Getting to know my boss," Nell said as Jase sat on the couch, the spindly legs creaking under his weight. "He's tricky. I may have to sneak some things past him." She opened the bag and tried not to recoil at the smell of the hot grease. *You look like hell*, she told herself. *Eat*. She took out a french fry. "So what's new? How's Bethany?"

"I wouldn't know. Haven't seen her in a couple of weeks."

"Again?" Nell put the french fry back. "Jase, that's your fourth girl this year."

"Hey, you don't want me getting too serious too young, do you?"

"No," Nell said. "But—"

"Then be grateful I play the field. That way when I'm ready to settle down, I'll settle down. No cheating." Jase faltered a little. "I mean, there's no point in getting serious now, two more years of undergrad to go, and who knows what after that. I don't even know what I want to be when I grow up." He smiled at her again, as sunny and as guileless as when he was six.

"I love you," Nell said.

"I know," Jase said. "You have to. You're my mom. It's part of the deal. Now eat something."

"I am." Nell reached in the bag for the french fries. "See?" She chewed a fry, trying not to gag at the taste of the grease. "Although I have to admit I'm not a big french fry fan."

"You used to be," Jase said. "You used to pour vinegar over them like Grandma did, remember? One of the best smells I know is vinegar and hot oil because of you two."

"Well, at least I gave you some good memories," Nell said.

"You gave me a boatload." Jase stood up and leaned across the desk to kiss her again. "I have to go. Promise me you'll eat that."

"I'll give it my best shot," Nell said.

When he was gone, she dumped the bag in the trash and went back to the computer and Gabe's datebook. It really was amazing the amount of work the man did. Imagine what he could accomplish once she'd organized him.

She began to type again, keying in words while she thought about all the things she could do to fix McKenna Investigations.

On Wednesday, Nell got to the agency at nine sharp, but Gabe wasn't there. She was surprised to feel vaguely let down, as if she'd braced herself for nothing. It was like pushing hard on a door that opened easily; she felt stupid and clumsy, all at once. She made coffee and poured Riley a cup and took it in to him, and then she went into the bathroom to start on the final frontier.

"What are you doing?" Riley called when he came out of his office half an hour later to give her his empty cup.

"Cleaning your bathroom," Nell said, drying her hands on a paper towel as she came out to find him staring at the four white garbage bags she'd managed to fill so far. "You won't let me do anything else right now, and you have dirt in there from the Cold War."

Riley frowned. "What did you want to do instead?"

"Fix the business cards. Repaint the window. Replace the couch," Nell said, her voice getting grim. "Speak sharply to Lynnie. But the boss says no." She looked up at him. "You're a partner in this place. Give me permission to do what I want." It sounded like an order so she added, "Please."

"Cross Gabe?" Riley shook his head. "No."

Nell turned back to the bathroom. "Fine, then go out and do something so I can type the report."

"We never talk anymore," Riley said, but he said it on his way out.

One hour, three shelves, and two phone messages later, the door rattled opened, and Nell came out of the bathroom, expecting Gabe.

A very young blonde came in, all but bouncing on her heels as she pushed the stubborn door shut with her tight little body. She beamed at Nell, and Nell smiled back, helpless not to.

"You must be Nell," the blonde said. "My mom told me about you. I'm Lu."

She held out her hand, and when Nell took it, her handshake was firm, almost painful. *Like Gabe's*, Nell thought. She had his smart, dark eyes, too, which contrasted with her blonde, cheerful openness. *Odd but attractive*, Nell thought. "Very nice to meet you."

"My mom thinks you're the best." Lu stuck her hands in the back pockets of her jeans, clearly prepared to make her own judgment.

"She's a nice woman," Nell said.

"Nice isn't everything," Lu said. "She's a Pisces. They never get what they want. Especially when they're married to Tauruses." She shot a disgusted look at her father's office door.

"You're not a Pisces," Nell said.

"I'm a Capricorn," Lu said. "We get everything we want." She jerked her head at Gabe's door. "Is my dad in?"

"Nope," Nell said. "He's out harassing the guilty."

"Maybe that'll put him in a better mood." Lu pulled her hands out of her pockets and plopped down on the couch, everything she had bouncing with her. As part of her miracle, the couch held. "He's being impossible about this Europe thing."

"Europe thing?"

"I want to go to France next month," Lu said. "Get a Eurail pass, see the world. He wants me to go to OSU. He's paid the tuition, which he feels is significant."

"I've paid tuition," Nell said. "It is significant."

"Yes, but I don't want to go," Lu said. "It's my life. I didn't ask him to pay tuition."

"You probably didn't have to," Nell said. "Your dad strikes me as somebody who takes care of his own."

"Exactly. That's pretty good for only knowing him three days."

"It's been an intense three days."

"That's what my mom said." Lu studied her, narrowing her dark eyes until she looked uncomfortably like Gabe. "Mom says you're going to run the place. She can't get my dad to do anything. I mean, she *divorced* him and they stayed together."

"They're divorced?" Nell said.

"Hard to tell, isn't it? He bought the house next door for her so she'd stay, and she did." Lu shook her head. "I think that's why my mom's decided to go to France with me, although she's not there yet. If Dad doesn't want her to go, she won't go." She set her jaw. "I'm going." She cast a careful look at Gabe's door. "I think."

The door rattled again. "Hello, trouble," Riley said as he came in, smacking Lu on the top of the head with the folder he was carrying. "Stop making your dad crazy. He's taking it out on me."

"It's good for you," Lu said critically. "You get things too easy."

Riley detoured around her to drop the folder on Nell's desk. "Everything you've ever wanted," he told her. "Last part of a background check. Type away." He looked back at Lu. "Would it kill you to spend a couple months in college and make your old man happy?"

"It is not my mission in life to make my father happy," Lu said airily. "I must follow my bliss." She came back to earth. "Tell me you love me."

"I love you," Riley said. "Now get out. This is a place of business."

"You know, if you have to tell people it's a place of business, it kind of loses its impact," Nell said.

Riley grinned down at her. "And that's enough lip from the help."

Nell smiled back and then caught Lu's expression.

"Hello," Lu said.

"Not hello," Riley said. "Good-bye. I thought I threw you out of here."

"Just when it was getting interesting," Lu said and left, yanking on the door to get it closed.

"That's an amazing child," Nell said.

"You have no idea. She's had Gabe and Chloe whipped since birth. Some guy is going to have his hands full with that one." Riley looked into the bathroom. "I can't believe you're still doing that. Go to lunch."

"One more shelf and I'm done," Nell said and went in to finish.

The bathroom was better, but it still needed to be painted. Maybe she could do that when they weren't looking, since she was permanent now. She climbed up on the toilet tank, balancing herself with one hand on the wall, and began to take old boxes and bottles down from the top shelf, dropping them into the trash can below and listening to them smash with satisfaction. Then she reached for the last box.

It was pushed into the farthest corner and she had to pry it forward with her fingernails, but she finally got it to the edge of the shelf. It was small, about four by five inches, covered in cheap red-tooled leather. She climbed down from the toilet to look at it in the light, brushing off the dust to see the picture on top, an engraving of some kind of imp or devil. She heard the street door slam, heard Riley say he'd finished the background check, heard Gabe answer him, and looked at the box again.

If there was trouble in there, Gabe was going to blame her. She took a deep breath and opened the box, but the only thing inside was a car title, its yellow paper blending with the yellow felt lining of the box.

This cannot possibly upset him, she thought and went out to give it to him.

"This Jack Dysart thing," Riley said as he followed Gabe into the office.

"There is no Jack Dysart thing." Gabe took off his jacket and sat down at his desk. "We have real work to do." He was about to go on, but his new secretary knocked and came in, slender in her gray suit, pale against the dark wood of the door.

"I found this," she said and brought a small red box to the desk. "It was on the top shelf in the bathroom, and there's nothing much in it, just a car title, but I thought—"

"A title?" Gabe opened the box and took out the paper. It was a title transfer to Patrick McKenna for a 1977 Porsche 911 Carrera, dated May 27, 1978, and signed by Trevor Ogilvie. He looked at it closer.

Trevor had sold the car to his dad for one dollar.

He felt his skin go cool. His dad had put the box on the top shelf of the bathroom in 1978 where it wasn't likely to be found by anybody working for him, certainly not by his twenty-one-year-old son or eleven-year-old nephew who might conceivably ask how he'd gotten such a cool car for a buck.

What the hell had his dad done for Trevor in 1978 that was worth a 1977 Porsche?

"What?" Riley said. Gabe pushed the box across the

desk to him and watched Riley's usual good humor fade from his face as he read the paper.

"Is that what you were looking for?" Nell said, and Gabe frowned at her. Jesus, it was like working with Chloe again. No train of thought at all, just random stations.

"What are you talking about?" he asked patiently, and he must have been too patient because she frowned back at him.

"I was cleaning your shelves," she said, "and I noticed patterns in the dust that looked like somebody had been pulling books out. So I figured you were looking for something."

"No," Gabe said and looked at Riley.

"Not me," Riley said. "But it was after the cleaners stopped coming. Lynnie?"

Gabe shook his head. "If she found the box, why not just take it?" He frowned at the box. "Actually, why look for this at all?" He picked it up again. It was small, but there was plenty of room inside for something besides a title. "Unless she took what she wanted." Something else about his dad and Trevor . . .

Riley was frowning. "Yeah, but what the hell could she want—"

"Thank you, Mrs. Dysart, you've been a great help," Gabe said, and Nell took a step back, looking as though she'd been slapped.

"All right," she said. "Listen, about the sign on the window—"

"What?" Gabe frowned at her, impatient for her to be gone. "What sign?"

"McKenna Investigations. It's flaked completely off in places. I was thinking we could redesign—"

"No, Mrs. Dysart. The window stays the way it has always been." He looked at the box and thought, *Although I may not know much about the way things have always been.*

"Then could I talk you into a new couch before the old one collapses?" she said, and he looked up, startled by the edge in her voice. Her eyes held a gleam that said she was repressing things best left unsaid and there was actually some color in her cheeks. Well, the hell with her, he had real problems.

"We don't get that many drop-ins," he told her. "The couch stays."

She stood there for a moment, and then she said, "Your front door sticks, too," and left.

That is one angry woman, he thought, and looked at the box again. *Hell*.

Riley took a deep breath. "So what did Patrick do for Trevor that he couldn't put on the books?"

"Here's another question," Gabe said. "How big a coincidence is it that we find a box with Trevor's name in it at roughly the same time a woman starts blackmailing him, which is also roughly the same time that Lynnie calls in sick?"

Riley sat very still, looking at the possibility from all sides while Gabe waited. "Maybe," he said finally. "It's sure not out of character for her." He looked up at Gabe, frowning. "Doesn't explain Jack and Budge."

"Jack, maybe," Gabe said. "He was a partner in '78." He pulled the box back and closed it so he wouldn't have to look at the damn title transfer, and the devil leered up at him. "My dad loved that car. The last fight he had with my mother was over that car."

"*You* love that car," Riley said. "Maybe this is a sign that it's time for a new one."

"There are no signs," Gabe said. "Stop talking to Chloe."

"Well, there are clues," Riley said. "I don't know about this one, though. If it was Lynnie, how the hell did she know the box was here?"

"Maybe she didn't," Gabe said. "Maybe she was just snooping around and found it and took what she wanted and then put it back." He shook his head. "No, that makes no sense. She was looking for something." He stood up and picked up his jacket. "You may now investigate Jack Dysart at will."

"What are you going to do?" Riley said.

"Find Lynnie," Gabe said grimly. "And then I'm going to talk to Trevor." He looked around the office and saw his dad everywhere. "About the good old days."

Nell watched Gabe leave and gritted her teeth. She'd never been evicted from anyplace as fast as he'd thrown her out of that office. And she could have helped, if he'd just—

"Back later," Riley said, coming out of his office and heading for the street door. "Much later."

Well, the hell with you guys, Nell thought and went back into the bathroom to wipe down the last shelf. She was just finishing when she heard the street door rattle and pop open. "Nell?" she heard Suze call, and she said, "Just a minute," and climbed down from the toilet, the last of the cleaning done. It wasn't very satisfying.

When she came out into the office, Suze said, "We have to talk to you," and Nell looked beyond her to see Margie's tearstained face.

"What's wrong?" Nell went to Margie. "What happened? Did Budge do something? Is it about the teashop? Because you don't have to—"

"Oh, *Nell!*" Margie threw her arms around her.

"What?" Nell looked over the top of Margie's curly head to Suze, who looked equally miserable, although her misery was mixed with rage. "Did Jack do something? What's going on?"

"Margie talked to Budge last night," Suze said grimly. "She suggested that since she was getting a job like you, maybe they shouldn't get married."

"I told him that marriage wasn't an answer," Margie said wetly into Nell's shoulder. "I told him you'd had a good marriage and it just ended for no reason, so I didn't see why we'd be any luckier, and that's why I needed a job."

"You shouldn't do that to Budge," Nell said, patting her shoulder. "You probably shouldn't marry him, either—"

"That's not the problem." Suze swallowed. "Budge told her your marriage didn't just end."

"What?" Nell said, going suddenly cold.

"Tim was seeing Whitney all along," Margie said, pulling her face out of Nell's shoulder. "Way before he left you. He was cheating the whole time."

I knew that, Nell thought, and then the office swooped around her and her knees buckled and light exploded in her head like stars.

Chapter Four

Nell felt Suze grab her before she hit the floor, easing her down to sit on the Oriental rug. *We should replace this rug,* Nell thought. *It makes the place look ratty.* She started to fall backward, but Suze held her and shook her.

"No, you don't," she said. "Stay with us."

"He cheated," Nell said, and saying it made her want to throw up.

"I hope he dies," Suze said, still holding onto her. "Are you okay? You look awful." She hooked her hands under Nell's arms and hauled her onto the rickety brown couch. "Put your head between your legs."

Nell obediently dropped her head between her knees. *He cheated. He made a fool of me.* "Did you know?"

"No," Suze said. "I swear, I would have told you. But it never made any sense that he'd fall out of love with you. You gave him everything. I couldn't believe he'd have the guts to leave you to do everything for himself. He's such a toad, and that kind never leaves without backup."

"I'm so *sorry*," Margie said.

Nell took a couple of deep breaths to get some oxygen back to her brain. Tim had cheated. She'd been fair and practical and adult, and he'd cheated. He'd cheated *twice*, first when he slept with Whitney and then when he'd told her there wasn't anybody else. The second betrayal was worse. That was the lie that he'd used to swindle her out of her anger. He'd taken her job and her house and half her china, and he'd broken her life, and then he'd lied so she couldn't even kill him for doing it. *The bastard.*

Nell sat up straight, rage making her blood thick. *"I hate him."*

"Well, it's about time," Suze said. "What are we going to do about it?"

I'm going to scream. "I have to go," Nell said, pushing herself up from the couch, and Margie moved out of her way as she headed for the door.

Gabe spent a frustrating hour getting nowhere, so when he got back to the agency and Nell was gone, he was not amused. *What the hell?* he thought and grabbed the phone when it rang. It was a client from out of town and he sat down at Nell's desk and took down the details with the gold pen that lay precisely to the right of her notepad. Everything on the desk was precise, right down to the expensively gold-framed photo of Nell and a much younger man who looked enough like her to be her son. The boy was good-looking, and Nell was flushed and happy and healthy. *What happened to her since then?* he thought as he hung up and then forgot about her as the phone rang again.

"What did you find out?" Riley said, when he answered.

"Not much. Lynnie wasn't home and her landlady was watching from next door so I couldn't go in on my own. And Trevor was not a help."

"He never is," Riley said. "The question is, was he not a help because he was clueless, or was he not a help because he was stalling?"

"Stalling," Gabe said. "He couldn't remember signing over the car."

"He forgot a Porsche?"

"His position is that he couldn't possibly remember it after twenty-three years."

"His position is flawed," Riley said. "Is Nell there?"

"No," Gabe said looking around. "Which is why I'm answering the phone."

"Well, when you find her, get her to dig out the '78 files," Riley said. "I know this is something Patrick was covering up, but there might be something in there, and if there is, she'll find it. That woman can find anything."

"If she ever comes back. She left some of her things, so I suppose we'll see her again when the mood strikes her."

"Will you get off her case?" Riley said. "She's probably at lunch, for Christ's sake. You're developing a fixation here."

"Speaking of fixations, how's Jack?"

"I'm just getting started," Riley said, his voice thick with anticipation.

Gabe sighed. "So am I. Oh, and before I forget, you have a decoy for tonight. Can you get your hort major to help?"

"She has a paper due," Riley said, and Gabe thought, *This is what you get for dating infants.*

"I'll get somebody," Gabe said and went to find Chloe in the tearoom. She was opening the oven behind the counter. "Can you do a decoy tonight?"

"No." Chloe said. "I hate those things. They mess with my karma."

"Right." Gabe said. "Have you seen our new secretary?"

"Nell? No." She pulled a cookie sheet out and then nudged him out of her way with her hip to put it on the granite counter.

"She didn't seem like the type to take a long lunch," Gabe said.

"She doesn't seem like the type to take lunch at all," Chloe said irritably, shoving a sweaty curl out of her eye. "Not that you'd notice."

"What did I do now?" Gabe said. Chloe shook her head and waved him away, but he stayed. "Chloe, do you remember much about my dad?"

She stopped, her irritation evaporating. "Patrick? Sure.

He was good to me. And he was crazy about Lu, remember? I hated it that he died so soon after she was born. He loved her so much."

"Yeah," Gabe said, trying not to remember. "Do you think he was bent?"

Chloe put the spatula down. "Like a crook?"

She hesitated, and Gabe thought, *Oh, hell.* He'd been hoping she'd say, "No, absolutely not, are you crazy?"

"More than you," she said finally.

"Me?" Gabe looked at her, dumbfounded. "You think *I'm* bent?"

"I think you do what you need to when you need to. I don't think you've needed to do anything particularly shady for a long while, but I think you're capable of it. I think you're capable of almost anything if the motivation is right."

"Jesus," Gabe said.

"Your dad was, too," Chloe said. "Except I think he liked money a lot more than you do. I think he liked women more than you do."

"Hey," Gabe said, insulted.

"Well, you've been faithful to me and you're not even particularly interested in me," Chloe said. "Your dad would have cheated on me on the honeymoon."

"We didn't have a honeymoon," Gabe said. "God, I love this conversation. So I'm crooked *and* undersexed?"

"I didn't say undersexed," Chloe said. "I said that wasn't a motivation for you. What's going on?"

Gabe felt the gloom close back over him again. "I think my dad may have done something really wrong. Something he didn't want me to know."

"Wow." Chloe leaned against the counter. "He told you everything. It must be pretty bad."

"It's something to do with the car."

"Really." Chloe tilted her head at him. "Something to do with your mom?"

"My mother?" Gabe frowned at her. "I don't—"

"You always said she left because of the car," Chloe said. "I never knew her, but I know you, and you don't get whatever morals you have from your dad. So maybe he did something really bad, and that's why she left and not because of the car."

"She left because he treated her like hell," Gabe said.

"She left a lot of times because he treated her like hell," Chloe said. "The car was the time she didn't come back."

"Maybe she just got fed up," Gabe said. "He did a lot of cheating and yelling."

"He shouldn't have been married." Chloe picked up her spatula again. "And from what he told me, she did things to get even with him and that made it worse. Marriage can be so awful."

"Thank you," Gabe said. Chloe began to take the cookies off the sheet, and Gabe inhaled the almond scent and thought, *That's always going to remind me of her.*

"Well, it's a gamble," Chloe said, as he picked up a cookie. "For women, anyway. Men can always start over again. The value of the male is based on money. The value of the female is based on youth and beauty. Men can always get more money, but women can't get back those years when they're gone. That's why they take men to the cleaners in a divorce."

"Cheap talk," Gabe said around a bite of cookie. "You wouldn't even take alimony."

"I wanted to be independent," Chloe said. "But I wanted Lu to grow up with you, too. I knew what you were doing when you bought the house next door for us, but it was so good for Lu. And then you gave me this place to run, and that was fun, too. But I should have said no. I should have gone."

The regret in her voice hurt. "If you want to go," he said, "go. I'll take care of Lu. You're still young. Close this place and go."

Chloe slapped down the spatula, and he stepped back in surprise. "See? That's why you're such a son of a bitch.

If you'd throw a fit, if you'd cheat, if you'd act like your dad, I could walk out and be free, but you're always so damn decent about everything and you make it so hard—" She broke off.

"Hey." Gabe put his arms around her. "I can be lousy. Let's talk about astrology."

"I have to go away," Chloe said into his chest. "Just for a little while."

"I've got you covered," Gabe said, his cheek against her hair. "How much money do you need?"

She pulled away and smacked him on the chest. "*Stop it*. I have to do this on my own."

"Okay." Gabe let go of her and took another bite of cookie. "Do you have any money?"

"Yes," Chloe said. "I know this place doesn't look like it right now, but it's been doing pretty good."

"Okay," Gabe said. "Are you going to get mad if I tell you to call if you need anything?"

"Yes," Chloe said. "But I'll call anyway."

She looked so sweet standing there, flushed from the heat of the oven and from her own frustration, and he knew it really was over, he'd known it for days, maybe longer than that. He bent and kissed her one last time, softly, and she put her hand on his cheek and said, "I really do love you."

"I love you, too," Gabe said. "Just do me a favor and make sure the guy who replaces me deserves you. I sure as hell didn't."

"You're doing it again," Chloe said. "Just *stop it*. Act like your dad for once."

"Astrology is crap," Gabe said, and she smiled and shook her head.

"Tell me that when I come back and you're madly in love with Nell," she said.

"God forbid," Gabe said and went back to his office.

*   *   *

When Nell had slammed open the door to the insurance agency an hour earlier, her old assistant Peggy had said, "Nell!" sounding pathetically grateful to see her, but Nell had kept right on going and banged open Tim's office door without knocking.

"Nell!" Tim looked up, as handsome as ever, and got to his feet. "How nice—"

"You *lied* to me," Nell said through her teeth, and his smile vanished. "You *cheated on me*."

Tim's surprise shifted to cautious sympathy. "I'm sorry, Nell. I was hoping you'd never find out."

"I *bet* you were, you *son of a bitch*," Nell said, and Tim jerked his head back.

"It wasn't like that," he said, looking wounded. "I didn't want to hurt you. And I didn't really lie. Our marriage had been dead for years."

"*Had* it? Well, *gee*, then why we were still *sleeping* together and *running a business* and—"

"Because I didn't realize it." Tim sat on the corner of his desk, professional, adult, calm, and understanding in a shirt another woman had picked out. "It wasn't until I met Whitney that I realized there was more to life than insurance and . . ." He spread his hands, helplessly. ". . . I had to follow my heart." He smiled at her sadly. "The heart has its reasons."

Nell looked around for something to throw, something to hit him with, something that would jolt him out of this calm, let's-all-be-adults hypocrisy and into something a little more satisfying. Like naked terror.

"Don't take it personally, it didn't have anything to do with you," Tim said, and Nell saw the Icicles lined up behind him—fourteen awards for best Ohio agent of the year—and felt suddenly, insanely calm.

"Well, don't take this personally, either, sweetie," she said and walked behind him while he slid off the corner of the desk to get out of her way. She picked up the first of the crystal statues and smashed it on the desk where he'd been sitting. It splintered into shards, almost exploding on impact, making a huge gouge in the mahogany, and she thought, *Yes*, as Tim yelled, *"No!"*

"I've just realized that you are a completely worthless human being," Nell said, picking up another Icicle. "I spent a year and a half in purgatory because you're such a lying coward that you didn't even have the decency to tell me the truth."

"Nell," Tim said, backing up, warning in his voice. "Be fair. You always told Jase when he was little that feelings are feelings and you have to pay attention to them."

"That's true, and right now *I'm feeling a little angry*." Nell raised the crystal over her head and smashed it into a thousand jagged pieces as Tim scrambled around her to grab up as many Icicles as he could.

Peggy came to the door and said, "What—" as Nell picked up an Icicle he'd missed. Peggy stopped, her eyes wide.

Nell ignored her to focus on Tim. "Although actually, if I was following my heart, I'd bury one of these suckers in your *spleen*."

Tim took a leap back as she smashed the third crystal, smacking it against his desk so hard that the pieces flew across the room.

"Oh, my," Peggy said as Nell picked up another one.

"Okay, that was dangerous." Tim drew himself up, his arms full of Icicles. "If you'll just calm down—"

"This one's for Jase," Nell said, brandishing the fourth crystal at him. "Because I think he knows the truth, which means you forced my son to *lie to me*." This one she threw all her body weight behind, and it splintered with so much force that one of the shards ricocheted into the window behind her and cracked it.

"Nell!" Tim yelled. *"Stop it!"*

What she needed was a rhythm. She grabbed and smashed a fifth one, swinging it like a tennis racket served at the floor. The tennis serve smash felt good, traveling up her arms, making her muscles sing. That was what she needed, good pacing and a smooth delivery.

"Goddamn it, I lied for *you!*" Tim said, trying to pick up another crystal even though his arms were full.

"You lied"—she grabbed the next crystal, swung it, and smashed it on the desk—"because you're a cheating"— *swing and smash*—"cowardly"—*swing and smash*—"spineless"—*swing and smash*—"slimy"—*swing and smash*—"son of a *bitch* who didn't want to take the *responsibility* for wrecking his marriage." She stopped to catch her breath and because there weren't any more Icicles on the shelf; Tim was holding the last four in his arms, his eyes defying her to take them.

Nell put her chin down. "Give me those."

"No." Tim stood stern and tall. "Absolutely not. You should see yourself, you look crazy."

"Give me those," Nell said quietly, "or I will take them from you and beat you to death with them."

Tim gawked at her, and Nell reached out and wrenched one from his arms and swung it into the desk, feeling stronger with each explosion.

"This is *crazy.*" Tim tried to scramble around her, and she grabbed another Icicle, tripping him as he went, and smashed it on the desk before turning to scoop up one he'd dropped as he'd staggered over her foot. She smashed that one, too, and then advanced on him for the last one, lusting after it more than she'd ever lusted after him.

"I need that," she said. "*Give it to me.*"

"Stop it," he said, clutching his last Icicle to his shirt. "For heaven's sake, look at this mess."

"You think this is a mess?" Nell said. "Have you seen our family lately? Have you checked out our business? You smashed everything we'd built, everything we worked for, because you wanted to screw a size six. *This*"—she gestured to the glass-strewn office—"is *nothing* in comparison."

Although now that she looked around, the place was a pretty significant mess. His desk was destroyed. The window was cracked. The gray carpet was full of crushed glass. She'd done some good work here.

"There's no need to be nasty." Tim's anger made him flush. "Whitney wears a two. And I lied for you and Jase," he said, backing toward the door. "I didn't want you to be hurt."

Nell stopped, dumbfounded, breathless with disbelief. "You didn't want me to be hurt? You spend twenty-two years living with me, working with me, having a family with me, not a cloud in the sky, not a hint that anything is wrong, and then on Christmas you leave me, no explanation, the world suddenly makes no sense, and you think that won't hurt?"

"It wasn't your fault," Tim said, taking a step forward. *"I know it wasn't my fault."*

"It wasn't because you weren't attractive or young or understanding," Tim went on. "I didn't care about that."

"I'm going to kill you," Nell said.

"If I'd said, 'There's another woman,' you'd have thought it was because you weren't good enough."

"No, I wouldn't have," Nell said. "I'd have thought you were an unimaginative son of a bitch having a midlife crisis."

"But it wasn't about you," Tim said earnestly. "I just fell in love. It had nothing to do with you."

"So it's all about you," Nell said. "I'm just an innocent bystander."

"Yes!" Tim said, relieved that she understood. "It would have done you no good to know about Whitney, it would only have caused you pain. I did it for you."

"Were you always this much of a weasel?" Nell said. "Because I honest to God can't remember."

"Nell, I know it's a shock, but really, everything's fine. You're doing great, Jase is doing great, I'm happy." He spread his arms to show forgiveness, the last Icicle in one hand. "'Course, I'm going to have to replace a lot of Icicles here."

Nell locked her eyes on the last Icicle and went after it, ignoring the crunch of the glass under her feet. "Give me that."

Tim shoved the Icicle at Peggy who was still standing frozen by the door. "*Quick!*" he said. "She's lost her mind. Go lock that up."

Peggy took the last Icicle and looked at Nell, caught, and Nell stopped, equally caught, this time by reality. She looked around the office and felt like hell, not because she'd destroyed it, but because destroying it hadn't helped. All she'd done was lower herself to his level. Now Peggy thought they were both scum.

Tim nodded, stern and in control, the Face of Reason in a mint-green shirt and coordinated tie. "I'm so disappointed in you, Nell. And I know Peggy must be, too."

"Not really," Peggy said and handed the last Icicle to Nell. "I quit."

She left as Tim said, "*Peggy!*"

"You are such a loser," Nell said, holding the last Icicle. "And I will *never* have to save you again." With one final swing, straight from the shoulder, she smashed the last Icicle—flinching as a piece of it flew up and caught her on the cheek—and with it the last of her life with Tim.

"You never saved me," Tim said, any pretense of friendship gone. "I was the brains in the business. You were *just the secretary.*"

"You can keep telling yourself that," Nell said, "but it's not going to help."

He stood behind the mutilated desk and looked at her as if he hated her, and she said, "Good. Now you know how I feel."

Then she walked out of her old office and her old life, completely at a loss about what to do next.

Nell tried to stay angry on her way to the McKennas, absentmindedly wiping blood from the cut on her cheek, but it didn't work. Back in the office, she sat behind her desk and felt the ice creep into her veins. She wasn't allowed to fix this place, wasn't allowed to get the money back from Lynnie, wasn't even allowed to go rescue that poor dog in New Albany. Every time she tried to get up to speed, some man slowed her down. She tried to be angry about that, but mostly she just felt tired. And she'd lost Peggy's job for her, too. She called the office and got Peggy as she was leaving.

"I'm so sorry," Nell told her. "Don't quit because of me."

"I'm not," Peggy said. "I don't want to work here anymore. Ever since Whitney took over your job, she's driving me crazy. She doesn't know what she's doing because she's just starting, and she makes mistakes and then gets mad at me if I fix them without checking with her, and then she gets even madder if I don't fix them. I can't win."

"I know how that feels," Nell said. "Are you going to be okay?"

"I'm going to be fine," Peggy said. "Tim's going to have problems, though."

"Good," Nell said, but when she'd hung up, she slumped in her chair again. She tried to concentrate on her work, but when Gabe came out of his office a few minutes later, she was staring hopelessly into space.

He started to say something and then stopped to stare at her. "What happened to your cheek?"

Nell touched the cut. *My old life happened to it.* "Flying glass."

"Oh, hell, stay there," Gabe said, his voice exasperated as usual. He went into the bathroom and came out with a damp paper towel and the first aid kit.

"Really, it's okay." Nell rolled away from the desk a little. "I'm fine."

"You're bleeding all over the office." He hooked his foot around the bottom of her chair and pulled her back. "Sit still. This is the closest we've got to medical benefits, so take advantage of it."

He dabbed the cut clean and then smoothed antibiotic cream on her cheekbone, his fingers surprisingly gentle even while he scowled at her, so she sat quietly while he cut a tiny butterfly bandage to hold the cut closed, and tried not to enjoy being taken care of since it was sure to be a fleeting moment. She watched his eyes while he worked, intent on her, and when he was finished, he glanced at her and the glance caught. She stopped breathing for a minute because he was so close, and he froze, too, and then he said, "You're done," and sat back. "Now, where the hell did you find flying glass?"

"You don't want to know." Nell touched the butterfly.

"Yeah, I do. Am I missing another window?"

"No," Nell said and flushed. He sat watching her, waiting for something, and she finally spoke just to fill the silence. "Thank you for the first aid. I owe you."

"Good." He stood up. "We're collecting. We need you to work tonight."

"Tonight?" Nell shrugged as he took the first aid kit back into the bathroom. "Okay. Tell me what it is and I'll do it now."

"Not secretarial," he said as he came out again. "Riley will pick you up at nine. Lose the bandage by then."

"Nine tonight?" Nell said. "What is this?"

"Decoy work. You sit down in a bar next to a guy to see if he picks you up." He turned back toward his office.

"Wait a minute. Some guy is going to proposition me?" She thought of herself in the mirror that day, looking like she'd been dead for months. "I think you've got the wrong kind of woman here."

Gabe shook his head. "Men in hotel bars are not that picky."

"Ouch," Nell said.

"Sorry. Didn't mean it that way. You're a very attractive woman."

He seemed marginally sincere, but she'd seen herself in that mirror. On the other hand, she didn't have anything better to do with her evening, except discuss her day with Suze.

"I'll do it," Nell said.

When Nell returned Gabe's datebook an hour later, she still looked flushed and stormy and even more unstable than usual with that cut on her cheek, all of which was oddly attractive. Of course, he'd always had a weakness for the odd and unstable. Look at Chloe.

He stood up. "Let me show you our freezer."

"Your freezer?" she said, but she followed him through the outer office and into Chloe's storeroom where he un-locked the door to the big walk-in freezer.

"This is where we keep our back files," he said, holding the door open for her.

"Why?" she said, peering in.

"Because it locks," Gabe said. "And because Chloe only uses the front part."

"Why does she have a freezer at all?" Nell said.

"The place used to be a restaurant. We use what we have." He flipped on the light and stepped inside and she followed him in. "Somewhere in here is at least one file box marked '1978,' possibly two. Find them and go through them and pull out everything that has Trevor Ogilvie's or Jack Dysart's name on it."

"All right," Nell said, looking around. "I can't get locked in here by accident, can I?"

"No. It's not an automatic latch."

"And how many years of files do you have in here?"

"Twenty or thirty. The rest are in the basement."

"You have a basement, too." She sounded depressed by that. "Okay, 1978. I'll find it." He turned to go and she said, "Are you ever going to tell me what's going on?"

"Sure," Gabe said as he stepped out of the freezer.

"About the time I let you redesign the business cards and repaint the window."

Searching through file boxes didn't do much to occupy Nell's mind, so she worried about the night to come; by five, she'd found at least two dozen files with Trevor's or Jack's name on them, and she was sick to her stomach with pre-performance stage fright. So on her way home, she stopped at Suze's and said, "I need a makeover," and when she opened the door to Riley four hours later, he was appropriately speechless at the sight of her.

"I had some work done," she said as she waved him into her apartment.

"It shows." Riley tilted his head and surveyed her. "Redhead, huh? It suits you."

"You don't think it's too bright?" Nell went back to the mirror. She couldn't get over it herself. With vivid color in her hair and some makeup, she looked semi-alive again. "I thought it was too much, but Steven said this would look natural."

"Who's Steven?"

"Suze's hairdresser. By the park. He's a genius."

"He certainly is," Riley said. "Everything looks natural."

Nell turned back to see him looking at her dress, an electric blue bandage that wrapped around her like a second skin. "It's Suze's," she said, and when he said, "What's Suze's?" she realized he was looking at her body, not the outfit. "The dress. My best friend, Suze, gave it to me."

"Suze has good taste," Riley said. "Jesus."

"So all I have to do is be nice, right?"

"In that dress, you don't even have to be nice," Riley said. "And now we have a problem."

"What?" Nell tugged at the dress. "Too tight?"

"For me, no. For the bug, yes." He held up a tiny tape recorder. "You need to put this somewhere where it can't be seen." He shook his head at her. "I can see everything."

"No, you can't." Nell held out her hand. "This is Suze's push-up bra that's at least a cup size too big for me. There's room in here for an entire stereo system."

"Imagine my disappointment," Riley said and handed over the recorder mike.

She managed to wedge the recorder into Suze's bra, but that was the only thing she was relieved about as she went into the elegant hotel bar half an hour later and crossed the room to the man Riley had pointed out to her from the doorway.

"Scotch and soda," she told the bartender, and then she looked around the mirrored bar before glancing at the man next to her.

He was an ordinary-looking guy in a nice-looking suit, and he was watching her. Or, at least, he was watching Suze's bra and Steven's hair.

"Hi." She smiled and turned back to her scotch and startled herself with her redheaded reflection in the mirror. It had been a long time since she'd looked this good. She wet her lips and smiled again into the mirror, into her own eyes instead of somebody else's, flirting with herself as she drank her scotch. Actually, she'd never looked this good. If she put back on some of that weight—

The guy caught her eye in the mirror. "Hi," he said and held out his hand. "I'm Ben."

"Hi, Ben," she said, taking it. "I'm Nell." *And I'm hot. Sort of.*

"What's a nice lady like you doing in a place like this?"

"Getting a drink." Her pulse was pounding. It was a miracle he couldn't feel the throb through her palm. "You?"

"Getting drunk," he said. "I'm in town on business, and it's boring as hell. You here on business?"

"Yes," Nell said, taking back her hand as the bartender put a second drink on the bar for her. "My job is definitely responsible for this."

"Well, here's to your job," Ben said, raising his glass. "It's certainly making my night better."

He was nice, Nell discovered as he bought her drinks and listened to her. Tim hadn't listened to her since she'd said, "I do." "I like you," she told Ben over her third drink, and then she remembered that he was married.

He smiled back at her. "I like you, too." He looked around the bar and added, "But this place is noisy, and I want to talk some more." He looked deep into her eyes. "How about coming up to my room where it's quieter?"

Was the whole world full of straying men? How did anybody stay married?

"I'm sorry," Ben said into her silence. "I shouldn't have asked."

"No, it's okay," Nell said. "I'm just getting over my divorce, so I'm a little shaky on this stuff."

He smiled at her, sweet if you didn't know he was a cheating scum. "I promise to go slow," he said and touched her shoulder lightly, and to her surprise, Nell flushed.

It had been just a little blip in her pulse, but it was there, and it made her realize there hadn't been any blip for a long time. She looked down at herself, wrapped in Suze's blue Lycra, and realized she'd become disconnected from her body. No hunger, no lust, she wasn't even sure she could feel pain. The cut on her cheek hadn't hurt at all, now that she thought about it. Maybe she was dead and she was just too damn dumb to lie down.

"Nell?" Ben said. "I'm sorry, I—"

"Yes," she said to him, suddenly desperate to feel something. She didn't want to die without having slept with anybody but Tim. She didn't want to die at all, she wanted to feel alive again. Ben was a cheat, he didn't count, he was from out of town, she'd never have to face him again. *Prove to me I'm still alive.*

"Yes," she said. "I'd love to come to your room with you."

"I'm glad," he said. "You're somebody I want to get to know better."

You don't want to know me, she wanted to say. *Just have sex with me, and then I'll rat you out to your wife.*

They caught the elevator as people were getting off, and Nell stood beside him, vibrating with tension. This was the right thing to do. She needed something to break through the ice that held her still, something to start her moving again.

The elevator doors opened, and Ben held them apart for her. She went down the hall with him and waited while he unlocked his door. "In you go," he said cheerfully, and in she went, trying not to hyperventilate.

He took off his coat and threw it over a brocade chair, looking like every guy she'd ever known in a shirt and tie. *Maybe I should try dating bikers*, she thought.

"How about a drink?" Ben said, and she put her hand on his arm and said, "No. Thanks."

She stepped closer so he could kiss her, and he stepped closer, too, smelling of whiskey, which wasn't unpleasant, and feeling warm under her hands when she put them on his arms, which also wasn't unpleasant. She had a feeling she should be getting more than "not unpleasant," but she'd been dead a long time, so she didn't want to ask for too much. And when he kissed her, a perfectly good kiss, that wasn't unpleasant, either.

Then he slid his hands down her back onto her rear end, and she didn't feel a thing, not a tremble, not a shudder. And for the first time she realized that could be a problem; unless he traveled with KY, there was no way she was going to be able to have sex with him. Not to mention when he peeled off her bra, he was going to find the microphone.

He kissed her again while she tried to figure out what to do. Maybe if she—

Somebody knocked on the door, and Ben whispered, "Sorry," and went to answer it.

"I think you have my wife in here," Riley said, and Nell thought, *Oh, thank God.*

"Your wife?" Ben said, and Nell went to the door, trying not to smile in relief.

"Hi, honey," she said brightly.

"Honey?" Ben said. "I thought you were divorced."

"Not quite," Riley said through his teeth, glaring at her. "She misses on the details sometimes."

"Really sorry about this," she said to Ben as she slipped past him. He looked at her the same way Riley had. Well, she couldn't blame him, she'd lied to him.

Although he had definitely lied to her.

"I really am sorry," she said, turning back at the door. "I think it's indefensible to lie to a prospective lover about your marital status. Don't you?"

The last thing she saw as Riley pulled her away was Ben flushing, whether in rage or embarrassment, she couldn't tell. It really didn't matter.

Riley was seethingly quiet all the way down High Street, waiting until they were back in Nell's apartment, and she'd turned to him and said, "Okay, so I probably shouldn't have done that," before he snarled, *"Probably?"* and launched into a tirade on her criminal negligence in not following orders that could have led to grievous consequences. "What are you trying to do?" he yelled at her finally. "Turn Gabe and me into *pimps?*"

"I think you're exaggerating." Nell felt close to tears. She hadn't wept for months, not since Tim had dumped her. She tried to listen to Riley's accusations, tried to goad herself into sobbing, but it wasn't going to happen. She could smash offices and dye her hair and pick up men all she wanted, but she was never going to feel anything again. Depressed beyond measure, she left Riley in midsentence and went into her living room and sat down on her daybed in the dark, still not crying. She hadn't even bought the daybed herself, Suze had. She was a ghost in her own life.

After a minute, Riley came in and sat down beside her. "I'm finished yelling," he said in a normal voice. "What the hell is wrong with you?"

"I can't feel anything," Nell said. "I haven't felt anything forever. I forget to eat because I never get hungry anymore. I find out my husband lied to me and cheated on me and I wreck his office—"

"What?" Riley said, alarm in his voice.

"—and by five, I'm back to numb. I end up in a total stranger's hotel room, and he kisses me and I feel nothing. Absolutely nothing. Not even revulsion or fear." She looked at him and said, "I'm dead. And I don't think I'm coming back. That man was kissing me and I felt *nothing*."

"He was also a total stranger who was cheating on his wife," Riley pointed out. "I don't think those are big turn-ons for you."

"Nothing is a big turn-on for me," Nell said. "I'm stuck in the 'off' position, and I think it's forever." She drew a long, shuddering breath. "I thought maybe changing the way I look would do it, but it's all on the outside. I'm still gray inside. And I can't break *out of it*."

Her voice rose up to a cry at the end, an ugly, fingernail-down-a-blackboard screech, and she expected Riley to pull away, but he put his arm around her instead, solid and strong.

"You are overdramatizing this," he said.

She pulled back, insulted. "Listen, you," she said, and he leaned forward and kissed her.

Chapter Five

She grabbed at him, first in surprise, and then because he felt good, hot on her mouth, solid under her hands. "What was *that*?"

"You think too much." Riley let his fingers slide down her neck and made her shiver. "See? Not dead."

"Hey, I have real troubles," Nell said, trying to get her indignation back, but he drew his fingers over her breast, and she lost her place in the conversation.

"You have no troubles," Riley said. "You got divorced from a guy who didn't deserve you, you have friends who are so worried about you they got you a great job, and tonight you have me. I see no problems here."

"Well, *I—*"

He kissed her again, this time full out groping her while he did, and the pressure of his hand felt so fine on her breast that she leaned into him while she kissed him back, wanting him to push against her, to struggle with her, to make her feel something again. "See?" he whispered against her mouth. "You were just with the wrong guy."

"Oh, and you're the right guy?" she said and surprised herself by laughing.

"For tonight, I'm the right guy." Riley slid his thumb into her neckline. "You're definitely at the disposable lover stage," he said and kissed her neck.

"There's a disposable lover stage?" Nell said, but he was leaning into her, and she smiled into his mouth as he kissed her again. "I don't believe this," she said when she pulled away. "I'm really *depressed*—"

"No, you're not. You're mad as hell." He ran his fingers lightly down the back of her dress. "You just think depressed is more ladylike. Time to blow off some steam. Where's the zipper to this thing?"

"I am not having sex with you," Nell said, moving away, but not too far. The kissing part was cheering her up too much for her to kick him out just yet. "It would be unprofessional."

"Oh, and you've been such a pro tonight." Riley pulled her toward him gently so he could look over her shoulder. "There is no zipper on this dress."

"It's Lycra," Nell said. "It pulls on. With a great deal of effort."

"Good thing I'm a strong guy," Riley said, reaching for the hem.

"Nope." Nell pushed his hand away. "I'm not having sex with you. You're an infant."

"An older woman," Riley said. "Good. Teach me everything you know." He pulled her to him again, and she put her arms around him and kissed him back because he was really good at it, and he fell slowly back onto the daybed with her on top of him. "I'm a beginner at this," he said, "so you'll have to tell me everything I'm doing wrong."

He slipped his hand between her legs and she said, "Well, *that* for starters."

"Too soon?"

His hand slid away and she felt vaguely disappointed.

"We'll start at the top and work down, then," he said and kissed her again when she opened her mouth to protest, touching her tongue with his. *As soon as this kiss is done*, she thought, but when the kiss was done, she was pressed against him, thinking, *Necking doesn't count, especially when you're with somebody who does it this well*, and ten minutes later, when he'd managed to pry the Lycra above her hips, she decided petting didn't count, either. And shortly after that, she wasn't thinking at all, just reacting to his mouth and his hands, feeling herself grow hotter the more he touched her, wanting his hands to be rough instead of gentle, but willing to take gentle if that was all she could get. When her dress and his shirt were off, he drew his fingers up her stomach and she shivered against him as he said, "It's a real shame the way you can't feel anything."

"Don't gloat," she said and pressed closer to him, trying to absorb his heat.

"Nothing to gloat about," he said. "Yet."

Then he began to kiss his way down her body, easing her underpants off with one hand. Nell said, "Uh, wait a minute," and he said, "No," into her belly button and kept on going. And ten minutes later, every nerve in Nell's body thawed and came screaming back to life.

"Now I'm going to gloat," Riley said, and then, while Nell tried to catch her breath, he shoved off his pants. *I really shouldn't be doing this*, she thought, but he rolled so she was on top of him, kissing her softly, and she clung to him while he slid hard up into her. And then to her amazement and relief, he rocked her back to another short, sharp explosion, clearing out her veins and her brain with cheerfully gentle efficiency.

"You do that really well," Nell said when she had her breath back and they were apart again. She felt weirdly good, as if she'd just had an out-of-body experience, sort of detached but pleased.

"I practice." Riley kissed her on the forehead, a brotherly kiss that was also weird, considering they were both naked and he'd just gotten rid of a condom. "You okay?"

"Yes," Nell said, not sure. Her body felt wonderful, but her mind was fogging up again, trying to match passion and Riley with anything in her previous existence and getting nowhere. Well, that was good. She was trying to start a new life. Except that now that the rolling around was over, she didn't feel much different. Cold and embarrassed, but not different. She felt around for her chenille throw, and Riley rolled away from her on the daybed and stood up.

"Looking for this?" he said, and flipped the throw over her.

"Thank you." She struggled to sit up, trying not to look at the large naked man in her apartment, and he dressed while she nonchalantly didn't watch.

"Uh, Riley," she said, when he was buttoning his shirt. "I think—"

"Well, stop it," he said, stooping to kiss her again. "Get some sleep, kid, and start again tomorrow. You'll be up to speed in no time."

He was gone before she could figure out a good answer, so she lay back in her bed, the soft chenille around her, and listened to her body. Her mind might be fogged, but her body was pretty clear. Good things had happened.

"What the hell," she said and, for the first time since the divorce noticed that there wasn't anybody there to hear her.

Maybe it was time to relearn playing well with others.

Not that she didn't already have Suze and Margie—

Suze and Margie. They'd *die* when they found out what she'd done. Nell laughed out loud, surprising herself again, and then curled up again to fall asleep, marginally cheered by life in general.

Nell smiled as innocently as possible at Gabe when he came down to the office the next morning, but he stopped and stared at her anyway.

"What?" she said, guilt making her cranky.

"Your hair looks good," he said.

She touched it, surprised. Right, she'd dyed her hair red. "Thank you."

"Any particular reason you changed it?"

"No," Nell lied, and he stood there, tall and unfathomable, staring at her with those eyes until she said, "Really. No reason. I mean, there was that thing last night, the decoy thing—"

Gabe nodded.

"—and Riley said I should look hot—" She flushed because it sounded stupid and because saying "Riley" reminded her of how *really* stupid she'd been. "—and it was time, I mean, I was looking pretty gray—"

He nodded again, patient, which made her temper flare.

"—and this is really none of your business," she finished, sticking her chin out.

"I know," he said. "Anything else you want to tell me?"

"I don't want to tell you anything at all," Nell said and turned back to the computer, ignoring him until he said, "Thanks for making coffee. You can start on the basement today," and went into his office.

A minute later, Riley came down from his apartment.

"Look," Nell said. "About last night—"

"It was fun, you appreciate it, you're feeling much better, but you don't want to do it again." Riley picked up his cup and saucer from the shelf and poured his own coffee.

Actually, I'm not feeling that much better, Nell thought, checking to make sure Gabe's door was closed all the way. "Right. How did you know?"

"I told you, you're in the disposable lover stage. The last thing you want is a relationship, but you do want to know you're still functioning. Happens to people all the time after a divorce." He took a sip and said, "This is really good coffee."

"Thank you." Nell sat back in her chair. "For everything."

"Oh, my pleasure." Riley grinned at her. "Just promise me next time you won't go upstairs with the guy."

"I'm not going upstairs with anybody," Nell said firmly. "I'm not doing that again."

"Probably a good idea. Got any friends who'd like to flirt for money?"

"Yes," Nell said. "But her husband would have a fit, so probably not."

Gabe came out of his office. "There was nothing in the '78 files," he told Riley. "So Nell's going to start on the basement. If you've got some time, help her."

"You bet," Riley said, not looking at Nell. "Well, I gotta go do the report from last night." He evaporated into his office, and Gabe turned to look at Nell.

"What's with him?"

"Late night last night," Nell said, keeping her eyes on the papers on her desk. "You know, the decoy thing."

"Right. How'd that go?"

Nell handed him the tape without looking at him. "Guilty as sin. Got it right here."

"Great," Gabe said, not taking it. "Make a copy for the files, get the pictures printed, and FedEx the originals to the client with Riley's report."

"Right."

"You going to tell me what's going on?"

"No."

"I will find out eventually. I'm a detective."

"No."

"Okay," Gabe said, "the basement is yours," and went back into his office.

Oh, yeah, she could see herself explaining this one. "I was trying to jump-start my life so I slept with Riley, but it didn't work, and I'm a little depressed, but I'm still in there fighting. Any ideas?"

No.

Okay, malicious destruction of property hadn't helped and neither had meaningless sex, even though both had been cheering in the short term. Maybe she was too inner-directed. Maybe she should try to help others.

There was a dog in New Albany. . . .

She got up and went into Gabe's office. "Listen, this woman came in on Monday and she had this dog problem."

Gabe nodded.

"I think we should do something about it."

"No," Gabe said and went back to the papers on his desk.

"You can't just say no," Nell said, wanting to smack him.

"Sure I can. I own this place."

He was ignoring her, dismissing her, and she felt her blood rise. "You could do it tonight. Just go right in there and grab it and the owner would never find out."

"No."

Nell pressed her lips together. "It would be the right thing to do."

"It would be breaking the law."

"It would still be the right thing to do."

Gabe looked up at her, his brows drawn together. "Do you want me to physically remove you from this office?"

Nell met his dark, dark eyes and, to her immense surprise, felt a shiver go through her. *Yes.* Then she stepped back. One night with Riley and she was looking for it everywhere. Honestly. "No, sir."

"Then leave under your own power," Gabe said.

Nell gave up and left, conscious he was watching her as she went. She closed the door behind her and went back to her desk to pick up the phone.

"I need some help tonight at ten," Nell said when Suze answered.

"Sure," Suze said. "What are we doing?"

Nell looked over her shoulder to make sure Gabe wasn't standing in his doorway. "We're kidnapping a dog," she whispered. "Wear black."

Gabe distracted himself with agency business and idle speculation about Nell's next move in the fight for the dog until she came in later that afternoon, holding a large green ledger, and said, "I may have found something in the basement, but I'm not sure."

Gabe looked at her, still immaculate in her pale gray suit. "In the basement. How do you stay so clean?"

"It's a gift." Nell put the ledger down on his desk. "I have a question first. The files from '78 show a break about halfway through. The first five months are really well organized, and then everything goes to hell. Did you shift secretaries?"

"Yes," Gabe said.

"Bad decision," Nell said. "You should have kept the first one because the files are garbage after that."

"The first one was my mother," Gabe said. "She left."

"Oh." Nell straightened a little. "Sorry. Well, the good news is that she didn't leave until June of that year, so if you're looking for something before or around the twenty-seventh of May, it's easier."

Gabe pulled the ledger toward him and opened it to the place she'd marked with a slip of paper. "What's this?"

"Financial ledger from 1978. That's the only Ogilvie entry that doesn't match something in the files," Nell said. "But then it wouldn't. It's for flowers."

"Flowers?" Gabe said, running his fingers down the page.

"For a funeral," Nell said, just as Gabe found it: *Flowers, Ogilvie funeral*, written in his mother's strong, dark hand.

A funeral. "Who died?" Gabe said, trying to stay calm. "We'll have to check the newspaper files—"

"Maybe not," Nell said, sitting down across from him. "I think I know."

He looked up at her and she swallowed.

"Okay, I'm not sure, I'll have to check," she said. "But that would have been a year after I married Tim."

Twenty-two years ago, he thought automatically. She must have been as young as Chloe.

"And Tim's brother, Stewart," Nell went on, "had married Margie Ogilvie that spring. And shortly after that, Margie's mother died. Helena."

"Trevor's wife," Gabe said and sat back. "Olivia is twenty-two. Helena died in childbirth?"

Nell shook her head. "Margie's parents were getting a divorce. And then her mother died, and Margie's dad married again, fast, and Olivia was born almost right away. I know Margie was really upset, but she never said anything about it and I never asked. We weren't close then."

"How did Helena die?" Gabe said, praying it was something straightforward, in a hospital, with a lot of doctors around.

"She shot herself," Nell said, and Gabe thought, *Oh, Christ, this is going to be bad.* "I'm not sure about the details," Nell went on, speeding up, "except that Margie was there and it was awful."

"Margie saw her shoot herself?" Gabe said, hope rising.

"No," Nell said. "I think she was in the next room. But she was there, and she found her mom. It must have been terrible."

"Yes it must have been," Gabe said automatically, sitting back.

Riley knocked and came in, and Gabe pushed the ledger toward him.

"Did you see this?"

Nell stood up. "I'll leave you alone," she said and left before Gabe could say anything.

"What's with her?" he said to Riley.

"She probably didn't want to get thrown out again," Riley said, taking the ledger. "What's this?" Gabe filled him in, and when he was done, Riley looked as lousy as he felt. "You think your dad helped Trevor cover up a murder?"

"I think we'd better start looking into the suicide," Gabe said. "I'm going to call Jack Dysart and see if this is what the blackmailer really hit Trevor for. You get the police report on Helena's suicide."

Riley looked at the clock. "Tomorrow. It's too late to-day. What about Lynnie? You think she has something that pins this on Trevor?"

"I don't know. I stopped by today and the landlady was there again. I think she lives in the other half of the duplex, and I think she doesn't have much to do. I'm going to have to stake out the place tonight. Which reminds me, what happened with Nell last night? If we're going to be sued for something, I want to know."

"She . . . misunderstood," Riley said.

Gabe closed his eyes. "How badly did she misunder-stand?"

"She went upstairs with him. I got her out before any-thing happened."

"This woman has no brains," Gabe said. "Why the hell—"

"She has brains," Riley said. "You give up on women too fast. She's a great secretary and a nice person."

"I'm glad you like her. You've got her again tonight."

"Oh, no, I don't. I have a date." Riley looked at his watch. "Your turn."

"Nope," Gabe said. "I'm stalking Lynnie."

"So can't this thing with Nell wait?"

Gabe studied him. "Is there a reason you don't want to see Nell tonight?"

"No," Riley said. "However, there is a reason I want to see the hort major."

"I see. No, it can't wait. She's going to kidnap that dog in New Albany."

"You're kidding."

"No."

"You don't know that for sure," Riley said.

"I got twenty says she goes for it."

Riley considered it. "No bet. I'll watch her." He put the ledger back on Gabe's desk. "Suicide, huh?"

"We certainly hope so," Gabe said and picked up the phone.

*   *   *

When Suze held the door to her yellow Beetle open for Margie that night at ten, Margie said, "So what are we doing?"

"Stealing a dog," Suze said, tugging up on her low-cut tank top, the only piece of black clothing she owned. Jack liked color.

"Okay," Margie said and climbed into the backseat, holding the skirt of her black halter dress around her. "When we get done, can we go unpack Nell's china?"

"Did you miss the stealing-the-dog part?" Nell said from the front passenger seat as Suze slid into the driver's seat.

"I don't care," Margie said. "I just wanted out of the house. Budge is mad at you. He says you shouldn't be dragging me out this late at night."

"Sorry," Nell said, and Suze thought, *Budge needs a hobby. Besides Margie.*

"Dog stealing," Margie said. "You have such an interesting job."

Suze headed for the highway, not at all sure this was a good idea. On the other hand, a dog was being abused, and she was against that. And since she'd gotten married the day after she'd graduated from high school, she'd never gotten to pull any college pranks. No tipping cows, no stealing mascots, no putting Volkswagens in dorm rooms. This was as close as she'd ever come to youthful indiscretion and she should be enjoying it. The problem was, there might be an age limit on pranks. She was thirty-two. "You're not young anymore, babe," Jack kept saying. "Get used to it."

"Why is that guy doing that?" Margie said, and Suze looked in her rearview mirror and saw a nondescript gray sedan behind them flashing its lights. Suze slowed and the car pulled up beside them.

Nell leaned over her to look. "Oh, *no*. Pull over."

"I don't think so," Suze said. "On a dark road and we don't know who he is? I don't want to be tomorrow's headline in the *Dispatch*."

"I know who he is," Nell said. "Pull over."

Suze pulled to the side of the road and parked, and the other car pulled in front of her. "Who is he?"

Nell shook her head and rolled down her window, and Suze squinted out the front. Whoever he was, he was big. Hulking even. "You sure about this?" she said to Nell, but then the guy reached the car and bent down to look in Nell's window. Suze couldn't see him clearly in the dark, but she got an impression of a lot of jaw made larger by a lot of frown.

"You are dumb as a rock," he said to Nell.

"I am out for a drive with my friends," Nell said politely. "You are not invited."

The guy looked past Nell and saw Suze and looked stunned for a minute, and then he scowled, not the reaction Suze was used to from men. Usually they looked stunned and then smiled.

"You can go now," Nell said.

"You are out to steal a dog," the guy said, transferring his disapproval back to Nell. "That is illegal. Turn around now or I'll call the cops."

"You wouldn't really, would you?" Nell said, and the guy sighed.

"There's a Chili's out on 161, right before you make the turn into this place. Go there. I will follow you. If you take any fancy turns, I'm hitting 911 on the cell phone. And yes, I really will."

"No, you won't," Nell said, but she turned to Suze and said, "Drive to Chili's, please."

When they were back on the road, the gray sedan following them every inch of the way, Suze said, "Give. Who is that?"

"Riley McKenna," Nell said. "One of the guys I work for."

"He looks familiar," Margie said from the backseat. "Have I seen him before? Maybe he came into Chloe's. I learned how to do the cash register today."

Suze ignored her to concentrate on the essentials. "Would he really call the police on you?"

"No," Nell said, "but he'd follow us and make it all impossible. So we're going to have to convince him to let us go."

Suze shot her a glance. "What do you have on this guy?"

"Nothing," Nell said. "We're just going to appeal to his better nature. I'm fairly sure he has one."

When Riley followed them into Chili's, Suze got a better look at him. Tall, blond, and broad, with plain, non-flashy Midwestern good looks and enough jaw for two people, he frowned with exasperation and still drew glances from the women who passed him coming in. He wasn't her type—Jack was her type—but Suze could understand the attraction.

When they were sitting in a booth, Riley next to Margie who looked pleased to be there, he said to Nell, "You are not going to steal a dog," and Suze felt her temper spurt.

"Sure she is," she told him. "Who died and made you God?"

"This is my sister-in-law Suze," Nell said, and Riley nodded at her, not impressed. That was irritating, too.

"And this is my other sister-in-law, Margie," Nell said, and Riley turned to Margie and smiled down at her.

What the hell? The world was getting strange if Margie was going to get a job and all the men.

"Very nice to meet you," Riley said to Margie and turned back to Nell. "Three rules and you want to break them all. Gabe'll fire you, you know. He has no sense of humor about this stuff."

"Three rules?" Nell said. "I thought there were two, and I didn't tell them who the client was, and rescuing an abused dog should not be against the law, so I think I'm still in clear." She lifted her chin at him as the waitress came for their drink order, and Suze thought, *Nell?*

When the waitress was gone, Nell added, "What's the third one? I don't want to trip over it by accident." She sounded cheeky, almost flirting with him, and Suze sat back to watch.

"You already tripped over it," Riley said. "And fell. Last night."

Nell blushed.

"Nell?" Margie said, and Nell's blush deepened while Riley grinned at her.

My God, she slept with him, Suze thought. *Hallelujah.* "I'm liking you more," she told Riley. "But we're still going to rescue that dog."

"I don't want Nell to lose her job," Margie said, looking at Riley with heightened curiosity. "It's doing such good things for her."

Riley smiled at Margie, and Suze caught the crackle in his eyes and thought, *Whoa. No wonder Nell fell. I would have, too.* Then she remembered she was happily married.

"There's no reason Gabe has to know," Nell was saying. "It has nothing to do with him."

"He turned down the job," Riley said. "You're part of the firm, so he turned it down for you, too."

"No," Nell said. "If I was part of the firm, you'd have new business cards."

"Don't start with the business cards," Riley said. "This is about the dog you will not be stealing."

He sounded very sure, which was very irritating. Suze cleared her throat, and he turned to look at her, frowning again. "I don't think you understand the situation," she said. There was no crackle in his eyes at all as he tried to stare her down, none of the warmth she was used to when men looked at her, and it threw her off a little. "You can stop us tonight, but we'll do it sooner or later. So you might as well help us tonight and get it over with so you can go back to whatever it is you usually do with your evenings." She looked at Nell to see if she'd blush again, but she was nodding at Riley.

"This is true," she told him. "I'm going to get that dog."

"How long are you going to be insane?" Riley said to her. "Not that I don't appreciate aspects of it, but you're going to get burned here pretty soon if you don't cool your jets. Your luck can't hold forever."

"I am not insane," Nell said. "I am reclaiming my life."

"And somebody else's dog," Riley said.

"Yes."

Riley looked around the table. "And this is your gang." He shook his head. "Three women dressed in black on a residential cul-de-sac in New Albany. What were you going to tell the cops when they picked you up? You're theater majors?"

"The cops were not going to come into it," Suze said. "We were going to move unseen through the night."

"In a yellow Beetle," Riley said. "That thing glows in the dark. What were you thinking of when you bought it?"

"I didn't know I was going into a life of crime," Suze said. "You got a better idea?"

"Yeah," Riley said. "Unfortunately, I do." He signaled to the waitress, who came over immediately and took his order for a hamburger to go.

Somebody should give this guy some grief, Suze decided. Women were making it entirely too easy for him.

Nell was smiling at him, compounding the problem, although it was lovely to see Nell smile again. "I knew you'd help," she said to him.

"It's a good thing you're cute," he told Nell and her smile widened, and Suze forgave him everything.

"I like you," Margie said.

"That's good," Riley said. "Because you're staying with me."

Margie beamed at him, and Suze felt annoyed again. Nell was cute and Margie got invited to stay, so what was she, chopped liver?

"We'll use my car," Riley said.

"That's a really boring car," Suze said. "Only a guy with no imagination would buy a gray car."

Riley sighed. "Think it through. It'll come to you." He turned back to Nell. "We'll drop you and the mouth one block from the address. If you're nabbed, you'll call my cell phone, and I will come and rescue you if I can. If I can't, I'll bail you out."

"Thank you," Nell said. "Why can't Margie come?"

"Too many people," Riley said. "It should be just you, but I'm not going to be yapped at for the next half hour, so the mouth goes, too."

"I do not yap," Suze said.

The waitress brought the hamburger, and Riley handed it to Nell. "Use that to lure the mutt. Make sure you take its collar off before you leave the yard. All these places have those invisible fences, and you don't want the dog yelping as you drag it through an electromagnetic field."

"What if it bites her?" Margie said. "We don't know anything about this dog."

"That's her problem," Riley said. "I'm just trying to keep her from getting arrested and fired."

"He'd really fire me?" Nell said.

"If you dragged the agency into this? Hell, yes, he would. So would I. We have a reputation to protect."

"Hard to believe," Suze said coolly and was rewarded when he flushed a little.

"Don't take shots at the family business, lady," he said to her. "How would Jack feel if you dragged the law firm into this?"

Suze felt herself grow red. "How do you know about Jack?"

"I know everything." His face softened when he turned to Nell. "You know, this is really not a good idea."

"I know," she said. "But I have to. This is bigger than the dog, although the dog is enough."

"Okay." Riley stood up and nodded toward the parking

lot. "It's quarter to eleven. If you're going to do this, we go now."

Nell stood up, too, and took the hamburger. "I'm going to do this."

"Wonderful," Riley said and headed for the door.

"What about the check?" Suze said.

"Pay it," he called back. "This is your party."

"I don't like him," Suze said to Margie.

Margie slid out of the booth. "Think of him as a growth experience."

"Oh, good, I've been wanting one of those," Suze said and tossed a twenty on the table. It was too much, but she was in a hurry to steal a dog.

Riley dropped them at the corner, and as Nell shut the door, she heard him say, "So tell me about yourself," to Margie. She and Suze walked across the lot lines until they found the address. Her watch said five till eleven when they ducked under the firs at the back of the dog's lot, and ten minutes later, the door to the huge glass sunroom at the back of the house opened, and a man shoved a shaggy, cowering dachshund out into the yard with his foot. "Go on," he said, sounding bored. "Make it fast."

He stood there in his expensive landscaping with his arms folded, and Nell whispered, "Oh, damn, he's going to watch it." She grabbed Suze's arm. "Go ring the front doorbell. *Go.*"

"I don't wanna," Suze said, but she ran off into the dark, looking like a rogue beauty queen in her low-cut black tank top, and Nell zeroed in on the trembling dachshund, now squatting not ten feet away from her, elongated and frumpy. She unwrapped the hamburger and waved it around, hoping the darkness under the trees hid her from Farnsworth, still standing in the doorway. While she watched him, he turned to look back into the house, and then he swore and went inside.

"C'mon, SugarPie," she cooed softly into the darkness, waving the hamburger in front of her. "C'mere, baby."

SugarPie froze in midsquat, her eyes sliding back and forth over her long narrow nose as if she were trying to decide between the house and Nell and wasn't liking either much.

"C'mere, sweetie," Nell said, trying to keep the edge out of her voice, and SugarPie began to creep back toward the door.

"No, no, no!" Nell swooped down on the dachshund who squatted even closer to the ground in terror as Nell grabbed her around the middle, both ends sagging as she picked it up. "Shut up," she said, balancing the flopping animal on her hip as she took off, leaping over hydrangea and low boxwood to get to the darkness of the trees while SugarPie squirmed like a stretched, greased pig. The dog flinched when Nell dashed across the lot line— *"Sorry,"* she said. "Forgot about the collar"—and then it bounced on her hip, quivering but silent, its back legs scrabbling to find purchase on Nell's butt as she sped through the dark backyards. She heard Farnsworth yell, "SugarPie, you little bitch, where are you?" behind her, and then she was out onto the street, changing course to get as far away as she could, forgetting entirely where she was supposed to meet Riley.

Anyplace was better than here.

When she was six blocks away, she stopped to catch her breath and shifted SugarPie off her hip. "Sorry about that," she said, and the dog looked at her, its eyes peeled back, huge as golf balls, shuddering in her arms until it almost vibrated free. "No, really, it's okay." She bent down and put it on the smooth, white sidewalk under the streetlight, keeping one hand on its collar in case it decided to bolt. Instead, SugarPie collapsed, rolling over on her back to let her head fall back against the sidewalk, limp with fear, giving out a high-pitched moan that sounded like air escaping from a balloon.

"Good grief, don't do that," Nell said, trying to prop up the dog's head. If things got any worse, she was going to have to give it mouth-to-mouth. She could see herself explaining to Deborah Farnsworth, "Well, the good news is, I got your dachshund back. The bad news is, she fibrillated on the sidewalk." "Come on, SugarPie," she said, looking uneasily back over her shoulder. "Pull yourself together. Be a woman."

She picked up the dog and cradled it in her arms and began to walk down the block toward the highway. "You'll be okay," she said to the dog. "Really, you just had to get away from that awful man. We'll have you back to the lady who loves you in no time."

SugarPie didn't seem convinced, but now that they were moving again, she tuned her vibrating down to an intermittent shudder.

"I swear," Nell said, walking faster, "you're looking at a life of hamburger and no yelling." She held the dachshund closer, and it sighed this time and put its head on her arm, and she stopped to look down into its eyes. "Hello," she said, and SugarPie stared back, pathetic and wide-eyed in the glow from the streetlight, her eyelashes fluttering like a Southern belle confronted by a Yankee. "I swear to you, everything is going to be all right."

A car pulled up beside her and she leaped in fear, starting SugarPie's shudder reflex again, but it was only Riley. She climbed in the backseat next to Suze, and Riley said, "Oh, good, you got the dog," with no enthusiasm whatsoever and drove them away from the scene of the crime.

"You were great," she told Suze as she put the dog on the seat.

"No, she was not," Riley said, watching them in the rearview. "She actually talked to this guy, and when he files the police report, he's going to describe her, assuming he ever looked at her face."

Suze tugged up on her tank top but it didn't do much good.

"Maybe he won't realize she was in on it," Margie said. "Maybe he'll never know."

"He'll know," Riley said. "And he'll remember her."

"There are a lot of thirtysomething blondes in this city," Suze said.

"Not like you," Riley said. "You stick in a man's mind."

SugarPie sat on the seat between them, shaking like a maraca.

"Could you knock it off?" Nell said. "You're scaring the dog."

"I can relate," Riley said. "You scare the hell out of me, too. From now on, you dognap alone."

Gabe had already left for his first appointment when Nell arrived the next morning at nine-thirty, ready with an explanation for her lateness that didn't involve taking SugarPie over to Suze's and then explaining things to an angry Jack. That was just like Gabe. She'd gone to all the trouble of constructing a good explanation and then he wasn't there to appreciate it.

"How's the dog?" Riley said when he came out for his coffee, and Nell said, "Suze has her," and dialed SugarPie's mother to tell her the good news.

"I can't take that dog," Deborah Farnsworth said when Nell had explained the situation. "I think it's marvelous that you got her, but I can't take her. This is the first place he'd look."

"But she's your dog," Nell said, feeling the cold clutch of panic in her stomach. "Don't you—"

"To tell you the truth, I don't like her much," Deborah said. "She was a cute puppy, but then she grew up and got sneaky, and frankly, I'm just not a dog person. My husband was the one who wanted her."

Nell clenched her jaw. "Then why—"

"Because he was yelling at her," Deborah said, her voice

righteous. "And also, I didn't want the son of a bitch to have her. How much do I owe you?"

"Nothing," Nell said, facing ruin.

She hung up and thought, *I stole a dachshund for nothing.* Another grand gesture shot to hell. Plus now she had a dog to cope with. She tried to comfort herself with the thought that at least SugarPie was unabused now, depending on what Suze was doing to her, but the fact remained, she had a hot dog on her hands. Maybe she could give it away. To somebody in another state.

She went back to work, trying to keep her mind off SugarPie, only surfacing two hours later when the phone rang. It was the cleaners, confirming that they'd be in the following Wednesday since they'd gotten payment for the previous two months. "Thank you," Nell said and apologized again. "Administrative mix-up."

She hung up and thought, *Lynnie.* Lynnie and Deborah and Farnsworth-the-dog-kicker and Tim . . . the world was full of selfish people lying and cheating and getting away with murder and letting other people clean up after them. And everything she'd done to make things right had left her with nothing but some vague guilt over vandalism, a slight glow after irresponsible sex, and a traumatized dachshund she didn't want.

If she went after Lynnie, at least she'd get the money back. She'd have something concrete to show people, to show Gabe. She'd be doing something *useful* again, something professional, something that was part of managing a business.

After some thought, she put the answering machine on and went out to visit her predecessor.

Chapter Six

When Gabe got back to the office, Nell wasn't there again. He spared one thought for what she could possibly be doing to complicate his life this time and then went into his office, leaving his door open in case she came in.

She didn't, but the police did.

The door rattled and popped, and when he went out to look, he saw a man and a woman in uniform. Not anybody he knew. That damn landlady must have called them, and now he was going to have to come up with a good excuse for stalking an ex-employee.

"We're looking for Eleanor Dysart," the woman said, smiling at him while her partner slouched behind her.

"Not here right now," Gabe said cheerfully. "Can I help?"

"We'd like to talk to her," the woman said, just as cheerfully. "Do you know when she'll be back?"

"I don't even know where she is," Gabe said. "What did she do?"

"That's—"

"You're Gabe McKenna," the man said.

"Yes," Gabe said.

"She vandalized her ex-husband's office," the man said. "His new wife swore out a warrant."

Jesus H. Christ, Gabe thought. *I hired a maniac.*

"Nice, Barry," the woman said, but she didn't seem too upset. They'd been partners for a while, Gabe realized, and wondered what it would be like to work with somebody you didn't want to strangle half the time.

"She smashed a bunch of awards," Barry said. "The husband didn't seem too happy about the warrant, but the new wife . . ." He shook his head.

"She's mad," the woman officer said.

"I can make this go away," Gabe said. "Give me a couple of hours."

"We would be grateful," Barry said.

"We would be surprised," the woman said. "The new wife is not a cream puff."

"Neither is the old wife," Gabe said. "Give me until five."

He went back in the office and called Jack Dysart and got his administrative assistant, a smart, tough woman named Elizabeth.

"Jack's not here," Elizabeth told him. "He got a call and left."

"Tell me it was from his brother, Tim," Gabe said.

"No," Elizabeth said. "I can have him call you."

"No," Gabe said. "Find him. Tell him his new sister-in-law, whatever her name is—"

"Whitney."

"Tell him Whitney has sworn out a warrant for Nell's arrest on vandalism charges."

"Nell?" Elizabeth sounded doubtful. "That doesn't sound like her."

"That sounds exactly like her," Gabe said. "Tell Jack we're going to have to lean on Tim until he drops the charge."

"God, yes," Elizabeth said. "Jack will have a fit."

"He likes Nell that much?"

"Suze likes Nell that much," Elizabeth said. "Jack will have Tim arrested if Suze is unhappy."

"Tell him I'm on my way," Gabe said and hung up. *Interesting day*, he thought and went out to O&D to see what he could do to save his secretary's butt before he fired her.

Nell knocked on the door to the old brick duplex that matched the address in Lynnie's file, trying her best to look vague and unthreatening. When no one answered, Nell looked around the narrow porch and knocked again and then again and yet again, and finally a woman came to the door, a pretty brunette in her thirties sporting a low-cut red sweater. Nell said, "Lynnie Mason?" and the brunette said, "I'm not buying anything, thanks," and began to close the door.

Nell put her foot in the door, the way she'd seen it done in the movies, and then stuck her shoulder in there, too, for good measure. "I'm from the McKennas," she said, smiling brightly. "We seem to be missing some funds. Thought you might have them."

"I have no idea what you're talking about," Lynnie said. "But if you don't get out, I'll call the police."

"Good idea," Nell said. "I'll wait here. That way I can show them the checks you forged when they get here." She patted her bag which did not have the checks in it, and Lynnie thought fast. Nell could practically see the wheels turning behind her eyes.

"Look, I'll call Gabe later—"

"No," Nell said. "If Gabe wanted to handle this, he'd be here. He wants the money back, and he doesn't particularly want the police involved, but if it's a choice of no money or the police, he'll invite them right in. If you give me the money, nobody gets arrested. I think it's pretty simple, don't you?"

Lynnie opened the door. "Why don't you come in?"

Her duplex was sparsely furnished with plain pieces that looked temporary and a few personal pieces that looked expensive, but it also had hardwood floors, and big old windows that let in lots of light, and *space*, lots of space, room to move, and for a minute, Nell envied her.

"The thing is," Lynnie said, when they were sitting down, her voice softer, prettier without the edge, "I've been sick, and there were medical bills. I didn't mean to hurt anybody, I just wanted to pay my bills."

She looked imploringly at Nell, her eyes huge and beseeching, and Nell thought, *If I were a guy, that might even work.* The red sweater she was wearing would have been particularly effective, and Nell wished for a minute she was the kind of woman who could wear a tight, bright sweater instead of gray suits.

"You can understand that, can't you?" Lynnie said. "A woman alone?"

I must really look pathetic, Nell thought. *She can tell I'm alone.* She gave Lynnie a brisk smile. "Oh, sure, but now that you're all better, we'd like the money back."

Lynnie shook her head, as if in disbelief. "I can't believe that Gabe would care about a couple hundred dollars."

"Five thousand eight hundred and seventy-five," Nell enunciated clearly. "At least, that's what we've found so far. We'd like it in cash."

"That's impossible," Lynnie said, widening her eyes. "I couldn't possibly have borrowed that much."

"Cute," Nell said. "Come across with the cash, or I'm calling the cops."

Lynnie looked startled for a nanosecond, and then she smiled at Nell, her lower lip quivering a little. "You don't look like a cruel person."

"I've had a very rough week," Nell said. "Forget cruel, I'm vicious."

Lynnie met her eyes, and then she transformed in front of Nell from a helpless, soft girl into a tough, tired woman.

"*You've* had a rough week." Lynnie laughed. "Don't get me started."

"Yeah, it must really take a lot out of you, ripping off the innocent," Nell said.

"What innocent?" Lynnie sat back. "Honey, there are

no innocent men. Just guys who haven't been caught." She lifted her chin and said, "So I pay them back. I'm a one-woman justice squad."

"What did Gabe ever do to you?"

"Gabe?" Lynnie shrugged. "Gabe's okay. That my-way-or-the-highway bit got old fast, but he's basically all right."

She had a point. Nell tried to resist it because she didn't want to bond with Lynnie. "That doesn't justify trying to destroy his business."

Lynnie looked surprised. "I wasn't trying to destroy him." She leaned forward. "Look, what did I take? The cleaning money? I cleaned."

Not very well, Nell thought, but Lynnie was on a roll.

"I was underpaid in that job. Hell, I've been underpaid in every job I've ever had. If I was a guy, I wouldn't be just a secretary, I'd be an administrative assistant at twice the salary. I worked for this guy once who was a lawyer, and I did all his work. Every guy I've ever worked for has been big on sacrifice and service." Her mouth twisted. "*My* sacrifice and service."

"Well, then, go after *them*," Nell said, trying hard not to say *damn right*. "Look, torture the bastards in your life all you want, I'll stand on the sidelines and cheer. I even have a bastard of my own you can have. But I need Gabe's money back. That wasn't fair, he didn't deserve it."

"They all deserve it. You were married, right?" Lynnie said, zeroing in on her. "You've got that I-used-to-be-married look. How long? Twenty years?"

"Twenty-two," Nell said, feeling sick.

"Let me guess," Lynnie said. "You worked for him and built a life for him and invested all yourself in him and sacrificed for a future when it would be your turn. Only he changed his mind, and now you're working for Gabe. How are you doing financially?"

"I'm okay," Nell said. "That's not the point—"

"Just okay," Lynnie said. "But he's doing better than that, isn't he? You're back at minimum wage, but your ex, he's still living like you used to, maybe better."

"He's had to cut some corners," Nell said.

"And he's got the future you built for him, only it's with a new woman, probably younger," Lynnie went on, and Nell flinched. "Honey, I've been there. It'd be different if they let you go and said, 'Here, take back that great skin you used to have, take back those high boobs and that flat stomach and all that energy, you just start all over again, honey, we'll give you a second chance.' But they don't. You get older and all your assets are spent, and they leave you broken and there's not a damn thing you can do about it."

Nell swallowed hard. "I'm not broken. I don't care. Just give me Gabe's money and I'll go."

Lynnie leaned forward. "You don't have to be a victim. You can get even. You can make them pay. You would not believe how good it feels to make them pay."

"I don't want to make him pay," Nell lied. "I just want Gabe's money back."

"I could help you," Lynnie said. "You could help me." She leaned closer, intent and sincere. "Your problem is, you're afraid to play dirty." She spread her hands. "Why? They do. You have to cheat like they do. Take them for everything they've got and keep moving so they can't slow you down."

"I'm moving," Nell said. *I trashed his office.* And a fat lot of good that had done her. "And I know it's no good to just move against them. That's not getting me anywhere. I have to move toward something."

"Exactly," Lynnie said. "You are exactly right. That's what I'm doing."

"By ripping off Gabe?" Nell shook her head. "If exactly what you want is five thousand bucks, you don't want much."

"I want it all," Lynnie said. "Gabe can spare what I took. And the rest is coming from somebody who can spare a lot more." She sat back. "I don't trust him, but I've got

him. I have trusted enough men." She met Nell's eyes.
"You know?"

"Yes," Nell said. "But I still want Gabe's money back."

Lynnie took a deep breath and sat back, defeated.
"Okay. But first I need to call . . . my lawyer." She went to
the phone and dialed, looking back at Nell over her shoulder. "It's me," she said after a minute. "There's a woman
here from the McKennas and she's accusing me of taking
some money. I was thinking—" She stopped and flushed,
growing redder as she listened. "I stopped letting you tell
me what to do a long time ago. I'm not going to hand
over—" She stopped again, and then she said, "Six thousand dollars." She waited again, and evidently she liked
what she heard this time better because she started to nod
and her voice lightened and became pretty again. "All
right, then. What?" She looked around the apartment and
then said, "Sure, why not? As soon as I get back. Where?
Fine."

She hung up and turned back to Nell, smiling. "So. My
lawyer advises me to give you the money."

"Your lawyer's no dummy," Nell said, standing up.

"But the money's not here. It's in the bank. So I'll go—"

"We'll go," Nell said, and Lynnie lost her smile for a
moment.

"I'm not your enemy," Lynnie said, taking a step closer.
"They are."

"Just give me the money," Nell said, trying not to listen.

Lynnie closed in. "You know, if women just wised up
and stuck together, they couldn't get away with this stuff."

"Some of them don't cheat," Nell said. "Okay, Gabe's
a little controlling, but he doesn't deserve to be ripped off
for it."

Lynnie closed her eyes and shook her head. "So that's
it. You've got it for him."

"Got what?" Nell frowned at her and then understood.
"Oh. No, I just met him a week ago."

"It only takes a minute, honey," Lynnie said. "You've

got your work cut out for you with that one. He'll use you without even noticing he's doing it. Look at poor dumb Chloe."

"I just want the money back," Nell said.

"Yeah, I got that," Lynnie said. "I'll just follow you in my car.

"I walked," Nell said. "So I'll just ride with you. Friendlier that way."

At the bank, a small branch office in the Village, Lynnie cashed a check and turned the money over to Nell.

"Thank you," Nell said and turned and walked out of the bank, leaving Lynnie as far behind as possible—*Get thee behind me, Satan*—but when she got outside, Lynnie called to her from the bank's concrete porch.

"You've just made a mistake," Lynnie told her calmly, and Nell blinked at her.

"Is that a threat?"

"No," Lynnie said. "You're fighting for the wrong side. You're tough and you're smart and you're giving it all to Gabe. Didn't you just do that for your ex?"

Nell swallowed. "This is different."

Lynnie shook her head. "It's the same. Listen, if you and I got together, we could really do some damage." She smiled at Nell, a smile that held more rue than anger. "My problem is that I've always been good with money but not with plans. I've needed somebody smart to handle the details, you know? I thought I found somebody once, but he took off." Her face fell a little at the memory. "He said he was going to get a divorce and marry me, and I believed him. Never get involved with your boss."

"Tell me about it," Nell said, thinking of Tim.

"Gabe would be the worst," Lynnie went on, watching her. "You just can't work with a man like that, you can only work *for* him." She leaned a little closer to Nell. "But you could work with me. You look like you'd know how to plan, and I'd never cheat you."

She wouldn't, Nell thought and walked back to her.

"Listen, I'm sorry men have been lousy to you. I really am. I hope you get what you want. Preferably without maiming somebody else, of course, but I hope you get it anyway."

"The maiming is the best part." Lynnie leaned on the wrought-iron balustrade. "Look, I'm working on this thing. You'd be all for it, this guy is such a user even I can't believe it. And I've got the goods on him, he's paying, and we can get more. He deserves everything we could do to him. We're talking justice with a profit here." Lynnie smiled at her, and Nell smiled back. "But he's tricky. I could use some backup. How about it? You and me, pay-back time, full speed ahead."

For a moment, Nell considered it, the two of them wreaking vengeance for all womankind, but it was a fantasy. "I can't do it, Lynnie," Nell said. "I'm just not built that way." She stuck out her hand, and after a moment, Lynnie took it. "Best of luck, really."

Then she walked out onto the street, not looking back, and headed for the McKennas, full speed ahead on her own.

Nell was in the office an hour later when Suze came in carrying a box of gourmet dog biscuits and a wicker basket that held a black short-haired dachshund in a red sweater.

"You've got to take SugarPie," she said to Nell. "Jack just called and he wants to have lunch. Do you suppose he heard about the dognapping? Maybe that Farnsworth guy recognized me."

"No," Nell said, not sure. "But give me the dog and go." She took the basket and eyed the dog. "What did you do to her?"

"Clip and a dye job," Suze said. "The clip didn't go too well, but the dye looks great. It's that gentle, wash-out stuff, so I figured it wouldn't hurt her, but I washed her twice afterward with dog shampoo to make sure."

SugarPie looked up at Nell, her eyes as pitiful as ever

over her still-brown nose. "It's okay," Nell told her. "I have no shampoo. Your washing days are over." She put the basket under her desk where it was hidden from the door. Once the basket was down, SugarPie stood up. She was wearing a red sweater with a white turtleneck collar and cuffs and a white heart centered on her back.

"Cute sweater," Nell said doubtfully.

"It's cashmere," Suze said, peering under the desk at the dog. "Not scratchy at all."

"It's also September, not January," Nell said.

"She needs something to cover up the bad clip," Suze said. "That was the lightest outfit I could find. I've got more in the car so she can change outfits."

"Change outfits," Nell said.

"You should see the leather bomber jacket I bought her," Suze said. "Fleece lined. Come winter, she's going to look very butch."

Nell looked back down at SugarPie. She looked like a miserable anorexic cheerleader. "Thank you," she said to Suze. "That was very nice of you."

Suze put the box of gourmet dog biscuits on the desk and then faded toward the door. "She loves those biscuits. Really, she's so pathetic that she's no trouble at all. It's just that Jack—"

"I know, I know." Nell waved her toward the door. "Go find out what he wants. We'll be here."

When Suze was gone, Nell slid SugarPie's basket farther under her desk so she could scratch her with her toe while she worked, and after a couple of minutes of rhythmic scratching, the dachshund sighed and stopped trembling and began to doze, and Nell began to feel much better.

Things were finally looking up.

When Suze got to O&D, Jack was waiting for her outside his office, vibrating with anger in front of a lot of marble and expensive paneling.

"Hi, Elizabeth," Suze said, smiling at his assistant, keeping Jack in her peripheral vision.

"You're late," Jack said, cutting short Elizabeth's greeting and earning a sharp glance from her in return. "Come on."

"I was dropping the dog off at Nell's," Suze said as he hurried her toward the elevator. "You told me you didn't want it alone in the house, so I took it to her at work."

"I don't want it in the house at all," Jack said. "It would have been nice if you'd asked me before you let your crazy friend bring it over, but you didn't think of that."

"Nell's not crazy," Suze said sharply.

"The hell she isn't," Jack said. "You wouldn't believe what she just pulled. She's not part of the family anymore. Go shopping with Whitney instead."

"She's part of *my* family," Suze said, but he ignored her to slam his hand into the closing elevator doors and pry them apart.

They got on the elevator, taking their place in the middle as the three men already there made room for them, smiling at Suze. "Hi, Suzie," one of them said, and she turned around to see Budge's round face beaming at her. "Heard you and Margie and Nell are going to the movies tonight," he said, clearly delighted to be chatting with the beautiful wife of a senior partner. "You make sure Nell doesn't keep her out too late."

"Oh-kay," she said, thinking, *Call me Suzie one more time and I'll have you fired.*

The doors opened, and Jack took her arm and hustled her out to his BMW. By the time he slammed his door and put the keys in the ignition, she was so mad that she reached over and yanked them out again, surprised at her own temerity.

Jack looked startled. "What the hell do you think you're doing?"

"Why are you being such a jackass?" she said, standing up to him for the first time in fourteen years.

"Don't use that tone with me," he said. "Where were you last night?"

"I told you, stealing SugarPie in New Albany," Suze said. "Where'd you think I got her?"

"I thought you were telling me the truth. God knows it was bizarre enough." He glared at her and she glared back.

"What is *with* you? If you have a problem with the dog, it's over, Nell has it. If it's something else, tell me about it and stop being such a bastard."

"All right, if that's what you want." Jack drew himself up, probably trying for dignified rage and looking like a petulant twelve-year-old instead. "You're having an affair. Admit it. You're cheating on me."

Suze gaped at him. "Have you lost your mind?"

"Pete Sullivan saw you having dinner with Riley McKenna."

"I've never—" Suze stopped. "Last night? Nell, Margie, and I went there to talk to him. We were in a diner for about half an hour arguing with him about SugarPie. I can't believe this. I was with *Margie and Nell*, for heaven's sake."

"They'd lie for you," Jack said, some of his indignation gone. "Hell, Nell's capable of anything."

"Yeah, and then she got me the dog as a cover story. I didn't even know Riley McKenna until last night, and having met him, I don't want to know him any better. What is *wrong* with you?"

Jack exhaled and let his head fall back against the headrest. "I'm having a bad week."

"And you thought you'd share it with me? Thanks a lot." Suze shook her head. "I can't believe you don't trust me. *I'm* not the one with the past here, buddy."

"Hey," Jack said. "Watch your tone. I have never cheated on you."

"Then why did you think I was?" Suze said. "Peter Sullivan is a horrible person, you know that, you know he just said that to get at you, and you fell for it. I think you're projecting. I think you want to cheat. I think—"

"Wait a minute," Jack said, alarmed.

"—you're tired of being married to a woman in her thirties and you want something younger—"

"Suze, I love you," Jack said, leaning toward her now.

"—and you feel guilty about it, and that's why you don't want me to get a job—"

He leaned across her and kissed her, stopping her mouth and making her reach for him, everything solid in her world for as long as she could remember. "I will *never* cheat on you," he whispered, holding her close. "I love you. We're forever."

"How could you think *I* would?" Suze said, trying not to forgive him. "How could you say those horrible things?"

"Suze, I'm fifty-four," Jack said. "Riley McKenna's thirty. He's my worst nightmare."

"How do you even *know* him?" Suze said, and Jack pulled away a little.

"They do a lot of work for us," he said. "Look, I'm sorry. I heard you were there with him, and I lost it. I was stupid. Let me make it up to you."

"All right." Suze handed him his keys back, wanting the whole mess over.

Jack put the key in the ignition and started the car, patting her knee before he pulled out of the parking lot, back to his old jovial self, almost giddy with relief. "I can't believe you think I'd cheat," Jack said, cutting off another car as he pulled out into the street. "I'm home every night. I give you everything. What's with you having a temper all of a sudden?"

Just something else you gave me, she thought and settled back in her seat, not reassured at all.

The office door rattled again at one, and Nell looked up, expecting Gabe and seeing Jase.

"Lunch," he said, grinning at her, his dark eyes flashing. "Come on. My treat."

"I'd pay," Nell said. "But I can't go. I had to go out this morning and now I'm swamped." *Also I have a dog stashed under this desk.*

"Okay," Jase said. "Tell me what you want and I'll bring it to you."

"I'm not hungry," Nell said. "I can—"

The door rattled again and popped open and hit Jase in the back.

"Hey," he said, and then Lu poked her head around the door and said, "Don't stand in front of the door, dummy." She cocked her head up at him, really looking at him this time, and then she smiled. "*Hello.*"

"Hello," Jase said, leaning around the door toward her, and Nell thought, *Uh-oh.*

"He was just leaving," Nell said.

"No, I wasn't." Jase pulled the door open wider. "Come on in. Tell us your troubles."

"My dad is driving me crazy," Lu said. "What are you here for?"

"My mother has to eat," Jase said.

Lu brightened. "You're Nell's son?" She looked toward Nell and nodded. "Very nice work."

"This is my boss's daughter," Nell said, trying to telegraph her disapproval.

"I'm Lu," Lu said, holding out her hand.

"I'm Jase," Jase said, taking it and holding onto it. "I was going to take my mother to lunch, but she can't go—"

Nell picked up her purse. "Sure, I can."

"—so I'm free," Jase said. "How about you and me? I'll solve your problem with your father."

"You can do that?" Lu grinned. "Have you *met* my father?"

"No," Jase said. "But I can do anything." He held the door open even wider. "Including pay for lunch."

"Cool." Lu waved to Nell. "We'll bring you back something. Don't tell Daddy I was here."

"Not a problem," Nell said, but they were already halfway out the door.

"*Jase!*"

Jase stuck his head back through the doorway.

"She's my boss's daughter," Nell hissed at him. "Do not do anything depraved."

"It's lunch," Jase said. "I don't do depraved until after dark."

"That's not funny," Nell said, but he was gone.

She thought about whether to worry and decided she had enough existing problems to think about without adding potentials to the list. And really, she was doing good. The glow from this one wasn't fading. She had over five thousand dollars to give to Gabe. Maybe he'd let her order new cards and repaint the window, maybe even buy a new couch now that she had the money. She just had to segue past his irritation at being disobeyed to get to the part where he owed it to her to—

The door to the office slammed open, and Nell looked up into Mr. Farnsworth's rabid eyes. "I want to see your boss," he snarled.

Nell swallowed hard and said, "He's not here," and scratched SugarPie a little more vigorously with her foot under the desk. The dog had jerked awake and was trembling again, but then so was she. Mr. Farnsworth had that effect.

"I don't believe you," he said and went past her to wrench the door to Gabe's office open.

Thank God, he's not here, Nell thought. *Thank you, thank you, God*.

"Where is he?" Farnsworth said, coming back to the front of the desk.

"Out on business," Nell said, trying to put some edge to her voice. "If there's nothing I can help you with—"

"You stole my dog," Farnsworth said.

Nell lurched a little in her seat, kicking SugarPie. "I most certainly did not."

"Not you, personally," Farnsworth said, annoyed. "This agency."

"I can assure you—" Nell began, and then Gabe banged the door open and came in, taking off his sunglasses and looking mad as hell, and she couldn't think of one thing to say to fix the situation.

"There you are!" Farnsworth said, rounding on him. "I'm suing you and this agency and—"

"Who the hell are you?" Gabe said, clearly not in a mood to be sued.

"I'm Michael Farnsworth, and you stole my dog." He faltered a little bit at the end, possibly realizing how absurd it sounded, especially with Gabe standing there enraged in his well-cut suit, looking like a pillar of the community with a gun permit.

"I beg your pardon?" Gabe said, and the temperature in the room dropped twenty degrees.

Don't ever let him talk to me like that, Nell prayed, fairly certain her turn was coming up shortly.

"My wife hired you to—"

"This firm does not commit crimes," Gabe said, his voice knife-edged. "We have been in business for over sixty years, and we have an impeccable reputation. Unless you want a countersuit for slander, I suggest you restate your position."

"My dog is missing," Farnsworth said, his bluster fading. "I know my wife came here to hire you."

"We do not discuss our clientele," Gabe said. "But I can assure you, no one at this agency accepted a commission that involves breaking the law."

"My wife," Farnsworth said, fading fast. "I know she's behind it."

"Then go talk to her," Gabe said, clearly finished with the conversation.

"Maybe I can hire you," Farnsworth said, and Nell

thought, *That's all I need. Gabe investigating me.*

"I have one clue," Farnsworth went on. "A hot blonde came to the door to distract me. It wasn't her in a wig," he added, jerking his thumb at Nell. "This one was built. She—"

"Mr. Farnsworth, nothing in the world would induce me to take part in this mess," Gabe said. "Go to the police. They can question your wife and get to the bottom of it faster than we can. And they'll do it for free. This is what you pay your taxes for."

Farnsworth nodded, and Nell nodded with him. Gabe always made sense. Unfortunately, this time he was siccing the police on her, but still, he made sense.

She had to get the dog out of the country. If only she knew somebody going to Canada—

Farnsworth went out, leaving the door open, and Gabe followed him to slam it shut.

"Well," Nell said, trying to sound virtuous when he'd turned back to her. "What got into—" She stopped when she saw the look in his eye.

"Where," Gabe said, "is that *goddamn dog*?"

Chapter Seven

Nell gave a quick thought to bluffing and decided against it. Somehow he knew, and her only salvation was going to be to come clean.

"She's under the desk," she said, and then Riley came in from the street and said, "Who was the asshole who just stormed out of here?"

"Back off," Gabe said, not taking his eyes off Nell. "I'll deal with you later."

"What?" Riley said. "What did I do?"

Nell pulled SugarPie's basket out and set it on the desk.

"Jesus, you brought it *here*?" Riley said. "What if the guy shows up looking for it? He knows his wife—"

"That was him, leaving," Gabe said, looking at the dog with distaste. "What the hell is that?"

"A former brown long-haired dachshund," Nell said. "Suze disguised it."

"Suze Dysart?" Gabe said. "That would be the hot blonde."

"Very hot," Riley said, and Gabe glared at him.

"Did it ever occur to you to say no to these women?"

"He did," Nell said. "But when we said we'd do it anyway, he helped so we wouldn't get in trouble."

"What a guy." Gabe looked down at the dog again and shook his head. "And I hired you. Where were you this morning?"

"Right here?" Nell said, trying to look innocent. She

could give him the five thousand later. Say on Monday. A nice Monday in December.

"Try again," Gabe said dangerously.

"Okay." Nell picked up SugarPie's basket. Maybe if he didn't have to look at the dog. "I was on an errand for the agency."

"Do not do this agency any more favors," Gabe said. "Where did you go? And if you broke the law, you're fired. I'm not kidding."

Nell's stomach went south at the word "fired." "I went to Lynnie's. I got the money back." She put SugarPie back on the desk and took the bank envelope out of the drawer to hold out to him. "See? Over five thousand dollars. I collected an agency debt."

"I'll be damned," Riley said. "Good for you."

"No, not good for her," Gabe said savagely. "I very much want to talk to Lynnie, which may be a little harder now that she knows we're on to her."

Nell put the money on the desk. "I'm sorry I let her know we knew, but I got you the money back. I *helped*."

He didn't look impressed. *I'm fired*, she thought.

"Okay, listen," she said, talking faster than she ever had in her life. "I know you're mad, but I still think I did the right thing. I think this is a great agency, but it needs some help with the office, and part of that is getting the finances back in shape, and they're in a lot better shape now because of what I did, and I did *not* break the law, I didn't even break all the agency rules, and anyway the third one doesn't count because I didn't know about it." She stopped as Riley closed his eyes, and Gabe jerked his head up.

"I really think this is a great agency," she finished.

"Thank you," Gabe said, his voice grimmer than she'd ever heard it. "I want to talk to you but I have to see Riley first. We are going into his office. When I come out, you will be here."

"Certainly," Nell said, sitting down.

He turned to Riley and pointed to his office. "In there."

"Don't take this out on me," Riley said. "You hired her."

Gabe slammed the door to Riley's office and said, "Here's some good news. Not only did our secretary steal that damn dog, she vandalized her husband's office. I just had to pull the cops off her. And Lynnie now has a pretty good case for extortion, so they may be back. She's out of control and she has to go."

"No," Riley said, and Gabe stopped, surprised. "Yeah, I'm surprised, too," Riley said, sitting down behind his desk. "But I'm going to fight you on this one. She's good. She's just having a hard time right now. Give her another chance."

"Why?" Gabe said. "So she can do something else to destroy this agency?"

"She's not the threat to this agency," Riley said, "and you know it. You're not mad at Nell, you're mad at Patrick."

Gabe stopped, caught, and then said, "No, I'm pretty sure I'm mad at Nell," but he sat down while he said it.

"You think Patrick helped Trevor cover up Helena's murder and you also think Lynnie found something he left behind that she's using to blackmail Trevor and possibly Jack and Budge. And you can't do anything about it, so you're taking it out on Nell."

"No."

"She's done more for this office in one week than my mother did in ten years," Riley said. "She works hard, she's efficient, and she deserves the job. She gets another chance."

"One more chance could bring us down," Gabe said.

"Talk to her," Riley said. "Stop bossing her around and acting like your dad. Take her to lunch and give her a chance to explain. And if you come back and still want her gone, I'll agree."

Gabe drew in a deep breath. He was not projecting his anger at Patrick on Nell, she was earning it all in her own right. But Riley was a good partner, and it wasn't a lot to ask. "All right," he said, and stood up.

"I don't think you're necessarily wrong about Lynnie," Riley said. "I think she found something, and I think she's a good bet to blackmail the O&D three. You want me to go roust her now? She might open the door for me. She has before."

"You and women." Gabe shook his head. "I can't believe you slept with Nell."

"I can't believe it, either," Riley said. "She kind of gets you when you're not expecting it. Watch yourself at lunch."

"Funny," Gabe said, and left.

Nell was sitting obediently at her desk, praying that when Gabe came out of Riley's office he'd see that she'd done the right thing and—

"Come with me," he said to her as Riley followed him into the outer office. "We're going to lunch."

He sounded threatening, so she picked up her purse. "What about the money? And SugarPie?"

"Riley will take care of the money and SugarPie." Gabe pointed toward the door. "Now."

Riley looked at Nell with sympathy. "Sorry about that, kid." He stuck the bank envelope under his arm, picked up SugarPie's basket, and went back into his office.

Gabe stood by the door, looking like Lucifer shortly after the fall, and Nell felt the hand of doom on her, all because she'd done the right thing, several times. It was so unfair.

"If you're going to fire me," Nell said, sticking her chin out, "just do it here. Get it over with."

"I'm going to feed you," Gabe said. "Then we're going to discuss the depth of your understanding of the rules here, and then if that understanding is deep enough, I will not fire you and we'll come back here and you'll to do the office work we hired you for. If your understanding is insufficient, however, you're going to need more copies of your résumé."

Nell tried to think of something scathing to say, but if there was a chance he wasn't going to fire her, discretion was clearly the better part of her financial future.

"Thank you," she said and went past him and out the door.

The two-block walk from the agency to the restaurant was fortunately short because Gabe was silent behind his dark glasses. "Nice day, isn't it?" she said once, and he didn't answer, so she shut up and picked up her pace to keep up with him.

At the restaurant, a local bar and grill called the Sycamore, they took one of the small tables near the front, and Gabe sat with his back to the light, leaving her the view around one of the big stained-glass panels that hung in the windows behind her. She twisted around to look at the place—lots of dark wood and Tiffany ceiling lights and old advertising prints on the walls—and then the waitress came for their drink order, and Gabe said, "I'll have a draft and a Reuben." He looked at Nell. "*Order.*"

The waitress looked taken aback.

"Black coffee," Nell said to her, smiling sweetly.

"She'll have an omelet," Gabe said to the waitress. "Four eggs, plenty of ham and cheese."

"I don't want an omelet," Nell said. "I'm not—"

"Do you really want to have this argument with me *right now*?" Gabe said, and the waitress took a step back.

"I'll have a Caesar salad," Nell said.

"Good." Gabe looked up at the waitress. "Put a double order of grilled chicken on it, and bring her a double order of fries."

"I don't want—" Nell began.

"*I don't care,*" he said, and Nell shut up until the waitress was gone.

Then she said, "You know, my lunch is none of your bus—"

"You trashed your ex-husband's office. His new wife swore out a warrant for your arrest."

"Oh, God," Nell said, every nerve in her body turning to ice.

"When I hired you, you didn't have a pulse," Gabe said. "Now you have a police record."

"Oh, *God.*"

"What the hell did you do? She kept snarling something about icicles."

"Awards," Nell said faintly. "Ohio Insurance Agent of the Year for the company. I broke them."

"Hope you enjoyed it. Jack and I spent the morning fixing that for you. He argued that since you still own half of the agency the warrant was no good. Your ex-husband finally gave in. The police are no longer looking for you."

"Thank you," Nell said politely and began to shred her paper napkin in her lap.

"Then there was Wednesday night when you tried to sleep with a client's husband."

"That was a mistake," Nell said. "I apologize."

"And I gather you did sleep with Riley."

"Hey, I'm clear on that," Nell said, rallying a little. "You didn't tell me not to fuck the help."

Gabe looked taken aback. "I know I didn't. I didn't tell you because I didn't think you would. Frankly, I didn't think you could say 'fuck,' let alone do it."

The waitress put their drinks in front of them and said to Nell, "Your food will be right out." She looked concerned.

"Thank you," Nell said, trying to look unabused.

When the waitress was gone, Gabe said, "Then yesterday you talked to someone outside the firm about a client, and last night you stole a dog. And this morning you extorted money from a former employee. All in all, you've had a full week."

"I did it for the firm," Nell said virtuously.

"You're out of control," Gabe said, and launched into a lecture about values and responsibility and the agency reputation that lasted until the waitress came to the table and started unloading food.

Nell's salad was enormous, brimming with chicken and extra cheese and croutons. Gabe pointed to it. "Eat."

"I'm not going to eat all of this," Nell said.

"Then we're going to be here a long, long time." Gabe picked up his sandwich.

Nell stabbed at her salad and took a bite. It was good, but who the hell did he think he was, anyway? She swallowed and said, "Who do you think you are, anyway? What I eat is not your business."

"Yes, it is," Gabe said, picking up a french fry. "You represent my office."

"So?"

Gabe pointed at her salad, and she stabbed it again. "So you look like death. If you don't put on some weight, clients are going to think I don't pay you enough."

"You don't," Nell said around a mouthful of salad. "And I look fine."

"You look like hell," Gabe said. "Shut up and eat while I explain the three rules to you."

"I know the three rules," Nell said, and Gabe pointed at her salad again. She thought about arguing, decided it would be faster if she just ate, and stabbed the salad again.

"The reason we do not talk outside the office is that people come to us with information that is confidential and they want it to stay that way."

Nell swallowed. "I know that."

"When you told Suze about the dog, you broke that confidentiality. Your friends are not part of the office. If I can't trust you not to tell them, I can't trust you."

Nell chewed slower. "You're right. I'm sorry."

"I'm always right." He waited until she'd forked up more salad and then he said, "Breaking the law is almost as bad. We have a good relationship with the police because they know we're straight. I do not want that good relationship jeopardized because you think you're above the law."

Nell swallowed her salad. "I don't think I'm above the law. I'm sorry about the office, and I won't do that again."

"You also stole a dog. And you still think that was right."

"You didn't make me give it back."

"Shut up and eat," Gabe said, and then before Nell could feel smug, he added, "Which brings us to fucking the help."

Nell slid down a little in her chair and ate more salad.

"I don't care if you sleep with Riley, that's your business," Gabe said, sounding mad.

"I'm not sleeping with him," Nell said hastily, feeling guiltier than ever. "Not anymore. It was a short fling. One night. Really." She smiled at him, trying to look innocent, and then picked up the mug of beer and drank. This wasn't one of the better lunches of her life. The beer felt good, tart and cold going down, and she drank again, feeling the alcohol ease into her bones a little.

Gabe signaled to the waitress.

"And it was my fault, not his," she told him, licking the foam off her lip. "I was being pathetic and he felt sorry for me."

The waitress came and Gabe said, "We'll need another beer."

"What?" Nell said and then looked down at his beer in her hand, half gone. "Oh, sorry." She tried to push the mug back to him.

"Keep it," Gabe said. "It has calories. And it wasn't because you were being pathetic. Riley has no interest in wimpy women."

"I didn't say 'wimpy.' "

"Eat," Gabe said, and Nell went back to forking salad.

When the waitress had brought the second beer and gone, he said, "Those three rules are there because of experience, Nell."

She looked up at him, surprised. He'd never called her Nell before.

"They were my dad's rules, but he made them for good reason," Gabe said. "They—"

"What was the reason for the no-sex rule?" Nell said, hoping to distract him.

"He married his secretary. The rules—"

"Your mother was his secretary?" Nell stopped chewing. "Wait a minute, wasn't Chloe your secretary?"

"*The rules*—" Gabe said, and Nell waved her fork at him and said, "I've got it. I'll never break another one, I swear." When he looked skeptical, she said, "No, really. I do understand. I like this job and I want to keep it. If anything like the dog comes up again, I'll bring it to you and then nag you until you do something about it."

"Oh, yeah, that'll be better," Gabe said, but he picked up his beer, so the yelling was probably over. "*Eat*," he said, and Nell stabbed a piece of chicken and ate, surprised at herself.

It had been years since anybody had told her to do anything, yelled at her about anything. Maybe never. She and Tim had settled into a life where she'd run everything and he'd gone with the flow. And then one day he'd found somebody else, somebody who wouldn't run his life so he could have the illusion he was in control. Only now, from all reports, Whitney was running his life. Which must mean Tim wanted a woman to boss him around, he just didn't want to admit he wanted a woman to boss him around. He wanted to be Gabe without the responsibility.

Her fork hit the bottom of her bowl and she looked down. The salad was gone.

"Good." Gabe shoved her french fry plate closer. "Start

on those. And say something. When you're not talking, you're thinking, and when you think, my life goes to hell. Eat and tell me what happened with Lynnie."

Nell took a deep breath. "Well, I went to her apartment and I told her that we were going to the police if she didn't give back the money. And then we talked."

"What did she say?"

Nell closed her eyes and put herself back in Lynnie's living room. "She said she'd been sick." She recited the conversation as best as she could remember, deleting the part where Lynnie had accused her of falling for Gabe. When she finished and opened her eyes, he was regarding her thoughtfully.

"How much of that did you make up?"

"None of it," Nell said, outraged. "I may have forgotten some of it, but everything I told you happened."

"Good memory. I'm 'my way or the highway,' huh?"

"Oh, yeah," Nell said and picked up a fry.

"Okay." Gabe took a fry, too. "What aren't you telling me?"

Nell thought about saying, "Nothing," and then decided that lying to Gabe McKenna was not a good idea. "She got personal. I don't want to talk about it."

"There might be something in it I can use."

"Nope."

Gabe dipped a fry in ketchup and handed it to her. "Eat."

"I like vinegar better," she said. He motioned for the waitress and asked for vinegar and the check, and then he went back to his own lunch, deep in thought. Nell relaxed, and when the vinegar came, she sprinkled it on the second order of fries, inhaling the sharp, sweet cider. Heaven.

"So she was putting the screws to somebody," Gabe said. "I don't suppose you got a name?"

"I got exactly what I told you," Nell said, and he nodded and finished his sandwich.

When the waitress brought the check, Gabe looked at

it for a minute before putting a few bills on the tray. When she was gone, he said, "How serious are you about this job?"

Nell stopped chewing. They were back to her. That couldn't be good. "Well . . ."

How serious was she? She liked Riley, and Gabe was growing on her. She'd felt good rescuing SugarPie, good about getting the money back even though she liked Lynnie. Even finding out that night as a decoy that Ben was a cheater was something; it would help his wife out. People should know when they were being lied to, it was wrong that they didn't know. You couldn't fix your life if you didn't know what was wrong with it.

"I'm very serious," she said.

"You have not demonstrated that you're a good risk," he said, not accusing her.

"I know," Nell said. "I've had a very rough week, but it was educational, too. I'm going to be all right now."

"What happened?" Gabe took one of her fries and winced when he bit into it.

"Vinegar," Nell said.

"What happened this week? Prove to me you're not insane."

Nell swallowed. "Okay." Where did she start? "I've been divorced for a while. Over a year."

Gabe nodded.

"It was hard. My marriage and my job were pretty much the same, so I lost everything all at once. I kept thinking I was all right, but I wasn't. I mean, he just left me, Christmas afternoon, just stopped right there, in the middle of all the wrapping paper, and said, 'I'm sorry, I don't love you anymore,' and left me to clean up the rest of it. It didn't make sense. I couldn't make the world make sense if that happened."

Gabe nodded again.

"Why do you do that?" Nell said. "Nod and not say anything. Those silences are killers."

"If I say something, you're not talking," Gabe said.

"Tricky."

"What happened?"

"Well," Nell said. "I tried to cope and be understanding and figure it out so it made sense, and then he met Whitney and married her and put her in my old job, and I ended up falling asleep a lot. And then Suze and Margie found out that he . . ." She put down the french fry she'd been holding as she remembered the way the world had rocked that day. Only two days ago. A lifetime ago.

"That there was another woman after all," Gabe said. "Whitney all along?"

Nell straightened. "How did you know?"

"Lucky guess. When did they tell you?"

"Wednesday," Nell said.

Gabe nodded. "Which would explain going upstairs with the guy on the decoy and sleeping with Riley and smashing your ex's office. I'm not sure how you ended up with the dog and Lynnie—"

"People kept doing lousy things and getting away with it," Nell said. "I was *mad*."

"You can't do that anymore," Gabe said.

"I know," Nell said.

"As part of this firm, your actions reflect on all of us."

"I'm part of the firm?"

"That depends."

He looked into her eyes, and she gazed back, trying to look steady and trustworthy. *I want to be part of this*, she thought. *Let me in.*

"I have an assignment for you," Gabe said. "You are hardworking and efficient and smart as hell, and I don't want to fire you. But you have to promise to keep your mouth shut and not avenge any wrongs you see. Can you do that?"

Nell nodded.

"This particular assignment is about someone you know," Gabe said, "which is why you can help."

"Will I have to betray anybody?" Nell said. "Because I won't."

Gabe shrugged and picked up another fry. "Depends on what you mean by 'betray.' I want the answers to some questions. I don't think the person you'll be asking is guilty."

Nell swallowed. "I can promise not to say anything to anybody about anything you tell me. I can't promise anything else until you tell me what this is about."

"Fair enough," Gabe said. "Somebody is blackmailing people at O&D. Trevor Ogilvie, Jack Dysart, and Budge Jenkins."

"Oh." Nell felt relieved. She didn't care what happened to any of them. She picked up another french fry. "You think it's Lynnie?"

"It's a guess."

"What is she accusing them of?"

"Budge of embezzling."

Nell laughed out loud. "Budge? She doesn't know him at all."

"Really?" Gabe said. "What would you accuse him of? If you wanted to scare him?"

Nell leaned back and looked at the ceiling as she thought. Nothing bothered Budge, except . . . "Something that would take Margie from him," she said. "He worships the carpet she walks on, has for years."

"What would do that?"

"If he broke a piece of her Franciscan Desert Rose earthenware," Nell said, only half joking. "Margie is pretty easygoing. She put up with Stewart for fifteen years, and I'd have killed him on the honeymoon."

"Stewart," Gabe said.

"Stewart Dysart," Nell said. "Jack and Tim's brother. Jack's the oldest and the big success, and Tim's the baby and the sweet one everybody loves, and Stewart would have been just pathetic in the middle except he was so obnoxious about everything."

He frowned at her. "Why does his name sound familiar? Did they divorce?"

"No. He went south with almost a million of O&D assets seven years ago."

"Got it," Gabe said, nodding. "O&D hushed it up. Why didn't she divorce him?"

"If she gets divorced," Nell said, "she'll end up marrying Budge, and she doesn't want to marry Budge."

Gabe looked at her in disbelief. "She can't say no?"

"No," Nell said. "Margie cannot say no. But she can say, 'Not yet, I'm married,' so she's covered. What did the blackmailer accuse Jack of?"

"Adultery. Trevor, too."

"I don't think so," Nell said. "Jack's bananas about Suze. Almost to the point of pathology. And Margie's dad cheated once before, but it was over twenty years ago, so I don't think that counts. Besides, that ended so badly, so much scandal when her mother killed herself, that I don't think he'd take the chance again."

Gabe nodded. "I need you to ask Margie some questions about her mother."

"Oh." Nell's good humor faded. "No."

"Somebody has to ask her," Gabe said, looking the way he had the first day she'd met him, dark and hard. "You don't want it to be me."

"Don't threaten me," Nell said. "And don't threaten her. I don't even know what this is about, and you want me to go asking horrible questions."

"I told you what it's about," Gabe said with exaggerated patience. "Blackmail."

"What does Margie's mother who died over twenty years ago have to do with Margie's dad being blackmailed now?"

"You'll just have to trust me on that."

"No, I won't," Nell said. "Look, if I have to promise to question Margie or you'll fire me, I'm fired."

Gabe sighed and stood up. "Come on. It's time to get back to work."

Nell stood, too, and looked down to take one last fry for the road.

There weren't any. She'd eaten a huge salad and two orders of fries.

"You ready?" Gabe said.

"Am I fired?"

"No," Gabe said.

"I'm ready," Nell said.

Chapter Eight

"Still employed?" Riley said to Nell when they got back to the office.

"Of course," Nell said. "How's SugarPie?"

At the sound of her name, the dog crept out of Riley's office, quivering and limping, a cashmere-clad basket case.

"What did you do to her?" Nell said, appalled.

"Absolutely nothing," Riley said. "I left her to go check on Lynnie, and when I got back, she was doing this. I ignored her and she snapped out of it. She does it for the effect."

"She does not. She's been *abused*." Nell crouched down to gather SugarPie into her arms, but she moaned and rolled over on the Oriental, her stubby little legs pointing off to one side, looking pathetic in their white cuffs. "*SugarPie?* What's wrong?"

"If this dog was human, she'd be leaping in front of buses, claiming whiplash." Riley looked down at her. "I won't play the sap for you, sweetheart. But the redhead will. Work it for all the dog biscuits you can get."

"That's not—"

"Give her a dog biscuit," Riley said.

"Biscuit?" Nell said to the dog, and SugarPie rolled her head to look at her pitifully. Nell reached up to the desk and got a biscuit. "Here, baby. It's okay."

SugarPie looked at her for a long dramatic moment. Then she took the biscuit carefully in her mouth, looked yearningly up at Nell one last time, and rolled over and devoured it with savage relish.

"You stole an unabused dog," Gabe said.

"He called her a little bitch," Nell said from the floor, indignant.

"Well, technically, she is," Riley said.

"And she looked awful." Nell looked down at SugarPie, now licking the rug to get the last of the biscuit crumbs. "She was traumatized."

SugarPie looked up at all of them, dropped her head between her shoulders, and moaned.

"Now what?" Gabe said, and she fluttered her eyelashes at him, quivering at his feet.

"Marlene Dietrich used to do that eyelash thing in the movies, right before she took a guy for everything he had," Riley said. "All this dog needs is a garter belt and a top hat."

"You've been had, kid," Gabe said to Nell. "It's an occupational hazard around here. Take the dog back." He looked down at SugarPie and added, "Preferably in the dead of night."

"That would be a good idea," Riley said. "Except she shaved it, dyed it black, and dressed it in Ralph Lauren. Its own mother wouldn't recognize it now."

"You shaved it?" Gabe sighed. "Don't tell me why. Just get it out of here."

"Before I forget," Riley said to Nell, "Suze Campbell called. I told her the dog was fine." He looked down at SugarPie. "I lied, of course."

"Suze who?" Nell said, surprised.

"Dysart," Gabe said, shooting an exasperated look at Riley, and went into his office.

SugarPie picked up her head and looked after him with interest and then, evidently realizing all remaining eyes were on her, collapsed again.

"How do you know Suze's maiden name?" Nell said.

"So Gabe calls you 'kid' now, does he?" Riley raised his

eyebrows at her. "What did you do, drug his beer?"

"We talked," Nell said, putting her chin in the air. "He saw the wisdom of my ways."

"He made you promise to change your ways or he'd sack you," Riley said.

Nell dropped her chin. "That, too. So how do you know—"

"Well, I, for one, am glad you're staying," Riley said and Nell smiled at him, feeling better than she had in months. On the rug at their feet, suffering deeply from a lack of attention, SugarPie moaned and fluttered her eyelashes at him over her long brown nose.

"Are you sure she's not abused?" Nell said. "She acts so weird."

"Biscuit," Riley said to the dog, and the eyelash flutter went into overdrive. He gave her a biscuit and she rolled over again to hold it between her paws as she crunched it into oblivion. "I'm sure." He picked up the biscuit box and said, "Come on, Marlene. Back into hiding in case somebody comes looking for you, although only God knows why anybody would."

"Marlene?" Nell said.

"I'm not calling anything SugarPie," Riley said. "That's obscene."

The dog gazed at them unblinking for a moment and then rolled to her feet, checked the carpet to make sure there were no missed crumbs, and trotted off into Riley's office, slowing only to flutter her eyelashes at him as she went by.

"I don't believe it," Nell said.

"I have this effect on a lot of women," Riley said.

"Wait a minute," Nell said. "How do you know—"

But Riley had already closed his door.

"Well, *that's* interesting," Nell said to nobody in particular and went back to work.

*   *   *

Nell walked to the grocery the next day because it was Saturday, and she didn't want to talk to Suze. If she stayed in the apartment, Suze would come over, and she wasn't allowed to tell her anything, wasn't allowed to say, "How am I going to ask Margie about her mom?" couldn't even say, "*Should* I ask Margie about her mom?"

She looked at the problem from all possible sides as she cruised the aisles at Big Bear, picking up yellow peppers and fresh spinach and Yukon Gold potatoes and tomatoes so ripe they glowed. The colors were amazing and she added more, vegetable pasta and papery garlic and red and white and yellow onions. Suddenly everything looked good, and she was starving.

It was only when she got to the checkout that she remembered she was walking. All that color turned out to be heavy, and two blocks from the store, she had to put the bags down just to get her fingers out of the plastic loops. While she worked her fingers, she looked around. Like most of the German Village streets, it was crowded with trees and brick houses with wrought-iron fences, but this one in particular looked familiar. When she got to the corner she realized why: It was the cross street for the lane Lynnie lived on. She checked to see if Lynnie was there and saw the door to her brick duplex standing open and a strange woman on the narrow porch.

Nell hefted her bags up again and went to see what was going on.

Lynnie's apartment looked empty. Some of the furniture was still there, but it was on its way out to a van that said CITYWIDE RENTAL on it. Nell moved aside as a guy carried out a chair, and then she went up the steps to the woman on the porch, feeling oddly bereft, as if a friend had moved without telling her.

"Hi," she said and gestured to the open door.

"Two bedrooms, eight hundred a month," the woman said, and Nell realized she was the woman from the other side of the duplex. "You want to look at it?"

"Yes," Nell said, planning on finding out more about Lynnie's whereabouts, and followed her into the apartment, putting her bags on the floor to rest her fingers again.

The landlady, Doris, lived in the other half of the duplex and didn't know anything about Lynnie except that she'd left a note on her screen door the night before saying she was leaving and that Doris could keep the rest of the month's rent. Doris was not happy that Lynnie had skipped out on her lease, even unhappier when the rental company had come and disrupted her chance to sleep late on Saturday morning, but, as she put it, she was not a gloomy person. "I'm one of those half-full-glass people," she said, looking like her best friend had just died. "I just can't help looking on the sunny side of things."

Nell had nodded, not really listening once she'd gotten the full story on Lynnie because the apartment had begun to appeal to her. It was a standard duplex, living room and kitchen downstairs and two bedrooms up. But the living room was big enough to take her grandmother's dining room set, and the kitchen had glass doors on the cupboards, and the bedrooms were real bedrooms with doors, and the bathroom had black and white tiles from the forties. She looked out the back door and saw a postage stamp of a yard with a fence around it. Marlene would love it.

She looked at the bags of food on the living room floor, more food than she'd consumed in the entire previous month, and she wanted to wash the vegetables in the old porcelain kitchen sink and put her plates in the glass-front cabinets, cut tomatoes on the drainboard and eat potatoes and vinegar on the tiny porch while she watched the Village go by. She wanted to see things and taste things and feel things, and she wanted to do it here.

"I have a dog," she said.

"Nine hundred," Doris said. "Assuming you make the credit check."

"Eight hundred and I write you a check for the first

three months now." Nell said. "You won't have to advertise the apartment. You won't even have to clean it."

"I don't know." Doris said. "A dog."

"She's a dachshund, her name is Marlene, and she sleeps a lot."

Half an hour later, she opened the door to her old apartment and found Marlene sitting by the door, looking as though she'd been marooned for days. "We have a new place," she told the dog. "Fenced-in backyard. Rooms to run through. You're going to love it."

"I still don't understand why you want this place," Suze said, standing in the middle of Nell's boxes the next day.

"Because I picked it out, not you and Jack." Nell looked around the place as if it were a palace. "Because I'm finally doing things on my own."

"Okay," Suze said, feeling underappreciated.

"Hey, I still love the daybed you found for me, and Marlene is absolutely crazy for your chenille throw," Nell said. "I can't get it away from her."

Suze looked at Marlene, languishing on the daybed on four hundred dollars' worth of indigo chenille. "That's good to know."

"Can we please unpack your china now?" Margie said.

Jase backed in the front door carrying one end of Nell's dining room table, and when the other end appeared, after much arguing and tilting and groaning, it was held up by the girl he'd brought with him in the rental truck. He'd been yelling at her all afternoon to be careful unloading boxes or she'd hurt herself, to wait for him, to just *wait a minute* with anything that was heavy, while she laughed at him and hefted things without breaking a sweat, and Suze had thought, *Was I ever that young?*

And then she remembered: She'd been exactly that young when she'd gotten married.

My God, she thought, watching them now, arguing

about where to drop the table. *They're like puppies. And that was me.*

"You okay, Aunt Suze?" Jase said.

Suze nodded. "Couldn't be better."

"Just the clothes left," the blonde said.

"Yeah, right, Lu," Jase said. "Like my mother doesn't have a ton of those." He pushed her gently out the door, laughing down at her, and she made a face at him and pushed back.

Margie gazed around the apartment. "Are you still going to sleep on the daybed now that you have a real bedroom?"

"Nope," Nell said. "I'm going to get a real bed."

The daybed is a real bed, Suze thought, but she said, "If you want, you can have the bed in our second guest room. We never have second guests anyway."

"Wonderful," Nell said and went to tell Jase he had another job.

"I put some of my clothes in the truck for you, too," Suze said when she got back, but Nell didn't hear; she was on her way to the kitchen to open the ancient glass-front cabinets and touch the panes as if they were something wonderful. Suze went out to the truck to help with the last of the boxes. She put one foot on the step at the back and then looked up.

Jase was kissing Lu in the back of the truck, his hands tight on her rear end. It wasn't a kid's kiss, and it took Suze's breath away. Jase shouldn't be old enough to kiss anybody like that, but he was. He was three years older than she'd been when she'd gotten married.

"What happened to my clothes?" Nell called from the porch, and Suze called back loudly, "I'll get them," and banged on the side of the truck and then kept her eyes averted until she'd climbed inside.

Jase handed Lu a box and said, "Work for your keep," and she said, "Like you wouldn't keep me anyway." She shot Suze a grin as she climbed out of the truck with the box, so sure and happy and young that Suze felt the envy in her bones.

When Jase and Lu drove the empty truck away to get Suze's second guest bed, Suze went inside and found Margie and Nell unpacking Nell's china. Nell handed her a bubble-wrapped piece, and Suze unwrapped it carefully, trying not to be depressed by Jase and Lu. She should be happy for them. She was a horrible person.

The last of the bubble wrap came off, and Suze looked at the teapot in her hands, startled out of her despair. It was round on the edges and flat on both sides, and it had a landscape painted on it, an eerie little scene with a weird bubble-shaped tree and two sad little houses, smoke curling mournfully up from their pointed chimneys. The bottom of the teapot was blue, a little stream between two tall hills, separating the tree from the houses forever.

"I thought your stuff had flowers on it," Suze said. "I've never seen this before."

"It was on the top shelf," Nell said. "I never used it."

"Crocuses," Margie said, frowning into space. "That's what they were." She looked at the three boxes marked "China" and said, "This can't be all of it."

"This is my share," Nell said. "Tim got the rest in the divorce."

"What?" Margie's eyes grew wide. "He took your *china*?"

"It's just dishes," Suze said.

"It's her *china*," Margie said, and Suze remembered Margie's ten zillion pieces of Franciscan Desert Rose and said, "Right. Her china."

"And he got more than half," Margie said. "You had *shelves* of it."

Suze looked down at the teapot in her hand. "What is this stuff, anyway? I only remember the flowers."

"It's all British Art Deco china," Nell said.

"Art Deco?" Margie said.

"From the twenties and thirties," Suze said, still fascinated by the teapot. "Very geometric, bright colors, styl-ized designs." They looked at her as if she'd said something strange, and she said, "Art History 102. I know the intro-ductory stuff about everything."

Nell nodded. "It's from my mom's family in England. That teapot is Clarice Cliff, my second favorite pattern of hers. It's called Secrets."

"I don't understand why Tim got so much more," Margie said.

"The stuff I loved best was the expensive stuff," Nell said. "Like the Secrets tea set. It has thirty-four pieces and appraised at seven thousand dollars."

"Oh, my Lord," Margie said, taking a closer look at the teapot Suze was clutching.

Suze held it out to Nell. "Take this, please."

Nell took it and put it in her china hutch. "So did you get your mom's china, Margie?" she asked, and Suze looked at her sharply. Nell had been the one to tell her fourteen years ago that questions about Margie's mom were off limits.

"No," Margie said. "What's this?" She held up the tea-pot she'd just unpacked, a round peach-colored pot with white crescents scratched in it.

"Susie Cooper," Nell said. "Not nearly as expensive. That's part of her kestral line. She owned her own pottery works in the late 20s and was still designing in the 80s."

"She lasted." Margie nodded down at the Cooper bowl in her hands.

"Her pieces were the best designed," Nell said. "She even had her own pottery works. But Clarice made beau-tiful things." Nell unwrapped another bowl. "This is Stroud, my favorite pattern. Just the green band around the outside and the cartouche at the bottom."

The bowl was cream with a wide green band bisected in the lower left-hand corner by a little square with a land-scape inside it—a fluffy cloud, an orange-roofed house, a puffy green tree, and two curved hills—a tiny perfect world.

A tiny perfect world. That sounded like Nell, arranging everything in her life and then maintaining it. If Nell could, she'd make sure the clouds in the sky looked exactly like that. Neat and comfy. Suze looked back at the creamer. "And this one is called Secrets."

Nell sat back and nodded again. "That was my mom's favorite." She looked at Margie for a minute and then went on. "I think it's autobiographical. According to gossip, Clarice was having an affair with her boss, the guy who owned the china works."

Margie sat up straighter, with a little gasp. "That's *terrible*. She must have been an awful woman, stealing somebody else's husband."

Suze tried not to flinch. Even after fourteen years, it was a sore point.

"That's the worst thing a woman can do," Margie said, visibly upset. "That's *unforgivable*."

"Margie," Nell said. "Have a heart."

Margie looked up. "Oh, not you, Suze." She frowned at Suze's creamer, and Suze handed it to Nell. "But that Secrets woman, well, really. Just snagged her married boss." She looked down at her Susie Cooper plate and said, "Tell me Susie wasn't like that."

"Susie was loyal and practical to the end," Nell said. "Married with a son."

"Good. A good wife." Margie handed Nell the bowl and began to unpack more.

Suze thought, *She owned her own company, too,* and began to dislike Susie intensely. She unpacked a Secrets sugar bowl, careful not to scratch the bubble tree or the quiet blue sea at the bottom. Poor Clarice. Loving a married man, working for him every day, knowing they couldn't be together, probably rejected by all the good wives around her, never able to start her own company because she had to stay with the man she loved. "What happened to Clarice?" she said, staring at the two lonely houses with great sympathy.

"When she was in her forties, her boss's wife died and he married her and they lived happily ever after."

In her forties. If that had been her, she'd be waiting another ten years for Jack. Would she? Would she do it all over again today? What kind of person would she have turned out to be if she hadn't gotten married? *Don't think about that.* "Well, good for Clarice," Suze said and handed Nell the sugar bowl.

"Wait, I have figurines of them." She began to take wrapped pieces from the box and put them on the floor until she found what she was looking for, handing them each a bubble-wrapped package.

"Who's this?" Suze said, stripping the wrap off hers first, and Nell peered at it and said, "Susie Cooper."

Susie sat on a piece of pottery with a flowered plate behind her, looking like a stylish Mary Poppins in a conservative mauve suit, her knees demurely together, holding a wide-brimmed hat on her head.

"Pretty," Margie said, unwrapping hers more slowly.

Practical, Suze thought, with definite distaste.

"Oh," Margie said.

Margie's figurine sat on a piece of pottery with a landscaped plate behind her, her ankles crossed and her low V-necked green flapper dress pulled above her knees. She looked over her shoulder with her back arched and a glint in her eye.

Suze smiled. "Clarice."

"I don't want her. Let me see Susie," Margie said to Suze, and Suze traded her, smiling down at saucy Clarice, the good-time girl with the impractical pottery and the married lover. *Maybe I should have stayed a lover,* she thought. Maybe she wasn't cut out to be the married Susie she'd ended up as, maybe she'd been born to be a good-time Clarice.

Of course, it was too late now. She handed Clarice to

Nell and watched her put the figure in the hutch.

"They all did really well," Nell said, straightening Clarice on the shelf. "They had work they loved and they excelled at it."

"Work," Suze said and felt overwhelmingly envious of Susie and Clarice and their pottery, and Margie and her teashop, and even Nell and her secretary job. Maybe she could take a pottery class. Or go to chef school. Jack would like that.

Except she was tired of school.

She unpacked some more Secrets, trying not to think about what else she was tired of. She had a good life. Everything was fine.

"What's wrong?" Nell said, and Suze turned around to tell her she was fine and saw her looking at Margie.

The plate in Margie's hand had a pink rose painted in the middle of it. It was pretty, but Margie was staring at it as if it had skulls on it.

"Margie?" Suze said.

"My mom used to have china like this," she said. "Not this pattern, but with roses."

Her mom. Suze looked at Nell, who was looking miserable. *This is what you tried to do before*, she thought, *get Margie talking about her mom*, and for the first time ever, she was angry with Nell.

"Do you want the plate?" Nell said. "I don't have a set of it or anything. It's called Patricia Rose. It's one of Susie's." She kept talking, her eyes on Margie's face, but Margie's expression didn't change, and finally she said, "What's wrong, Margie?"

"She was breaking them," Margie said finally. "They were my Grandma Ogilvie's china and really expensive, and she'd kept them for years and only used them on the holidays and then my dad told her she was boring and left, and there she was with all that china."

"Margie?" Suze said, putting out her hand.

"And I came home one day to make sure she was all

right because she'd been so quiet since Daddy had left. And when I got there, she was dressed in her best clothes, wearing her good jewelry, and breaking them with a hammer."

"I feel that way about the Dysart Spode," Suze said, trying to defuse the tension. "I'd love to take a mallet to that stuff."

"I was scared, and Daddy called and I told him he had to come right over, and he argued with me that I should take Mom to the hospital, and while I was talking to him, she went out to the garage and shot herself," Margie said, still staring at the plate.

Suze went cold. "Oh, honey," she said and put her arms around Margie, hugging her soft little body to her, and Nell gently took the plate from Margie's hands and said, "I'm so sorry, Margie. I really am."

"I gave the china to my dad's new wife," Margie said, her voice muffled by Suze's shoulder. "She really hated it, but she was stuck with it because my dad thought it was so nice of me, welcoming her to the family like that. I wanted to throw up every time I saw it." She took a deep breath. "I just hope Olivia inherits it, that's what I hope."

Suze tightened her arms around her.

"Margie—" Nell began

"I've been so scared for you," Margie said to her from Suze's arms. "She looked just like you did, like she couldn't figure out what had happened. And then you wouldn't unpack your china—"

"It's almost all unpacked," Nell said soothingly. "I'll do the rest of it, no, *we'll* do the rest of it later. We'll do it together and none of it will get smashed. I'm okay, Margie. I wasn't, but I'm okay now. You wouldn't believe all the food I've got in the refrigerator, and I'm eating it, God, I can't stop eating, everything tastes so good."

Margie sniffed, and Suze said, "Well, stop because I cleaned out my closets and brought you all kinds of clothes I can't get into anymore. You're going to look great in bright blue."

Margie straightened a little. "Nell in bright blue?" she said doubtfully, but she left the china without a backward glance to go upstairs with Nell, and Suze took the Patricia Rose plate and hid it in the bottom corner of the hutch, as far away from Margie as she could get it.

A little later, while Margie was frowning at herself in a pink sweater in Nell's mirror, Suze followed Nell down to let in Jase and Lu with the second guest bed. "I put the plate in the bottom of the hutch," Suze said. "That was too freaky. She just looked at that pink rose and went off."

"Freakier than you think," Nell said. "Ever wonder why Margie has so much midpriced earthenware when she could afford real china?"

"No," Suze said. "I don't think about dishes much."

"Think about it now," Nell said. "Franciscan Desert Rose."

"Ten million pieces of it," Suze said, horrified. "Oh, God. Should we say anything to Margie?"

"No, we should not," Nell said. "I've become a big fan of coping strategies in the past eighteen months. Leave her to her earthenware."

"I love this sweater," Margie said, coming down the stairs in one of Suze's pink sweaters after Jase and Lu had gone up with the bed frame. "Especially the color. What are you going to do with all these clothes? Your closets are small."

"I don't know," Nell said, clearly grateful for the change of subject. "Take the ones I want right now and put the rest in storage, I guess."

"In my basement," Margie said. "Because I like trying on this stuff. In the suits, I'm you, and in the sweaters, I'm Suze."

She sounded wistful, so Suze said, "Take my extra stuff, too. Then we'll have a slumber party at your place and be each other for a night."

"Good idea, now how about coffee?" Nell said, her

voice perky as all hell. *Feeling guilty*, Suze thought and forgave her.

Somebody knocked on the door, and Suze went to get
it as Margie said, "Yes, please. Where's my purse? My
thermos is in there."

Soy milk, Suze thought. *Personally, I could use a Scotch*.
Then she opened the door and saw Riley McKenna, bigger
and blonder than she'd remembered him, gawking at her
in disbelief, and thought, *Make that a double*.

"You are *kidding* me," he said. "How the hell did you
get here?"

"I drove," Suze said. "What's your problem?"

"An old friend used to live here," he said. "I stopped by
to see if she was in."

"If your old friend is Nell, she's unpacking." Suze
stepped back. "Come on in and say hi."

"Nell rented this place?" Riley shook his head as he
came in. "Somebody else lived here two days ago."

"Well, people change," Suze said, and shut the door,
watching him navigate the boxes in the living room to get
to Nell. From the back he looked like a blond Robert Mit-
chum. From the front, of course, he was Babyface Nelson,
but he looked very noir from the back, broad and hulking
and sort of menacing. Not somebody you'd want to meet
in a dark alley. Maybe.

He sat and talked and laughed with them, flirting with
Nell and making Margie blush, and Suze felt almost sorry
for Budge when he came to take Margie away. Budge was
warm to Suze, polite to Riley, and chilly to Nell who had
corrupted Margie by getting her the job at The Cup, but
all the while his eyes went from Margie to Riley and back
again, as if he knew that Riley had more than an extra five
inches in height and ten fewer years on him. "We have to
get you home," he finally said to Margie, and they loaded
the extra boxes of clothes in Budge's station wagon. Then
Margie left, looking wistfully back over her shoulder as
Budge held the door open for her, like a footman instead

of a lover. *He's Prufrock*, Suze thought, afraid to force the moment and his future because he knew Margie would say, "That's not what I want at all."

Later that evening, when Suze got home, she told a suspicious Jack about the unpacking, about the thorough cleaning that Nell was going to give the place before they met to unpack the rest of her stuff on Tuesday, about Margie and the plate, about Marlene on the chenille throw, about the marvelous stir-fry Nell made and then ate half of by herself, but she didn't mention Riley.

Jack just didn't appreciate noir the way she did.

While Suze was giving Jack the abridged version of the evening, Marlene lounged at the foot of Suze's second guest bed, nestled in Nell's chenille throw, evidently recovered from the move.

"Just look at all this room you have to run in," Nell said, trying to distract herself from her guilt over Margie. Then she remembered that Marlene didn't run. She sank back into her pillows and watched the dog stretch and wriggle deeper into the chenille. Nell had gotten used to thinking of her as a small, badly raised, manipulative child, but Marlene was an animal, tooth and claw down there in the chenille, and her ancestors had once roamed free. *Maybe I should take her to the park*, Nell thought, *let her rediscover her wild side*.

Marlene caught Nell watching her and began to flutter her eyes.

Nell shook her head. The only place any ancestor of Marlene's had roamed free was Canyon Ranch.

Marlene rolled her head back and moaned a little.

"Biscuit?" Nell said flatly.

Marlene moaned louder.

Nell got up and went down to the kitchen, jumping a little when she heard a knock on the door. She stuck Marlene's biscuit in her pajama pocket and went to look through the lace curtain Suze had rigged up over the window.

Gabe was standing there, tall and dark in the night, and she felt a chill go down her spine just looking at him.

As chills went, it was fairly warm.

Don't be stupid, Nell, she told herself and opened the door. "Hi. You lost?"

"Housewarming gift," he said, handing her a bottle of Glenlivet. "Riley said you'd taken over this place."

She stood back so he could come in, belatedly aware she was wearing ancient flannel pajamas covered with Eeyores that Jase had given her for Christmas when he was ten.

"Cute pajamas," he said. "Had them long?"

"I suppose you want a drink of this," Nell said and went to get glasses.

"What I really want is you telling me Lynnie left a lot of stuff behind," Gabe said, following her out to the kitchen. "Riley went through her trash on Friday night and there wasn't a damn thing in it for us, and then today we find out she moved. I think God owes me something good on this case."

He stopped as she turned around with the glasses in her hands.

"What?" she said, trying to fathom the look on his face.

He shook his head and took one of the glasses, looking good in the middle of her kitchen, like he belonged there. Maybe it was because the duplex had a period look to it. The white cabinets were forties, and so were the black and white squares of linoleum, the same period as Gabe's office with all that World War II furniture. He even looked a little like a forties movie star, she thought; he had that William Powell thing going for him, only taller and broader and edgier and without the mustache.

"So you didn't find anything here when you moved in?" Gabe said, and she brought herself back to 2000.

"I'm not in all the way yet," Nell said. "But there wasn't

anything in any of the drawers or cupboards we've opened so far."

Gabe lifted his glass to her. "Cheers."

He drank some of his Scotch and then leaned against the drainboard, smiling at her, and after a minute she said, "Knock it off, I'm not falling for that anymore."

"What?"

"Those long silences you lay on people so they'll fill them and incriminate themselves."

Gabe grinned at her. "Anything in particular you want to come clean about?"

She thought, *Margie*, and felt like hell again.

"Spill it," he said.

"I'm mad at you," she said. "I asked Margie about her mom today, and it was awful. I won't do that again." She went back into the living room to sit down on the daybed and drink her Scotch.

He followed her out and pulled a chair around to face her. "Give it up."

She told him everything while he drank his Scotch, and when she was finished, she said, "I feel like hell. You should have seen the look on Suze's face when I asked Margie about her mom's dishes."

"Helena was dressed up and she had her good jewelry on," Gabe said.

Nell nodded.

"She really did kill herself." Gabe sighed and sat back, and she scowled at him.

"You sound relieved."

"I am. I was afraid she'd been murdered."

"Murdered?" Nell said. "What's going on?"

"That car title was dated two weeks after Margie's mom died. And there's no record of any case that my dad was working on for Trevor at that time, plus he would have billed him for anything straight."

"Oh," Nell said.

Gabe nodded. "We still don't know why Trevor handed

over the car, but at least it wasn't to help him cover up a murder."

Nell thought about it. "And you think this is all connected to the blackmail at O&D. And to Lynnie."

"That's one guess."

Nell sighed. "I wouldn't have your job for anything. No wonder you've been in such a lousy mood all week."

"Hey," Gabe said. "I think I've been very open-minded, considering your track record."

"You've been a bastard," Nell said. "But you're right, I deserved it."

"No, you didn't. You're right. I've been in a lousy mood."

"So what are you like when you're not in a lousy mood?" Nell said, settling back to sip her drink.

"Pretty much the same," Gabe said. "My way or the highway."

"That stung, did it?" Nell shook her head, remembering. "She was something else. You know, at the bank, when she offered me that partnership, I almost wanted to take it. She was really seductive. She kept saying if we worked together we could really do some damage."

"You told me," Gabe said. "It was my least favorite part."

"The thing is, I liked her," Nell said, remembering Lynnie's sharp face and vibrating energy. "I knew I shouldn't, but I really did. She was so alive. She didn't let any guy get her down. I wanted to be like her."

"May I just say thank you for the rest of my gender for not joining her? Talk about a nightmare." He tossed back the rest of his Scotch as she frowned at him.

"Oh, thank you *very much*. Could you please remember I'm on your side?" She looked at him, squared for battle, and met his eyes.

They weren't hostile.

"I not only remember," he said, "I'm counting on it."

After a long moment during which she tried to remember what they'd been talking about, he put his glass on the floor and stood, saying, "I'm keeping you up." She followed him to the door, and he turned back when she opened it for him. "Just a suggestion, but you might not want to open the door to strangers in your pajamas."

"I knew it was you," Nell said. "And these things cover everything I've got. Big deal."

Gabe shook his head and went out into the night, and Nell locked the door behind him and went back upstairs to crawl into bed with Marlene. Marlene looked at her with unimaginable pain in her eyes. "Oh, right, I owe you a biscuit." She fished it out of her pocket and held it out to the dog.

Marlene's eyes were half-lidded and she looked as though she were on her last breath.

"I'm sorry it took so long," Nell said, still holding out the biscuit. "The boss showed up. Looking pretty damn good, I might add. And here I am in old pajamas. He complained. Maybe I should get some new ones. Snazzier ones."

Marlene's half lids began to look more like contempt than death.

"You're right," Nell said. "What are the chances he'll ever stop by after bedtime again?" She stretched farther to give the dog the biscuit, and Marlene turned her head away, overcome.

"Take it or lose it," Nell said, and Marlene took it gently and lay on her back, staring woefully into space.

"Chew," Nell said, and Marlene gave up and rolled over and scarfed the biscuit down. Then she sighed and snuggled down into the chenille, and Nell scooted over and patted the bed next to her. "Come here, baby."

Marlene picked up her long nose, considered the spot, and lay back down again.

"Oh, *thanks*," Nell said, and pulled the chenille throw up farther on the bed, next to her. Marlene sighed and staggered to her feet, dragging her long body up the bed to flop on top of the chenille against Nell's stomach. "There," Nell said, scratching her behind the ear as she snuggled down next to her. "Isn't that better?"

Marlene yawned, but she didn't flutter, so Nell took it as assent.

"We're proud, independent women, Marlene," Nell said, trying not to think of Gabe standing dangerous in the dark. "We don't need men."

Marlene looked at her with definite contempt and then buried her face in the chenille and went to sleep.

Chapter Nine

"Thank you," Gabe said when Nell brought in a package the next morning. She was wearing a bright blue sweater and a short navy skirt, nothing like the slim gray suits she'd been sporting since he'd hired her, and not much like the tissue-thin flannel pajamas she'd had on the night before, either. He was never going to be able to look at an Eeyore with innocent eyes again. And now there was this new outfit to contend with: The blue sweater made her hair seem even brighter, and the short skirt showed a lot of her legs, which were terrific.

"A guy just dropped this off," Nell said, and he stopped looking at her legs to take the package.

"Tell Riley this came," he said as he opened it.

"What is it?"

"Police report on Helena Ogilvie's suicide."

"Oh," Nell said and went to get Riley.

An hour later, he looked at Riley and said, "It's not tight."

Riley raised his eyebrows. "She got dressed up. Margie was on the phone with Trevor when she shot herself. The gun had been in the house for years. *She left a note*, for Christ's sake."

Gabe shook his head, wanting it to be a suicide and less sure than ever before. "I don't like the coincidence that Trevor was on the phone when she pulled the trigger. I don't like any coincidences, but that one in particular stinks."

"Not necessarily," Riley said. "Margie was telling him that Helena was acting strangely. He told Margie to take her to a hospital. That's logical."

"He made the call," Gabe said. "At exactly the right time."

"Maybe Helena heard them on the phone and decided she wasn't going to a hospital. Maybe she figured if Margie was on the phone, she'd have help when she heard the shot."

Gabe pulled the photos back from Riley's side of the desk. They were hard to look at, not because of any gore, which was minimal, but because Helena Ogilvie was so pathetic, a small, chubby woman dressed in a good silk suit who should have been at a garden show or a bridge game and not sprawled dead in her garage, her diamond-encrusted hands splayed on old oil spots. "I don't think the cop who did this report thought it was a suicide, either," he said. "Look at all these photos. Look at all the interviews he did. Jack Dysart, for Christ's sake. He was looking for something."

"And he didn't find it," Riley said. "I vote for suicide."

"I want a second opinion," Gabe said and buzzed Nell.

"I'm not asking Margie anything else," she said when she came in.

"Come here," Gabe said. "Look at this."

Nell came around to his side of the desk and looked over his shoulder and took a step back. "Oh, no."

She turned away, and he said, "Stop being such a baby."

"Don't spring stuff like that on me," Nell said. "*Warn* me."

"This is Helena Ogilvie," Gabe said patiently.

"I guessed that," Nell said. "The hole in her head was a dead giveaway."

"She wrote three suicide notes, threw two into her wastebasket, got dressed in her best suit, went downstairs, smashed some china, talked to her daughter, went out into her garage and shot herself," Gabe said. "What's wrong with that story?"

"I'd never kill myself if Jase was there," Nell said promptly. "You don't do that to your kids."

"People do," Riley said. "Plus, she was clearly nuts. That china bit?"

"No, I understand the china bit," Nell said. "That wasn't crazy. Getting dressed up sounds crazy."

"No," Riley said. "Suicides like to look nice."

"That's it?" Gabe said to Nell, feeling let down. "She wouldn't have killed herself in front of Margie? That's all you've got for me?"

Nell looked at him with exasperation, which was understandable. "Look, I didn't even know this woman." She pushed the photos away. "And I'm not going to get to know her from these. From what I have gathered, she wasn't very bright, but she was nice, and she just couldn't cope after Trevor left her, and I can understand that, too."

She looked back at the photos, clearly miserable, and Gabe felt a pang of guilt.

"Okay," he said. "Sorry. You can go." He shook his head at Riley. "So Trevor didn't give Dad the car to cover up a murder. We should celebrate."

"I can see you're thrilled." Riley leaned forward and picked up one of the photos. "Okay, if you're that uneasy, let's do this again. What in all of this mess doesn't sound right? No matter how loony."

"Killing herself in the garage in a silk suit?" Gabe said. "I can't get those oil stains on the garage floor out of my mind." He spread the photos out on the desk. "She could have gone upstairs and locked herself in the bathroom. Why kill yourself in a garage?"

"Maybe she didn't want to get the bathroom messy," Nell said, wincing as she looked at the photos. "Maybe—"

"You've got to do better than that," Riley said to Gabe. "Suicides do strange things. Hell, she was shooting herself in the head. What did she care if her suit got dirty?"

"It's such a cold place to kill yourself," Gabe said. "And—" He stopped, aware that Nell was staring at one of the pictures, a close-up of the entry wound. "Don't look at that one." He shifted the pictures, trying to find one from farther away, but Nell picked up the close-up.

"Where are her earrings?" she said.

"What?" Gabe took the photo from her.

"She's not wearing earrings. If she was dressed up, she would have had earrings on." Nell swallowed. "Margie said her mom put on her best jewelry."

"Diamond rings," Gabe said. "She had them on both hands." He shuffled through the photos to find the ones of Helena's hands. "Three rings," he said, showing the pictures to Nell. "Her wedding and engagement rings on her left hand, and this ring with diamonds in a circle on it on her right."

Nell shook her head. "Not enough. She'd have had earrings on." She shuffled through the photos until she found one taken from farther away. "And I would bet there was a necklace, too, and maybe a bracelet or a brooch. There, see? She's wearing a diamond circle pin. But no earrings. She wouldn't have dressed up and not put earrings in."

"That ring is weird," Riley said, and they both looked at him, and he pointed to the circle ring on Helena's right hand. "Well, look at it. It's not a normal setting. It's a flat circle with diamonds embedded in it, and the band doesn't run under the circle. That's not something every jeweler would carry."

Gabe leaned forward to look at the picture of Helena's right hand, and Nell leaned to see, too, warm against his shoulder. The ring was too small for Helena's pudgy finger, and her flesh puffed up through the center of the diamond-encrusted circle.

"It's ugly," Nell said. "Why would anybody design a ring like that? The circle pin, sure, but a ring?"

"Part of a set?" Riley said. "To match the pin?"

"Ask Margie," Gabe said to Nell.

"No," Nell said. "If that ring was part of a set, there are other ways to find out. I'm not upsetting her again."

Riley said, "Maybe she just forgot the earrings," but he didn't sound sure anymore.

"Maybe." Gabe opened his desk drawer and pulled out his phone book. "Take that picture of the ring and hit jewelers who have been in business since before 1978," he told Riley as he leafed through the white pages. "Talk to the oldest employee. See if anybody recognizes it." He ran his finger down the page and picked up the phone.

"Who are you calling?" Nell said.

"Robert Powell," Gabe said.

"Who?" Riley said.

"The cop on the case." Gabe said, gesturing to the signature at the bottom of the report. "I think we need to talk."

An hour later, while Nell was still trying to get rid of the memory of the pictures, Lu came by the office.

"He's in there," Nell said. "Don't annoy him, he's having a rough day."

"I'm not going to annoy him," Lu said. "I've decided to stay and go to school."

"Really?" Nell sat back. "Well, we're all grateful. What changed your mind?"

"In a way, you did," Lu said, smiling at her. "Thank you."

"I did?"

Lu opened the door and went in, and Nell heard her say, "Good news, Daddy," before she closed the door.

"I didn't do anything," she said to the empty office. She'd met Lu three times, and she hadn't said much of anything the second or third times because Jase—

"Oh, no." *Don't let it be Jase.* They'd date, and then Jase would break up with her because he always did, and Lu would be devastated because what girl wouldn't be devastated at losing Jase, and Gabe would . . .

She picked up the phone and dialed Jase's apartment and got his machine. "This is your mother," she said. "If you're dating Lu McKenna, stop it right now. I'm not kidding." She started to hang up, and then added, "I love you." Then she banged the receiver down.

Lu came out of the office, smiling. She nodded at Nell and whispered, "He's really happy. Ask him for something."

"Tell me this is not about Jase," Nell whispered back.

Lu's smile widened. "I don't need to go to Europe. I have all the excitement I need right here. Really, you did an *excellent* job raising that man."

"Boy," Nell said. "He's a boy. You're children."

Lu shook her head. "Parents," she said, and went out the door with a backward wave of her hand.

"Oh, God," Nell said.

"What's wrong?" Gabe said, and Nell jumped a foot in her chair.

"Don't do that," she said, clutching the desk.

"I just wanted to say thanks," he said, looking at her, mystified. "Lu said you're responsible for her changing her mind about Europe."

"Not true," Nell said. "Absolutely not. I had nothing to do with it."

"Okay," Gabe said. "What's this about?"

"Nothing." Nell turned back to her computer. "I'm just typing here. Go back to work."

"Look, I'm *grateful* you talked Lu out of Europe."

"I didn't," Nell said, keeping her back to him. "Not me. Go away now, I have to work."

"Sooner or later, you'll tell me," Gabe said.

Over my son's dead body, Nell thought.

"Okay, fine, be that way." He turned to go back into his office. "Oh. I've got an appointment at nine tomorrow morning with Robert Powell."

"Got it," Nell said, opening the appointment file. She concentrated on work the rest of the day, trying to ignore Jase and Helena lurking in the back of her mind. By the time she got home to Marlene, she was so unsettled that she sat on the daybed with the dog in her lap and just cuddled her until she felt better. Really, she didn't see how people got through the day without a dog. She spared one guilty thought to Farnsworth, getting through his days without Marlene, and then decided she was being oversensitive. He'd called her a little bitch; clearly he didn't love her. Marlene moaned in Nell's lap, and Nell said, "Yeah, that's the kind of day I had, too. Biscuit?"

A little later when Nell was chopping peppers on her drainboard for dinner and eating half of what she chopped, Jase called.

"I have this really weird message from you on my machine," he said. "Are you on medication or something?"

"No, but I will be if you don't stay away from Lu McKenna," Nell said. "I'm not kidding. Her father is nobody to mess with. That man has guns registered in his name."

"Mom," Jase said. "Chill. This is between me and Lu."

"Until her father finds out. Then it's you and the emergency room."

"Well, then, don't tell him," Jase said, completely unfazed. "You worry too much."

"I have things to worry about," she told him, but when she'd hung up, she looked around her cheerful kitchen and thought, *Maybe not*. Maybe the bad times were over. She'd survived her first week at work, she had a new place to live, things could only get better. Maybe Lynnie was in a better place, too. Maybe she'd blackmailed Trevor Ogilvie and was now living the good life. Nell had no regrets about Trevor Ogilvie losing money to Lynnie. He was the one who'd driven Margie's mother to suicide. The hell with him.

She and Marlene reclined on the daybed and ate salad and dog biscuits, crunching together companionably, and then they went upstairs to Suze's bed, Nell carrying Marlene's chenille throw. She changed into the plain blue silk pajamas that Suze had given her for her birthday—"Where's the black lace in my life, Marlene, that's what I want to know"—and then climbed into bed and read until they both fell asleep.

Nell woke up several hours later to a pitch-black bedroom and a strange sound in her bed. It took her a moment to fumble through her sleep and figure out the noise, but then she woke up completely.

Marlene was growling.

It was a weird little growl, which was par for Marlene, a sort of whiny purr with menace, but there was nothing weird about the way Marlene crouched on the bed in the moonlight. It was the first time Nell had seen her looking like pure, unaffected canine.

"What?" she whispered to the dog, and Marlene crouched lower and growled deeper.

Nell sat very still and listened and at last heard what Marlene had heard, a faint shuffle from the floor below, so faint she listened longer just to make sure as her skin went cold. There was somebody downstairs, opening drawers and closing cabinet doors.

"Shhh," she said to Marlene and eased up the phone. She hit 911, wincing at the tones in her ear, and when the dispatcher picked up the phone, she whispered, "There's somebody in my kitchen."

When she'd whispered everything she knew into the phone, the dispatcher told her to stay on the line, and she sat in her welter of covers, her hand on the still-tense Marlene, praying whoever it was would stay downstairs until the police came or he found whatever he was looking for—

She sat up a little straighter. What was he looking for? She didn't even have a TV or a stereo. Surely by now any burglar would have taken one look at her dearth of electronics and decided she was a bad risk. Unless the burglar wasn't a burglar. Unless . . .

She disconnected from the 911 line and punched in the speed-dial code for the office. She was pretty sure it was the same phone Gabe had upstairs.

"*What?*" Gabe said on the third ring, sounding half asleep and mad as hell.

"There's somebody here," she whispered into the phone.

"What?" he said again.

"This is Nell," she whispered.

"I know it's you," he snapped. "Why are you whispering at three A.M.?"

"There's somebody here. In the apartment. Downstairs."

"Jesus, *call 911.*"

"I did," Nell said, exasperated. "Do you think I'm stupid? But I thought since this was Lynnie's old place—"

Marlene growled again, and Nell stopped, putting her hand on Marlene to quiet her so she could listen.

Somebody was on the stairs.

"What's going on?" Gabe said. "Damn it, Nell—"

"I think he's coming up the stairs," she whispered, her voice cracking. "And I'm really scared."

"Turn the light on," Gabe said. "Do it now. Warn him you're awake. Is your bedroom door locked?"

"It doesn't have a lock."

"Shove something in front of it."

"Right," Nell said and put the phone down to push off her covers. Her hands were shaking, and as she kicked off the last of the blankets, she caught her foot in the Marlene's chenille throw and tripped. Marlene went wild as the phone slid off the bed with a clatter, and Nell tried to catch herself on the bedside table and fell against the door instead, smacking her head on the doorknob as she went down, hearing somebody run down the stairs at full speed as she fell.

"Shhhh," she said to Marlene who was now in full-fledged snarl, flinging herself against the door and scrabbling at it with her nails. Sirens filled the air, and then lights swung across her wall from the street below, and Nell heard her back door slam. She rubbed her head once and then crawled back across the floor to the phone. "Gabe? It's all right, I think. Gabe?" But he was gone.

"Thank you for taking twenty years off my life," Gabe said an hour later when the police had gone. He was sitting in Nell's living room on the daybed, drinking Glenlivet and trying to get his pulse under a hundred and twenty before he yelled at her for scaring the hell out of him.

"I thought you'd want to know," Nell said. "Since it was Lynnie's place and all."

"I'd want to know because it's your place," Gabe said. She was in pajamas made of some kind of slippery bright blue stuff that slid all over her when she moved and made her red hair look even wilder, especially next to the Technicolor bump she was sporting on her forehead. She was completely unconcerned about her pajamas, her bump, or the fact that she'd just had a near-rape-or-death experience, and she sat next to him on the daybed, pale and fine-boned and delicate, devouring whole-wheat toast with peanut butter and jam with a single-minded appetite that was disconcerting.

Gabe took a piece of ice out of his Glenlivet and handed it to her. "Put that on the lump on your forehead," he said and drank the rest of the Scotch.

She held the ice to her forehead, frowning as it began to melt and the water ran down her arm.

"Thank you for calling 911 first," Gabe said, using a pillow to mop off her arm.

"I'm not stupid," Nell said.

"Never thought you were," Gabe said. "Just nuts. Do you think it was Lynnie?"

"I don't know," Nell said, and then she thought about it while she chewed toast, her face getting that intense look that usually made him nervous. "No. Whoever it was stayed downstairs at first, and then came up. So he was looking for something down there—"

"—and didn't find it. Lynnie would have known where it was." Gabe put his glass down. "Come on."

"Where?" Nell said.

"Your bedroom," he said.

"Your technique needs work," Nell said and made him wait until she'd finished the last of her toast.

He stood inside the doorway and stared at the room. There were clothes and books tossed everywhere, her quilts were twisted in a heap on the massive bed that almost filled the room, and in the middle of it all, Marlene sat on the floor on a dark blue nubby-looking blanket and looked balefully at them.

"Nice," Gabe said, looking around the room. "I'll look in the register grates. You find the floor so we can tap the boards."

Two and a half hours later, Gabe knew the upstairs of Nell's apartment like no other place on earth, but they hadn't found anything. Nell stretched in exhaustion as she got up from the guest room floor, her pajamas doing interesting things while she moved, and then she said. "I'd love to stay and play with you, but I have to be at work in an hour."

"Me, too." Gabe sat with his back against the wall, frowning at the empty room. "Lucky for me I have a secretary who handles the office if I'm late."

"She might call in tired," Nell said.

"That might be a good idea," Gabe said. "Let's not leave this place empty until we've taken it apart."

"What did we just do?" Nell said. "A quick once-over?"

"Riley might have some ideas. He doesn't miss much. And then there's the downstairs." He pushed himself off the floor and went into her bedroom and picked up the phone. He punched the numbers in and frowned at her when she came in. She was even paler than usual and the bump on her head was turning purple. "You look terrible."

"Thank you." Nell sat down on the big bed and flopped back against the pillows.

"The pajamas are better than the Eeyores," he said. "But your forehead is a mess."

"I was injured in the line of duty," she said, crawling under the quilts.

"I told you to keep ice on that bump," Gabe said while the phone rang. "You should—"

"What?" Riley said, grumpy and half asleep.

"It's me. Open the office today. Nell's not coming in."

"I can be in there later," Nell said, fighting sleep. "I just—"

"And cancel whatever plans you have for tonight. Nell had a break-in last night and we need to search this place."

"A break-in?" Riley said, awake now. "Is she all right?"

"She's fine. Just clumsy. All she needs is some sleep and some *ice*," he said, directing the word to her, but she was asleep, her face serene for the first time since he'd met her. She looked pale and fragile and fine, like the woman in the Roethke poem, lovely in her bones.

"Gabe?" Riley said.

"I'll be in later," he told Riley. He hung up and pulled her quilt over her, taking care not to wake her. Marlene jumped up on the bed and then hung her head over the edge, moaning at the blue thing she'd been lying on. He picked it up and tossed it at the foot of the bed, and she promptly curled up on it and dozed off.

"Not much bothers you girls, does it?" he said and took one last look at Nell before he went downstairs.

The Powell residence was a tidy bungalow in Grandview, a good neighborhood that wasn't obnoxious about it. Gabe knocked on the door and was surprised when the man who opened it was younger than he was.

"Robert Powell?" he said.

"That's my dad," the man said, offering his hand. "I'm Scott Powell. You must be Gabe McKenna." He nodded toward the side of the house. "My dad's had an apartment over the garage since he retired. This must be some great old case. He's really jazzed to see you."

His dad had a terrific apartment over the garage, Gabe saw when he went up the stairs. Big skylights, thick carpet, comfortable furniture, and enough electronics to rival Radio Shack. Scott was obviously making sure Robert had the best retirement possible, and Robert was just as obviously enjoying it.

"Some place, huh?" he said, grinning at Gabe from under grizzled brows. He was built like a bear, an older version of the slimmer Scott, and Gabe relaxed a little, liking them both.

"Great place," he said, taking the seat Robert waved him to. "Thanks for seeing me."

Robert shook his head. "My pleasure. You looking into the Ogilvie suicide?"

"Not officially," Gabe said. "I have a personal interest."

Robert nodded. "You related to Helena?"

"No," Gabe said, and took a deep breath. "Was it a suicide?"

"No," Robert said, and Gabe sat back. "I'm not saying she wasn't thinking about it," Robert went on. "I'm not saying she might not have done it anyway. But she didn't shoot herself."

"Why?" Gabe said.

"She had pills," Robert said. "A lot of them. She'd been saving them for almost two months, telling her doctor she needed tranqs and sleeping pills and filling the prescriptions."

"Not conclusive," Scott said from where he leaned against the wall.

"My boy's on the force, too," Robert said proudly, and Gabe felt a throb of jealousy that Scott still had his dad, had him living close, could see him whenever he wanted, watch the game with him on the wide-screen TV, kick back with him and have a beer. Robert looked up at Scott and said, "There's more, hotshot." He looked over at Gabe. "She wrote three suicide notes, practicing."

"Two of them were in the wastebasket," Gabe said, remembering the police report.

"Yeah, but they were all drafts," Robert said. "They had words marked out, smudges. And she had good stationery on the desk in that room. She hadn't written the final one yet."

"Still not conclusive," Scott said, but he was looking a lot more interested.

"Then there were her earrings," Robert said. "She was all dressed up, but she wasn't wearing any."

"We noticed that, too," Gabe said. "You didn't happen to get a list of the pieces in the set, did you? Besides the ring and the pin she was wearing?"

Robert shook his head. "The daughter couldn't remember all of them, and by the time I'd talked to her, her mother was buried wearing them."

"Buried in diamonds?" Scott said skeptically.

"Big diamonds," Robert said. "Worth maybe a hundred grand back then. Now . . ." He shrugged. "I did not believe the husband would put those stones six foot under, but I wasn't about to dig her up to see. By the time I managed to get a description to get to pawnshops, a week had passed. Nobody ever came forward and said they'd seen them. Of course, some of them wouldn't."

"You think somebody killed her and took the jewelry?" Gabe said. "You think it was a robbery?"

"No," Robert said. "I think it was a murder, and whoever did it grabbed the diamonds as an extra. And then I think he was stuck with them because they were so unusual. All circles like that? Anybody would recognize those. Unless he broke the stones out and sold them that way."

Scott picked up a dining room chair and swung it around to straddle it. "Anybody have a motive?"

"She was holding her husband up on the divorce," Robert said. "The dumb bastard had a mistress with a baby on the way, and he wanted to marry her. But the wife was holding out for half of his half of his law firm. It would have ruined the place and, according to everybody I talked to, she knew that and didn't care."

"So the husband," Scott said.

"Or the husband's partner," Robert said. "He didn't have an airtight alibi, and he really couldn't afford to lose any income. He was paying alimony to one wife and supporting an expensive trophy, too. I talked to her. Not a nice woman." He looked at Gabe. "He still with her?"

"Jack?" Gabe shook his head. "No. He divorced Vicki about eight years later and married another trophy. He's still with that one."

"So now he's paying double alimony." Robert laughed. "Dumb bastard. He struck me as the type who figured that if he wanted it, he should have it, damn the consequences. He was slick about it, but he had the look. You know?"

Gabe thought about Jack. "I know. How about Trevor?"

"Trevor?" Scott said.

"The husband," Robert said. "He was on the phone with the daughter. We checked, and he was standing in his law office at the time, secretary there and everything."

"Convenient," Scott said. "How about the daughter? Did she inherit anything?"

"A nice chunk, nothing spectacular," Robert said. "But you can forget her being in on it. She was a sweet little thing. She went to pieces when she found her mother's body. They had her sedated for a couple of weeks afterward, and when they finally took her off the pills, she was still rocky. She didn't do it."

"Did she know who did?" Gabe said.

"If she did, she wasn't remembering it," Robert said. "I'd swear she wasn't lying to me, but she wasn't the kind to face reality. At least she wasn't then."

Gabe thought of Margie, playing tea party at The Cup with Chloe. "She still isn't."

"She still married to that son of a bitch?" Robert said.

"No," Gabe said, interested. "Stewart was a son of a bitch?"

"Arrogant asshole," Robert said. "Dumber than snot. If I could have pinned it on somebody, I'd have pinned it on him, but I'd never have made it stick. He couldn't have planned a picnic, let alone a murder."

"So who did it?"

"I don't know," Robert said. "There was nothing there, I mean, there were even powder traces on her hand. My only real hope was the diamonds, and they never turned up. So the daughter divorced the creep, did she? Good. I liked her."

"Margie?" Gabe said. "No. He embezzled close to a million from Ogilvie and Dysart and left, seven years ago."

"That dumbass embezzled?" Robert said. "I don't think so. He couldn't have embezzled from his own checking account."

"Really?" Gabe said. "That's interesting. Because O&D was sure it was him."

"Not unless he had help," Robert said. "And he'd have needed a *lot* of help. Did he have an accomplice?"

"Not that we know of," Gabe said. "O&D didn't hire us for that one."

"You look into it," Robert said. "There's gonna be somebody else standing behind him, telling him what to do." He sat back. "So your interest is personal, huh?"

Gabe thought about ducking it, and then said, "My dad was Trevor's best friend."

Robert nodded, waiting.

"I think he knew something," Gabe said. "But he died in '82, so it's gone with him."

"McKenna," Robert said. "We didn't question anybody named McKenna."

"I think he might have been called in after the shooting," Gabe said. "I don't know."

"Maybe you don't want to know," Robert said.

"He deserves better than that," Gabe said.

"If you don't look, it's because you think he's guilty."

"Something like that," Gabe said and felt like hell.

When Gabe had thanked Robert, Scott walked him back to his car. "Listen, if you need any help, give me a call."

"Thanks," Gabe said, surprised.

"Hey, if something turned up about my old man, I'd want to know."

Gabe nodded back toward Robert's apartment. "He's a great guy."

"The best." Scott stood back and gazed at the Porsche with envy. "Great car. What year?"

"1977," Gabe said, and watched Scott's eyes narrow a fraction.

"Year before the suicide. Any connection?"

"Trevor sold it to my dad for a dollar two weeks after the shooting."

Scott whistled. "When'd you find that out?"

"A week ago."

"Bad week," Scott said as Gabe got in the car.

"And it's not getting better," Gabe said.

That evening, Suze helped Nell and Margie finish the unpacking, while Riley and Gabe tore apart the kitchen. "So what are they looking for again?" Suze asked Nell.

"They're not sure," Nell said, handing her another piece of bubble-wrapped china to untape. "They figure they'll know it when they see it."

"I think they're exciting," Margie said. "Detectives."

"Ha," Suze said and unwrapped the china, only to stop and stare. It was a small, round white china cup, but it had feet, honest-to-God people feet with blue spotted socks and black shoes. Margie had another, with black striped socks and yellow shoes. "What *is* this stuff?"

"Walking Ware," Nell said. "Novelty china from the seventies. I forgot I had it until we had everything appraised, but then when it came time to divide the china, I couldn't part with it."

"I've never seen anything like it," Margie said over Suze's shoulder. "And I was around in the seventies."

"It's English." Nell unwrapped another piece, a long-legged sugar bowl, the spindly legs crossed at the knees and the feet shod in huge yellow shoes. "My mom was English. We'd go over there to spend a couple of weeks every summer. These made me laugh, so my aunt and grandmother started sending pieces to me for birthdays and Christmases."

Suze unwrapped another little round cup, this one with longer legs, stretched out as if they were running.

"That's called Running Ware," Nell said and then looked up startled when something thudded in the kitchen. "Where's Marlene?" she said, and Marlene picked up her long, narrow head on the daybed and looked to see if food was involved. "Just checking, baby," Nell said, and Marlene sighed and put her nose into the chenille again.

Suze put the running cup on the floor beside her. It looked as though it was covering ground. "I love these. Do they all look like this?"

"Different-colored shoes and socks," Nell said. "I think I'm going to have to keep them in the kitchen, assuming I still have a kitchen when they're finished in there." She was unpacking a teapot with striped socks and black Mary Janes. "The hutch is full of Clarice and Susie."

"Do you have room in the kitchen?" Margie said.

Nell frowned. "I don't know. Maybe if I put up a shelf—"

"Chloe has the most darling shelves in The Cup," Margie said. "She edged them with the plastic stuff that looks like crochet. . . ."

While Margie burbled on about the teashop, Suze unpacked the rest of the pieces, matching teacups to teapots and sugar bowls and creamers. At the bottom of the box, Suze found Nell's family photo album and passed it over to her, and Margie took it and began to leaf through it as Suze lined up the running egg cups in a line and laughed. There were nine of them, some with striped socks and some with checked and some with dots, all running hell-bent for leather someplace else.

"I have to have copies made of all those pictures," Nell was saying to Margie. "Jase should have an album, too."

"Where do you get these cups?" Suze said, breaking into the conversation. "I want some."

"England," Nell said. "Antique and secondhand stores mostly. Or eBay, the online auction site. They show up there pretty often."

"How much?"

"Plain egg cups are about thirty or forty dollars," Nell said. "The running ones come a bit higher. Maybe fifty."

"Fifty dollars for an egg cup?" Margie said.

"I want these in my china cabinet," Suze said, tracing the fat, smooth edge of the nearest cup. "It's full of butt-ugly Spode."

"You can have them," Nell said. "Early birthday present."

"No, they're too much," Suze said, and thought, *If I got a job, I could pay for them myself.* In the kitchen, something else thudded. Detective work. Nell had told her that the McKennas could use her as a decoy, but she'd known Jack would have a fit, so she'd said no. But now there were these cups. . . . "Can I buy these one at a time? Pay for them as I go?"

"Sure," Nell said, looking a little taken aback. "Or take them now and pay me later."

"No," Suze said. "I want to earn them. One at a time."

"The Dysart Spode is beautiful," Margie said, sounding a little grumpy. "I don't see why—"

"You want it?" Suze said. "It's yours."

"I have my Desert Rose," Margie said. "But that beautiful blue—"

"Have you ever *looked* at those plates?" Suze picked up the cup with the mauve shoes, and her heart beat faster. It had thin blue lines around the top of the socks. It was going to look great running amok among the Spode. "They're from a series called the British Sporting Set, and the pictures on them are awful. There's one called 'Death of the Bear.' "

"You're kidding," Nell said. "I've been eating off it for years at holidays, but I never looked at it."

"There's another one called 'Girl at the Well,' " Suze said. "She looks like she's going to throw herself in. I get very depressed looking at my china."

"The running cups are yours," Nell said.

Suze put the mauve cup down and felt immeasurably lighter. She was going to have to get a job now. She had a future that didn't involve going to school and waiting for Jack to get home. She was *doing something*.

"Thank you. I will." She took a deep breath. "So Margie, how many days a week is this shop open? Budge is going to go nuts without you on the weekends."

"Just on Saturdays," Margie said, her face clearing. "And only in the afternoons all week. It's a *darling* job. . . ."

Suze stared at the egg cups while Margie burbled on. They strode across the floor, confident and sure. On the move.

"You know, Margie," Nell said, and her voice sounded so odd that Suze looked up to watch her. "If you have a photo album, I could take it in when I take this one in to get the duplicates. You, too, Suze. That way if anything happened, you'd have a spare."

Suze stared at her, and Nell's eyes slid away. *She put that album in the bottom of the box on purpose*, Suze thought.

"Is it expensive?" Margie was saying. "I'm sort of broke. Budge says I should declare Stewart dead and collect his insurance since Stewart spent all my inheritance, but that doesn't seem right. I'm not even sure he's dead."

Suze shifted her surprise from Nell to Margie. "You need money?"

"I don't *need* it," Margie said. "Yet. And he could be dead. Of course, he could not be, too."

"The photo place might give me a deal if I took two in," Nell said, her voice overly bright. "You could pay me later, like Suze. It's no trouble."

"Well, okay," Margie said. "It is a good idea. I'll bring it in to work tomorrow."

"Good," Nell said, her voice so chirpy it broke.

Suze tried to catch her eye again, and Nell said, "We should have coffee," and stood up.

Suze stood up to follow her, but then Gabe came out of the kitchen, and she pulled him aside. "Listen," she said as he looked at her, startled. "Nell said once that you might need some help on your decoy work. Is the job still open?"

"Sure," he said, a little wary. "We've got one Thursday night."

"Where and when?" Suze said. "I'll be there."

Nell kept an eye on Gabe and Suze from the kitchen doorway. If she knew Gabe, he was pumping her for something. "Hey," she called out to him and heard Suze say, "Thank you," before Gabe came over to her, and she drew him into the kitchen. "What are you to talking to Suze about?"

"She was talking to me," Gabe said. "She wants to do decoy work."

"What?" Riley said, from behind them.

"Jack's not going to be happy," Nell said.

Gabe shrugged. "That's Suze's problem."

"And *mine*," Riley said. "I do most of the damn decoys. Why—"

"Ignore him," Gabe told Nell. "He's frustrated because we have found exactly nothing. We had high hopes for the basement, but the door to it has been nailed shut since World War II."

"I asked about that," Nell said. "Doris likes the basement to herself. She makes wreaths down there."

"Wreaths," Gabe said, as if he wasn't sure what to do with that. "Okay. You're sure Lynnie didn't leave anything that you threw out?"

"If she left anything, Doris took it," Nell said. "The place was empty when I moved in.

"Doris," Gabe said and looked at Riley.

"Oh, thank you very much, no," he said. "Make Nell do it. It's her landlady."

"Ask Doris what she found," Gabe said to Nell.

"Sure," Nell said. "And then when she evicts me for suggesting she stole from Lynnie, Marlene and I will come live with you."

"Good idea," Gabe said, and he sounded serious. "You should come back with us, just in case your prowler comes back to search again. Chloe's place has locks that'll keep out anybody, and she'd love to have you."

Nell looked around her apartment. *Her* apartment. "I just moved in. My china's unpacked. Really, I'm fine."

"You'd be safer next door to us," Gabe said. "If anything happened, we could get to you in a minute."

That did sound appealing, but it wouldn't be her place. "No," she said. "Thank you, but no. We don't even know that the guy who broke in here knew I was here."

"I'd still feel better with you next door," Gabe said, but Nell wouldn't go.

Later that night, when Budge had collected a reluctant Margie, when Suze had climbed into her yellow Beetle with a parting shot at Riley and a fishy look at Nell, and when Gabe had tried one more time to talk her into moving to Chloe's and then left, Nell patted Marlene and said,

"Okay, puppy, anybody who comes through that door, you go for the throat."

Marlene sashayed her butt deeper into the chenille.

"Unless it's Gabe," Nell said. "He's on our side."

Chapter Ten

With her china unpacked and her apartment livable and her midnight invader foiled, Nell turned her attention to the office. Gabe had been grateful when she'd brought him Margie's photo album since it had several good pictures of Helena wearing her diamonds—earrings, necklace, bracelet, brooch, and ring—and even more grateful when she started organizing the freezer full of files. Unfortunately, he wasn't grateful enough to give her a free hand with the office, so she took matters into her own hands and painted the bathroom walls a pale dove gray with gold trim along the ceiling. "Very fancy," was all Gabe said, so she went on, surprising him one afternoon when he came back to find her on a ladder and Suze underneath, painting the reception room walls a soft gold. She braced herself, but all he said was, "If you fall off the ladder, you're on your own," and went into his office. "Not chatty, is he?" Suze said, and Nell said, "He's depressed about a case that's not going well." She did her damnedest to cheer him up, keeping his business running seamlessly and his coffee cup filled, playing Dean Martin and Frank Sinatra in the outer office and swiping almond cookies from Margie for him in the afternoon, but he didn't seem to notice, ignoring her if she worked at something he asked her to do, yelling if she changed something without checking with him first. "I could dance naked for that man on his desk," she told Suze at Halloween, "and all he'd say is, 'Damn it, Nell, you're stepping on the reports.' Not that I want to dance naked for him. That's just an expression."

"Try it," Suze said, adjusting Marlene's pumpkin costume while Marlene glowered. "There, doesn't she look cute?"

Marlene looked like a rabid orange marshmallow peanut.

"Gabe looks like that every time I improve something," Nell said.

Still, he let her get away with small things, and the place started looking a lot better. The only effective opposition she encountered was from Riley when she moved the ugly bird on the filing cabinet to the basement. "This," Riley said when he brought it back, "is the Maltese Falcon, and it stays." "Oh, please," she'd said, but when she appealed to Gabe, he said, "Leave the bird alone, Eleanor," so she gave up and it brooded over her once again from the filing cabinet.

The rest of the agency work went well, the background checks and routine divorce work that both Gabe and Riley did so well that they turned away jobs because they couldn't handle it all. Even the decoy work with Suze was a success, although Riley made her wear suits after the first one. "It is just not fair to send that woman into a bar in a sweater," he told Gabe and Nell. "It's entrapment." So the next time Suze went out, she wore one of Nell's gray suits, her pale hair pulled back in a chignon, and, if anything, looked even sexier. "It's that Grace Kelly thing she's got going," Riley said, but all Suze said was, "I love this look," and Nell gave her all her old suits, the grays and grayed-blues and charcoal blacks that made Suze look like a sophisticated and potentially dangerous woman instead of a college kid. Suze said Jack hated them, but she seemed to feel that was a plus, so Nell didn't worry. In return, Nell inherited Suze's electric wardrobe and woke up every morning to a choice of cashmere sweaters and silk T-shirts in every color of the rainbow. Gabe didn't notice that, either.

Nell also woke up every morning to Marlene who, while still milking her traumatic past for every biscuit she could get, had given up moaning and rolling over as a way of life and occasionally even broke into a fast trot if food was involved. Nell had meant to leave her in the apartment while she was at work, but the first day she tried it, Marlene had complained the entire day, and Doris had not been amused, and she was already unamused from Nell's carefully worded inquiries about any of Lynnie's leftover stuff. So Marlene now walked to work with Nell, clad in the tan trenchcoat Suze had bought her, investigating the six blocks of concrete and ground cover between the apartment and the agency with the same pessimistic suspicion with which she viewed the world in general. Once at the agency, she stayed with Riley if he was in, fluttering her eyelashes at him while he fed her dog biscuits and scratched her stomach with his foot. "Women," Riley would say as she fluttered, and she'd whimper a little in return. "That's a really sick relationship," Gabe said once, but he didn't bar Marlene from the office, and since Farnsworth had never called again in search of her, Nell felt fairly safe bringing her to work, if a little guilty that she'd taken the dog. "If he really wasn't mistreating her, I stole his pet," she said to Riley. "*Now* you think of that," he said.

In the meantime, and in spite of Budge's opposition, Margie was loving the teashop, which meant that Chloe could leave without worry, so she did, flying to France with Lu's Eurail pass. "She went where?" was all Gabe said, and Nell wondered at first if maybe he wasn't hiding his despair at losing her as she put postcard after postcard on his desk. They all said, "Having a wonderful time" and burbled something about whatever scenic wonder was on the front of the card, and none of them said, "I miss you." That had to hurt, Nell thought, but after working for him for six weeks, she realized he wasn't the type to hide anything. If he was mad, she knew about it; if he was depressed, she knew about it; if he was on the track of something, she knew about it. It was exhilarating to work for somebody that direct, and the days went by on high octane, occasionally revved up by the inevitable clashes as she fixed his agency for him.

"Don't think I don't know what you're doing," he told her in November when she stuck the old Oriental from the reception room in the closet under the stairs and put down a new gold and gray Morris-patterned rug.

"It looks nice, doesn't it?" Nell said.

"No," Gabe said. "It looks new and we didn't need it."

"Now about the business cards—"

"No," he said and shut his office door in her face.

A day later, trying to move the wood filing cabinet to a different place so the damn bird wouldn't be looming over her shoulder, Nell got a splinter in her right hand and couldn't get it out with her left. She went in to Gabe with her tweezers and said, "Help."

"How the hell did you get a splinter?" he said, putting his pen down.

"The filing cabinet," she said. "The back edge was rough."

"The back edge was against the wall," he said, taking the tweezers.

"Yes, it was," Nell said brightly. "Now if you could get that piece of wood out of my palm . . ."

He took her hand in his and stuck it under his desk lamp, and she held her breath.

"There it is," he said and used his thumb to draw the flesh of her palm tight so he could see it better. "Brace yourself, Bridget." He drew the splinter out carefully and let go of her hand. "Now keep your mitts off my filing cabinets. They've been there for sixty years and they're staying there."

"Bridget?"

"What?"

"Brace yourself, Bridget?" Nell repeated.

"Old joke." Gabe gave her the tweezers. "Go and move my furniture no more."

When Riley came back, Nell said, "Do you know a joke about 'Brace yourself, Bridget'?"

"That is the joke," Riley said. "It's the answer to 'What is Irish foreplay?' "

"Irish foreplay," Nell said. "Oh. Never mind."

The phone rang as Riley went into his office, and when she picked it up, it was Trevor Ogilvie. She tried to give him Margie's number at The Cup, but he wanted to talk to her.

"Jack says you're overqualified for that job, my dear," Trevor said. "With your background, you shouldn't be just a secretary."

I'm not just a secretary. "Oh, it's a little more complicated than that."

"Well, we still think of you as family," Trevor said.

You never thought of me as family, Nell thought and began to wonder what the hell was going on.

"So we'd like to offer you a job here," Trevor went on. "We could certainly use your organizational skills."

"Well, thank you, Trevor, but I think—"

"Don't be hasty, Nell. Gabe can't be paying you that much."

The certainty in his voice annoyed her. "Actually, the pay is pretty good," she lied. "And it's a very interesting working environment. But I do appreciate the offer."

When she'd hung up, she went in to see Gabe.

He looked up and said, "What did you try to move this time?"

"Trevor Ogilvie just offered me a job."

"What?"

Nell sat down across from him. "I swear to God. He said Jack said I was overqualified for this one, and they could give me something better. He promised me more money, too."

Gabe's face was impassive. "What did you say?"

Nell was indignant. "What do you mean, what did I say? I said no, of course. What is he up to?"

Gabe leaned back. "He said Jack talked to him?"

Nell nodded.

"Maybe Jack's upset about Suze working and thinks if you quit, Suze'll quit."

"Jack doesn't know Suze is working. She tells him she's going out with me."

Gabe was quiet for a moment, and then he said, "Thanks for not quitting."

"Quitting?" Nell said. "I'm just getting started. I'm tearing apart the basement next."

"Oh, good," Gabe said. "We don't have enough upheaval around here."

But for the first time, he didn't sound exasperated, and Nell went back to work feeling positively cheerful.

Gabe's life was not as tidy.

For one thing, he couldn't find Lynnie or any evidence of where she'd gone or who had broken into her apartment, and he considered that a personal affront and a professional failure. Riley's canvassing of the back records of jewelers and pawnshops wasn't getting anywhere, either. "The damn diamonds could have been pawned anywhere," Riley told him. "In fact, if the guy who had them had any brains at all, he'd have gone out of town. Give it up." But Gabe couldn't, even though he had other problems more pressing.

Budge Jenkins, for example, called regularly, miserable about Margie taking over The Cup. "It's not safe for her," he said, the only man Gabe had ever known who could fidget over the phone. "She could get robbed." Gabe had said, "Budge, it's a teashop not a 7-Eleven. She's closed by six every night," but Budge continued to fuss and nag until Gabe thought seriously about kicking Margie out just to get Budge off his back.

Then there was Riley. "Suze is a menace," he told Gabe after the first decoy with Suze. "She walks in a bar and everybody comes on to her." "Considering her line of work for us, that's a plus," Gabe said. Suze herself was a complete professional, and Gabe saw her in the office most days, either helping Margie close the register at six or aiding and abetting Nell in her ceaseless efforts to transform an agency that didn't need it. He'd decided to let Nell have her way on the rest of the place as long as she left his office alone, a decision reinforced by her matter-of-fact refusal of Trevor's offer of a job and a pay raise, but in the second week in November, she made her move.

"Your furniture needs work," she told him, facing him down across his desk, blinding him with her red hair and an orange sweater with a bright blue stripe across the bust. "It'll only be for a day, two at most."

"Stay out of my office," Gabe said, trying not to look at the stripe. "You can have the bathroom and the outer office, but this is mine. I know it's out of date, but the fifties are due to come back any day now."

"This stuff isn't fifties, it's forties. And it's already back. I don't think you should get rid of it, I think you should have it cleaned and repaired." Nell sat down, aiming the stripe right at him. "But you've got to clean the leather and the wood on the furniture, and some of it's wobbling and needs to be reglued." She looked at the ceiling. "There's even one with a broken arm."

"I know," Gabe said. "You broke it."

"And we need to replace the blinds in here—" Nell said brightly.

"Damn it, Nell," he said, "could you please leave something here alone?"

"—but it wouldn't be a change at all." She smiled at him. "It'd be a *restoration*." She looked cheerful but tense, and he realized she was braced for him to yell.

He'd been yelling a lot lately. He took a deep breath and waited until he was calmer. "All right," he said finally. "If it doesn't cost too much, and you're not changing anything, go ahead with the furniture."

"And the blinds."

"And the blinds."

"And the rug."

"Don't push your luck, Eleanor."

"*Thank* you," Nell said and headed back to her desk to start phoning repair people.

"But you can't *change* anything," Gabe called after her, and she stuck her fiery head back in the door to say, "I'm not changing anything around here. I'm *improving* it." Then she disappeared again.

"Why is that not reassuring?" Gabe said to the empty space that vibrated with her afterimage.

When he came in a week later, all his office furniture was gone.

"*Nell!*"

"The restorer came," she said, materializing in his doorway in a violet sweater this time. There was a red heart knitted into the fabric above her left breast. *Why doesn't she just wear bull's-eyes?* he thought. "He said the wood just needed to be cleaned and waxed," Nell went on, chipper as hell, "but that restoring the leather upholstery and reinforcing the loose joints might take longer."

"Restoring the leather? That sounds expensive."

"It is, a little, but not like buying new," Nell said brightly. "And think of what a difference it'll make."

"Nell—"

"And when that's done we have to talk about the couch in the reception room—"

"The couch is fine."

"—because it isn't period, it's just ugly and falling apart. We—"

"*Nell,*" Gabe said, and something in his voice must have gotten to her because she stopped and looked at him war-

ily, a redheaded, wide-eyed Bambi in purple cotton knit.
"*Stop it,*" he said and felt guilty for saying it.

"A new couch and I'm done," Nell said. "I swear. That
and the business cards and the window, but the new couch
first. Somebody's going to fall through the old one and
then where will we be? Sued, that's where. Really, I know
what I'm doing."

"I never doubted it," Gabe said. "I'm just not sure you
know what we're doing. That would be running a detective
agency. We do not have the kind of clientele that notices
the decor. By the time they get to us, we could be meeting
in Dumpsters and they wouldn't care as long as we got the
answers they needed."

"The couch will be the end of it," Nell said and crossed
her heart, both of them. "I swear."

"No couch," Gabe said. "I mean it."

Nell sighed and nodded and went back to her desk as
the phone rang and then stuck her head back in. "Riley's
on one and your phone is over there on the floor by the
window."

"How many days?"

"Larry said tomorrow, Wednesday tops."

"Who's Larry?" Gabe said as he picked up the phone.

"I don't know," Riley said on the other end. "Who's
Larry?"

"The guy doing the furniture," Nell said. "You'd like
him. He liked your stuff."

She disappeared back through the door as Riley said,
"You did not send me out to find any Larry."

"Forget Larry," Gabe said. "Where are you?"

"Cincinnati," Riley said. "The pawnshops here also have
no record of the diamonds in 1978. And I'm tired of this.
Trevor said he buried them with Helena, and I've decided
to believe him."

"Don't stop until you've hit every damn shop in the
city," Gabe said.

Riley sighed his exasperation into the phone. "So who's Larry?"

"Some guy Nell has redoing the furniture in my office."

"You know, you and Nell have a lot in common," Riley said. "Neither one of you ever gives up."

"Maybe I'll send Nell after Lynnie."

"She got her the first time," Riley said. "I'd give her a shot at it."

Nell knocked on the door and came in again. "Client to see you," she said and then stood back to let Becca Johnson in.

Becca looked miserable, which was par for her; she hired the McKennas to check the background of every man who came along that she thought might be The One, but unfortunately Becca's intelligence and common sense were equaled only by her lousy taste in men. Now as she stood in front of him, her breath coming in shudders as she bit her lip, Gabe knew Becca had picked another winner.

"I'll talk to you later," Gabe said to Riley and hung up. "What's wrong?"

"I'll get a glass of water," Nell said and disappeared through the door.

"His name isn't Randy," Becca said, and then her face crumpled and she walked into Gabe's arms.

"Okay," Gabe said, patting her. "Whose name isn't Randy?"

She lifted her pretty face from his shoulder. "He's really wonderful, Gabe. I was so sure this time, I didn't even hire you because I knew. But his name isn't Randy at all. He *lied to me*," Becca wailed, and Gabe winced as her voice rose.

Nell came back in with the water and then stopped, raising an eyebrow. *Don't start with me*, he thought and crossed his eyes at her over Becca's shoulder. She crossed hers back at him, put the water on the windowsill, and left the room with a nice swing to her walk. *I should annoy her more often*, he thought. *It puts some bounce in her step.*

"I really trusted him," Becca said, reminding him he had a problem on his hands. "I was *so sure*."

"Did you ask him about it?" Gabe said, patting again.

"Ask him?" Becca pulled back. "*Ask him?*"

"Yes," Gabe said patiently. "How did you find out?"

"His suitcase," Becca said, sniffing. "In the back of his closet. I was looking for an extra blanket and found it. The initials on it are EAK."

"Maybe it's a secondhand suitcase," Gabe said. "Maybe it was his maternal grandmother's."

"It's his," Becca said. "It's almost brand-new. He doesn't buy secondhand. Everything in his place is brand-new."

"Maybe he borrowed it," Gabe said, and she stopped hyperventilating. "Becca, ask him. Then call me and tell me what he says, and we can investigate that if you want. But don't jump all over the guy because of initials on a suitcase."

Becca sniffed again. "You really think that's it?"

"I don't know," Gabe said. "But it's time you talked to him. If you're really serious about him—"

"I am so serious about him," Becca said.

"—then you're going to have to learn to talk to him."

"We talk," Becca said, and then when Gabe shook his head, she said, "Okay, I'll ask him." She swallowed once and said, "I really will. Tonight."

Gabe found his notebook on the bookshelf and took down all the particulars about Randy, his background as far as Becca knew it, and his suitcase. Then he took her elbow and steered her toward the door. "Okay, I've got all I need. Call me when you've talked to him, and if you're still not happy, we'll find out everything."

"Thank you," she said, with the tiniest catch in her voice. "I'm sorry, Gabe, but I really thought this was it, and then I saw those initials."

"Don't panic yet," he said, urging her gently through the reception room.

When she was out the door, he turned back to Nell. "Was there something you wanted to say?"

"Me? No," she said, all innocence. "You groping clients is no business of mine."

"Remember that," he said, going back to his office. "And try to send in only really built women from now on. They're more fun in a clinch."

He closed his door just as something hit it. Probably a paper wad, he thought, and went back to work smiling until he realized he didn't have a desk or a chair.

Later that evening, waiting for the last callback from California on a background check, Gabe sat on the floor in his office and ate Chinese next to Nell while he looked at her legs stretched out beside his. At least sitting beside her, he couldn't see that damn heart.

"What would you do if you went after Lynnie?" he said.

"Find some guy with money, stake him out like a goat, and wait for her to show up," Nell said. "Do you have the potstickers? Because I—" She broke off as he handed the potsticker carton to her.

"You know, I remember when I had furniture," he said, reaching for the garlic chicken carton. "It was nice in here then."

"I called and Larry's bringing it back tomorrow," Nell said. "You're going to love it. Tell me about Becca."

"What about Becca?" Gabe said, willing to fight but not really up to it. It was so much more pleasant to savor the garlic and look at the scenery.

"Riley calls her the Check-Out Girl, so I gather she checks out the men she dates?"

"Becca comes from a small town where everybody knows everybody else," Gabe said. "She now lives in a big town and works in a big university with a huge transient population. Nobody knows anybody. So she hires us to do the work that her mother and grandmother would do back home."

Nell considered it around a fork full of sweet and sour pork. "That's not dumb."

"No, but this time she didn't want us to investigate. This time it was the real thing. Stop hogging the pork."

He stretched out his hand and she passed the carton over.

"So what happened?"

"She thinks he lied about his name." Gabe took a bite of pork and let the tang of the sauce linger for a moment before he swallowed. The good things in life deserved to be savored. No point in moving fast.

"You don't sound too convinced," Nell said.

"No reason to panic yet." Gabe picked up his paper cup, and just as he realized it was empty, Nell passed him another one full of Coke. "Thank you."

"So who else is a regular besides Becca the Check-Out Girl?" Nell said, prying open the potsticker carton. "Boy, this smells good."

"Trevor Ogilvie," Gabe said, watching her ankles. "He hires us every three or four months to find out what Olivia's up to." He put down his plate to find the hot and sour soup. There were two small containers of it, so he handed one to Nell and opened the other for himself. "Riley calls her the Quarterly Report. He likes her because she goes to places with loud music and cheap beer. She's due again next month." He tasted the soup, thick and hot, and the sourness reminded him of Nell's french fries. He'd been having all of his fries with vinegar lately because the tartness woke up every taste bud he had.

"And then there's the Hot Lunch," Nell said.

"Harold Taggart and his lovely wife, Gina." Gabe pointed his spoon at her. "You get them the next time. Riley's fed up."

"What do I have to do?"

"You sit in the hotel lobby and watch to see if Gina

shows up with her newest, which she will. Completely dependable, our Gina is."

"Then I point my finger and say 'I Spy'?"

"Then you point the camera and take the picture. Harold likes pictures."

Nell shook her head and jostled his shoulder a little. "That's sick."

"That's what Riley says. I try not to pass judgment."

"You're an example to us all," Nell said.

"I like to think so," Gabe said, gazing at her legs again.

Nell uncrossed her ankles. "They're good, aren't they?"

"Yep."

"They were the only part of my body that didn't go to hell when I lost weight," Nell said. "I think it was because I kept walking."

"You look a lot better," Gabe said, passing the sweet and sour back to her. "You were a little scary when you started here."

"I feel a lot better," Nell said, peering into the carton.

The top of her head brushed his chin, feather soft and surprisingly cool. *Hair that red should be hot*, he thought.

She held up the carton. "You want any more of this or can I finish it off?"

"It's yours," Gabe said. "Hard to believe we used to have to force you to eat."

"So what other regulars?"

"Nothing else colorful," Gabe said. "We do a lot of background checks for some firms in the area."

"Like O&D."

"Especially O&D. We got a lot of their work because my dad and Trevor were buddies." Gabe lost some of his good mood thinking about them. "And then we did such a crackerjack job nailing Jack in both his divorces that he sent us work from his department, too."

"That's open-minded of him." She frowned into space. "I'm having trouble seeing Trevor as anybody's drinking buddy."

"Trevor was not always a thousand years old," Gabe said. "He and my dad really tore up the town." He tried not to think about what else they might have done. "There's a picture of them on the wall. Over there, behind the coatrack."

Nell pushed herself up off the floor and went to look, and Gabe watched her legs as she crossed the floor. Great calves. He considered leaning over to look up her skirt and decided the light wasn't good enough to bother.

"My God," Nell said, bending to squint at the picture, which Gabe appreciated. "Trevor looks positively dashing."

"Well, back then he was. He was a tough litigator, too. He could stonewall with the best."

"Your dad looks like you."

"Actually, I look like my dad, but thanks."

Nell looked back at him and then at the picture again. "Not exactly. You look like somebody I'd trust."

"Thank you," Gabe said, surprised. "I think. Does that mean 'boring'?"

"No," Nell said. "That means your dad looks like a player."

"Good call," Gabe said.

She stepped back and took the blue pinstriped jacket from the coatrack. "Was this his? It looks like the one in the picture."

"It was his," Gabe said. "Don't know about the picture. He liked pinstripes. Ring-a-ding-ding."

Nell shrugged the coat on, and it hung down past her hips, almost covering her skirt. *Take the skirt off*, Gabe thought, and then thought, *Oh, no*. It was one thing to idly appreciate a woman's legs; it was another thing entirely to start fantasizing about loss of clothing in conjunction with a McKenna secretary.

"This is a great jacket." Nell turned back to him as she pushed the sleeves up her arms. "Why don't you wear it?"

"Not the pinstripe type," he said, enjoying the slash of

her red hair above the deep blue of the jacket. She looked more than cute, she reminded him of somebody: gamine face, almond eyes, pale skin, a smile that could melt concrete. Somebody old-fashioned but hot. *Myrna Loy*, he thought. She brushed her hands over the front of the jacket, and he said, "That's a good color for you."

"You think? Where's a mirror?" She left the office, probably heading for the bathroom, and Gabe thought, *Don't go.*

He put his fork down and shook his head, trying to get the image of her—those long, long legs and that bright, bright hair—out of his mind, but he still wanted her back.

It was the secretary thing, he decided. Decades of McKennas chasing secretaries and catching them. It was in their DNA by now. But he was an adult, a mature, careful, intelligent adult. All he had to do was concentrate, and habit wouldn't get him this time.

"You're right," she said, coming back and smiling at him, a great smile, a great mouth with a full lower lip that—

"I'm always right," Gabe said, getting up. "You want any more of this stuff?"

"All of it if you don't," Nell said. "I can't get enough lately."

She put the coat back on the rack and then crouched down to gather up the cartons on the floor, and her purple sweater rode up a little so he could see a thin strip of her pale back above the skirt now pulled tight across her rear.

Stupid tradition to have, he thought. Why couldn't the McKennas have been born with a genius for making money instead of secretaries?

"What?" Nell said, looking up at him.

"Nothing," he said. "Just thinking." And then the phone rang and he went back to work.

*   *   *

Across the park, Suze was having problems of her own.

"What the hell is this?" Jack said, and she looked up from her book to see him coming out of the dining room, holding one of her running cups.

"British novelty china," she said. "I'm collecting it."

"You've got these things crammed in with our good china."

"Your mother's good china," Suze said and went back to her book.

"I don't think it's a good idea to put this cheap stuff in there, too," Jack said, and she looked up to see him turn the cup over to look at the bottom and lose his hold on it. It hit the hardwood floor, and the bowl broke in half, separating from the legs at the same time.

"*Jack!*" Suze threw her book to one side as she went down on her knees to gather up the pieces.

"I'm sorry," he said, not sounding sorry at all. "It's that cheap stuff—"

"This is a Caribbean Running Cup," she said, trying to fit the pieces back together. "It's from the 1970s and it was worth seventy-five dollars."

"That thing?" Jack sounded incredulous.

Suze ignored him to carry the cup pieces through the dining room and into the kitchen, looking for glue.

He followed her. "Is this something else Nell's talked you into? You don't need her china, you have the Dysart Spode."

Suze put the pieces on the counter and looked at them, sick to her stomach. Even if she glued it back together, it would be broken. She touched the big yellow shoes and noticed a chip in one. "Damn it," she said and went back to the living room to search for the missing piece of yellow glaze.

Jack followed her again. "I can't believe you're spending my money on these stupid cups."

"I'm spending my money." She got down on her knees

and searched the floor, tilting her head to see if the shiny chip would catch the lamplight.

"You don't have any money," Jack said.

She squinted at the floor and said, "Yes, I do. I'm working."

"You're what?"

There it was. She moistened the tip of her finger and picked up the chip. Then she stood up and said, "I've been working part-time for the McKennas for a while now."

"*Working?*" Jack said, making it sound like cheating.

"Yes," Suze said, and went back to the kitchen. She put the chip on the counter and unscrewed the orange plastic top on the glue bottle.

"Suze," Jack said following her, "you can't be—"

"I'm a decoy," Suze said, trying to figure out the best order for gluing. She squirted glue on the Formica counter and dipped the white side of the chip in it. "People hire the McKennas to find out if their partners are cheating on them, and I'm the one who gives the guys the opportunity to cheat."

"*You're doing what?*"

She put the chip back onto the yellow shoe carefully, moving it into place with her fingernail. Maybe she should glue the shoe and the cup separately and then glue the shoes to the cup later when the first mends were dry.

"Suze," Jack said, and she turned to see him flushed with anger. "I told you I didn't want you seeing Nell so much, and now you're *working* with her? Picking up guys in *bars*?"

"Nothing happens, Jack, I just talk." She turned back to the counter and picked up the two halves of the cup, dipping their edges in the white glue. "Riley's there the whole time, and he'd kill me if I ever went too far."

"Riley *McKenna*?"

"In fact," she added, ignoring his roar while she held the two pieces of the cup together, "that's why I'm doing it. Nell screwed up, and they won't let her do it anymore so—"

"Well, you're not doing it, either," Jack snapped. "Jesus Christ, Suze, have you lost your mind? You are not—"

"Yes, I am." Suze leaned against the cupboard, holding the cup pieces together. "I like working for the McKennas, and there's no reason for you not to trust me, so I'm not quitting." She took a deep breath and said, "It's not fair of you to ask me to."

"*Not fair?*" Jack looked apoplectic. "You're sleeping with Riley McKenna, that's why won't you quit, and I won't—"

Suze sighed. "I am not sleeping with Riley." When he didn't look convinced, she added, "Nell's sleeping with him. And I won't quit because I like having a job, and it doesn't get in the way of anything I have to do for you or with you, and if you don't trust me enough to let me work then I think we'd better see a marriage counselor because we're in big trouble." She ran out of breath at the end and stopped to recoup.

"Nell's sleeping with him?" Jack sounded taken aback and then scowled down at her again. "I don't believe it. She's at least ten years older than he is. Nobody in his right mind would sleep with her when he could have you."

"*Hey!*" Suze met his eyes. "That's my best friend you're talking about, and you are a big hypocrite. You're twenty-two years older than I am and that's never bothered you."

"It's different for women," Jack said. "Trust me."

"Trust you?" Suze said. "Why should I? You don't trust me, and I'm starting to think maybe you're projecting."

"Psych 101?" Jack said, and Suze kept talking right over him.

"You're thinking about cheating on me and so you're extra suspicious, which is really rotten of you. And there are a lot of reasons somebody would rather have Nell than me because she's smart and funny and independent and allowed to go out at night without some jackass accusing her of adultery and breaking her china. What are you going to do when I get to be Nell's age and you meet somebody who's younger than I am? Dump me because nobody

would choose a forty-year-old over a thirtysomething? Because if that's true, you can just leave now and spare me
the suspense."

"Calm down," Jack said, clearly taken aback. "Just calm
down. Of course, I'm not cheating. I'm just surprised about
Nell, that's all. Tim said she was lousy in bed."

Suze felt herself grow hot. "I'd be lousy in bed, too, if
that son of a bitch was there. *Riley* seems to be pretty happy
with her, and I gotta tell you, Nell sounded surprised when
she talked about the way he makes love, so I'm betting
Tim is just a crummy lover. And she was stuck with him
for twenty-two years so she deserves some good stuff with
a younger guy who knows what he's doing."

"How do you know he knows what he's doing?" Jack
said, his face darkening with suspicion again.

"You know, if you get any dumber . . ." Suze put the
glued cup carefully on the counter and turned back to him.
"If you want to talk about this again, you act like an intelligent adult and not a tantrum-throwing baby. This is
the dumbest fight we've ever had, and you started it because you didn't trust me. I'm not kidding, we need coun-
seling if you really honest-to-God think I'd cheat. Don't
you know me at all?"

Jack closed his eyes. "I don't know. I just hear Riley
McKenna's name and I go crazy." He looked at her again.
"But you did lie to me. You got a job."

"Yeah, well, I knew you'd do this I-am-master thing and
tell me I wasn't allowed to," Suze said. "I'm tired of that.
I want a husband and a partner, not a daddy. I'm thirty-
two years old and I have a job. That's not abnormal. Hell,
all I wanted was to buy some egg cups." She looked down
at the counter, at the legless cup and the chipped shoes
and gritted her teeth to keep from screaming at him.

"You don't need to work," Jack said, stubbornly. "If you
want the damn cups, just buy them. It's not the work, anyway, it's that you didn't tell me. You lied to me, and you
wonder why I think you'd cheat on me?"

"Keep this up, and I will." Suze picked up the two china pieces and left him standing in the kitchen, taking the living room stairs two at a time to get away from him. She locked herself in Jack's office, called Nell, and got her machine.

"I just told Jack about the job," she said. "He thinks I'm sleeping with Riley, can you believe it? I told him you were. Go have sex with Riley again, so I'm not stretching the truth."

She hung up the phone and logged onto eBay to take her mind off her anger and what she thought might be fear. Too much, too soon, that was the problem with that conversation. She did a search for Walking Ware and found three plain running egg cups, selling for too much, but she didn't care. She put an eighty-dollar reserve on each of them—you'd have to be nuts to pay eighty dollars for a plain egg cup, which meant she probably had them— and sat back to contemplate her bids. She was shaking, she realized, and it wasn't from overpaying for egg cups.

I'm really glad I did that, she told herself, as she touched the broken pieces of cup. It was insane that he didn't want her to have a job. Insane and controlling and paternalistic and anti-feminist and—

What if he leaves me?

She shivered at the thought, her entire body going cold. She'd be alone. She'd been lonely before she met him, her mother always at work, her father long gone, and then Jack had been there, swearing he always would be there, that she'd never be alone again. And she hadn't been, ever.

But he could leave her over this. And it'd be her fault.

Suze slumped back in her chair. There was a distinct possibility that she'd just been really stupid. Had she just jeopardized her marriage for a part-time job and some china? That was going to be cold comfort if she lost the only man she'd ever loved. Okay, yes, he was being a bastard, but he was afraid, she'd seen it in his eyes. He thought he was too old for her. He thought he was losing her. *He might be*, she thought, and then she thought, *No*. She knew exactly how he felt. She'd been afraid for fourteen years that he'd betray her the way he'd betrayed Abby and Vicki, that she'd be alone like they were. It had been awful, and now he was feeling it, too.

She disconnected from the network and slowly pushed her chair back. She didn't need a job if it did that to Jack, if it made them fight like this.

She went back down the stairs slowly and found Jack in the kitchen, hanging up the phone. He looked at her defiantly, and she said, "If it bothers you that much, I'll quit."

"That's my girl." Jack held out his arms, and when she didn't walk into them, he went to her, and she let him hug her. "I'm sorry, Suze, I just lost it. I know you wouldn't cheat, you didn't deserve that. You deserve an apology, something better than an apology. How about if we go out and get you a little something later?"

As long as it's not a divorce, Suze thought and disentangled herself as soon as she could to go back upstairs and glue the last two pieces of the cup together, trying not to feel depressed, and trying even harder not to be angry.

Chapter Eleven

The next afternoon, Suze called the agency to tell Riley she was quitting.

"He's not here," Nell said.

"You sound awful," Suze said. "What's wrong?"

"Another run-in with Gabe," Nell said. "Usually the yelling doesn't bother me, but I'm tired today. At least his furniture is back. That should help."

"Maybe you should stop doing the stuff that makes him yell," Suze said, thinking of Jack.

"I don't think so," Nell said. "Then he'll think yelling is a solution. He apologized before he left and he's taking me to dinner, so it's all right."

"Really?" Suze said.

"We're meeting Riley at the Sycamore at six-thirty. Is Jack going to be home then?"

"No," Suze said. "He has some business thing. We're eating at nine."

"Meet us there," Nell said, and Suze thought, *What the hell.*

She got to the Sycamore a little early and saw Riley sitting at a table by the window. He waved at her, and she went over and sat down across from him.

"Nell said you wanted to talk." He sounded mad, but his face was blank.

"I'm quitting," she said. "The decoy stuff."

"Okay."

"That's all? Just 'okay'?"

"Jack found out, right?"

She wanted to smack him. "Maybe I'm just tired of working for you." The waitress came by and she said, "Iced tea, no lemon, please." Then she looked at Riley, nursing a beer with his back to the stained-glass panel in the window, staring past her as if she wasn't there.

"You know, I'm glad Nell's late," Suze said, "because I want to know your intentions."

"What intentions?" Riley said. "I have no intentions."

"Your intentions for Nell," Suze said patiently. "You remember, the redhead you're sleeping with?"

"Slept with," Riley said. "Three months ago. That's over. It was over after one night, which she undoubtedly told you."

Suze narrowed her eyes and leaned across the table, looking for a fight with somebody she could afford to fight with. "You *dumped her*? Do you know what she went through with that jackass she married? And now you—"

"Back off, Barbie. All she wanted was a one-night stand. It's part of the recovery process."

"Don't give me that."

"She was just trying it on. Happens all the time."

"And you know this how?"

"Because my job puts me into close proximity to people who have just discovered that their relationships are over. Which often leads to me getting hit on by those who prefer men in their beds."

Suze shook her head in disbelief. "And you perform this service—?"

"Usually, no. Nell's a good woman who was having a bad time."

"And you wanted sex."

"I had a date that night. If I just wanted sex, I could have had sex."

"You had sex with somebody else after you slept with Nell?"

"No," Riley said, his patience clearly wearing thin. "I

called and canceled. Now I'm tired of this conversation. What's new in your life? Assuming Jack lets you have anything new in your life."

"So Nell's all alone again," Suze said. "You gave her a one-night stand—"

"Nell is not alone. Nell has you and Margie and me and Gabe and her kid and probably a cast of thousands I don't know about. She went a little nuts because that's what happens after a breakup, but she's moving in the right direction now. She's eating again and ripping the office apart and fighting with Gabe, and she looks pretty good to me. Give her time, she'll find somebody new."

"How much time? I don't want her to be alone, it's awful to be alone."

"How would you know?" Riley said, looking past her again.

"I can imagine," Suze said. "I know it's awful. She should have found somebody by now."

"Two years," Riley said, lowering his head a little.

Suze turned around to see what he was looking at and saw a restaurant full of people eating. "What?"

"That's the average recovery time after a divorce. Two years."

"Oh, God." Suze counted back. "She got divorced a year ago last July. That's another seven months yet. That's too long."

"*Susannah*," Riley said, with enough gravity that Suze paid attention. "Leave her alone. She's doing fine."

"I can't stand it that she's alone," Suze said.

"No, you think you couldn't stand it if *you* were alone." Riley smiled past her.

Suze turned around again and spotted a brunette across the room, smiling back. She faced Riley again, annoyed. "What kind of a woman would flirt with a man who was with somebody?"

"I'm not with you," Riley said, keeping his eyes on the brunette. "We're just sitting at the same table."

"But she doesn't know that." Suze looked back at the brunette with contempt. It was women like this who broke up marriages.

"Sure she knows."

"How? What'd you do? Send her a note?"

"Body language. We're both leaning away from each other. Plus you've been yapping at me for fifteen minutes now, so even if we were together, it would not be for long."

"God knows, that's true," Suze said, settling even farther back from him. "I can't imagine what Nell saw in you."

"You don't have to," Riley said, still smiling at the brunette. "She told you. Blow by blow, I'll bet."

"This is what I need," Suze said. "You talking dirty to me at the Sycamore."

"That's not what you need." Riley stood and picked up his glass. "But what you need, you can't get because you married a dickhead." He took her glass, too, and said, "I'll get you a refill," and was gone before Suze could say, "I don't want a refill."

She watched him while he stopped by the brunette's table, watched the brunette's smile widen as he talked, and then watched her laugh as he went on to the bar.

How very cheap of that brunette, letting him pick her up like that. Well, thank God she wasn't looking for somebody if this was what it was like in the world of dating. Thank God she had Jack.

Suze turned back to look out the window at the brick street in front of the restaurant. The sun was going down, and the Village was getting the timeless look it always took on at sunset, beautiful and moody. *I love it here*, she thought. *Why aren't I happy?*

Except she was happy. It was the twilight. Twilight was always melancholy, and melancholy beauty could make anybody a little heartsick. She'd be fine when the sun came up again.

Riley put her glass in front of her and sat down across

from her again, blocking her view of the dusky street.

"You didn't even ask me what I was drinking," Suze said.

"Taste it."

She took a sip. Iced tea, no lemon.

"I pay attention," Riley said.

"So she let you pick her up in front of me. Has she no ethics?"

"God, I hope not," Riley said. "Also, I told her you were my sister."

He looked so calm across from her, so confident that he knew everything, and she felt the sudden urge to disconcert. If she leaned over and kissed him, the brunette would know she wasn't his sister. That would fix him.

"What?" Riley said, looking less confident.

"I didn't say anything," Suze said.

"No, but your expression changed," Riley said. "Whatever you're thinking, stop it."

"I wouldn't do it anyway. No guts."

"Good. I hate women with guts. I like 'em pliant."

"I am not pliant," Suze said.

"Another reason we're not together," Riley said.

The chair beside her scraped, and Nell said, "Why are you frowning at each other?" as she sat down. She looked tired but relaxed, so the fight with Gabe must have ended.

"Low-class company," Suze said, moving her feet so Marlene could hide out under the table.

"Thank you very much," Gabe said, taking the seat beside Riley.

"So how was your day?" Suze said brightly and then didn't listen, choosing to watch Riley laugh with Nell and make eye contact with the brunette instead, clearly not caring that she was out of his life.

When Riley and Nell went to the bar for refills, Gabe said, "So how's your life?"

"I have to quit the decoys," she said. "I'm sorry. I really, really am."

"So are we," he said. "You were great to work with."

"Thank you." She looked away so he wouldn't see how much it mattered to her and saw Nell, laughing with Riley at the bar. "She looks wonderful, doesn't she?" Suze said, turning back to Gabe. "So bright and happy."

Gabe nodded, watching Nell, too. " 'The shape a bright container can contain.' "

Suze blinked at him, amazed. In a million years, she wouldn't have suspected Gabe McKenna of quoting poetry. "Roethke?"

Gabe looked taken aback, too. "Yeah. He was my dad's favorite. He used to recite that one to my mother all the time. Nell makes me think of it sometimes." He frowned at her. "How do you know Roethke?"

"English 361," Suze said, "Introduction to Poetry." When she got home, she was going to find her old anthology and see if that poem was as erotic as she remembered. Even if it wasn't, she was sure it was a great love poem. Maybe Nell wasn't alone after all.

It would be too terrible if Nell was alone.

Two hours later, Suze and Riley had both gone, and Nell was finishing off the last of her French Silk pie and trying to figure out the undercurrents of the evening. Gabe nursed a beer across from her, looking mildly annoyed because Trevor had called earlier and offered her a job again.

"Okay," she said. "I don't get what all that tension was about. Riley was a lot more upset about Suze quitting than he let on. What's up with that?"

"There's some history there," Gabe said. "Listen, when Trevor called, did he say Jack had told him to offer you that job?"

"No," Nell said. "And there is no history. Suze never met Riley before the night we stole Marlene. Their entire relationship is fourteen decoy jobs."

"True," Gabe said. "I'm asking about Trevor because

it's not like him to take direct action. Jack, yes, Trevor, no. Trevor waits."

"He didn't say." Nell leaned forward over her empty plate to look him in the eye. "You told me you investigated Jack's divorces. Are you telling me, you investigated *Suze*?"

"You sure you've told me everything you know about Margie?"

"Vicki hired you to find out about Suze and Jack," Nell said. "My God. That's when Riley saw Suze?"

Gabe nodded, giving up as she knew he would. "Through a motel window stripping for Jack in a cheerleader uniform. At eighteen. It permanently damaged him." He stared into space for a moment, looking thoughtful.

Nell narrowed her eyes. "And you know this how?"

"There are pictures," Gabe said, coming back to earth. "It must be something big because Trevor is really hot to get you away from us."

"There *are* pictures?"

"*Were*," Gabe said hastily. "*Were*, there *were* pictures."

"You are ducking me," Nell said, leaning closer.

"Like that's possible," Gabe said. "Of course, there's always the possibility that it's Jack manipulating Trevor. What do you know that Jack doesn't want you to tell me?"

"Nothing. You have everything I know. Listen, I'm going to be finished in the basement by the end of next week. Want me to start on your car?"

Gabe narrowed his eyes. "Stay away from my car." He stopped, thoughtful. "Maybe that's it. Maybe they're afraid you'll find something. God knows, you've been everywhere."

"Just to clean the car." Nell pushed her plate away. "I wouldn't dream of driving it."

"I clean it. There's nothing in there. And don't even talk about driving it."

"I said I *wouldn't* dream—" Nell began, but he was

standing up, ready to go, his keys in his hand, the Porsche insignia tantalizing her.

"I can't think of any other reason to hire you away," Gabe said. "It's got to have something to do with this blackmail mess."

"Maybe they just need a good office manager," Nell said, pushing her chair back, careful not to hit Marlene. "So are those pictures still around?"

"You will never know," Gabe said. "The furniture looks great, by the way."

"You are much too sensitive about that car," she said and picked up Marlene to follow him out into the cold November night.

Nell was disappointed that Suze had quit, but not surprised. "It's a miracle Jack let her do it this long," she told Riley. "At least now you're off the hook. I know you didn't like working with her." She waited for him to come clean, but all he said was, "She wasn't that bad." Shortly after that, he began dating a dental technician who did regional theater and thought decoy work was performance art, and nobody mentioned Suze again.

Suze didn't take the change nearly as well. "I'm fine with it, really," she told Nell, but by the time Thanksgiving rolled around, she'd stopped smiling and her temper had frayed.

"Jack insisted on inviting Tim and Whitney," she'd told Nell the week before. "And I told him if you weren't coming, I wasn't coming. And then he said I wouldn't need you because he'd invited Margie and Budge and Margie's dad and his wife and Olivia. *Five of them.* And then there's my mother and his mother."

"I can stay home," Nell had said, not wanting to make any more trouble between Suze and Jack. Jack had taken to glowering at her whenever they met, and she was tired of it.

"No, you can't," Suze said. "You and Jase are the only people I want to see. You have to be there."

So Nell had arrived early with pumpkin pies and Marlene, and had helped finish the cooking while Suze snapped Marlene into a turkey costume she'd found. Nell had been cheerful to Whitney when she looked resentful, sympathetic to Jase when he got stuck with the sulky Olivia, and patient with Tim's mother when she made veiled comments about people getting on with their lives and not holding on to their pasts. The low point of the day had come right before they'd sat down to eat when Mother Dysart had counted the place settings, said in horror, "We can't have thirteen at the table!" and stared pointedly at Nell. The high point had come immediately after that when Suze had stared pointedly at Mother Dysart and said, "Shall I fix you a tray?" Jase had saved the day by hauling Olivia off to the kitchen—"We'll eat at the kids' table just like old times"—but Jack hadn't been amused, and he'd punished Suze by spending the entire afternoon laughing with Olivia and ignoring her. Suze hadn't seemed to care. The family had mercifully dispersed by nine when Jack took his mother home, and she evidently decided to keep him for a while, because at eleven that night, Suze and Nell were alone in Suze's guest room, savoring the solitude and their ninth eggnogs. Even Marlene seemed relieved.

"Thanks for spending the night," Suze said. "I couldn't face cleaning that up by myself."

"Not a problem," Nell said, stretching out on the bed in her blue silk pajamas. It felt good to stretch, good to use her muscles, and she thought, not for the first time, that she had other muscles she'd like to use, too. Celibacy sucked. There were times when she almost considered jumping Riley again, just for the exercise. "Thanks for having both me and Whitney in the same room so Jase didn't have to split a holiday again."

"She's an interesting woman," Suze said. "For a

midget." She sat cross-legged on the bed beside Nell, un-snapping Marlene's turkey costume.

"She's petite."

"She's a nasty little cockroach."

"That's loyalty talking," Nell said. "She's not that bad. And I actually don't care about her anymore, although I'm still hoping Tim dies. The only thing I have against her now is that she's having sex and I'm not."

"You know," Suze said, as she frowned at a stubborn snap, "if we had any brains, we'd be sleeping with each other."

"What?" Nell said. "Us?" She thought about it. "It would make things easier."

"You do think I'm cute, right?" She stopped unsnapping Marlene to hold out the hem of her ancient OSU T-shirt.

"As a bug," Nell said. "Too bad it's wasted on me." *Where the hell is Jack anyway?*

"You look good in blue silk, too, sweetie," Suze said. "I'm telling you, we're missing a good bet here."

Nell looked down at her blue silk pajamas. She did look good in blue. Maybe she should get a blue nightgown. In lace. Just in case somebody stopped by sometime. She shifted uneasily on the bed, looking for a distraction. "Have you got anything to eat that doesn't scream Thanksgiving?"

They went downstairs to the kitchen, Marlene clattering behind them in hopes of food, and Suze peered inside the refrigerator. "Leftover lasagna from yesterday. Celery and carrots. Cheese. I think there's rocky road ice cream in the freezer. Everything else is holiday stuff."

"Yes," Nell said.

"To what? The ice cream?"

"To all of it. I'm starving. Got any wine?"

Suze began unloading the refrigerator. "This is a nice change for you. We got very tired of trying to force-feed you last summer."

"I was getting tired of being harassed," Nell said, going

for the carrots. "And then suddenly I was hungry, and now I can't catch up fast enough." *Also when I eat, I don't think about sex.*

"Well, you're looking a lot better." Suze took a bottle of red wine off the shelf and went looking for a corkscrew. "Are you back to your original weight?"

"No, and I don't want to be," Nell said. "I like your hand-me-downs. But I'm healthy again. Well within government guidelines."

Suze handed the bottle and the corkscrew to Nell. Then she dumped the lasagna on a plate and shoved it into the microwave. "Carbs coming up. There are probably steaks downstairs in the freezer. Want me to thaw a couple for breakfast tomorrow?"

"Sure." Nell popped the cork on the wine. "Steak and eggs. Do we have to wait for breakfast?"

Suze went down to the basement and came back up with three steaks, which she set in the sink to thaw. "I can't imagine being a vegetarian," she said, taking the glass of wine Nell handed her. "How does Margie stand it?"

"How does Margie stand Budge?" Nell said, thinking of the way Budge had hovered over her all day and trying not to think of what he must be like in bed. That thought alone called for a drink.

"He worships the ground she walks on," Suze said. "Lots of women like that."

"Sort of like Jack," Nell said.

"So, really," Suze said, "have you ever thought about being a lesbian?"

"Excuse me?"

"You know, you and me. Easier than guys."

"Oh, right. Nope." Nell unwrapped the cheese and cut off a chunk. "I'm heavily into penetration. Or at least I used to be. It's been a while. Months. Years."

"Not that long," Suze said. "Or didn't Riley penetrate?"

"He certainly did," Nell said. "But that was only once and he doesn't count. He was a disposable lover."

Suze stared silently at the microwave as it counted off the seconds, and when it dinged, she pulled the pasta out and put it on the table. Then she took two forks from the drawer, handed one to Nell, and they sat down with the lasagna plate between them.

Suze stabbed the lasagna on her side. "Disposable lover?"

"According to Riley," Nell said around a mouthful of cheese and noodle, "women who are getting over a divorce go through a disposable lover stage when they sleep with men just to prove they can."

"Well, he'd have access to divorced women," Suze said. "So who else have you disposed of?"

"Just Riley." Nell cut into the lasagna again. "This is really good."

"There should be more than just Riley," Suze said sternly.

"Nobody else I'm attracted to," Nell said, and then Gabe flashed before her, standing in the doorway, looming over her, arguing with her, pushing back when she pushed him, enjoying the fight as much as she did, and she stopped with her fork halfway to her mouth.

"Think of somebody, did you?"

"Nope," Nell said and ate some lasagna. "So lesbianism. This interests you?"

"Maybe. I've never tried it. I got married very young, you know."

"I know," Nell said. "I was at the wedding. When the minister said, 'Does anyone here object?' I wanted to stand up and say, 'Has anyone here noticed the bride is an infant?' but I didn't." She leaned over and put a piece of bread on the floor for Marlene, who looked at it as if it were broccoli. "If you're holding out for lasagna," she told the dog, "you can forget it."

Marlene ate the bread.

"Thank you for not ruining my wedding," Suze said.

"Don't mention it. This is really good lasagna."

"It has tofu in it."

Nell slowed down long enough to look at the pan with doubt. "I can't taste it."

"Then pretend it isn't there, the way you're pretending this guy isn't there."

"There is no guy," Nell said. "Tofu, huh?"

"Forget I mentioned it." Suze refilled their wineglasses. "Ever kiss a girl?"

"Nope." Nell reached for the butter. "You?"

"Nope." Suze put her fork down. "We should try it."

"I'm eating," Nell said. "Maybe later, for dessert."

"So what's new at work?"

"Not much. Gabe let me fix the furniture in his office, can you believe it? Next I'm going to get a couch and then I'm going to get that window repainted. And new business cards."

Suze sat back and observed her. "Gabe always seems dull to me."

"Gabe? Good heavens, no." Nell forked more lasagna. "Riley says he's repressed from too many years of trying to keep the firm afloat because his dad almost ran it into the ground, but I think he's just dry. You know, the old traditional private detective cool."

"I thought so," Suze said. "It's Gabe."

"What?"

"You have the hots for Gabe. That's why you keep pushing him, to get him to pay attention to you."

"No, I do not," Nell said, putting her fork down. "Are you insane?"

Suze shook her head. "I can hear it in your voice. Come on, it's me. Admit it."

"Well." Nell picked up her wineglass. "I have had a few fleeting inappropriate thoughts." She drank half her wine and then added, "But I'm sure it's just because he looks like Tim."

"He doesn't look like Tim," Suze said. "Besides, you don't feel that way when you look at Tim now, right?"

"Classical conditioning," Nell said, thinking about how stupid Tim had looked at dinner, holding hands with Whitney and trying to pretend he didn't have two wives at the same table. "I think I just look at tall, rangy guys with dark hair and think 'I should be sleeping with you' because I slept with Tim for so long. It'll go away." She shook her head and drank again.

"Tim's not that tall," Suze said. "And I repeat, you don't feel that way about Tim anymore, right?"

Nell considered it. Did she feel lust when she looked at Tim? Well, God knew, not today she hadn't. He'd looked softer than she'd remembered, as if she'd left him out in the rain. Not somebody she'd want to touch, not somebody she could move against and feel bone and muscle. He looked as though, if she'd pushed a finger in him, the dent would stay.

"No," she said.

"Well, then," Suze said, exasperated. "I don't see that as a setup for lusting for Gabe."

"I just don't want to be like Margie and her interchangeable blonds."

"They weren't interchangeable," Suze said. "Stewart was a jackass, and Budge is a doormat." She seemed depressed by that and finished off her wine with a sigh.

"Well, that's what I mean," Nell said. "She responds to a certain look in men and that's what she falls for no matter what they're really like, and then she's stuck."

"What's Gabe really like?"

"Smart." Nell pictured him standing in the office doorway again. "Tenacious. Charming when he wants to be. Exasperated. Dry. Sweet. Obnoxious. Kind. Controlling. Brave. Sloppy. Patient." *Hard. Strong. Lean.* "And lately, really, really hot." She shook her head and reached for the wine bottle. "Go figure."

"This does not sound like lust."

"Thank God."

"This sounds like *luv*."

"Oh, no, it doesn't." Nell straightened. "Don't even start that. Absolutely not." She grabbed her glass and drank.

"The thing about love is, you don't get to choose," Suze said. "You just wake up one day and there it is, sitting at the foot of the bed, going 'nyah, nyah, *gotcha*,' and there's not a damn thing you can do about it." She shook her head at the thought and drank, too.

"Absolutely not. No. I'm not going back to that again."

"And the fact that you think he's hot doesn't hurt," Suze said. "He is very appealing. Nice body."

"Excuse me?" Nell said.

"He wears those suits damn well." Suze picked up a carrot stick, nonchalantly not looking at Nell. "And that master of the universe thing he's got going for him is sexy, too. I do love a man who's in control."

"You're married to one of those," Nell pointed out.

"Right. Doesn't mean I can't appreciate it in others."

Nell picked up her fork and stabbed the lasagna. "So go for it."

"You wouldn't mind?"

"Not at all," Nell said airily. "Although you are married."

"Well, then, if I ever decide to cheat, it'll be with Gabe," Suze decided. "He really is darling."

"You're trying to make me mad, right?" Nell said, reaching for her wineglass.

"Is it working?"

"Yes. Damn it."

"I don't see a problem," Suze said, putting the carrot down. "You're both single. Go for it."

"I am not sleeping with my boss," Nell said. "And he's not sleeping with me. It's against policy."

"What policy?"

"Don't fuck the help. The McKennas have a history with their secretaries."

"He slept with Lynnie?"

"No, that was Riley."

"Riley." Suze shook her head over her wine. "What a complete waste of manhood that boy is."

"No, he's not." Nell straightened a little. "Riley is a good man."

"I thought you said he slept with everything that moved."

"With a few flaws," Nell admitted. "But he's a great guy, really. I'd trust him with my life. You just need to know him better." She regarded Suze carefully. "Or maybe not."

"Definitely not."

"So you're getting bored with Jack?"

"Ice cream?" Suze said brightly and went to the refrigerator.

"Okay. Hit a nerve, did I?"

"I am not bored with my husband." Suze said, thunking the half gallon of rocky road down next to the lasagna.

"Of course not," Nell said. "Got a spoon?"

Suze got two spoons out of the drawer and handed Nell one. "So you gonna make your move on Gabe any time soon?"

"Never."

Nell scooped a chunk of rocky road out of the carton and bit into it, leaving some behind on the spoon. The chocolate smeared her lower lip, and Suze bent over and licked the chocolate off, her tongue touching Nell's as Nell jerked back a little in surprise.

"C'mon." Suze grinned evilly at her, and Nell thought about it through a haze of eggnog and red wine and laughed. What the hell.

"Okay. Marlene, close your eyes." She leaned forward and kissed Suze, her mouth soft on soft, sweet on sweet. It was different, smooth and cool, like vanilla ice cream.

Suze pulled back after a minute. "What do you think?"

"Nice." Nell ate the rest of the ice cream on her spoon. "No zing, though. I don't think we'll be buying Marlene the 'My Two Mommies Love Me' T-shirt."

"Yeah." Suze slumped into her chair. "I want to have an affair."

Nell stopped, wide-eyed for a moment. "I have Riley's number in my purse."

"I can't cheat on Jack," Suze said miserably, picking up her wineglass.

"So why are you necking with me?"

"I don't think he'd count you. I think he'd probably get turned on if I slept with you."

"I think he'd probably want to play, too," Nell said, scooping more ice cream. "That's where I bow out."

"I just . . ." Suze sat back. "I haven't kissed anybody but Jack in fourteen years."

Nell's mouth was full of ice cream, so she held up her hand.

"And you. But that wasn't for real. It's like you said, I miss the zing. I want some zing."

"Well, zing is good," Nell said, swallowing. "But it doesn't last."

"It should." Suze folded her arms. "I don't expect it to be fireworks forever, I know that stuff goes, but shouldn't I still feel a little zing when he kisses me? A little *hello*?"

"I don't know," Nell said. "I think the zing went with the fireworks with Tim and me. Ask Margie. She's had more zings than I have."

"You had Riley. There was zing, right?"

Nell considered. "Not really. He's an excellent, excellent kisser, and there was buzz to the novelty of it all, but zing? Nope. I think you have to have pre-zing to get zings."

"Huh?"

"You know," Nell said, thinking of Gabe. "You look at his hands when he's writing and you get hot just watching the pen move. You hear his voice and have to take a deep breath because you stopped breathing the minute you heard him. He leans over your shoulder and you close your eyes so you can enjoy it more. Pre-zing."

"That's not pre-zing," Suze said. "That's full zing."

"Well, I didn't have that with Riley."

"Oh." Suze looked thoughtful. "I figured Riley was universal zing. Margie sure responded that night in the car."

"But you didn't," Nell said and grinned at her.

"Of course I did," Suze said. "Obnoxiousness doesn't negate animal magnetism."

"I do not get the animal magnetism," Nell said.

"Natural zing," Suze said. "Some guys have it. Like Riley and Jack."

"Nope," Nell said. "Don't get either one. That must be your zing. You didn't start thinking about cheating until you met Riley, right?"

"I am not thinking about cheating now," Suze said, holding her glass so tightly that her knuckles went white. "I wouldn't. I really wouldn't."

"Right. But you didn't start thinking about it until you met Riley, right?"

"I don't even like him."

Nell sighed in exasperation. "But you didn't start thinking about it until you met him, *right?*"

"A while after that. But I'm not going to do it. It's a fantasy." Suze put down her wine and dug into the ice cream instead. "It's not even that. I mean, I don't have fantasies about him. That would be wrong." She swallowed some ice cream and choked a little. "So what's he like?"

"Who?"

"Riley. In bed."

Nell thought about it. "Very gentle. And thorough. He pays attention, crosses all the i's, dots all the t's. Slow but steady." She tilted her head, thinking about what she'd said. "That sounds boring, doesn't it?"

"Not really," Suze said, her voice a little strained.

"Because he wasn't. Boring, I mean. Very gentle but very intense. Lot of power there. Great hands."

"Oh. Not that I care." Suze scooped out more rocky road and stuffed it in her mouth.

"So you're thinking about Riley."

"I think about the zing," Suze said, her mouth full of ice cream. "And unfortunately, he comes to mind. Which annoys me. But I'm not going to do anything about it."

"Me, neither," Nell said, scooping more ice cream and trying not to think about Gabe.

"We should try that kiss again," Suze said, putting down her ice cream spoon.

"Why?" Nell said around her rocky road.

"Suppose there was a plague that wiped out all the men."

"No more wars and lots of fat, happy women. Nicole Hollander already did the cartoon."

"No, I mean would you give up sex?"

"I'd still have electricity, right?" Nell said. "Me and my vibrator. Not a problem."

"It's not the same," Suze said. "There's no touching, no bodies—"

Nell imagined Gabe, stretched lean and hard beside her, and put her spoon down.

"—no heat, no slide—"

"Shut up," Nell said, and reached for the lasagna plate again.

"We'd only have each other," Suze said.

"And Margie," Nell said, trying to imagine a three-way with Margie. "The sheets would always be clean."

"Imagine all the men are gone in the plague, and it's just you and me. Margie's doing the laundry."

Nell shook her head and stabbed the lasagna. "I don't think I have the psychology for this. I think I'm wired for testosterone." She looked at Suze. "I don't think you have the psychology for it, either. I think you're using me to distract yourself from Riley. And I don't think it's going to work." Nell went back to the lasagna. "Are you sure there's tofu in this?"

"Positive," Suze said and picked up her ice cream spoon. "Lot's of tofu, no zing. Like my life."

"I've got Riley's number," Nell said, reaching for the bread.

"Positively not," Suze said. "I'm a happily married woman."

I'm not, Nell thought, and toyed with the tantalizingly idea of Gabe while they finished off the lasagna and the bottle of wine.

Chapter Twelve

A week later, Nell was still refusing to act on her attraction to Gabe, so Suze cornered Riley at the Sycamore while they were waiting for Gabe and Nell and grilled him.

"Nell and Gabe," she said to him as the waitress put her ice tea in front of her.

"Should be here very shortly," Riley said. "Where's your husband?"

"In a meeting," Suze said and then frowned as Riley concentrated on something behind her. "Another brunette?" she said, exasperated.

"Blonde. Keep talking. You will anyway."

"Gabe and Nell. I think they need a push."

"Don't interfere. They'll get there, assuming they stop fighting long enough to notice they want each other."

Suze sat back in surprise. "You know about this?"

"I work with them," Riley said. "When he didn't fire her the first week, I knew something was up. Also, he was not happy that we'd slept together."

"Nell's pretending she doesn't care."

"She cares," Riley said. "And I'm bored with this conversation."

He was still trying to make eye contact with the blonde, or maybe he already had. She didn't care enough to turn around and look, but she wanted his attention, so she leaned forward.

"Listen, Scooter," she said, and he frowned at her. "They're going to need help. The French have this saying that in every relationship there is one who kisses and one who is kissed."

"What French?" Riley said. "You're French?"

"I took French 101. It means in every couple, there's one who calls the shots and one who obeys."

"I got that," Riley said with palpable patience. "Why should I care?"

"Gabe and Nell are both kissers," Suze said. "Nell ran Tim, and Gabe ran Chloe and the office and you."

"Not me," Riley said.

"You and I are kissees," Suze went on as if he hadn't spoken. "Other people come after us. That's why nothing is ever going to happen with us. We'd spend the rest of our lives waiting for the other one to make a move."

"You, maybe," Riley said. "I move. Just not on you."

"But Gabe and Nell are forever going to be kissing, trying to be the one on top. They're so caught up in fighting over who gets to call the shots, they're never going to connect and kiss for real."

"So they'll learn to share," Riley said, starting to look grumpy. "I am not a kissee." He looked beyond her and his face cleared.

Suze gave up and turned to see. The blonde was getting up to go, smiling at Riley.

Riley smiled back.

Suze turned back and picked up her tea. "I rest my case."

"What?" Riley said. "I'll make my move when I want to."

From the corner of her eye, Suze watched the blonde pick up her purse and move toward the door, slowing as she went past Riley. He lifted his face to say something to her, and she handed him a business card.

"Call me," she said and left, pushing past Gabe and Nell, who were on their way in.

"Kissee," Suze said to Riley.

"I prefer to think of it as 'popular,'" Riley said, stowing

the card in his pocket. Gabe pulled out the chair next to him for Nell, and Riley looked up and said, "What took you so long?"

"Places to go," Nell said.

"Things to do," Gabe said and sat down beside Suze. "What's new?"

"Some woman just picked up Riley," Suze said.

"It happens," Gabe said. "He sits there and they throw themselves at him."

"Kissee," Suze said to Riley.

"Kiss off," Riley said. Later, when he was helping her on with her coat, she leaned back and whispered, "*Push* him, will you?" Riley sighed and rolled his eyes, but after fourteen nights of decoy work, she could read him like a book. He'd do it.

Now all she had to do was get Nell in motion, and at least *somebody* would be getting zing.

The next night, Gabe listened to Nell out in her office ask Riley if there was anything else he needed before she went home. Marlene's nails clicked on the hardwood floor as she made her last tour of the reception room, stopping longest at the Christmas tree Nell had put up after he'd told her not to, and Gabe felt the early evening melancholy that had been taking him lately. The place was always different after Nell was gone, as if she took sound and light with her, but that was probably because she always left after five when the whole world got quieter and darker.

Riley knocked on the door and came in. "I'm quitting for the night. You need anything else?"

"Lynnie," Gabe said. "Helena's diamonds. Stewart Dysart."

"Jesus, Gabe, get over it," Riley said.

"She was not the type to go quietly away," Gabe said. "She's somewhere planning something. And I'd really like to know where the hell Stewart is, too. I'd love to find a link between them, find out that he was the one who sent her in here to look for something, the one who told her who to blackmail at O&D. I asked, but no Lynn Mason ever worked at O&D. She forged her reference from there, and of course your mother never checked it."

"Maybe she was there under another name," Riley said. "Listen, I've been thinking. Nell's a very attractive woman. That red T-shirt she's wearing—"

"Don't fuck the help," Gabe said.

"Not for me," Riley said. "You."

"Oh, no. I can only imagine what all that ruthless efficiency would be like in bed." The thought held a perverse kind of appeal, so Gabe shoved it out of his mind.

"I bet you can," Riley said. "You're pathetic."

"Go away."

"You're also in denial."

Gabe sat back, exasperated. "Do you have a point?"

"This thing you have with Nell—"

"There is no thing."

"—is so obvious that you're the only one who hasn't noticed." Riley stopped and reconsidered. "Although I'm not sure she's caught on, either."

"Which would leave you to do the noticing. No, thank you."

"Suze Dysart mentioned it."

Gabe raised an eyebrow. "When did you discuss this with Suze Dysart?"

"We had a drink last night," Riley said. "Waiting for you, remember?"

"I noticed Jack wasn't there."

"He had a business meeting."

"At night?"

"I didn't mention that."

Gabe sighed and rubbed his forehead. "He was very sincere about not cheating on her when he talked to us about the blackmail thing."

"That was three months ago. Jack's not known for his attention span."

"Well, until Suze hires us to catch him, we don't care. Don't you have something to do? What about the Hot Lunch?"

"Nell did it," Riley said. "Here's something fun. Gina's dating a girl this time."

"Really?" Gabe said. "Good for Gina. That should rev Harold up some."

"More than some. This time he's upset. He says it's disgusting."

"Harold should broaden his horizons."

"That's what I said. I told him if he played his cards right, he might get them both in bed as an apology."

Gabe winced. "And he said . . . ?"

"That he wants to deal with you from now on," Riley said, cheering up some. "I'm a pervert."

"We already knew that." Gabe sighed. "Okay, what are you doing while I talk Harold down from the ledge?"

"The Quarterly Report," Riley said, losing his smile. "Trevor says Olivia is acting more suspicious than usual. He's worried."

"And Merry Christmas to you," Gabe said. "At least you get to go to bars for the holidays."

"Spare me," Riley said. "Olivia is a complete vacuum, which was okay when I first started watching her, but it's been three years now and she's still dumb as a rock, going to the same stupid, noisy places, falling into bed with the same moronic guys, which wouldn't bother me except that then I end up listening to them when I eavesdrop, and sooner or later I'm going to kill one of them just to shut him up."

"Never thought I'd see the day," Gabe said.

"What?"

"You're maturing. Way to go."

"Never say that," Riley said, and got up to make his escape before Gabe could accuse him of adulthood.

When Riley was gone, Gabe tried to concentrate on the reports in front of him, but Riley was right. Nell kept intruding, the same way she kept barging into his office and his life: abrupt and defiant and maddeningly efficient, snapping back up at him whenever he tried to put her down. She couldn't have been more different from Chloe if she'd tried, but Chloe had never lurked in his subconscious. Chloe had always just been there, warm and loving and sure, part of the wallpaper of his life. She'd known what she'd been talking about when she said they both deserved better. She had certainly deserved better.

He shook his head at his own obtuseness and resolved to be better to Chloe when she came back, if she ever came back; her last postcard had been from Bulgaria. That filed neatly away, he ignored Nell—standing in the center of his mind in her red T-shirt with her hands on her hips—and went back to business. Maybe he should call Trevor, see if he could worm out of him exactly what he was worried about with Olivia. That would make Riley's life easier. Maybe he could also worm out of him whatever the hell Lynnie had been blackmailing him for. He needed his appointments for tomorrow, too; and Harold was going to need extra time since the Hot Lunch had taken a turn for the different, so better tell Nell—

Nell knocked on the door and came in, carrying papers and a blue folder.

"About tomorrow," Gabe said, trying not to look at her red silk T-shirt. Unfortunately looking down gave him her legs. She had phenomenal legs.

"Here's your schedule," Nell said, putting it in front of him. "I've given you extra time at lunch with Harold. He seemed a little upset when I talked to him."

"He's married to Gina. That would upset any man." He frowned at her, realizing what she'd just said. "What do you mean, you talked to him?"

"He called back. You were on the phone with Becca."

"Right. Which reminds me—"

"You're going to see her tomorrow. Here's her folder." Nell dropped the blue folder on top of his itinerary. "Arranged latest job to earliest. Also the stuff Riley and I got on Randy, the phantom Texan, which is nothing. On the other hand, we didn't find anything bad."

"Nothing is bad enough," Gabe said. "Also I need—"

"The Quarterly Report folder." Nell held it out to him.

"*Stop that!*" Gabe jerked it out of her hand. "Jesus, you read minds, too?"

"No," Nell said, looking taken aback. "I just figured you'd want to look at it since Trevor called twice."

"Thank you." Gabe took the folder. "Sorry I yelled. Get him on the phone for me, will you?"

"Line one," Nell said, and when he jerked his head up, she held her hands up in defense and said, "Pure dumb luck. He called right before I came in here."

"You are getting a little creepy," Gabe said, reaching for the phone.

"*Hey,*" she said, and he looked up at her, caught in the dusky twilight from his window, her hair on fire over her snapping brown eyes, her slender shoulders braced back for his assault, her body arched in her tight red T-shirt curving down to hips that were undeniably rounder than they'd been six months before, tapering into impossibly long, strong legs planted firmly apart on his Oriental rug. "I am not a little creepy," she said. "I am *efficient.*"

That's not all you are. He tried not to look at her, but it was impossible.

"And Trevor just offered me that job again, so watch it, buddy, or you'll be short a secretary."

"Sorry. I'm having a bad day."

"Oh, hell, Gabe." She let her hands fall from her hips. "I'm sorry, too. I'm just tired and cranky. You want a cup of coffee before I go?"

"No."

"Well, what can I get you? Tea? Beer? What?"

You, he thought and gave himself the luxury of one

shiny fantasy of Nell on his desk with his hands sliding up the pale, smooth skin under her T-shirt before he said, "Nothing. Go away."

"Your people skills need work," Nell said and then mercifully went back into the reception room.

He picked up the phone and punched "one." "Trevor? Sorry to keep you waiting. Good to talk to you." *To anybody but Nell.* He opened the bottom drawer and took out his bottle of Glenlivet. "I understand you're worried about Olivia." Nell. *Jesus.*

"She's up to something," Trevor said. "I know that junior partner of yours is good, but I think this might be something for you to handle."

Gabe cradled the phone between his chin and his shoulder as he looked for something to pour the whiskey into. If Nell had been there, she'd have had a glass under the bottle by now. Of course, if Nell had been there, he wouldn't want the whiskey. He'd want—"Riley's not a junior partner, Trevor, he's a full partner. And most of the time he's a hell of a lot better than I am. He's the guy you want on this one." He looked around the room for a glass, an old coffee cup, anything, but he knew better.

Nell had been there. The place was spotless. He gave up and took a swig from the bottle.

"If you're sure," Trevor said.

Gabe savored the heat of the scotch going down. "I'm sure. Riley is the best there is."

"Call me if you find out anything," Trevor said. "I know I'm overprotective, but damn it, she's my little girl."

"Right," Gabe said, screwing the top back on the bottle. Olivia Ogilvie was a little girl the way Britney Spears was a teenager. "Count on us. Oh, and Trevor? Stop trying to steal my secretary."

He hung up on Trevor's unrepentant chuckle, and Riley spoke from the doorway. "Thanks."

Gabe looked up, surprised. "I didn't know you were still here."

"I'm the best there is, huh?"

Gabe eased back in his chair. "Yeah, you are. Should have told you that before."

"It's good to hear any time." Riley slouched into his chair and regarded him steadily. "What did you say to Nell?"

"She was fussing. I kicked her out." Gabe thought about it and unscrewed the Glenlivet again. "I'll apologize."

"She seemed a little annoyed."

"She's always annoyed," Gabe said and drank.

"You okay?"

"Never better." He capped the bottle. "Trevor wants the report on Olivia tomorrow. Is that a problem?"

"Not unless Olivia stays home and behaves herself. Since it's Friday night, I'm guessing that's not a problem." Riley studied him for a minute, and just as Gabe was about to say, *"What?"* Riley said, "I think you're right." He straightened in his chair and looked open and forthright, which made Gabe narrow his eyes in suspicion. "I do have a more mature outlook on life."

"Okay," Gabe said, waiting for it.

"And just now talking with Nell and her T-shirt, I realized what I walked away from," Riley said. "Mature men need mature women. I'm going to make a move on her again. That okay with you?"

Gabe looked at him with loathing. "You couldn't let it alone, could you? You had to keep pushing."

"Just wanted to make sure it's okay."

"I will rip your throat out with my bare hands."

"There you go," Riley said, standing up. "Big day for both of us. I'm into maturity and you're out of denial."

"And the sad thing is, you're on my side," Gabe said. "Imagine what my enemies are doing to me."

"Forget about your enemies," Riley said. "Investigate your secretary."

Gabe thought about Nell on his desk again. Now he knew why his dad had kept the whiskey in the bottom drawer. Secretaries, the bane of the McKennas. "When did she get divorced?"

"A year ago last July," Riley said, and then he said, "No, you're not going to wait for the two years to be up."

"Smart thing to do," Gabe said. "Statistics show—"

"Cowardly thing to do," Riley said. "That's seven months from now. I got twenty says you don't make it."

"You're on," Gabe said. "Now go away."

Fifteen minutes later, Nell came in with her coat on and said, "I'm leaving. Anything you need before I go?"

Ask me again in seven months, Gabe thought, but he said, "Nope. Sorry I yelled earlier."

"Not a problem," Nell said. "That's pretty much your major mode of communication."

Gabe winced. "You really are a terrific secretary. Best we've ever had."

"Thank you," Nell said, surprised into a smile, and Gabe felt the heat spread as he looked at her. "Have a good night."

"You, too," he said as she faded through the door, taking the heat with her.

Seven months.

He got out the whiskey again.

At nine the next morning, Becca called and canceled for the fourth time. "I just can't ask him, Gabe," she said. "Maybe after Christmas."

"When you've asked him, call us," Gabe said, feeling sorry for her, but sorrier for himself: He had the mother of all hangovers. "Have a good holiday." He hung up the phone just as Riley came in and sat down across from him.

"I did the Quarterly Report last night," Riley said, his face grim.

"Oh, good for you," Gabe said around his headache and then looked at him closer. "What's wrong?"

"Trevor was right, Olivia's up to somebody new."

"How bad?"

"Real bad," Riley said. "It's Jack Dysart."

"Oh, *hell*." Gabe yanked open his desk drawer and found his aspirin bottle. He'd already taken two, but he was pretty sure it was impossible to overdose on aspirin. "Are you sure?"

"He went back to her place with her and they didn't close the drapes. And no, he wasn't checking her homework."

"Jack Dysart is an idiot." Trevor was going to have Jack's head on a platter, which was only right. And then there was Suze. She didn't deserve this. "Son of a bitch."

"I have stronger words," Riley said. "You going to tell Trevor?"

"Unless you want to," Gabe said. "Get the report together . . ." His voice trailed off as he saw what Riley had already seen.

"We don't give this to Nell," Riley said. "She'll tell Suze."

"She'll suspect something if you don't give her a report. Write a dummy for her to type and then do the real report yourself."

"If she ever finds out we lied to her, she'll kill us both," Riley said.

"Then see to it she never finds out," Gabe said. "And be careful. She's sharp."

Riley got up to go. "So you going to do anything about her?"

"No," Gabe said. "Go away."

"Look," Riley said. "You've had it for her for months now. Given the kind of guy you are, you're always going to have it for her. Why can't you just admit that and get it over with?"

"Thank you. When you've fixed your own life, then you can criticize mine."

"My life is fine."

"Your life is fine."

"Yes, my life is fine."

"Well, you've never been a hypocrite," Gabe said. "So I'm going to have to go with tragically stupid here."

"What hypocrite?" Riley looked mystified. "I don't have it for Nell. I was just trying to get you moving when I said that last night."

"Susannah Campbell Dysart," Gabe said, enunciating each syllable carefully. "For fifteen years."

"Entirely different situation," Riley said. "She was a fantasy of my youth. I'm over that."

"Tragically stupid," Gabe said and went back to his reports, and then, as an afterthought, prompted by the news about Olivia, he added, "Have you seen Lu lately?"

"Uh, no," Riley said and headed for the door.

"Hold it," Gabe said. "What's going on?"

"Nothing," Riley said. "She's your kid. Talk to her."

Gabe put his pen down, suddenly cold. "Drugs?"

"Jesus, no," Riley said. "I'm not saying I'd be surprised if she did a little weed now and then, but she's not stupid."

"Then what is it?" Gabe said, and when Riley hesitated, he said, "Someday you're going to have a kid of your own. Cut me a break now."

"She's dating a really nice guy."

Gabe frowned. "So what's the problem?"

"She's been dating him for a while."

"How long?"

"Since school started."

Four months. A new record for his scatterbrained child. "Anything wrong with him?"

"Nope."

"Then why are you scaring the hell out of me?"

"It's Nell's kid," Riley said. "Jason. Nell says he's not much for long-term relationships."

"Good," Gabe said, picking up his pen again, and Riley escaped into the outer office.

Nell came in a few minutes later with the previous day's paperwork to sign.

"How'd the Quarterly Report go?" she said.

"Same as always," Gabe said. "I've got lunch with Harold today."

"I know, I have it already," Nell said. "Don't forget the appointment at Nationwide at three."

She turned to go and Gabe said, "One more thing."

"Yes?"

"Were you aware that your son is dating my daughter?"

Nell froze, her bright green sweater stretched tight everywhere. "Oh?"

"Yeah, I thought you were," Gabe said, and went back to the paperwork. If Nell had raised the kid, he'd have to be decent, although that idiot she'd married wasn't a good indicator. He stopped to think about it and decided that it didn't matter who the kid's father was. Nell would have raised him right.

Besides, anybody was better than Jack Dysart.

December was the busiest month the McKennas had had since Nell joined them, and it depressed her a little. Weren't people supposed to trust each other more at the holidays?

"More suicides this time of year than any other," Gabe said when she mentioned it to him. "It's all that expectation. Everybody wants to live in a Norman Rockwell painting, and everybody's really living in *The Scream*. It gets to people."

"I'm happy," Nell said, trying not to look at him. His tie was loosened and his shirtsleeves were rolled up and his hair looked rumpled, and he looked like an unmade bed. A really inviting, really hot unmade bed. When she mentioned it to Suze the next day, Suze said, "Well, *do* something about it."

Nell shook her head, "There's a word for secretaries who seduce their bosses."

" 'Bimbos'?" Suze said.

" 'Fired,' " Nell said. "I like my job, and I'm not going to lose it by making a pass at Gabe."

They were decorating The Cup for Christmas for Margie—Martha Stewart would have taken Margie and her shop to her bosom, it was that classy-cute now—and Margie came up with a tray of intricately iced cookies and said, "What do you think?"

"They're works of art," Nell said, and meant it. The cookies were cut in classic Christmas shapes, but the icing that covered them was shiny and smooth as a new snowfall, and the piped decorations were immaculately done. "Those must have taken you hours."

"Just all morning," Margie said. "I'm thinking of opening in the mornings, too. Maybe just for Christmas. What do you think?"

"I think Budge will have a fit," Suze said. "Do it."

"He's not around in the mornings," Margie said. "And people like tea in the morning, too."

Nell was still stuck on the cookies. "These are really beautiful, Margie. People could give them as gifts."

"Do you think?" Margie's round little face flushed with pleasure. "I've been practicing. I've gone through pounds of royal icing, but I think I'm getting pretty good."

"I think you're great," Suze said. "What do they taste like?"

"Take one," Margie urged, and Suze said, "God, no. Don't you have any broken pieces?"

"I've got some that aren't pretty enough to sell," Margie said and went to get them.

"What's with the crack about Budge?" Nell said.

"I'm sorry," Suze said. "He's driving Margie crazy, calling her here all the time, trying to get her to quit, and it's so selfish of him when she loves it so much. I think he's afraid she's going to meet somebody else and leave him, but Margie doesn't have that kind of luck."

"Sort of like Jack," Nell said.

Suze shook her head. "You know, he bullied me into

quitting the decoys, and now he's working late all the time so he's not home anyway. I don't miss him that much, I just think if he's not going to be there, why do I have to be?"

Not good, Nell thought. "So what did you get him for Christmas?"

"Nothing," Suze said. "What's the point of buying him a present with money he gives me?"

"Okay," Nell said.

"What are you getting Gabe?"

"We don't exchange presents. We're not that close."

"Right. What did you get him?"

"Nothing," Nell said. "But I did have some of the pictures on his wall blown up bigger and framed in gold so we can put them in the outer office. Come here, you have to see them."

She took Suze into the storeroom and Margie followed them in with the cookies.

"These are really good," Nell said after one bite. "They taste like the almond cookies." She took another for later and began to unpack the picture boxes.

"I adapted the recipe," Margie said. "I thought if we only sold these at Christmas, people would appreciate them more."

"And pay more for them," Suze said. "Margie, you're a genius."

"I am, aren't I?" Margie said, delighted. "I'm freezing the dough so I can make it once a week but bake them fresh every morning. It's so much better that way."

Nell stopped unpacking pictures to look at her, surprised at her confidence. "Good for you," she said. She put the pictures on the box. "This one's your dad, Margie." She finished off her cookie and watched Margie smile as she recognized her dad in the twentysomething, scotch-clutching Trevor.

"I should get a copy of this for him for Christmas,"

Margie said. "He's been really depressed lately. This would cheer him up."

"Who's the guy who looks like Gabe? His dad?" Suze said.

"Yes." Nell pulled out another picture. "Here's Gabe and his dad together."

"My God, he's young," Suze said.

Nell looked at the slender boy in the picture. "He's eighteen there. He started working here at fifteen. Can you imagine?" She pulled out another one. "This is Patrick and Lia, Gabe's mom. Their wedding picture."

"She's pretty," Margie said.

"Her jacket's a little tight through the stomach," Suze said.

"She was expecting Gabe," Nell said, looking at Lia's vivid face above her practical pinstriped suit. "She is pretty, isn't she? Gabe's got her eyes."

"Oh, look at this," Margie said, picking up the next one. "Chloe's just a baby."

"Chloe *has* a baby," Suze said, looking closer at the picture. "Is that Lu?"

"Yes," Nell said, and recited the names as she moved her fingers across the picture. "Gabe, Patrick, Riley, and Chloe and Lu in front."

"That's *Riley*?" Suze said and took the picture from her.

"At fifteen," Nell said. "1981. Gabe said Lu had just been born, so they took a family picture. His dad died a couple of weeks later."

"Riley was a cute kid," Suze said.

So was Gabe, Nell thought, looking at Gabe at twenty-five.

"Chloe was the secretary," Suze said.

"Yep. So was Gabe's mom."

"Hmm," Suze said and handed it back.

"I've been thinking about Chloe's china," Margie said, apropos of nothing. "I think it's too plain with just the star on it."

"China?" Nell said, coming back from 1981.

"It's white," Margie said. "And I think something with color would be good, but I want to keep it in period, too. What do you think?"

"Don't ask Nell," Suze said. "You can't afford her taste."

"Fiestaware," Nell said. "It's really bright and it comes in a lot of colors. You used to be able to get it cheap at garage sales."

"EBay," Suze said. "I'll show you how to look for it tonight, Margie."

"Tonight?" Margie said. "Won't Jack mind?"

"No." Suze bit into her cookie again. "These are really good. Can I have the recipe?"

"If I give you the recipe, will you come here and buy them?" Margie said. "No."

"My God," Suze said, "we've created a monster," and Margie beamed at her.

Nell watched Suze instead. Not a happy woman. And she didn't get happier as the month progressed. Margie's cookies were mentioned in the *Dispatch* and her business doubled, much to Budge's dismay, and Suze began to help her out, eventually working full days without telling Jack. "It's not worth the fight," she told Nell. "And he's never there, so why should he care?"

"Can't think of a reason," Nell said and hunted up her divorce lawyer's card, just in case.

Christmas Day at Suze's had its high points—Margie gave them the almond cookie recipe on the condition they'd tell no one—but it also had its lows—Trevor barely spoke to Jack, Budge was rude to Nell in retaliation for The Cup, Olivia was more obnoxious than usual, and Jack gave Suze a diamond bracelet identical to one he'd given her the Christmas before and then left to take his mother home, disappearing until after midnight again.

"Let's spend New Year's Eve together," Nell said, as

they sat in the guest room, freeing Marlene from her angel wings.

"Jack might actually show up on New Year's Eve," Suze said. "But hell, yes, come over here. I'd rather kiss you than him anyway." She set Marlene free. "There you go, puppy. Holiday's over."

Marlene rolled over on her back and squirmed until the memory of the wings was gone, her long brown coat grown out from the indignity of her September disguise, and Nell scratched her tummy until she stretched out and sighed.

"Sometimes I feel guilty," she said.

"About what?"

"Marlene." Nell stroked the dog's tummy again, watching the dog's face. "I love her so much, but I stole her from somebody."

"Who didn't appreciate her," Suze said.

"We don't know that," Nell said. "I love her, but she's a drama queen. People probably think *I* abuse her."

"Think about something else," Suze said. "How'd Gabe like the pictures?"

"He really did," Nell said, smiling as she remembered. "Riley liked them, too, but Gabe looked at them on the walls for a long time, and then he said, 'These are great, thank you.' "

"That was it?" Suze said.

"That's a lot for Gabe," Nell said. "I could tell. They meant a lot."

"I was hoping he'd sweep you into his arms and say, 'My darling!' " Suze said. "What's wrong with him?"

"Evidently photos of his family don't turn him on. There's nothing wrong with him." Nell thought about Gabe, standing in the office, staring at the pictures. "There's not a thing wrong with him."

Suze snorted. "So what did he get you?"

"Me?" Nell came back from her memory. "A desk chair. From him and Riley both."

"Oh, *God*," Suze said. "The man is *hopeless*."

"No, really, it's perfect. It's just like the one I had in my old office." When Suze didn't look impressed, she added, "It's ergonomic and expensive as hell. I'd never have asked for it. I think Riley asked Jase about it."

"Good for Riley," Suze said.

"Riley also gave Marlene a huge box of dog biscuits," Nell said, scratching the dog's stomach again. "He and Marlene have a *very* close relationship."

"Has he ever met a female he hasn't had a very close relationship with?"

Nell patted Suze's knee. "Why don't we go downstairs and eat something? What do you have besides ham?"

"I think there's lasagna again," Suze said. "But food is not love."

"No, but it is food." Nell stood up.

Marlene rolled over and looked at them both, clearly expecting the worst.

"Biscuit," Nell said, and Marlene leaped from the bed and trotted off to the stairs and the kitchen.

"That's the way we should go after life," Nell told Suze, following the dog down the stairs. "Just lunge for it."

"Cheap talk," Suze said, and Nell gave up and concentrated on talking about everything except Jack and his resounding absence from the scene.

At five on New Year's Eve, Nell took the last of the reports in to Gabe to sign before she left for Suze's. She watched him, his face serious in the pool of light that his green-shaded lamp cast on the desk. It threw the planes of his face into relief, made his eyes even darker than they really were, and highlighted his strong hand as it slashed away across the page, signing his name with the same passion and determination he did everything.

He finished and put the pen down, and she said, "Thanks," and gathered the papers up clumsily, trying to get out before she lost it and went for him like Marlene after leftover ham. "Uh, have a nice holiday."

She retreated as fast as she could, but he said, "Nell?" and she turned at the door, fumbling the papers into order, trying to look bright and efficient instead of incandescent with lust.

"Yes?"

"Are you all right?" He frowned at her from behind his desk, and even frowning he looked hot. She really was losing her mind if disapproval made her pant.

"I'm fine," Nell said gaily. "Couldn't be better. Gotta go. Going to meet Suze. New Year's Eve, you know. Parties."

She shut up as he stood and walked around the desk. "What's wrong?"

He was standing a good six feet away from her, next to his desk. *You're too far away. I want you touching me.*

She closed her eyes at the thought of his hands on her, and he said, "Spill it."

"There's nothing wrong," she said, opening her eyes to look confidently into his, but she couldn't, and her eyes slid away at the last minute. "Stop being a detective."

"I've known you for four months," Gabe said. "If you're not yapping at me, there's something on your mind. Tell me what it is and for God's sake don't try to fix it on your own. This place can't take any more of your successes."

"There is no problem," Nell said, and met his eyes. Mistake. That dark, level gaze made her breathing come from deep inside her. He stood very still as the blood rose in her face, and she said, "I'm fine," but it came out faintly, on a breath, and the moment stretched out into a hot empty eternity before he shook his head.

"I was never going to make it to July anyway," he said.

He stepped toward her, and something gave inside her and she met him halfway, in the middle of the worn Oriental, clutching at his shoulders as he slid his hand around her waist, bumping noses with him as she went up on her toes and he bent down, and finally, finally tasting him as his mouth found hers.

Chapter Thirteen

Nell held on as he kissed her, clutching his shirt to pull him closer, and when she broke the kiss, he ran his hands over her, tracing heat, until she was breathless. "Wait a minute," she said, and he said, "No," and bent to her again.

"Hey," she said, ducking away, trying to get her breath. "What happened to 'Don't fuck the help'?"

"You're not that much help," he said and took her mouth again before she could answer, his body hard against hers, his hands hot on her back under her sweater. She thought, *Oh, God, yes*, and pulled his shirt free so she could slide her hands up his back and touch him, too, making him draw in his breath and then kiss her harder. He backed her against the door and she let him, needing it to push back and hold her own, only once stopping to think, *Maybe I should pretend to be soft and let him lead like Tim.* Then she thought, *No, it's Gabe*, and she knew she'd never have to be careful again. She took his face in her hands and kissed him again, and he held her as if he were never going to let her go, his hands on her everywhere, kissing her for long minutes until she was dizzy and aching for him. Finally he said breathlessly against her mouth, "I have this apartment upstairs," and she shuddered a little at the thought—*private, naked, rolling on cool sheets*—feeling him hard against her as she pressed closer, and that made her moan, a tiny moan that he must have heard because he said, "Or here's good, too," and pulled her down onto the ancient Oriental.

He was heavy on top of her, and she wrapped her legs around him as her skirt rolled up to her hips, arching against all that hard muscle and lean length, pressing back, no hesitation at all, doing anything to get him closer as his mouth moved down her neck and his hands slid under her sweater. She raked her nails down his back and he held her down, kissing her so hard that her blood pounded in her ears.

Then Riley knocked and opened the door and smacked her in the head.

"Very nice," he said, looking down. "You owe me twenty."

Gabe slammed the door shut with the flat of his hand and said to Nell, "You okay?" He sounded breathless and looked hot and disheveled and worried and turned on and everything she'd ever needed, and she said, "I want you so much I'm insane with it."

"That would explain the past four months," he said, leaning down to kiss her again, but she sat up from underneath him, knocking him off balance and grabbing him by the collar as she rolled him over on his back to climb on top of him.

"No insults," she said, straddling him, trying to catch her breath. "You're supposed to be *seducing* me."

"You should have just *told* me you wanted this," he said, running his hands down to her rear end to pull her tighter against him. "You didn't have to steal the dog to get my attention—"

"Or sleep with Riley?" she said, pushing his shoulders down.

His eyes darkened. "That you're going to forget." He put his hand on the back of her neck and pulled her down to kiss her, his mouth hard on hers.

"Make me," she said, her mouth still pressed to his, and he slid his fingers up under her skirt—*my God, this is Gabe*—and into her underwear—*don't stop*—and then slickly into her, making her shudder against him again while he breathed heavier because of her heat.

"Forget," he said, and she caught her breath and said, *"Not enough,"* and he rolled her onto her back and began to strip her clothes from her with such ruthless efficiency that it took her a moment before she did the same for him, ripping his shirt open to bite into the hot flesh of his shoulder. He jerked away and pinned her down again, his hands hard on her hips, his mouth hot on her breast, and she dissolved into the blurred tangle they made, losing her boundaries as he moved against her, feeling only heat and friction and pressure as she twisted in his arms, loving the hot slide of his body on hers and needing him so much that when he finally came into her, she shimmered in his arms, trying to consume him the way he consumed her, moving fast against him, until she finally broke, biting her lip as every nerve in her body surged.

When they were quiet on the floor, fighting for breath, Gabe said, "Sweet Jesus, is it always going to be like that?" and Nell said, "Oh, I hope so."

He laughed and kissed her. "Some day let's do something where we cooperate." His voice broke off as she let her hand trail down his back, and she watched him close his eyes, still breathless.

"I'm hungry," she said. "Is there food in your apartment?"

"Everything you've ever wanted is in my apartment." He pushed himself off her, and the cool air rushed in to take his place, making her nerves sing again. He stood and reached down for her hand, completely unselfconscious in his nakedness, and she let him pull her to her feet so she could put her arms around him again and touch all that heat and muscle, skin to skin, knowing he was hers, at least for tonight.

"Prove it," she said and kissed him again, tasting him again, falling into him again, feeling as though she'd finally come home to a man strong enough to love her the way she needed to be loved.

*   *   *

When Nell hadn't shown by eleven and there was no answer except for the machine at the agency, Suze shrugged on her coat and walked across the park to see what was up. If Nell was working late, she would have called—which was more than Jack ever did—so something must be wrong. It was Suze's duty as a best friend to go find out what.

Also, she had to get out of that big empty house.

The park was beautiful in the moonlight, the ice on the trees gleaming silver and the melting snow making a patchwork on the ground. Except for the occasional reveler driving by on his way to a party with people and noise and laughter, she was all alone.

She was alone a lot lately.

The heels of her boots clicked on the concrete walk as she picked up speed, passing the big stone pillars that marked the end of Riley's side of the park. It wasn't strange that Jack was away so much, even on New Year's Eve; it was a tough job being partner in a law firm. And besides, she'd made it past her thirtieth birthday. Jack had left Abby when she'd turned thirty and dumped Vicki at twenty-eight, but here she was at the ripe old age of thirty-two and he still loved her.

She was sure he still loved her. She just wasn't sure she loved him.

When she walked past The Cup and turned down the dark side street to the agency door, she realized she'd been stupid to walk around the Village that late. She knocked on the door and peered through the big window into the darkness. Nell wasn't there.

She was going to have to walk back home alone. It was suddenly a lot darker and a lot colder, and she didn't want to walk home alone.

She pounded on the door one more time, and the door opened and Riley stood there.

"What the hell?" he said.

"Nell never showed up," Suze said, her teeth chattering a little from the cold. "I was worried."

"So you went out walking through the city at night," Riley said. "Jesus. Get in here."

He turned on the light as she came in, and she saw he was dressed in a dark suit and tie, looking as close to distinguished as she'd ever seen him. Or maybe she was just desperate for company and not as picky as usual.

"Party?" she said.

"Always," he said. "What's Jack doing letting you wander around in the dark?"

Suze lifted her chin. "Jack doesn't let me do anything. I let me."

Riley shoved Nell's phone toward her. "Call him for a ride home."

"He's not there," Suze said.

Riley said, "Oh," and put the phone back.

"Nell's not at her apartment, either," she said to change the subject. "Do you know where—"

"Upstairs. With Gabe."

"Really?" Suze said, brightening a little. "Tell me they're not talking about the agency."

"I don't think they're talking at all. Although given their mutual passion for work, they could be running spreadsheets by now."

"But they weren't earlier."

"Not when I walked in on them."

"I forgive her for not calling me." Suze said, and turned back to the door.

"Wait a minute," Riley said. "You are not going to walk home in the dark. I'll give you a lift."

"I can—" Suze began and looked out at the dark street. "Thank you," she said. "I'd love a ride."

She got into his car and sat quietly while he put it in gear and turned down Third Street. "You going to be late for your date?"

"Don't have a date," he said. "Just a party."

"Nobody to kiss on New Year's Eve?"

"There will be somebody to kiss," Riley said as he turned to make the circle around the park. "There's always somebody to kiss on New Year's Eve."

Suze thought about her big empty house for a couple of blocks. "Not always."

He was quiet for a minute, and then he said, "Jack is an idiot."

"Jack's been married for fourteen years. The zing goes."

"Not yours."

"Oh, yeah?" Suze lifted her chin. "You think I've got zing?"

"You don't seem too pleased about Nell and Gabe. Or are you just being cool?"

"It was inevitable," Suze said, accepting the subject change. She'd been pushing her luck, anyway. Pathetic. "I don't know what she was waiting for." *I don't know what I'm waiting for.*

"Gabe was waiting for July," Riley said. "The dumbass."

"Why July?"

"Two-year recovery period."

Suze thought about it. "You know, Tim dumped her two years ago Christmas. She didn't get the divorce until July, but he left her on Christmas."

"So Gabe wins again," Riley said. "The guy's a master."

He pulled up in front of her house, and Suze felt like saying, "Take me to the party with you." But she couldn't. Jack might come home.

Jack wasn't coming home. He was with somebody else. Nobody left a wife alone on New Year's Eve unless he was with a mistress. She knew that from having been a mistress.

"You okay?" Riley said.

"Kiss me," Suze said, and he froze. "I mean it. I'm going back to that house alone and it's New Year's Eve and I want to be kissed. Feel sorry for me and kiss me."

"No," Riley said.

"Ouch," Suze said. "Sorry." She yanked on the door handle.

"Look," Riley said. "It's not—"

She stopped and looked back at him. "What?"

"You deserve better."

"Than you?"

"Than Jack. And God knows, better than me."

"I didn't mean to put you in that position. You know, a married woman coming on to you—"

"Any guy would be glad to be in that position." He sounded sorry for her, which made her mad.

"Yeah, right. Thanks for the ride."

She turned to open the door and looked up to see Jack, standing beside the car with his fists in his jacket pockets.

"Uh-oh," she said, and Riley bent to see past her out the car window.

"Oh, good," Riley said. "You want me to stay?"

"I don't think that will help," Suze said, pushing the door open.

He caught her arm. "Is he—"

"He doesn't hit," Suze said. "He yells, but that's okay. I'm all right."

Riley let go of her, and she got out of the car and slammed the door shut.

"Very nice," Jack said. "I come home to celebrate New Year's Eve with my wife—"

"Damn big of you." Suze said and pushed past him to go up the steps.

"*Who is that?*" Jack said.

"Riley McKenna." Suze reached the porch and put her key in the lock. "He brought me home when I went looking for Nell."

"*Good story*," Jack said, following her up the steps.

Suze went inside and turned on the light and waved to Riley to go on. "Not a story. You got one for me?"

"I told you, I was at work—"

"I called," Suze said, watching Riley's taillights skim

down the street toward his party. "You didn't answer."

"The switchboard shuts down at night."

"I called your cell phone."

"I turned it off."

"Really?" Suze said. "Why?"

"Are you sleeping with him?"

"With Riley?" Suze started up the stairs, suddenly so tired she could hardly move. "No. I barely know the man."

He grabbed her arm and jerked her off the steps, and she sucked in her breath, shocked out of her exhaustion.

"You're *fucking him*," Jack said, and she looked at him and didn't care anymore.

"If I was sleeping with Riley," she said, "*I'd be with Riley.* I wouldn't be standing here pretending I still had a relationship with you." She jerked her arm away and rubbed it and waited for him to raise his hand and hit her because then she could leave him.

"You told me you were going to be with Nell," he said. "You told me—"

"Nell's with Gabe," Suze said, "which is good. Nobody should be alone on New Year's Eve." She started up the stairs again, daring him to stop her.

"This is her fault," Jack said. "Budge was right, she's a bad influence. You were never like this before she moved down here."

"I'll have to thank her for that," Suze said, and climbed toward the darkness at the top because it was better than the light he was standing in at the bottom.

Six blocks away, through a postcoital drowse, Gabe listened with only half his attention to the celebrations on TV.

"This is great," Nell said. "One big party everywhere, no trauma."

"Good." Gabe settled deeper into his bed, too damn tired and much too satisfied to care.

"I still feel bad about Suze, though. She sounded so down when I called her. I'm a terrible friend."

"Umhm," Gabe said into his pillow, praying she'd run down soon. She'd put as much energy into them as he had, and now she was sitting up naked beside him, eating potato chips and doing a play-by-play of the fireworks. If she didn't shut up in the next five minutes, he was going to have to drug her.

"Hey." She smacked his shoulder, and he rolled back to see her grinning down at him, the potato chip bag in her hand, her hair making her look like a firecracker in his bed. "We are too new for you to take me for granted. Let's have a little courtship here, shall we?"

"Why?" he said. "I scored. It's over."

She let her mouth drop open in mock rage, and he laughed and pulled her down to him while she fought him the whole way, sending the potato chip bag flying.

"I am not taking you for granted," he said in her ear as she squirmed. "I'm exhausted from not taking you for granted."

She stopped fighting, and he closed his eyes in pleasure at all her suddenly pliant softness pressed against him. He heard a rustle and realized that Marlene had crept up from the bottom of the bed and was dragging the potato chip bag back with her while the TV chanted the countdown for the new year. *There's a dog in my bed*, he thought and wondered when she'd jumped up. He was fairly certain she'd waited until all the thrashing was over or they'd have kicked her into a wall. Marlene had excellent survival skills.

"I'm happy," Nell whispered in his ear, her voice all smiles, and he thought, *I can sleep later*.

He rolled so they were side by side, pulling her closer, still amazed that she was there with him, that he'd finally done all the things he'd been trying not to think about and that they'd turned out to be so much better than he'd tried not to imagine. "Me, too. Happy New Year, kid."

He kissed her softly this time, and she relaxed into him

and then said, "Look!" He followed her eyes up to the skylight now filled with fireworks like shooting stars. "Everything is perfect," she said to him. "Absolutely everything."

"Don't say that," he said, feeling a chill. "You're tempting fate."

"I don't believe in fate," Nell said, and he remembered that four months ago Chloe had said they'd be here, that it was in their stars. He started to tell her and then thought, *Not a good time to mention Chloe.*

"What?" she said, and he said, "Nothing," and she raised herself up on one elbow, prepared to argue it out of him.

"Truce for one night," he said, pulling her back, "just for tonight," and when she said, "But—" he kissed her quiet again, and then held her until she fell asleep, watching the fireworks fade above them.

"So you slept with Gabe," Suze said at brunch the next day at the Sycamore.

Nell tried to look innocent but she had too many good memories, so she grinned instead and cut another piece of French toast. "And Happy New Year's Day to you, too."

"Really?" Margie cocked her head and surveyed Nell, looking a lot like a dim little bird. "Imagine you married to a detective."

"Imagine me not married to a detective," Nell said. "I'm not doing that again."

"Nell McKenna," Margie said. "That's pretty." She poured extra syrup over her chocolate-chip pancakes. "Romantic."

"Beats Dysart," Suze said, stabbing her eggs Benedict.

Nell and Margie looked at her and then at each other.

"I never liked Margie Dysart," Margie said.

"She was okay once you got used to her," Suze said, and Nell laughed.

Margie was considering things. "I think Margie Jenkins would be okay, although it sounds sort of low class."

"Don't tell Budge," Nell said. "He'll change it."

"Margie Ogilvie is still my favorite, though," Margie said.

"So keep your name." Suze sounded annoyed with the whole conversation.

"Nobody would know I was married," Margie said.

"Which would make it all the easier to cheat," Suze said.

Margie frowned at her. "What is wrong with you?"

"Jack caught me coming home last night with Riley Mc-Kenna," Suze said, still torturing her eggs. "I was looking for Nell and he brought me home. It's past eleven on New Year's Eve, and Jack accuses *me* of fooling around. So I locked myself in the bedroom. The hell with him."

"Oh, no," Nell said, feeling horrible. "That's my fault. I am so sorry about last night, that was a terrible thing, I just forgot you—"

"Under the circumstances, no," Suze said. "Way to go, Eleanor, that's what I think about that."

"Men always know," Margie said. "Stewart was jealous of Budge."

Suze swung her head around to Margie. "What?"

"Stewart. He was jealous of Budge. Because I liked Budge better, the way you like Riley."

"I am not having an affair," Suze said coldly.

"Well, of course not," Margie said. "But you like Riley better than Jack."

"Uh, Margie," Nell began.

"It's a terrible thing to be married to the wrong man," Margie said. "It's like being trapped at a bad party that never ends. The voices are always too loud and the jokes are dumb and you end up standing against a wall, hoping nobody notices you because it's so much easier that way. It's like you're trying to avoid somebody who's the only other person at the party. I hated it."

She took out her thermos and poured more soy milk in

her coffee, while Nell and Suze sat stunned.

"Leave him," Margie said to Suze. "Don't try to make it work when it's that bad. It's just too awful, you end up doing terrible things because you can't stand the pain anymore."

"Margie." Nell stretched out her hand. "We didn't know it was that bad."

"I know." Margie drank her coffee, straight down to the bottom of the cup, and then put the cup back in its saucer. "I hit him once."

"Good," Suze said.

"No," Margie said. "But it turned out okay. He left. Are you okay?"

"I don't know," Suze said. "I have to think about it. I can't imagine not being married to Jack, but I don't think I can stand the tension anymore, either. He really thinks I cheat, and I don't. I really don't."

"We know," Nell said.

"But I really want to," Suze said.

"We know," Margie said.

"Sometimes I wish Jack would disappear like Stewart did," Suze said. "Just evaporate."

"No, you don't," Margie said. "Because what if he came back?"

Nell drew in her breath. "Do you think Stewart's coming back?"

"Budge wants me to file the insurance claim," Margie said. "He says I can buy a lot of Fiestaware with two million dollars. He says I shouldn't just leave it lying there."

"If you don't want to file, don't," Suze said sharply. "It's none of Budge's business."

"He's just looking out for me," Margie said. "But what if I file and Stewart comes back? I'd have to give it back. And you know I wouldn't have all of it."

"Has he come back?" Nell said, hating herself for the question.

"I don't think so," Margie said. "But it would be just like him. He was such a prick."

"*Margie!*" Suze said and then laughed, shocked out of her self-pity.

"Well, he was," Margie said.

"So you think he's alive," Nell said, feeling like a rat for pushing it.

"No," Margie said. "I think he's dead. But sometimes I'm *afraid* he's alive."

Nell sat there nodding, waiting for her to say something else, but it was Suze who spoke.

"So," she said to Nell. "Was there zing?"

"Merciful heavens, yes," Nell said, and let them tease her for the rest of brunch while she wondered how things had gotten so turned around that she was the happy one and they were the ones in trouble.

Two blocks away, Riley poured a cup of coffee from Nell's coffeemaker and said, "So. You and Nell."

"Figured that out, did you?" Gabe drank his coffee and squinted at the framed blowup of his dad and Trevor, touched again that Nell had thought of this way to decorate the office.

"I have great powers of deduction." Riley sat on the edge of Nell's desk and sipped his coffee cautiously. "Suze came by last night looking for her."

Gabe nodded, moving on to the family group portrait, a little chagrined at how young Chloe was in the picture, even younger-looking in the blowup than she had been in the original, like a very pretty egg, smooth and round. *Somebody should have slapped me*, he thought. She was Lu's age and holding a baby, for Christ's sake. But there hadn't been anybody there to protect her; her parents were dead, and so was his mother by then, and all his father had said was, "Good choice, she'll never give you any trouble." And she never had.

"I took her home and we ran into Jack," Riley said, and Gabe looked around.

"What?"

"Suze. Jack was there when I took her home."

"How bad was it?"

Riley shook his head. "Bad. But she didn't want me to stay. She said he didn't hit."

"No," Gabe said. "He's just arrogant and selfish."

"And cheating on her," Riley said.

"Did you tell her?"

"No."

Gabe nodded and turned back to the picture. "I can't believe how young Chloe is in this picture. What the hell was I thinking?"

"The same thing you were thinking last night," Riley said, coming to stand beside him. "Hell, look how young I am. And you sent me out on the streets to work."

"I didn't, Dad did," Gabe said. "And you wanted to go."

"I know," Riley said. "Damn, she was young. What were you thinking?"

"Not the same thing I was thinking last night." Gabe tried to imagine what his father would say about Nell. Probably "Run the other way, boy." With Chloe, he'd had no idea of what he was getting into, what marriage meant, but last night with Nell, he'd known exactly how much trouble he was heading for. And he hadn't cared.

He didn't care this morning, either.

He moved to the next picture, one of his mother and father on their wedding day, his mother dark-haired and vivid in a wasp-waisted suit, the buttons straining over her stomach, his father dark-haired and vibrant in his pin-stripes, happier than Gabe had ever seen him. They leaned into each other but not on each other, both of them tense with energy, smiling at the future, already knowing they had a baby on the way, not knowing they had twenty years of fights and slammed doors and shouted good-byes ahead of them. Gabe looked at his dad and thought, *He would have done it anyway. He loved her that much.*

"Gabe," Riley said.

And it's going to be like that with Nell, he thought, looking at the light in his mother's dark eyes. *And I'm going to do it anyway, too.*

"Gabe," Riley said. "Come here and look at this."

Gabe glanced his way and saw him standing in front of the family portrait. "What?"

"Look at Chloe."

Gabe squinted at the picture. "What am I looking at?"

"Her earrings," Riley said, and Gabe looked and said, "You are kidding me."

Chloe was wearing diamond circles.

Gabe headed for the door. Five minutes later, they were standing in Chloe's bedroom, her jewelry box dumped out on her dressing table, staring at a pile of silver ankhs and gold stars and enameled moons and—tangled in the middle of the miscellaneous chains and loops—two perfect gold circles the size of nickels, closely studded with diamonds.

"Are those it?" Riley said.

"Those are Helena's," Gabe said, picking them out of the mess. "And now I get to start the new year with Trevor."

"You already started it with Nell," Riley said.

"So I did," Gabe said, feeling a little better even as he stared at the evidence of his father's perfidy. "So I did."

Nell waited until after nine that night to call Gabe, knowing that he and Riley were spending the day with Lu because Jase had complained about it when he'd called to wish her a happy new year. She let the phone ring half a dozen times and was about to hang up when Gabe said, "Hello?"

"I found out a little more about Stewart," Nell said. "Not much, but some."

"Good," he said. "I'll come over. You want Chinese or pizza?"

"Chinese," she said, smiling into the receiver in spite of Suze and Margie's trauma. It was disloyal, but on the other hand, there was nothing like a man who fed you. And possibly slept with you later.

"Wear those blue silk things," he said and hung up.

Definitely slept with you later. The thought of it made her breathless. Everything about him made her breathless, including the sweeping way he just assumed they'd be back in bed. If he'd fumbled, she'd have been self-conscious and they'd have been awkward. And they weren't awkward, hadn't really ever been since the first day when she'd looked at his desk and realized how much work he was going to be.

Little had she known.

She ran upstairs to put on her blue silk pajamas and pick up the bedroom, pushing Marlene off the bed to straighten her quilt. Marlene moaned at her, so she dropped the chenille throw on the floor, and Marlene stuck her nose in it and shoved it around a little, stood on it and wiggled her butt, turned in circles four or five times, and then settled down with a tortured sigh.

"Yeah, you have a rough life," Nell said and went to clean up the bathroom.

When the doorbell rang, half an hour later, she caught her breath and took one last look in the mirror. Color in her hair, sparkle in her eyes, heat in her cheeks, and silk on her body. "God, I'm hot," she said to the mirror, and then she went to let him in.

Chapter Fourteen

Gabe came in, dropped the Chinese on the bookshelf by the door, put his arms around Nell, and kissed her until she was breathless.

"Do you have any idea how long I've been waiting to rip these pajamas off you?" he said, running his hand up her side.

"No," she said, her voice coming out as a squeak.

He kissed her again, his hands sliding all over the blue silk, and then he said, his voice husky, "So do we eat Chinese while I stare at you with lust, or do we go upstairs where I throw you down on the bed and have my way with you?"

"Bed," Nell said.

Half an hour later, Nell grabbed onto the headboard of her bed and pulled herself up, trying to get her breath back. "My God. Maybe we should try moving that down a notch."

"I wasn't the one moaning, 'Harder,' " Gabe said, pulling her down so that her back burned against him. The man was a furnace. "If you'd go a little slower, I'd have time to think."

Nell stretched against his muscle and bone, memorizing how strong and solid he was. "You want me to be passive?"

"Hell, no." Gabe ran his hand down her side and made her curl up again. "I'm just saying you're not an easy woman to love."

"Also, I don't moan." Nell shivered under his hands. "That was Marlene."

"That would explain the stereo effect." He kissed her neck and she shivered again, and then he drew his fingers across her stomach so that she pressed back, harder against him.

"Stop it," she said. "This is supposed to be afterglow."

"I like my afterglow with you in motion. I measure time by how your body sways." He bit her earlobe and she rolled to look up at him. "Okay," he said. "I just like my afterglow with you."

His eyes were dark as ever, but now they were hot, too, intent on her, and he took her breath away. *Good grief*, she thought. *Look at him. He's beautiful.*

"By how my body sways?" she said instead.

"It's from a very hot poem," he said. "It comes to mind whenever I watch you move."

Poetry, she thought. *He'll be surprising me forever.*

Not that she was counting on forever.

"What?" he said, and when she didn't answer, he slid his hand up her body again to make her shudder. "You make me nervous when you get that look in your eyes."

"It's hunger," she said, rolling out of bed and picking up her pajama top from the floor. "Time to eat."

"Bring it up here." He rolled and snagged her pajama bottoms from the floor before she could. "I'll wait."

"Lazy." She tugged on the hem of her pajama top, and he grinned at her.

"Conserving my energy," he said, and she lost her breath again.

When they were both in bed, forking garlic chicken from the same carton, he said, "By the way, we found some diamonds today."

Nell stopped with her fork in midair. "The Ogilvie diamonds?"

"Well, the Ogilvie earrings. They were in Chloe's jewelry box."

Nell listened as he filled her in and then said, "And I suppose you couldn't find Chloe in Europe."

"Not a chance. But I know what happened. My dad was crazy about her. He gave them to her, and she wore them for the family picture and then put them away. They're not her kind of jewelry. I called Trevor and he said he'd see me tomorrow. I'm *really* looking forward to that."

"Diamonds are everybody's kind of jewelry."

Gabe shook his head. "Not Chloe's. I'd bet she didn't even know they were diamonds, or if she did, she didn't have a clue what they were worth. She was only nineteen when Lu was born. Her idea of fiscal magnificence was a restaurant with cloth napkins."

His voice was affectionate, and Nell stomped on the jealousy that stirred in her. He'd be a real clod if he didn't still care about her. "You must have been really happy," she said. "Chloe's so sweet and then a new baby."

Gabe looked at her as if she were insane. "I was twenty-six and I had not planned on getting married, let alone being a father. Chloe could have been Marilyn Monroe and I wouldn't have been happy."

"Oh, come on," Nell said, feeling guilty because that was cheering.

"Stop romanticizing," Gabe said. "Everything turned out fine. Chloe was great, but it was not a fairy tale. Now tell me what Margie said."

"She talked about Stewart," Nell said. "She hated him." She filled in the details and inhaled chicken while Gabe ate and listened, finishing with, "She thinks he's alive but if she doesn't collect the insurance money, he won't come back. She's having a hard time."

"How are you doing?"

"Me?" Nell started to laugh. "I've had the greatest sex of my life two days in a row."

"That good, huh?" Gabe leaned over her to put the carton on her bedside table. "And we're just getting started." He kissed her, keeping his weight off her with his arms, and she pulled him down on top of her, wanting something solid to push against.

"I like the way you fight back," she murmured against his mouth.

"I have to." He moved his mouth to her ear. "If I don't, you'll destroy me."

"I was talking about the sex," she said, pulling away a little, and he reached for another carton.

"So was I." He sat back and opened the carton. "You're a strong woman."

"I didn't feel like it sometimes," she said, thinking of all the years when she'd played passive so Tim would feel as though he was in charge, all the lost months after Tim when she couldn't eat. She looked in his carton. Crab Rangoon. Excellent.

Gabe took one and gave it to her. "Yeah, but how do you feel now?"

"Powerful." She bit into the pastry, savoring the creamy filling. "Strong. Exciting."

"That's what you feel like to me, too," he said. "Must be you."

"Might be you," she said. "It's a pretty new feeling."

"I find that hard to believe." He picked up a pastry and bit into it. "I'd bet you've been kicking butt all your life."

Nell thought back over her old life. "I never really had any butt to kick. Everything went my way." Her friends had always deferred to her, the agency clients had obeyed her every suggestion, her kid had known better than to cross her, Tim had done what she'd told him to—

She stopped with another piece of Crab Rangoon halfway to her mouth as the realization hit.

"It's you," she said. "You're the first person who ever pushed back."

"Only because it feels so good. What else is there to eat over there? I could have sworn I bought—"

She took the Crab Rangoon carton away from him and put it back on the bedside table, and then she shoved him over onto his back. "I want to be on top this time."

"Maybe," he said, not fighting her. "But later. I had a long day, I fucked your brains out on an empty stomach, and I know there are potstickers over there. I want to eat."

"So do I," she said, and began to lick her way down his stomach.

"You can be on top," he said, and then he shut up.

"So how are you?" Nell asked Suze on Tuesday as they helped Margie close the teashop.

"I'm fine." Suze didn't look at her as she punched register keys.

"I mean you and Jack."

"We're fine."

"Okay," Nell said, switching gears. "You know, the weirdest thing happened today."

"Tell all," Suze said as she printed out the register tape.

"Gabe and I had a fight over the new rug for his office. He honest to God thinks if his father picked it out, it's sacred. And I'm not sure he even *liked* his father."

"Okay." Suze frowned at the tape.

"So I told him, look it's got a hole in it," Nell said. "And he said, 'You should know, you put it there.' The guy has eyes like an eagle. And I said if it hadn't been so old, I wouldn't have been able to, and he said getting rid of things based on my ability to destroy them would clean out the building, and we were just glaring at each other." Nell stopped to stare in front of her, remembered the way Gabe's eyes had snapped at her, the way he'd leaned over the desk to yell at her. "And I got so hot I grabbed him by the tie and kissed him."

"I'm still not getting the weird part," Suze said. "Sounds like business as usual to me."

"You know, it's not the fighting that turns me on," Nell said. "I hate the fighting. It's the way he looks when he's trying to dominate me. He doesn't have a hope, but he sure looks good trying."

"Interesting relationship," Suze said.

"Anyway, then we did some heavy necking, and then he asked me if I wanted to have dinner at the Fire House and kissed me again and went back to work."

"Sounds like a good provider," Suze said. "So?"

"So we didn't have sex," Nell said. "I know, I know, it was the middle of the day and we were at work, but do you know how long it had been since I've necked? I mean, *just* necked? Tim and I never did that. We talked about work and we had sex, but we never fooled around and then didn't do it." Nell shoved the last of the chairs under a table. "I'd really gotten to the place where if I got kissed, I started taking off my clothes."

"Which would explain Riley," Suze said, zipping shut the bank deposit bag.

"Do you and Jack neck?" Nell said, and Suze stopped.

"Oh," she said. "Now that you mention it, no."

"It must have something to do with marriage," Nell said. "I don't think I'm ever getting married again. You lose such good stuff."

"Yeah," Suze said, slowly. "We did a lot of fooling around before we were married."

"Well, you were eighteen. It's appropriate to do that when you're a teenager."

"We did more than that."

"That's what I heard." Nell brought the broom around to the back of the counter. "You need me for anything else? Because I necked today, and I think my boyfriend is going to expect me to go all the way tonight."

"What do you mean, you heard?" Suze said.

"Oh." Nell tried to think of a good lie, but it was Suze. "Well, you know, Vicki divorced Jack for adultery, so I assumed—"

"You didn't say 'assume,' you said 'heard.' " Suze folded her arms. "From whom?"

Nell looked at the ceiling, trying to think of a way out. Suze followed her eyes up. "From Riley?" she said.

"Riley?" Nell pulled back, confused. "Why Riley?"

"That's his apartment," Suze said, nodding at the ceiling.

Great. "I was just looking at the ceiling," Nell said. "Pressed tin. You don't see that much anymore."

"Unless you live in a historic district," Suze said. "Then it's pretty common. How—" Her eyes widened. "Gabe? The agency? Did they get the evidence for Vicki's divorce?"

"Yes," Nell said, "but don't you dare tell anybody I told you. I'm not allowed to talk to anybody about agency business."

"What kind of evidence? What did they do?"

"I think they just followed you."

"I want to see the report. They keep their files in the freezer, right?"

"I don't know where—" Nell began, and Suze went into the back room. Nell followed her in time to see her open the freezer. Margie had been warned about leaving it unlocked, but warning Margie was always an exercise in futility. "Uh, Suze?"

Suze started shifting through boxes, looking at dates. "Spring of 1986," she said. "It has to be . . . here it is."

"Okay, that's agency property," Nell said, but Suze already had the box open and was tabbing through folders.

"Dysart." She pulled out the folder and flipped it open and then grabbed for some pictures that slid out. Nell caught them as they hit the floor and straightened to put them back in the folder, only to be caught by what she saw.

They'd been taken through a window, through a space where the curtains hadn't been pulled completely shut. Jack was stretched out on a cheap motel bed, looking more handsome than Nell could ever remember, forty and fit and in his prime. No wonder Suze had fallen.

But the camera wasn't focused on Jack. Beside the bed, standing with her pom-poms on her hips, was Suze, eighteen and amazingly pretty in her cheerleading uniform, looking at him with head tilted and lips parted. She was laughing, and she looked shiny and new and exhilarated.

"My God," Suze said from beside her.

Nell said, "Yeah. You were a babe." Then she added hastily, "You still are, of course—"

"Not like that," Suze said. "I didn't know what I had. Look at that."

Nell looked again. "Honestly, you're better now."

"Oh, yeah, sure I am." Suze took the photos from her to leaf through them, and it was almost like a flip book, watching Suze-at-eighteen take off first her skirt, and then her sweater, and then her virginal cotton white bra and underpants until she stood there naked, flaunting a high, tight body that would have brought a stronger man than Jack Dysart to his knees.

"I may never take off my clothes again," Nell said, looking at the last picture in disbelief.

"Who took these?" Suze said.

"Riley," Nell said. "It was one of his first assignments. Gabe said it scarred him for life."

"Damn good thing I'm not sleeping with Riley," Suze said. "I'd never be able to compete with myself."

"Oh, please," Nell said. "Riley slept with me."

Suze jammed the photos back in the folder. "Don't ever let Jack see those."

"Listen, sweetie, *you* didn't see them. Just because I'm doing the boss doesn't mean he won't fire me." Nell filed the folder back in the box and put the lid back on. "Forget you ever saw these."

"I'd love to," Suze said. "But I don't think I'm going to."

*   *   *

January turned into February. Nell continued to fix the agency behind Gabe's back and then fight with him about it, Margie stalled Budge about the wedding and the insurance, Suze stayed with Jack and pretended she wasn't miserable, and Gabe remained fixated on the diamonds. He'd gone to see Trevor about Chloe's earrings and had the riot act read to him: Patrick had bought the earrings for Lia at the same time Trevor had bought the entire suite for Helena, and that kind of generous husband did not deserve a posthumously suspicious ingrate for a son. Gabe had come back even more determined that something was wrong— "If he bought those for my mother, I'd have seen them on her; that woman liked jewelry"—and now he was driving everybody crazy, mumbling about it. It really wasn't healthy for him to obsess on the past, Nell thought, and she did everything she could to distract him, including badgering him about the reception room couch, which was only getting more slovenly as the weeks passed. All they needed was for one really heavy client to drop down on the damn thing and they'd be picking splinters out of a lawsuit.

And it wasn't as though they didn't have enough to think about without some phantom diamonds. The agency was swamped with work, including a new wrinkle on an old client when Riley got a phone call and came out of his office to say, "Gina wants us to follow Harold tonight. I'm calling it the Hot Dinner."

"Gina thinks Harold is cheating?" Nell said.

"I think he owes her a couple," Riley said. "But I don't think she feels that way."

"Yeah," Nell said. "People get so sensitive about adultery."

The following Monday, Nell was typing the Hot Dinner report—Harold was definitely cheating—when Suze came in. "Hey," Nell said. "You're too early if you want lunch."

"Not lunch," Suze said, and Nell looked at her closer and went cold.

"What's wrong?"

"I need to hire the McKennas," she said. "Family tradition."

"Oh, no."

"Oh, I think so." Suze nodded toward Gabe's office. "Can it be him? I don't think I can face—"

Riley opened the door to his office and stood in the doorway. "Thought I heard your voice."

Nell looked from him to Suze. "Suze just dropped by."

Suze took a deep breath. "I need a detective."

"Okay," Riley said. "Stay home tonight until I call you."

Suze nodded and opened her purse. "How much retainer—"

"This one's on the house. Just be home." He went back inside and closed the door, and Suze turned to Nell and swallowed.

"He didn't even ask me what I wanted."

"I noticed that. Are you okay?"

"No," Suze said and sank down on the couch, tears spilling from her eyes. "We had a big fight last night about me working at The Cup. I refused to quit and he walked out. And he didn't come back at all last night."

"Hang on," Nell said, and ran to Gabe's office to get his Glenlivet. "Here," she said to Suze, splashing some into a Susie Cooper cup. "Drink this."

Suze gulped some of the whiskey and then inhaled sharply.

"Take it easy," Nell said. "Gabe only drinks the good stuff."

"I really thought I'd be different. Not like Abby and Vicki."

"You are different." Nell patted her shoulder and hated Jack. "Maybe he's not cheating. You don't know."

"I know," Suze said. "I just want to know for sure."

When Suze had gone, Nell banged on the door of Riley's office and went in. "What the hell is going on?"

"Jack Dysart Is Cheating on His Wife, Part Three," Riley said. "Sequels suck."

"Don't get cute with me," Nell leaned over his desk. "How long have you known?"

"A couple of months."

"And Gabe?"

"A couple of months."

"And you didn't tell me."

"Do we look stupid?"

"Yes," Nell said. "More than stupid. Why the hell—"

"Because you would have told Suze. Remember the first rule?"

"Don't pull that junior high crap on me," Nell said. *"This is my best friend."*

"Which is why we didn't tell you." Riley sat behind his desk, impassive and calm. "You couldn't have done a damn thing for her, anyway."

"I could have let her know—"

"She knew," Riley said. "She just didn't want to know. You knew before that Christmas that your husband was screwing around."

"I did not."

"You knew the whole time you were explaining to people that he hadn't cheated. You just didn't want to know." Riley sighed. "It's a coping device. I can show photos of a spouse cheating and if the client doesn't want to believe it, she won't. Or he. Denial goes both ways." He stood up and came around the desk. "Except by the time they hire us, they're usually ready to face the truth. That's why Suze didn't show up until now. So tonight I'll show her the truth. On the house." He put his hand on her shoulder. "Trust me."

Nell stepped away from him. "Never again." She turned to see Gabe standing in the doorway.

"You know," he said, "I'm not the jealous type, but—"

"Go to hell," she said and walked past him to get her purse.

Riley said, "Jack Dysart."

"Oh, hell," Gabe said and came after her. "Wait a minute."

"You knew and you didn't tell me," Nell said, purse in hand, trying to push past him to get the door.

"Yeah," Gabe said, blocking her. "Would you just listen, please?"

"No," Nell said, and Gabe grabbed her arm and dragged her into his office, slamming the door behind him.

"Listen to me," he said when she turned on him, ready to yell. "We found out doing the Quarterly Report for Trevor back in November."

"It wasn't in the report *I* typed," Nell said.

"We gave you a dummy."

"I am a dummy," Nell said. "I thought we—"

Gabe pointed his finger at her and said, "Don't even start on that. What we are has nothing to do with the agency."

"What are you talking about? We are the agency. The agency and sex. You lied to me and you betrayed Suze."

"No." Gabe said. "We lied to you so you wouldn't betray the agency."

Nell felt cold. "So you and Riley are the agency and I'm not?"

Gabe closed his eyes. "Look, it's simple. We didn't tell you because you'd tell her. You know the rules."

"I know the rules, and I know you break them all the time," Nell said. "This wasn't about the rules. This was about you keeping me out, you not trusting me. Well, the hell with you."

"*You would have told Suze*," Gabe said, but she'd already detoured around him and was heading out the door to Suze.

*   *   *

Riley called Suze that night at ten and picked her up fifteen minutes later. He took her up High Street to the campus and then parked in front of a bar off a side street.

"Here?" she said when they were inside. The place was a typical undergrad hangout, dirty, noisy, and cramped.

"Here," Riley said and went to the bar while Suze looked around and thought, *So this is what I missed by not being single as an undergraduate*. It didn't cause much of a pang, but then her stomach was already tied in knots so pangs were probably not physically possible. She found a booth and slid into it, taking care not to snag her sweater sleeve on the splintered tabletop.

My husband is cheating on me.

Riley came back with two mugs of beer in one hand and a bowl of unshelled peanuts in the other. He slid one of the mugs across to her and sat down.

"I don't see why we're here," Suze said, and Riley said, "Wait," so she shut up and sipped her beer. After a long silence broken only by the crack of peanut shells, she said, "Do you have to be this quiet?"

"Yes," Riley said, his jaw tight.

"Are you mad at me? Is it because I made a pass at you on New Year's Eve?"

"No."

She looked around the bar and thought, *I will not cry*. "You're not quiet with Nell."

"Nell is different."

"Because you slept with her."

"No," Riley said, pretty much ignoring her to look at the crowd, and Suze felt her temper rise.

"I can't believe you took advantage of her," she said, watching him to see if he'd flinch. By God, he was going to pay attention to her tonight or she'd know the reason why.

"I didn't take advantage of her."

"You seduced her," Suze said, and Riley turned to her with great and obvious patience and said, "Shut up."

"She said you were a really gentle lover," Suze said, trying to get some kind of reaction, any kind of reaction. "I find that hard to believe, considering the way you treat me."

"Nell was fragile. You're not." Riley cracked another peanut.

"I'm fragile. You wouldn't believe how fragile I am right now." She watched him crack another peanut, and added, "But since it's me, you're not inspired like you were with Nell. I'm not the type you'd be gentle with."

"No, you're the type I'd fuck against a wall," Riley said, and she slung her beer in his face.

He turned to her, the beer dripping onto his shirt. "Feel better now?"

"That was a lousy thing to say," Suze said, her heart racing.

He picked up a napkin and wiped some of the beer from his face. "You wanted a fight."

"Not like that." Suze handed him another napkin. "Is my husband cheating on me?"

"Yes."

"How old is she?"

Riley looked at her with sympathy, and that was worse than anything.

Suze closed her eyes in pain. "Oh, God, call me a whore again, just don't look at me like that."

"I didn't call you a whore. She's twenty-two."

Twenty-two. "Well, that explains it, I guess." She looked down at herself, remembering the photos Riley had taken fifteen years before. "Nothing on me looks twenty-two." She reached for her beer and realized she'd thrown it all at Riley, but before she could sit back, he'd shoved his mug in front of her. "Thank you."

She stole a look at him while she drank and found him still watching the room. Even in a beer-splashed shirt, he looked dependable. Big and dependable. Great hands, Nell had said. Maybe she could get him to beat up Jack. Of course, what she really wanted was to beat up a twenty-two-year-old. "Could I take her?"

Riley turned back to her. "What? In a fight?" He surveyed her. "Probably. You'd have rage on your side."

"How long?"

"For you to take her?"

Suze shook her head. "How long has he been seeing her?"

"End of November is the first we knew."

"And you didn't tell me?"

"No."

"And Nell didn't tell me."

"Nell didn't know until today."

"Why not? If—"

"Because we knew she'd tell you." Riley took the mug back. "We found out about it working another job. We do not go causing trouble, so we did not tell either of you." He drank, and Suze felt betrayed.

"I worked for you," she said finally.

"You quit because your husband threw a temper tantrum," Riley said. "Not that we're not grateful. He called the night before you quit and threatened to pull business from us if we didn't fire you, so you saved us having to compromise our ethics."

"But you would have."

"Suze, you'd worked for us for a couple of months. Ogilvie and Dysart have been giving us work for years. It wasn't much of a choice."

"You dumped me just like he's dumping me."

Riley shoved the mug back to her. "Drink up."

She reached for the mug and then froze as Jack came through a door in the back marked "Game Room." There was another woman with him, and she was young and she had dark hair, but it wasn't until they were farther into the room that Suze recognized her. "That's *Olivia*. That's his partner's *daughter*."

"Yeah, Jack goes for what's close and easy," Riley said,

and Suze glared at him. "Not you, dummy. Olivia Ogilvie."

Jack pulled out a chair for Olivia, and she laughed up at him as she sat. He bent and kissed her on the top of her head, and Suze was torn between pain and rage.

"I'll kill him."

"I'd work out a plan on that one," Riley said. "Unless, of course, you want to go to jail."

Jack went to the bar, and Suze watched Olivia. She wasn't strictly beautiful, but she was young and slender, and Suze felt like a lump. "No wonder."

Riley glanced at her. "What? Olivia? Stop beating yourself up. You're a class act. She's a promiscuous moron."

"Sort of like Jack," Suze said savagely, and Riley laughed.

"Exactly," he said.

Suze felt a little cheered, even as she watched Olivia. "I thought you wanted to fuck me against a wall. That doesn't say class act to me."

He didn't say anything and she turned to see what was wrong. "You make too many assumptions," he told her.

"Is he sleeping with her?"

"That assumption you can make."

"Are you positive?"

"Yes."

His voice was sure, and Suze felt sick. He'd seen them, and now she could see them, coupling in her mind's eye, and it was horrible, gross, disgusting, shameful . . . excruciating.

Riley nodded toward the bar where Jack was standing. "You want to confront him?"

The thought made Suze sicker. "No."

"Then my work is done. I'll take you home."

Jack sat down across from Olivia and raised his glass. What would he do if he glanced over and saw her? He'd told her once that he always knew when she walked into a room, even if his back was to her, he always knew.

The bastard.

"Yes," Suze said. "Take me home."

They were halfway across the bar when she looked back at Jack one more time and caught his eye. He froze for a moment and then put his beer down and headed for them, his face flushed.

"Hold it," she said to Riley, and he looked back and said, "Oh, hell."

"I knew it," Jack said when he was in front of them. "I knew—"

"I hired him," Suze said flatly, cutting him off. "Just like Abby and Vicki. This guy is going to retire on your lack of morals."

Jack looked past her to Riley, lowering his head a little, so mad he must have forgotten he was there with somebody else, too. *Who the hell does he think he is?* Suze thought, and then he took a step toward her, and Riley pushed her out from between them, blocking her from Jack with his shoulder.

"Don't even think about it," he said to Jack, his voice loaded with contempt. "I'll take you apart while they both watch."

"You've been waiting for this," Jack said, sounding as cocky as ever. "Fifteen years I've had her and you've wanted her. You think you're going to get her now?"

"I think now she gets what she wants," Riley said. "I think that's not you anymore. And I think it's about time."

"I want to go home," Suze said to Riley, and Riley turned his back on Jack, putting his hand on the small of her back to push her gently toward the door.

"It's my home, too," Jack said from behind her. "I'll—"

"Not anymore," Suze said. "The dead bolts will be on." She looked past him to Olivia, watching them with her tongue touching her top lip like a little cat, and then she turned toward the door, Riley behind her like a wall, blocking out disaster, steadying her when she stumbled.

When they were outside in the cold, he said, "Are you okay?"

"No," she said. "Take me home."

When he pulled up in front of her house, she got out and was surprised when he did, too. "Go on," he said, giving her a gentle push toward the house. "Not a good time for you to be alone. Call Nell and I'll stay with you until she gets here."

She unlocked the door and let him into the house, trying not to cry, trying to concentrate on her anger. "You probably think I deserve this."

"Did I say that?" Riley said, annoyed.

"I did it, too, I did this to Vicki."

"Aren't you in enough pain without beating yourself up?" Riley said, following her into the dining room. "Jack's a lowlife asshole, he's always been a lowlife asshole, and he always will be a lowlife asshole. Blame him."

"How about you?" Suze said, wanting to fight with somebody. "You spied on me in a motel room. You're not exactly on high moral ground yourself."

"I was working. You were the one stripping for somebody else's husband in a rented cheerleader uniform." Riley stared at her china cabinet. "What the hell are those things with feet?"

"I didn't rent it," Suze said. "It was my uniform. I was a senior cheerleader."

Riley exhaled on a sort of sigh. "I don't believe you. Here's a guy in his forties—"

"He was thirty-nine."

"—chasing a high school senior. That didn't strike you as wrong?"

Suze sat down, miserable. "Nothing about him struck me as wrong. He was the most amazing man I'd ever met." *Oh, Jack.*

Riley snorted. "Pederast."

Suze frowned at him, distracted for a moment. "I was eighteen. And weren't you just dating a college junior?"

"Don't change the subject."

"And you're what? Thirty-five?"

"Four," Riley said. "It didn't work out. She was too so-phisticated for me."

"Hard to believe." Suze slumped back into her chair. "Give Jack her number. Maybe he'll leave Olivia for her." She felt her throat tighten and swallowed. "You know, I really believed him when he said I was different. When I turned thirty and he didn't leave the way he'd left Abby and Vicki, everybody was amazed, but I wasn't because I knew he loved me." Her eyes got hot and she could hear her voice thicken. "And then he left me anyway." She bit her lip to keep from crying—crying in front of Riley would be just too damn vulnerable, the hell with him—and then she heard him say, "Oh, hell."

"I'm not crying," she said.

"I know I'm going to regret this," Riley said, "but he didn't leave you."

Suze glared up at him through her tears. "He didn't? Well, that's great news. What the hell is he doing with Olivia then?"

"He's making a preemptive strike. He's been faithful for the whole fourteen years he's been married to you. I know because I tried my damnedest to find another woman. There wasn't one. There really isn't one now. He knows you're going to leave him, so he's booking first. It makes him look like a scum, but it doesn't make him look like a middle-aged loser."

Suze surged up from her chair, enraged. "*I wasn't going to leave him. I loved him.* You don't know—"

"Did he want you to get a job?" Riley said.

"Oh, come on. Sitting on a barstool while you eaves-drop is not a job. It's not even an adventure."

"Did he object?"

"Yes," Suze said, getting madder as Riley got calmer. "So you're saying I should have stayed unemployed—"

"What did you do with your paycheck?" Riley said.

"What difference—"

"You opened a checking account, didn't you? Not a joint account. One just for you."

"I was making a hundred bucks a night," Suze snarled. "I don't think he missed it."

"You got a job without telling him, you opened a checking account without telling him—"

"Women do that every day. It does not constitute desertion."

"Who bought the cups with the feet?" Riley said, pointing toward the china cabinet and Suze saw her twenty-seven little pottery cups running in front of the china, running *over* the china, the whole cabinet in flight.

"If I was afraid somebody was going to dump me," Riley said, "and she started to collect those things, I think I'd start dropping them."

"He did." Suze swallowed. "He dropped one, but I glued it back together."

"When did you start buying them?" Riley said.

"September." Suze let her shoulders slump, rocking a little on her feet, and then she felt Riley's hand on her back, warm and solid.

"He didn't start seeing Olivia until the end of November," Riley said.

She winced at the name, the pain slicing through her because she wasn't braced for it. "If he wanted to leave, he didn't have to go to her," she said. "You can't tell me that he didn't look at her and notice she was younger and firmer and—"

"No guy would prefer Olivia to you," Riley said, sounding disgusted with her. "Stop wallowing."

Suze ignored him and faced the truth: She'd ended her own marriage, and now she didn't even have Olivia to blame for it. *Jack.* "I hate this." She turned around to face Riley, a little surprised to find that he wasn't standing close. He'd seemed so close. "And it's all my fault."

"No, it isn't," Riley said, exasperated. "You married a

guy who was so controlling that normal everyday life threatened him. You quit your job and close the checking account and then what? You going to sit in this dining room for the rest of your life, looking at those blue plates? Because I'm pretty sure you'll have to give up all those cups with feet, too. They creep me out, and I'm not trying to hold on to you."

Give up the cups? "I need Nell," Suze said and burst into tears.

"Hold on." Riley backed up a step. "Just *wait a second*." She heard him retreat into the kitchen and dial the phone. *I traded in the only man I've ever loved for a checking account and a bunch of egg cups*, she thought, and then she put her head down on the dining room table and howled.

A few minutes later, when the worst of it was over, she lifted her face and Riley stuck a box of Kleenex under her nose. "Nell's on her way," he told her, sounding as if he couldn't wait.

"Sorry about the crying," she said and took a tissue to blow her nose. "That must have been awful."

"Yes, it was. Don't do that again. Would you like a drink? Or something?"

She sniffed again and tried to smile up at him. He looked trapped and wary. "Oh, for heaven's sake, Riley, I just cried, that's all. My marriage died, I'm allowed to cry."

"Sure you are. Save it for Nell. She'll be here in about half an hour. You sure you don't want a drink? Because I do."

"Why half an hour? It's not that far."

"Gabe was with her at her place. They were fighting over us not telling you and then they . . . stopped. She's getting dressed."

There, Suze thought as she sniffed again. Nell had found somebody else. She hadn't curled up and died when her marriage ended that Christmas, she'd—

"Oh, God," Suze said. Nell had waited *two years*. It was going to be another *two years* before she wasn't alone again.

And all Nell had had to get over was that worthless Tim. She was going to have get over *Jack*. *"Oh, God."*

"What?" Riley said.

"It's going to be two years before I have sex again," Suze wailed.

"I'll just get those drinks," Riley said and escaped into the kitchen.

Chapter Fifteen

Suze sat on the stairs at midnight and patted Marlene while she listened to Nell tell Jack exactly what kind of cheating, disgusting, degenerate weasel he was through the locked door. She'd put the dead bolt on, and she wouldn't let him in, and eventually, he'd given up and gone somewhere else, probably to Olivia.

"Tomorrow you get a lawyer," she told Suze, coming up the stairs to her.

"Tomorrow I have to go to work," Suze said. "I have a teashop to run."

"You can call a lawyer from the teashop," Nell said, and then stood by her the next day while she did.

Suze's days dissolved into a blur of blended teas and Margie's cookies, drinks at the bar as a decoy for Riley, painful discussions with the lawyer, and long talks with Nell, who never got tired of listening, even when Suze kept going back relentlessly to the same themes.

"I'd be ready to kill me," she told Nell on Valentine's Day. "I know I keep saying the same things, but I just can't seem to get unstuck. I know I should file for divorce, the lawyer says it's time, but I just can't seem to—" She broke off. "I'm so *sorry*."

"You're doing better than I did," Nell said. "I didn't say anything at all for a year and a half. What do you want for dinner?"

They were at Nell's, something that made Suze feel guilty because here was Nell, finally happy with a good man to love her, and there was Suze, planted in the middle, like the toad in the fairy tale, spoiling everybody's good times. "Listen, it's Valentine's Day. I can go home."

"Over my dead body," Nell said. "How about stir-fry? I can do that fast."

"Sure," Suze said and wandered into the living room to pat Marlene again. It was amazing how therapeutic patting a dachshund could be, even one with an attitude as bad as Marlene's. She stopped by Nell's china cabinet and looked at Clarice's dishes. The Secrets houses stood alone on the hill with their lonely smoke plumes and depressed the hell out of her, so she looked at the Stroud cartouches instead, the cheerful little orange-roofed house inside the perfect little squares. For some reason they were worse, that lonely little single house trapped inside the square, everything so tidy, everything so impossible. Maybe that was what she was doing, trying to keep everything tidy, outlined in black. Your husband cheats, so you get rid of him. That was cartouche life, not real life. Real life was messy, complicated by doubts and regret.

Maybe she should go home and call Jack. Maybe they should talk without the lawyers there.

"You okay?" Nell said when Suze came out to the kitchen to help set the table.

"Maybe I gave up too soon," Suze said. When Nell didn't say anything, she turned to look at her. "What do you think?"

"I think that whatever you decide, I'm behind you one hundred percent," Nell said. "And Margie will be behind you one hundred percent with a thermos of soy milk."

"What would I do without you?" Suze said.

"That you'll never have to know," Nell said, putting a plateful of food in front of her. "Now eat. I worry you'll be as dumb as I was and do the sleepwalking thing."

For all Nell worried about her, Suze worried about Nell. Working at The Cup with Margie and moonlighting at the agency gave Suze a ringside seat on Nell's new relationship, and as far as she could see, if Nell didn't wise up, they were both going to grow old alone.

Because in spite of her obvious ecstasy, Nell wasn't living a new life. Nell had remade her old life, running her new boss the way she'd run her old boss. The problem was, her old boss had been a wuss and her new boss wasn't. Nell would ask for something, Gabe would say no, and Nell would work around him. Then Gabe would yell, Nell would drag him off to bed, and the whole thing would start all over again with something else Nell wanted, including her last three great goals, the ones even she was afraid to do an end run for: the couch, the business cards, and the new window. She and Gabe were either fighting or making love or on the way to one or the other, and while Suze could understand the exhilaration, she couldn't understand how they kept going. She'd have needed medication long ago.

"I don't understand them," Suze said to Riley when he came into the teashop to get away from the arguing one afternoon. She poured him a cup of tea and set out the plate of broken cookies she kept behind the counter for him, and he picked up half a star and nodded.

"You had it right," Riley said. "They're both kissers. And if Nell doesn't knock it off, they're going to have real problems."

"Oh, it's *Nell's* fault, is it?" Suze said.

"Yes, it is, and I'm not fighting with you so don't even start." Riley bit into the cookie, and Suze took a deep breath and calmed down. "Gabe owns the agency," Riley went on, "she's his secretary, she doesn't get to make decisions and just assume he'll rubber-stamp them. I can't believe the crap he's let her get away with so far, but it's getting to him."

"How can you tell?" Suze said. "He looks the same to me."

"I can tell because they fight every goddamn day, and he doesn't need that with this thing about his dad driving

him crazy. He's going to crack, and I don't want Nell to
be his breaking point. She's good for him, or she would
be if she quit acting like she owned the place."

"Yeah, those pushy women," Suze said. "You gotta keep
slapping them down or they'll run right over you."

"Why do I talk to you?" Riley said and went back to
the agency, his cup still in his hand, while Suze sat over
her tea and broken cookies and tried not to think about
the mess everything was in.

The argument in Gabe's office had ended the way their
arguments usually ended, and Nell was feeling wonderful.

"You know," Gabe said, putting his pants back on, "my
coffee breaks used to be a lot more relaxing."

"It's the caffeine." Nell stretched naked in front of his
desk to feel her muscles move. "I used to be modest."

"I must have missed that era." Gabe tossed her sweater
to her and she didn't bother to catch it. "Not that I'd be
particularly interested in it."

She walked over to the bookcase, feeling the muscles in
her legs flex. There was nothing like sex to remind you
that you were an animal. Damn, she felt good. She drew
her fingers along the edge of one of the shelves and said,
"I bet this office has seen a lot of naked secretaries."

"I don't think so," Gabe said, looking around for something. "Most women insist on beds."

"So I'm bringing something new to the tradition," Nell
said, moving along to the coatrack.

"God, yes. Where the hell did you throw my shirt?"

"Over my head, I believe." She unhooked the old blue
pinstriped jacket from the coatrack and slipped into it,
shimmying a little to let the silk lining slide on her skin as
she wrapped the jacket around her. "You should wear this.
You'd look great in it."

He stopped looking for his shirt. "Not as great as you
do."

"Yeah?" She smiled at him, so happy she felt like bouncing. She caught sight of the cassette player and went over and pushed Play, and Dino began singing "Ain't That a Kick in the Head." She laughed and did a fast two-step to it to "I kissed her and she kissed me," and then jumped when Gabe caught her hand a couple of bars later and spun her around into his arms.

"You can dance?" she said, amazed as he moved with her, as graceful as he was shirtless.

"I can if you let me lead," he said, switching steps on her and laughing when she caught up right away.

"What fun is that, following somebody around all the time?" She danced away a step and he caught her again.

"Well, you get my arms around you," he said, and when she cuddled closer, he tightened his grip on her and put his cheek against her hair.

"Big price to pay," she murmured into his chest.

"It's just dancing, Nell," he said, swaying with her.

"It's all dancing," she said and slipped out of his arms to do a jazzy shuffle, her hands in the pockets of the jacket, pulling it tight against her body, feeling free again.

He leaned against the bookcase and watched her, and she missed his arms. "There must be some way you can dance with both people leading."

"You can," Gabe said. "It's called sex."

When the song ended, she stopped, breathless, and stretched her arms out to feel her muscles, and he pulled her back to slow dance to "You Belong to Me."

"Just give me one," he said, and she relaxed into his arms, grateful for the way he felt against her.

"You're really good at this," she said.

"My mom taught me."

He sounded sad, and she pulled him closer. "I'll tell you what," she said. "I'll let you lead if you don't slow me down."

"Deal," he said and kissed her, still moving to the music, and when she broke the kiss, she put her cheek against his chest and thought, *So this is what it's like to be in love*. Except he'd never said he loved her. They'd been together for more than two months now, and he never said it. He held her closer, and she had one small moment of panic—that it would end, that he would never love her, that one day he'd say, "The fights are just too much," that she'd lose this feeling—and then she thought, *Well, at least I'll have had it*.

But later that night, when Gabe was spooned against her back, half asleep, she knew that wasn't enough. She needed forever, and she needed to hear it. She knew that was desperate and pathetic of her, she knew it was too soon, but she been torturing herself with a thousand reasons why he didn't love her, why he'd never love her, and she wanted reassurance now. The worst of the reasons was, *Maybe he still loves Chloe*. He never talked about Chloe, wasn't particularly interested in the postcards she kept sending, but Nell knew Gabe didn't show his emotions much. Maybe he was repressing his longing for Chloe. Maybe he pretended *she* was Chloe when they made love.

She bumped her rear end against him to get his attention, and he stirred and patted her hip. "Do you ever think about Chloe?"

"Sure," he mumbled against her neck. His hand curved above her head, his fingers caught in her hair, and she snuggled back closer, wanting him more tangled with her, more caught.

"When?" she said.

He moved against her back and let his other hand fall down across her stomach. "When I smell the almond cookies," he said and yawned.

Suze baked almond cookies every day. "Do you miss her?"

"Umhmm."

She could hear the sleep in his voice. "Do you wish she was back?"

"She'll be back." He yawned again. "She just wanted to see something besides Ohio for a while."

He was too tired to be ducking her, so she decided on the blunt approach. "Do you still love her?"

"Umhm."

"Oh." Nell felt sick. "Do you—"

Gabe sighed and pushed himself up on one elbow and away from her, and she fell back flat onto the bed. "No," he said, looking down at her, still half asleep, "not like you," and then he kissed her, and she was so startled, she held onto him, even when he ended the kiss.

"Not like me?" she said.

"I love you. Not like Chloe. Different."

He loves me. "Oh," she said, swallowing. *How different? Don't ask.*

"Chloe was easy," he said, as if he'd heard her. "Chloe was sweet. Chloe did exactly what I told her to. Chloe never caused me any trouble at all."

"Now say something nice about me," Nell said, feeling panic start.

"You drive me crazy," Gabe said, finally awake, sliding his hand across her stomach. "You never do what I tell you to, and you challenge everything I say, and I wish to hell you'd stop it. You make me so mad I yell at you, and then I look at you, and I can't get enough of you, and I know I never will. If I come down to the office and you're not there, the whole day goes to hell. If I'm having a lousy day and you come in, the sun comes out. I—"

"*I love you.*" Nell sat up next to him and clutched his arm. "Like *nothing* ever before. You let me be strong. I don't have to pretend. I don't feel *guilty* with you."

"Honey, I don't *let* you be anything," he said, with laughter in his voice. "You just are."

She kissed him, holding his face in her hands, loving him so much she ached with it. "I'm sorry about the third degree," she whispered. "I'll let you get some sleep now."

"Like hell you will," Gabe said. "You wake me up, you

put me back to sleep." He bent her back down into her pillows, and she curled around him, thinking, *He loves me, this one's forever*, even while she knew it might not be, that nobody knew forever until the end. *That'll have to be enough*, she thought, and then she closed her eyes and loved him back.

The next morning, Gabe woke with his arm draped over Nell and fought through a fog of sleep, trying to figure out what had jarred him awake. Marlene was sitting up at the foot of the bed, her ears pricked, and then he heard something that sounded like muffled screaming coming from next door.

"What the hell?" he said and rolled out of bed, grabbing for his pants,

Nell sat up, and said, her voice sleep-fogged, too, "Doris."

By the time he got downstairs, Doris was pounding on the front door, practically falling in when he opened it. "What?" he said, and she said, "The basement. Oh, my God."

"*What?*" he said, and she said, "In the freezer," and started to shriek again. He passed her over to Nell and went cautiously into her apartment and down the narrow basement stairs, thinking, *The freezer? What the hell?* but when he walked past a table full of pinecone wreaths and opened the narrow chest freezer, he sucked in his breath and almost screamed, too.

Lynnie was crammed in there, blue and desiccated and long dead, on the run no more.

"How long?" Nell said, when the police had gone, leaving yellow crime scene tape all over Doris's door, and Doris had left for her sister's, claiming she wouldn't spend another night in that house. "How long had she been there?"

"Long time," Gabe said, splashing Glenlivet into a glass for her. "My guess is, since last September. She was going off to meet her lawyer after you talked to her, right?"

"That's what she said." Since last September. *I moved in on top of her body.*

"And we never heard from her again." Gabe handed her the glass. "Drink up. You look like hell."

"You didn't tell the police about O&D," Nell said and sipped the scotch.

"Lynnie's blackmailing O&D is a guess," Gabe said. "I think it's a good guess, but it's not fact."

"But the embezzlement from you, that was a fact."

"What's your point?"

"You're protecting Trevor, but not yourself."

"No," Gabe said. "I'm giving the police all the information I have. They want facts, not hunches."

"You don't want your dad's name smeared," Nell said. "You're afraid Lynnie was blackmailing Trevor and Jack about Helena's death and you're afraid the police will find out your dad did it."

"Don't interfere in what you don't understand." Gabe went into the kitchen to put the Glenlivet back in the cupboard, and when he came out, he was putting his coat on. "I have to go talk to Riley. I'll see you later."

Nell watched him go and thought, *You're so smart about everything else, but you can't let go of the past.* She shook her head and stroked Marlene's silky head and tried not to think about Lynnie or anybody else for a while. *So much pain everywhere*, she thought, and then Marlene snuggled closer, and she felt a little comforted.

"She was *frozen*?" Suze said the next day at brunch.

"I'm so glad I never use my freezer," Margie said.

"Stewart wanted one because he liked steaks, but I think fresh food is important."

Nell looked at her, dumbfounded, and Suze nodded toward Margie's orange juice glass. "Mimosa," she said to Nell. "She ordered before you got here. That's her third."

"If she'd been a vegetarian," Margie said, oblivious, "she wouldn't have died."

"It wasn't her freezer," Nell said, not amused. "It was her landlady's freezer. She didn't have a freezer."

"So somebody just put her in there?" Suze sat back. "At least Jack left me, he didn't freeze me."

"Gabe said it looked like there was a bruise on her forehead, but it was hard to tell. She was . . ." Nell swallowed, thinking about what Lynnie must have looked like, and Margie shoved her mimosa toward her.

"Here," she said. "It helps."

Nell took the glass and drank.

"Are you okay?" Suze said. "I didn't realize you knew her that well."

"I didn't," Nell said, pushing Margie's glass back to her. "Just that one morning. But I liked her. She was a fighter. She fought dirty, but I think she was probably fighting with guys who fought dirty."

"What guys?" Margie said. "Was she engaged?"

"Gabe thinks she was blackmailing somebody," Suze said, and Nell kicked her on the ankle. Margie didn't need to know the "somebody" included her father and her fiancé.

Margie looked sadly at the bottom of her empty mimosa glass. "Somebody blackmailed me once."

"What?" Nell said.

Margie waved to the waitress. "Another mimosa, please."

"Make that a black coffee," Suze told the waitress, who looked at Margie and nodded.

"Who tried to blackmail you?" Nell said to Margie.

"Some woman." Margie sighed as the waitress brought

her a cup and filled it. When the waitress was gone, she said, "She wanted twenty thousand dollars, but I didn't have it. Budge says I should declare Stewart dead now, before I get any broker, but it just seems wrong. I mean, he's missing, not dead. I think."

"Margie," Suze said, her voice carefully reasonable. "Why did she want twenty thousand dollars?"

"She said I'd killed Stewart." Margie took her thermos of soy milk out of her bag and topped up her coffee. "She said if I didn't pay her, she'd tell everybody." She sipped her coffee until the level had dropped half an inch, and then she poured more soy milk in. "Which was ridiculous. I mean, clearly we didn't know the same people. What did I care if she told her friends that?"

"Just how hard did you hit him?" Suze said.

"When?" Nell said.

"Any time," Margie said, sipping her soy and caffeine. "I was never going to know her friends."

Nell took a deep breath. "No, when did she call?"

"Last year." Margie put her cup down and went back to her vegetarian eggs Benedict. "I never make this because the Hollandaise sauce is such a pain."

"When last year?" Nell said.

"Hmmm? Oh, it was before you got your job because I was worried about you not eating and I was looking at a recipe for cheese crepes when she called. I remember looking at the picture when she asked for the money. Do you like crepes?"

"Margie," Nell said. "When did she call?"

Margie frowned, thinking. "When did you get your job?"

"September," Nell said.

Margie shrugged. "Then it was August. But it didn't matter because she never called back."

"Did you tell anybody?" Nell said.

"Daddy and Budge," Margie said, reaching for the coffee again. "They said it was a prank. Budge said to forget it, it was over. So I did." She sipped from her cup and then said, "Oh. Was it Lynnie?"

"Hard to say," Nell said. "But it doesn't matter. Budge was right, it's over."

"Budge is always right," Margie said and put her cup down. "He says we should get married as soon as I declare Stewart dead. It's really a problem because I would like the insurance money, but it's wrong to declare Stewart dead if he isn't, and once he's dead I'll have to tell Budge I don't want to marry him, and that's going to be awful. Could I have one more mimosa, please?"

Suze signaled the waitress. "Three mimosas," she told her.

"You, too?" Nell said.

"It's the freezer," Suze said. "If he'd just killed her, that would have been bad enough, but he put her body in the freezer."

"Actually, it's worse than that," Nell said. "Gabe said the bruise on her forehead didn't look bad, that she probably hadn't been killed first, that whoever hit her had probably put her in the freezer unconscious but alive and she froze to death."

"Oh, God," Suze said.

"That's like Jack," Margie said. "He put you in that big house and didn't want you to work or anything. He froze you to death, too."

Suze winced and Nell said, "Margie, shut up," and Margie jerked back a little, looking hurt. "I'm sorry," Nell said, "I'm really sorry I said that. This thing with Lynnie is just . . . I liked her and somebody killed her." She took a deep breath and tried again. "I felt so stupid about sitting around for a year and a half after Tim, and I really admired her for fighting back."

"Don't feel stupid," Suze said gloomily. "I understand perfectly."

"But Lynnie didn't sit around," Nell said. "She went after people. And they killed her. I mean, you really have to think, are those our choices? Sit still and be nice or get killed?"

"More women get killed by men they know than by strangers," Margie said. "It was on Oprah. I like Oprah, but sometimes she's depressing."

Suze let her breath out. "Lynnie was blackmailing people, for heaven's sake. That's a high-risk career."

"It was some guy who did it," Nell said. "I will bet you anything. Some guy from her past who had betrayed her. She was getting even with him."

"Jack," Suze said.

"I don't know." Nell stared at her French toast. "Do you think Jack would kill somebody?"

"No," Suze said. "But he's got the betrayal thing down pat."

They sat silent until the waitress brought their mimosas, and then Margie said, "Do you think you could come by and show me that eBay thing you were talking about? The place that has the Fiestaware? You can sell things on there, too, right?"

"Sure," Suze said. "You can look at the running cups, too."

"No," Margie said. "They're not my style."

The police came to talk to Gabe again on Monday, and he told them the truth: He didn't know who'd hit Lynnie. Then they questioned Nell in the outer office, and that made him edgy; they couldn't possibly think she had anything to do with it. It took everything he had not to say, "Get away from her," and by the time they left, he was as annoyed at Nell as he was with them. If she hadn't taken it upon herself to go after the damn money, she'd never have met Lynnie, she wouldn't have been around when Doris had found her, and she wouldn't be on the police's top-ten favorite witness list now.

So when she came in, he scowled at her, and when she

said, "The cops almost fell through the couch, we have to get a new one," his temper flared.

"*No.*"

"Gabe, it's horrible. The rest of this place looks great, but that—"

"The rest of the place does not look great, the rest of the place looks like every goddamn office in the city. The couch stays."

She folded her arms, her deceptively delicate face scowling at him. She was about as delicate as a sledgehammer. "Let me guess. Your dad bought the couch."

He closed his eyes. "Why do you have to change everything? I don't even recognize that outer office anymore. It looks like some fucking doctor's office."

"It's tasteful," Nell said.

"It's slick," Gabe said. "And it's not me and it's not Riley—"

"And it's not your dad," Nell finished. "And it's also not 1955."

"And it's my office," Gabe said. "Not yours." He leaned forward, staring her down. "Remember this. You are just a secretary. You—" He stopped because she'd gone even paler than usual.

"I am not just a secretary," she said, her voice low and breathless. "*Nobody* is just a secretary, you *jerk.*"

Gabe cast his eyes to the ceiling, knowing that if he looked at her, he'd lose it. "Goddamn it, Nell, *this is my business.*"

"I know it's your business. You tell me that every damn day. I'm just trying to run it for you. I'm an office manager. You have an office to manage. I'm doing that. If you'd stop getting in my way—"

"I'm not Tim," Gabe said, and she shut up. "Stop assuming this is the insurance agency and that you can run me the way you ran him."

"I'm not Chloe. Stop assuming you can run me the way you ran her. What is it with men? Budge is making Margie quit the teashop because he'll worry too much if she's down here with murderers. What do you guys think, that you just acquire us and put us in the background and that we'll just *stay there*, so you can be comfy?"

He drew in a deep breath so he wouldn't yell again, using everything he had *not* to yell again, and she pressed her lips together and said, "Lynnie was right. You'd use me without even noticing me if you could," and left, her back poker-straight, practically shaking with fury.

Riley came in a minute later when Gabe was still trying to get his temper back. He didn't use her, goddamn it, he—

"The cops weren't too bad," Riley said, "and I just got a very interesting phone call." Then he looked at Gabe's face and said, "Oh, hell, tell me you're not fighting again."

"The couch," Gabe said, grimly. "Nell has problems with the chain of command. She'll learn."

"I wouldn't count on it." Riley closed the door and came in to sit across from Gabe. "Are you all right? You look like hell."

Gabe realized he was sweating. From rage, probably. Jesus, she was going to kill him. "I get so mad at her I can't stop yelling. And at the same time I want to grab her and—"

"I know," Riley said.

"And she just stands there, her hands on her hips, daring me to do it. I swear to God, she thinks it's foreplay."

"I know."

"And a lot of the time it is," Gabe said, thinking about it. "That woman is a fucking miracle in bed."

"I know," Riley said.

Gabe felt his temper flare, and Riley said hastily, "No, I don't. I've forgotten. I can barely remember her name." When Gabe still glared, he said, "Hey, I'm not the one who wants a new couch."

Gabe put his head in his hands. "I finally understand why men hit women."

"What?"

"You wouldn't understand. It's all a game to you. But I swear to God, when you can't make her do what you need her to do, and you can't live without her—"

"This is not like you," Riley said, straightening in his chair. "Jesus, get a grip."

"I can't," Gabe said. "There's nothing to grip. There's my life that's disappearing under ten coats of paint, and the woman who's burying it is the center of it." He looked up at Riley who was staring at him with real alarm, and he said, "I'd never hit her. But she starts in and I can feel it all slipping away from me, and I can't do a damn thing about it because I crave her. I just want to slow her down—"

"Okay," Riley said. "Could I suggest therapy? Because this is not like you. In fact, if it's that bad, fire her. Get her out of your life. I mean, I love her—platonically of course," he added when Gabe glared again, "but she's not worth this."

"I can't," Gabe said, feeling like a fool because it was true. "Sometimes I think it *would* be better if she'd just go away, but I need her. If she'd just stand still for a minute. If every damn minute didn't have to be about change—"

"I suppose compromise is out of the question."

"I tried that. I ended up with these goddamn yellow walls."

Riley looked at him as if he were insane.

"I didn't want yellow walls," Gabe said. "I liked the old walls."

Riley shook his head. "Okay, you have to stop yelling because it's frying your brain cells."

"The yelling is what's keeping me from killing her. I think it's what kept my dad from hitting my mom. He was so crazy about her, and she was so hot-tempered and stubborn and *contrary*—"

"I don't suppose you're seeing a pattern here," Riley said.

"God, I hope not," Gabe said. "She left him." He sat back in his chair, exhausted. "If she'd just let me run this place, we'd be okay. I'm her boss, for Christ's sake."

"Kissers," Riley said. "Who calls the shots in bed?"

"I have scars," Gabe said, "but I think I may be ahead on points."

"So you don't solve anything there, either."

"No. The better it gets, the worse it gets."

Riley was quiet for a long while, and Gabe finally said, "What?"

"Are you sure you won't hit her?"

"Yes."

"Try not to say anything about this to anybody else. I get chills thinking about what the cops could do with this conversation."

"I know. I get chills thinking about it myself. It's like I know the guy who hit Lynnie. He's like me."

"No, he's not," Riley said.

"I just wonder if that's how she died, if she pushed too hard, and he broke and hit her. I try to picture Trevor doing it, or Jack, and it's easy. Not so easy with Budge," he added as an afterthought.

"Depends," Riley said. "He gets a look in his eye when he's around Margie that is not good."

"Even Stewart," Gabe said. "I can see Stewart being dumb enough to kill her. The part I cannot see is putting her in the freezer. What kind of sick—" Nell knocked and came in, and he closed his eyes. "No more. I honest to God can't take any more today."

"It's just your schedule for tomorrow," she said, and she sounded as tired as he was.

"Okay," he said. She looked awful. "I'm sorry I yelled."

"I know," she said. "It's not you."

She smiled tightly at Riley and left, and he turned to Gabe and said, "If you two don't get therapy, I'm holding an intervention."

"It's just a bad day," Gabe said. "It'll get better. What

were you going to say when you came in here?"

"Oh, right. I don't know if this is better, but here's something new: Gina is divorcing Harold for adultery. It's the end of the Hot Lunch as we knew it. Can you believe it?"

"Yes," Gabe said. "He changed the rules on her. They had a deal and he messed with it and now there's nothing to keep them together."

"It wasn't much of a deal," Riley said.

"You don't get to judge other people's deals," Gabe said. "You just get to make your own and hold on."

"I don't think you and Nell have the same deal," Riley said.

"I'm still holding on," Gabe said.

Suze was washing down tables when Nell came into The Cup, looking like hell.

"What?" Suze said. "What did he do?"

"He called," Nell said. "He wants to meet me at the Sycamore. I think he's bringing Whitney."

"Whitney?" Suze said, and did a fast readjustment. "Tim called."

"He wants to have dinner." Nell drew a deep breath. "I haven't seen him for weeks, I actually forgot about him, and now this. I don't know."

"Are you going?"

"Well, yes," Nell said. "It could be anything. We still own a business together. We have a son. I can't just say no."

"Sure you can," Suze said. "And if you can't, I can. I'm going with you."

At five-thirty that night, Gabe came out his office and said, "I'm done for the day. You?"

"I don't think so," Riley said. "I think I need a beer. Let's go to the Sycamore."

"Any particular reason?"

"Nell didn't tell you?"

Gabe shook his head. "She said she and Suze were going to the Sycamore for dinner. I thought maybe Suze needed some time with her. Or maybe she just needed time away from me."

"They're meeting Tim," Riley said. "Suze figures Whitney is going to be with him and they're going to put the screws to Nell for something."

Son of a bitch. The irony of his hating Tim for being lousy to Nell was not lost on Gabe, but being angry with somebody else felt really good, so he ignored it.

"I definitely need a beer," he said.

Chapter Sixteen

Suze followed Nell into the restaurant, ready to watch her back. Tim and Whitney were already there, holding hands on one of the benches that divided the restaurant down the middle, and Nell took a chair across from Tim, leaving Suze to stare down the latest Mrs. Dysart. She was a pretty little thing, but her jaw was tense, and she stared at Nell as if she were the Antichrist.

"I'm really glad you could meet us," Tim said, doing his best insurance salesman impression, and Nell nodded. "There are a few things we need to get cleared up, nothing major, then we can all relax and have a nice dinner."

In what universe? Suze thought. There was denial and then there was Tim's world.

When Nell didn't say anything, Tim nodded and went on. "Well, it's about the Icicles. They're a hundred fifty bucks each to replace, and you broke fourteen of them last September so that's . . ." He turned to Whitney, frowning.

"Two thousand one hundred dollars," Whitney said crisply.

"Right, two thousand one hundred dollars," Tim said. "And then we had to replace the desk and that was five thousand six hundred, with tax."

"Five thousand dollars?" Suze said incredulously. "Where the hell did you get this desk? The Pentagon? And why now?"

"Taxes," Nell said, relaxing as she said it. "It's six weeks to tax time. They need cash."

"What we need is a check for seven thousand seven hundred dollars," Whitney said. "We've talked to a lawyer and we've been advised to proceed against you for the money and that we will succeed."

"You think?" Nell said, still serene.

"I think," Whitney said, still tense. "Or our lawyer says we call the police again and refile that warrant for malicious destruction and assault. He says they'll be very interested to know about your violent past since you are known to have threatened a woman found dead in your basement this weekend."

"I think you're a bitch on wheels," Suze said.

"Suze, this has nothing to do with you," Tim said.

Suze opened her mouth, and Nell put her hand on her arm. "I think your lawyer's wrong," Nell said. "In fact, I think your lawyer is a vengeful idiot."

Tim's eyes went to Suze and then back to Nell. "Look, we don't want to be mean, but you destroyed property we had to replace. It's only fair—"

"Tim," Nell said, a faint smile on her face. "I stopped letting you tell me what was fair months ago." She leaned forward. "First of all, I'm still half owner of that agency, even though it mysteriously did not show a profit for the first time last year. So I'd only be liable for half of those Icicles, which would put my obligation to you at one thousand fifty dollars."

"But we have to replace all of them," Tim said.

"No," Nell said. "I don't particularly want mine replaced, thanks. I like them better broken. And as for the desk, you cannot make a major expenditure without my okay, and a five-thousand-dollar desk is a major expenditure. I'm not okaying it. Therefore, it's a personal expenditure and you'll just have to cover it."

"Now wait a minute," Whitney said, and Suze braced herself to deck her if needed.

Nell ignored her to reach out and cover Tim's hand with hers. "I know how hard this is for you, sharing the agency with me."

"It makes it harder," Tim said, nodding. "I didn't think about you owning half the awards. You're right."

"Tim," Whitney said, her voice low.

"But the desk," he said, "that's not personal, Nell, that's my business desk."

"Here's what I think we should do," Nell said, still calm, looking into his eyes without heat. "I think I should sell you my half of the agency. I've been thinking about it for a while, and then after you called today I thought some more, and then I called Budge Jenkins, and he'll be over on Monday to begin an audit and to evaluate the monetary worth of the business as a whole."

"What?" Tim said, his jaw going slack.

There you go, Suze thought, feeling her entire body flood with glee.

"Then if everything's all right with the audit, you can give me half of what the agency's worth and write off your desk as a business expense." Nell sat back and finally turned to Whitney. "And that way, if I show up at the agency and smash something again, you can have me arrested and shot. Everybody's happy."

"I can't afford to buy you out," Tim said. "We have expenses—"

"Borrow," Nell said. "Tighten your belts. Live the way we did when we were first married. Shared tribulation can really strengthen a union."

"You're just being vindictive," Whitney said.

"I prefer to think of it as justice with a profit," Nell said a little sadly.

Whitney gazed at Nell, evaluating the situation, and Suze watched Whitney. "Our lawyer," Whitney said, "says we have a case."

"Your lawyer," Nell said, "is Jack Dysart, and he's blaming me for the breakup of his marriage." Suze flinched, and Nell patted her hand and said to Tim, "Your brother is not giving you advice based on your best interests. He wants revenge."

Tim exchanged glances with Whitney. "Nell, be reasonable. Debt is not a good move for me right now."

"All right," Nell said. "I don't think it's going to be a problem. Budge seemed to think he could find investors to buy me out. You'd lose control of the agency, of course, because they'd expect regular audits and reports, but you wouldn't have to worry about me anymore." She smiled at him. "And you can just take that one thousand one hundred out of my half before you write the check. I'll tell Budge that's okay."

"What a coincidence," Riley said, sliding in beside Tim before he could answer, pushing him into Whitney. "You guys are here, too. Who'd have thought?"

Suze relaxed, taking a deep breath for the first time since she'd sat down.

Gabe picked up a chair from another table and sat down at the end of theirs, his elbow close to Nell's. "We thought we'd have a beer," he said to Nell.

She let her shoulders ease back and smiled back at him. "Did you now?" She leaned a little closer, and Suze could see him relax, too.

"So what's going on?" Riley said. "Everybody happy?"

"Nell just sold her half of the agency to Tim," Suze said brightly. "Budge is going to do the audit and the estimation of value."

"Good man, Budge Jenkins," Gabe said, waving to the waitress. "We're celebrating," he told her. "We need two pitchers, six glasses, and four orders of french fries with vinegar."

"We haven't agreed to anything," Whitney said.

"You don't have anything to agree to," Nell said. "All the divorce settlement says is that we have to give each other the first chance on a buyout. And that's what I'm doing. If you don't want it, Budge's investors will. Either way, we're free of each other." She looked at Tim. "Finally."

"I'll drink to that," Gabe said as the waitress set down the pitchers and glasses. He poured Nell a glass and slid it to her, and she passed it down to Suze who slid it across the table to Whitney.

"Cheers," she said flatly, looking Whitney in the eye.

Whitney lifted her glass and said, "Cheers to you, too. Heard your husband left you."

Suze clenched her jaw, but before she could say anything, Riley said, "I don't think I've had the pleasure, I'm Riley," and reached across Tim to offer Whitney his hand. Whitney took it, not quite sure what to do, smiling faintly in confusion when he held her hand a minute too long.

Then he let go and said, "Don't be a bitch to the blonde. She'll cut you off at the knees and feed you your feet."

Whitney flushed, and Suze unclenched, and Gabe poured the last of the beers and said, "What shall we drink to?"

Nell looked around and said, "Good grief. Drink to me. I just realized I've slept with everybody at this table."

"And God knows we *appreciate* it," Riley said, while Tim gawked.

"Except for Whitney, of course," Nell said.

"To Nell," Gabe said, raising his glass.

"To Nell," Riley said and drank, and Suze clinked her glass with Nell and drank, too.

Whitney tried to share a superior eye-roll with Tim, but he was still staring at Nell. She turned back to Nell and leaned across the table to her, looking condescending and amused. "That's really *wild* of you. Three men in, what? *Fifty years?*"

Die, bitch, Suze thought, and said, "And me." She held up her hand, and all three men turned to her on the instant, leaving Whitney with no audience at all. Suze beamed on the table impartially. "She's a terrific kisser.

And when you consider she's nailed three of us in less than seven months, that's pretty good." She patted Nell's arm, thinking, *Do not tell them we only necked. This is payback time*.

Gabe had already turned to Nell, a grin splitting his face. *"Hello?"*

"After Riley, before you," Nell told Gabe solemnly. "I don't cheat."

"We don't care if you cheat," Riley said. "We just want the details." He raised his eyebrows at Suze, and she sat back, satisfied with the stunned look on Tim's face and the annoyed look on Whitney's.

"This is a joke," Tim said.

"I am never a joke," Suze said. "Especially not in bed."

"So you were in bed . . ." Riley prompted.

Nell sighed and turned to Gabe. "It was like this."

Don't tell them the truth, Suze thought. *Come on. For once, be nasty and get even*.

Nell looked at Gabe under her lashes. "We were alone one night, and we, uh, have needs—"

Gabe and Riley nodded.

"—and we like each other a lot. And we're very attractive. So we . . ." Nell finished with a shrug, smiling up at Gabe under her lashes.

"About those needs," Gabe said with great seriousness. "I want you to know you can always come to me. Any time, day or night. Bring Suze."

"You're *serious*," Tim said. "You really did this?"

You are such a boob, Suze thought. "It wasn't just lust. We got to thinking about what we'd do if a plague wiped out all the men." She shrugged at Riley and Gabe. "No offense."

"None taken," Riley said. "Be prepared. So what exactly did you do?"

"We experimented," Nell said. "Suze is an exceptionally good kisser."

"Good to know," Riley said, and Tim frowned at him. "Okay, then what did you do?"

Whitney looked at them sourly. "We don't need the details."

"Oh, sure we do," Gabe said, not taking his eyes off Nell. "Start at the beginning. What were you wearing?"

"My blue silk pajamas," Nell said. "You know, the slippery—"

"God, yes," Gabe said.

"Just the top, though," Nell lied.

"Good, good," Gabe said.

"Did you get the bottoms?" Riley said to Suze.

She shook her head. "No. I was wearing an old T-shirt."

"Not as good as the silk thing," Riley said, "but acceptable. Was there a pillow fight? You get extra points if there's a naked pillow fight."

"Some things are private," Nell said primly. "Mostly it was just fun."

Suze said, "Yes, it was."

Nell met her eyes, and Suze thought, *I'm so glad I have you*. On a impulse she took Nell's hand and kissed her cheek. "Best relationship I've ever had," Suze told her.

"Me, too," Nell said. "Absolutely."

When the silence stretched out, they turned back to the table to find the others watching them. Then Gabe said, "Right," and stood up. "Nell and I have to get back to the office now."

Nell blinked at him. "We do?"

"Yes, Bridget," Gabe said, looking straight into her eyes. "We do."

Nell flushed. "Right." She pushed her chair back so hard it tipped over. "Sorry." She righted the chair and picked up her coat. "I was just excited. About getting back. To the office." She looked at Gabe and said, "I live for my work."

Gabe laughed and put his arm around her as she slid past him, and when they went out the door, Suze craned her neck to see around the stained-glass panel into the street. Gabe had pulled her close, fighting a smile as he spoke sternly to her, and Nell laughed up at him. She looked so transcendently happy that Suze felt a pang watching them. *I want that, too*, she thought. *I had that once, and I want it again.*

"Check, please," Riley called. "And cancel the fries."

"Unbelievable," Tim said.

"Exactly," Whitney said. "I don't believe a word of this. They're just being childish, trying to get attention."

"If I want attention," Suze said coldly, "I do not have to make up stories. I just walk into a room."

"This is true." Riley moved from the bench to take the chair beside Suze that Nell had vacated. "So when was this again? And where was I?"

"Thanksgiving night," Suze said, leaning into his shoulder a little. "You were probably with the infant horticulture major."

Whitney shook her head at Suze. "And you wonder why Jack left you."

Riley snorted. "If you think that story would make a man leave her, you know nothing about men, honey." He turned to look down at Suze. "So you were in your T-shirt—"

"I've had enough." Whitney slid out of the bench and stood up, looking at Tim with concern. "They're just doing this to upset you, Tim."

Tim ignored her to look at Suze. "You really did it, didn't you?"

"Yes," Suze said. "I kissed your wife and I really liked it and so did Riley, and Gabe is dragging her off to bed even while we sit here. And you are a fool, but then, as Riley says, we knew that." Tim drew back and Suze went on, suddenly fierce in her determination to tell him the truth, to tell *somebody* the truth. "I loathe you for what you did to her, but I'm also glad because you set her free. She's so happy now, she's got something besides that stupid insurance agency to live for, and she wouldn't have you back as a gift, so it's all right now, but I will never forgive you for cheating on her and hurting her. You are scum."

Tim said, "Now wait a minute," and Whitney tugged at his arm.

"That's what I mean," she said to him, her distress clear in her voice. "They're just doing this to upset you. It's all lies. Don't listen to them. They're just trying to pay you back." She stroked his sleeve, and Suze thought, *She really loves him.*

Tim looked from Suze to Whitney to Riley, relieved. "Sure. That's not like Nell. I don't believe—"

"Believe it," Riley said. "What's the scar under her belly button from?"

"Laparotomy," Tim said automatically and then stopped.

"I noticed it while I was down there," Riley said. "And from her reaction to what I was doing, I'm surprised you even knew it was there."

"Ouch," Suze said and turned to Whitney. "All my sympathies, honey."

Tim stood up. "You people have no morals."

"You fucked a chippie and betrayed your wife and son," Suze said. "Get your own morals, slimeball."

"That's it," Whitney said and dragged Tim toward the door.

" 'Get your own morals, slimeball'?" Riley said to Suze when they were gone.

"I hate him."

"Understandably," Riley said. "That's no reason to descend to his level."

"I couldn't get to his level with a backhoe. He's beneath contempt."

"See, that was better. Not great, but more imagination than 'slimeball.' Want another beer before I walk you home?"

"Nope." Suze slid her chair back. "I've had enough stimulation for tonight."

"Too true." Riley looked at the check and put a couple

of bills on the table as he stood up. "I can't believe Gabe stuck me with the check."

"He had places to go and Nell to do."

Riley held the door for her, and she stepped out into the cold street. "That guy was born for monogamy," he said, as he took her arm. "First Chloe for nineteen years, and now Nell for eternity even though she drives him crazy. He just keeps holding on."

"It better be for eternity." Suze thought about jerking her arm away, but it was nice being supported like that. Firm. Warm. She could be independent when she got home again since that was her only option anyway. Independence should be a choice, not a punishment. She thought about Nell, about the months she'd spent frozen in shock, and then remembered her tonight, laughing up at Gabe. If he betrayed her, too . . . She stopped and turned to Riley. "If Gabe's just playing around—"

"Does he *look* like he's just playing around?" Riley sounded exasperated as he tugged on her arm, making her walk with him again. "Does he *act* like it? If anybody else had pulled the stuff she's pulled, she'd have been fired long ago. He's in this for good."

"Maybe." Suze slipped a little on a patch of ice and felt his grip on her arm tighten until she had her balance back. "He looks like he's nuts about her. But so did Tim once." *So did Jack about me, once.*

"You want guarantees?" Riley said. "There are no guarantees. But Gabe is not a cheater or a liar, and he's taken Nell into his life, not just his bed. He's not Tim." He sounded more than annoyed, but before she could apologize, he added, "He's not Jack."

"I'm sorry," Suze said. "I forgot he's your friend."

"He's my friend, my partner, my mentor, and my family," Riley said. "Do not criticize Gabe."

"Right. Forget Gabe. We've still got six blocks to walk to my house. How's your life?"

"Hell. The place I work has turned into the WWF

crossed with *Sex and the City*. Gabe's a quiet kind of guy, he wasn't born to be that mad or that happy. Let's talk about something else."

"Okay. What do you want to talk about?"

"So you're wearing the T-shirt and Nell is in the pajama top," Riley said, and Suze laughed and told him everything and then some, embroidering the story as they walked, implying that she and Nell had visited places they hadn't. By the time they were through the park, she was a little breathless from her own story, and by the time they climbed the steps to her cold, empty house, Riley had been silent for some time.

"I may have made some of that up," Suze said as she fumbled for her key.

"No, no," Riley said. "If there is a God, that was all true."

She unlocked the door and pushed it open, hating the dark emptiness inside. "The point is, it was fun. This divorce stuff isn't so bad," she told herself, as much as him. "Look at all the things I'm discovering about myself."

"And sharing with others," Riley said. "That's important."

It was dark on the porch so she couldn't see his face, but she could hear the smile in his voice, and something more.

"I'd like to share it with you, too," she said, exasperated, remembering the kiss he'd turned down on New Year's Eve, "but you're not interested." On an impulse, she stretched up on her toes and kissed him before he could duck, meaning to make it quick, so she could say, *Isn't that better than just thinking about it?*

But he kissed her back, hard, following her as she sank back on her heels, and her blood went hot on the instant. He pulled her to him and she leaned into his solid bulk and lost her breath. When he finished the kiss, she held on to him, tighter, gripping his coat because she knew he was going to step away, and she didn't think she could stand to be alone again.

Don't make me go into that house alone.

"That was dumb," Riley said, his breath coming hard. "I apologize." He tried to pull back, and she held on for dear life.

"If I push this," she said, "if I kiss you again and stick my tongue in your mouth and climb all over you, will you go to bed with me?"

Riley took a deep breath. "Yes."

Suze's heart skipped a beat. "Should I?" she said, wanting him to stop being such a passive clod, such a kissee, and tell her yes.

"No."

"*Why?*" Suze said, letting go of him. "I don't *get* this."

Riley leaned back against the brick wall, and when he spoke, he had his breath back and sounded angry. "When we were talking tonight, did you want me?"

"What? At dinner? No, I wanted to make Tim and Whitney pay."

"Yeah. That was clear. So did Nell. But she wanted Gabe more. She was a lot more interested in turning Gabe on than in making Tim sorry. Everything she said, she pitched to Gabe."

"Oh." Suze tried to remember. Maybe she'd been reading Nell wrong. "Okay. So?"

"You had no interest in me, which is okay. Many women have no interest in me. The only time you want me is when you're alone. You're going into the big empty house, so you reach for me. In most cases, I'd be all for it, but this is not most cases, this is you and you are a mess right now, and you're trying to take me down with you. Which does not mean I won't go if you ask again. I'm only human, and you are hot, kid, no doubt about it. But it's going to be bad afterward, and you know it."

"It's not just being alone," Suze said, trying to be honest. "I really want the sex, too. I *miss* it. It's been *weeks.*"

Riley let out a stifled sigh. "You want to wake up with me tomorrow?" he said, and Suze thought about it, about dealing with the reality of him in the daylight.

"No."

"That's okay," Riley said. "I don't want to wake up with you, either." He reached past her to shove the door all the way open. "So we'll go in there and fuck each other because it feels good, and then I'll leave." He gave her a push. "After you."

"You bastard," Suze said, standing firm. "You make it sound horrible. Why can't you just take advantage of me like any other guy would?"

"Because I am not any other guy," Riley said. "Although if you don't get your ass in there and lock the door, I will become him."

"You really do want me?" Suze said, and Riley said, "Oh, Christ, that's it, I'm coming in. Find a wall, and brace yourself." He pushed her harder toward the door, but she pushed him back as she stepped inside.

"No," Suze said. "You win."

"If I win, why am I outside?" Riley said.

"But you're wrong about me not wanting you for you," Suze said. "I do, sort of. I'm still not over Jack, although if he really did sic Whitney on Nell, I hate him—"

"What?" Riley said.

"—and I really could use the sex, and I hate being alone, and I'm looking for somebody to save me, you're right about all of that, but you're in there, too. There is definite zing with you, and I'm not getting it with anybody else."

"Really?" Riley said. "Maybe we should talk about this."

"No," Suze said. "Because if we talk much more, I will sleep with you for all the wrong reasons, and then you'll be right and I'll be wrong again."

"Maybe they're not the wrong reasons," Riley said. "Maybe—"

"Good night," Suze said a little breathlessly, and shut the door in his face before she could do something stupid.

Through the glass she could see him wait a minute, and then he went down the steps, his broad back disappearing into the darkness of the street. She thought, *I wish you weren't going, I really do.*

She watched from the front window as he turned down Fourth Street, heading back across the park to the agency, half hoping he'd turn around and come back. When she couldn't see him anymore, she dropped the curtain and heard a car start up across the street. She drew the curtain back again and watched a BMW pull away, gunning its motor.

Jack.

I hate you, she thought. *Watching me. Hurting Nell.* And even then she remembered how sweet he could be, how passionate, how good most of that fourteen years with him had been. That was the problem with marriage. It sunk its hooks into your soul and left scars that were with you forever. They should warn the people who were getting married about what it was going to do to them. How it shaped your life and changed your mind and altered your reality until you didn't know who you were anymore. How it hooked you on the presence of another person, maybe somebody you didn't even like very much, maybe somebody you didn't even love anymore, and made you need that person even when you didn't want him at all.

Marriage was a drug and a trap and an illusion, and kicking it was hell.

I'm glad Riley didn't stay, Suze thought. *I'm glad I'm alone.* And then she went upstairs to bed.

An hour earlier, Nell had kissed Gabe in the darkened agency office, exhilarated that she'd faced down Tim and relieved she and Gabe weren't fighting anymore. He'd caught her around the waist and pulled her to him, smiling down at her in the dim light from the street, and she thought, *I have to stop making him so mad.*

It was the same thought, she realized, that she'd had way too many times with Tim. That was sobering enough to make her step away.

"What?" he said, some of the light fading from his voice.

"Nothing," she said. "Have I mentioned that I'm crazy about you?"

He slid his arms around her again. "So tell me the rest of the Suze story."

"There wasn't any more. She kissed me. She wasn't you. Since then I've been kissing you."

"Thank you," Gabe said. "Anything I can do to show my appreciation?"

"Yes," she said, and shoved him toward the couch. He stumbled back in the dark and sat down on it hard, and she straddled him before he could stand up again.

"This is probably not a good idea," he said, testing it with his hand. "This is not the sturdiest—"

"Which is why I keep asking for a new one," she said, settling against him closer. "A safe couch that won't collapse under us. Or the clientele, for that matter. Kiss me and tell me we can get a new couch."

He put his hands on her thighs, moving them up under her skirt. "We've had this conversation. You don't get a couch. Come upstairs with me and you can have something else."

He leaned toward her, and she put her hands on his chest and pushed him back. "Wait a minute. I have an idea."

"Always bad news for me," Gabe said.

"Here's the deal, Dino. I am now in golddigger mode. I will let you do unspeakable things to me on this couch, right now, but you have to buy me."

"With a new couch," Gabe said, looking up at her in the dim light, his eyes hot on her and his hands hotter under her skirt, and she thought, *Oh, hell, with a paper clip, anything, take me.*

"Yes," she said, her chin in the air. "I live for my job."

"And you fuck for it, too." Gabe shoved her skirt up to her waist and then pulled her close, and she shivered as she felt him hard against her. "Very professional," he said. "Did I lock the street door?"

"Yes," she said and licked into his mouth, and he said, "You do realize this is in front of a window."

"It's dark. You want me or not?" She bounced on him a little, and the couch creaked, and he caught his breath, and so did she.

"Tell you what," he said, his voice husky, "if this couch breaks in the next half hour, you can have a new one."

"Deal." Nell pulled him down on top of her, rotating her hips to slide under him, figuring the couch would go that much sooner with him on top. Everything went according to plan for the next twenty minutes, both of them doing their usual good work until they were both too hot to stand it anymore and her underpants had been tossed somewhere on the other side of the desk. Then Gabe kissed her deeply and slid into her, and she braced herself for the storm to come.

It didn't. Instead he kept her still, imprisoned under him, while he pulsed against her, barely moving but hitting everything that counted with a rhythm that made her skin itch and her breath come short. She swallowed her gasp and said, "What are you *doing*?"

"Getting you there," he said in her ear, and she could hear the laughter in his voice.

She tried to bounce under him and couldn't, he had her pinned against the damn couch cushions so that she couldn't even get leverage on the floor.

"*Harder*," she said, and he said, "Nope," and slowed even more. She breathed deep as her blood thickened and said, "This isn't doing it for me," while she thought, *If he doesn't stop I'm going to come my brains out on an intact couch*.

"You lie," Gabe said in her ear, pulsing inexorably against her. "I can always get you there and I always will."

He kissed her neck and moved his hand to her breast, and she tried to bounce under him again, only to have him tighten his hand on her instead of picking up speed. She tried writhing, which he appreciated, and rocking, which he quelled with hot hands, and then finally, frustrated by her enforced stillness, she raked her fingernails down his back, lifting him off the couch with her hips and kicking herself into the first shudder of her climax. She jerked against him, and he sucked in his breath as she surged up from the couch, needing to move as much as she needed to come, and he bore down on her, pounding her into the creaking couch as she went mindless, everything in motion at last.

When she got her brain back, she realized the couch was still standing. "I am so disappointed," she said as her blood sang. "We'll have to do this again."

"Another reason not to get rid of the couch," Gabe said against her hair. "I'm going to have it reinforced when you're not looking."

"Get off me," Nell said, and he pushed himself off her and stood up. She shoved her skirt down as he zipped his pants, and then she said, "I can't believe this damn thing held."

"They made stuff good in the fifties," Gabe said. "Me, for instance. And, God knows, you."

Nell had turned on the desk light and was behind the desk retrieving her underwear when the street door opened. She straightened and saw Riley, holding his key.

"What are you doing here?" Gabe said, tucking in his shirt.

"I work here," Riley said. "You used to do that, too, before you gave it up to sexually harass your dognapping secretary. What a night." He tossed his keys on the desk and collapsed onto the couch.

It held.

"I can't believe it," Nell said, staring at it in disgust.

"I'm going to jump up and down on it before we do it the next time."

"What?" Riley said. "You just did it *here*? There's a window here, for Christ's sake."

"You have no flair," Gabe said. "Also it was her idea."

"Does it ever occur to you to say no to her?"

"No," Gabe said, but he was frowning, his head tilted. "Look at the legs on that thing."

"See, I told you," Nell began, but then she looked at the couch legs and shut up. They were splayed out sideways, as if the couch were slowly doing the splits, and the long seat had skewed as if it were warped. "Ooh. It's never done that before."

Riley pushed himself off the couch and it sank a little farther. "What did you do?"

"Now we have to get a new couch," Nell said, but Gabe ignored her.

He went over and grabbed the couch by the front edge, tipping it back until it rested against the window and he was looking at the bottom of it. "What the hell is that?"

"That" was a long piece of pipe, jammed tightly along the length of the seat at an angle.

"Well, no wonder it wasn't breaking," Nell said. "Of course, that also explains why it was so damn uncomfortable."

"It's not even welded in," Gabe said, looking at it closer. "It's just jammed in there. Give me a hand."

Riley came to stand beside him. "You know, if you jerk that out of there, the couch is history."

"Jerk it out of there," Nell said.

"Brace the couch," Gabe said, and Riley leaned against the seat, while Gabe grabbed the bar and yanked. "Damn it," he said, "one more time." Riley leaned harder on the back, and Gabe yanked again, and this time the pipe popped out, making him stagger back a step.

Riley let the couch drop back into place. "You want me to take this out to the Dumpster? Because it really is going to go if anybody—" He stopped because Gabe had the pipe upended and was shaking it. "What are you doing?"

"There's something in here." Gabe said, trying to peer into the end. "We need more light in this place."

"Good," Nell said. "I'll buy lamps when I get the new couch."

"Give me something with a hook on it," he said, and Nell thought, *Yeah, I have one of those*, but then he said, "Wait a minute," and dug out his pocketknife. He stuck the blade in the end of the pipe and began to lever something out.

"I repeat," Riley said. "What—"

"My father was not a fixer-upper," Gabe said. "And he jammed this pipe in the couch."

"How do you know?"

"Well, it wasn't you or me." Gabe frowned as he worked on the pipe. "And I don't see your mother or Chloe cramming it in there. And the likelihood of somebody else sneaking in here and jamming pipes in our furniture—" He stopped as he maneuvered a wad of white cloth out of the end of the pipe. He put his knife away and pulled on the cloth and it came out easily, unfurling as he pulled, until something heavy fell out at his feet and glinted on the floor.

"Diamonds," Nell said, looking at the spilled pile of glittering circles.

"I can't wait for Trevor to explain this one," Riley said.

"I can," Gabe said. "But I'm not going to."

Chapter Seventeen

"You gave Margie the pin and the ring," Gabe said half an hour later when he had the jewelry spread out on Trevor's dining room table. "You gave my dad the necklace, the bracelet, and the earrings. And I want to know why. No lies this time, no crap about ungrateful sons. The truth."

Trevor sat down at the table, looking older than Gabe had ever seen him. He felt no sympathy for him at all.

"There's brandy there on the sideboard," Trevor said.

Gabe picked up the brandy bottle, keeping his eyes on Trevor. "Who killed Helena?"

"Stewart," Trevor said, and Gabe almost dropped the bottle.

"Stewart? Margie's husband?"

Trevor nodded. Gabe splashed some brandy into a snifter and handed it to him, and he drank, not deeply, and then took a breath.

"Sit down," Trevor said, "and I'll tell you what happened. And then I hope you won't tell anyone else."

"Trevor, it's murder," Gabe said. "That's not something—"

"You'll never prove it," Trevor said. "If I could have proved it, I would have. I was divorcing Helena, but I didn't want her dead. She was Margie's mother. Margie's never really gotten over it, you know. Imagine if it were Chloe and Lu."

"Talk," Gabe said, staving off sympathy.

"I had an affair," Trevor said, sadly. "With Audrey. I

loved her, but I wouldn't have married her, Helena was my wife, after all. But then Audrey got pregnant and I wanted my child to have my name, and my marriage had really been over—"

"Trevor," Gabe said. "Get to the part where Stewart shoots Helena, and my dad helps."

"Helps?" Trevor looked revolted. "You should be ashamed of yourself. Your father was a fine man."

"With a hundred thousand dollars' worth of diamonds in his couch," Gabe said. "Explain."

"That's where he put them?" Trevor laughed, but without much humor. "In that cheap couch? That was Patrick for you. Smart as hell." He picked up the snifter again. "You could have thrown that couch out any time and then nobody would ever have known. How did you find them, anyway?"

"Nell wanted a new couch," Gabe said. "I want the story. Spill it."

"Nell's an industrious woman," Trevor said. "Helena wasn't. She took the divorce badly."

And most people take them so well, Gabe thought, wondering if Trevor had any idea of what a fathead he could be.

"I was prepared to provide for her, but she wanted half of my share of the firm, which was ridiculous. She wasn't going to get it, of course, but the litigation was going to kill us. Jack had just married Vicki, and he didn't have any spare cash since Abby had taken half of his assets. Stewart had just married Margie and wanted more money from the firm, but that wasn't possible with the cash flow. And then he came to me and said he and Jack had talked and they had a way out of our problems, that he could shoot Helena while I had an airtight alibi. I said no." Trevor stared at Gabe across the table. "I told them both no. I told him if we waited, she'd get tired and give up the fight, and we'd be fine."

"I believe it," Gabe said. Trevor would have suggested

waiting during the Chicago Fire because the flames were sure to die down on their own.

"I didn't want her dead," Trevor said again. "And about a month later, he called me. He said Margie had gone to her mother's and now was the time, that if I called her there and kept her on the phone, he could take care of Helena in the next half hour. I told him absolutely not. He said if we waited anymore, we'd lose everything. Then he hung up."

"So you rushed right over to warn Helena," Gabe said. "You called the police."

"The police?" Trevor looked aghast. "You're joking. No, I called Helena and Margie answered. She said Helena was acting strangely and she asked me to come over, but I knew I'd be too late. I told her to take Helena to the hospital right away, that I'd meet her there, and she said, no, that if I just came over—" Trevor closed his eyes. "While we were arguing, she heard the shot. And then I went over."

"Was Stewart there?"

"No," Trevor said, his voice flat. "Margie had found her mother and she was hysterical, so I put a blanket over Helena and called the paramedics." He took a deep breath. "And then I went upstairs and found Helena's suicide notes. Three of them. She'd been practicing." His face flushed and he sounded angry. "She'd been planning on killing herself all along. If Stewart had just waited. . . ."

So much for Trevor not wanting Helena dead.

"He was a fool," Trevor said. "I should never have let Margie marry him."

You shouldn't have let him shoot your wife, either, Gabe thought, but he said, "She was shot with your gun."

"He'd taken it earlier," Trevor said. "Jack had everything planned."

Gabe leaned against the liquor cabinet. He'd buy that Stewart hadn't planned the murder, but the accusation against Jack was fishy, coming as it did on the heels of the

Quarterly Report. And that "he'd taken it earlier" bit had been rushed. "I'm still not seeing Patrick in this."

"Margie had told me that her mother had on her good jewelry. When I saw the body, Helena had on her rings and her pin, but the rest was gone."

"Stewart had taken it," Gabe said, playing along.

"Just the pieces he could grab before he ran," Trevor said, distaste making his voice curdle, and Gabe began to believe him. "The pin would take too long to unlatch and the rings were embedded in her fingers because she'd put on so much weight. I knew he'd do something stupid with the other pieces, he was a stupid man, so I called Patrick."

"And still nobody tells the police," Gabe said.

"The scandal would have ruined us," Trevor said.

"Your daughter was married to her mother's murderer," Gabe said.

"Exactly," Trevor said. "Imagine what that would do to her if she ever found out."

Gabe stared at him, Margie's maybe-they'll-never-know mantra made flesh.

"Your father was magnificent as always," Trevor said. "He followed Stewart for days until he went into a pawn-shop. Then he took most of the agency's capital and bought the diamonds back."

"And he told my mother and she left him," Gabe said, thinking, *What fools the two of you were.*

"Of course not," Trevor said. "Lia wouldn't have understood. But she didn't understand anyway, didn't understand what had happened to the money and didn't understand why he wouldn't tell her. She wasn't a good wife, Gabe. I'm sorry to say it, but it's true. Not trusting at all."

Gabe looked at him and thought, *You must be from Mars.*

"And Patrick wasn't the kind of man to let himself be run by a woman," Trevor went on.

"I'm sure that kept him warm at night after she left," Gabe said.

"I didn't have the capital to pay Patrick back in full," Trevor said, ignoring him, "so I gave him the Porsche. I knew he liked it, and it was my second car."

"Jesus," Gabe said.

"And then we did dummy invoices for the balance of the money, billing the law firm for fake background checks. I'd paid him back for all of it by the end of the year. Your mother was gone by then and your aunt was keeping the books. Nobody noticed."

"But he kept the diamonds," Gabe said.

"Well, I couldn't take them," Trevor said. "I was living with Audrey by then and I couldn't risk her finding them. I'd told everyone they were buried with Helena. If Margie had found out I had them, she'd have gotten the entirely wrong idea."

No, she wouldn't have. "So they were just going to stay in the couch?" Gabe said.

"No. We were going to wait five years and then break the stones out of the settings and sell them. But then—"

"Dad had a heart attack without telling you where they were," Gabe finished.

Trevor nodded. "And then Stewart embezzled and left, and it was all over. So we went on with our lives until Nell started to tear up your agency. You should have hired a lazy secretary, my boy." He tried to chuckle, but his heart clearly wasn't in it. "I tried to hire her away before she found the jewelry but . . ." He sighed. "And now it's all over."

Gabe shook his head in disbelief. "All over? Trevor, it is not all over. Stewart is still alive and, let's not forget, guilty of murder. And he didn't leave for *fifteen years.* Jesus, the holidays must have been fun with him across the table from you."

"There's a lot you could learn from your father," Trevor said gravely. "He was never judgmental."

"*Which explains this entire mess,*" Gabe said. "If he'd dragged you off to the police—"

"Gabriel, the police were not then and are not now a possibility." Trevor's voice took on the strength of his youth, and for once he was impressive. "Without my testimony, you can't prove anything, but you can hurt my daughter and my business, so I'm asking you, as the son of my dearest friend, to let this go. It was twenty years ago—"

"Twenty-three."

"—and nothing can be gained by dredging this up. Even if the police believed you, they can't find Stewart. He's been gone seven years. Margie's going to have him declared legally dead. It's over. Let it go."

Gabe stood up. "Trevor, I'm not the only one who knows."

"Nell will do what you tell her," Trevor said.

"Obviously, you don't know Nell," Gabe said. Trevor looked at him with contempt, and Gabe flushed. "And I wouldn't tell her to keep quiet even if she did listen to me."

Trevor shook his head, clearly disappointed in him and his way with women.

Gabe tried a new tack. "So where does Lynnie fit in all of this?"

"Who?" Trevor said, looking legitimately mystified.

"Lynnie Mason. Our former secretary. The one who turned up in a freezer a week ago."

Trevor blinked at him. "She doesn't. Wasn't she quite young?"

"Early thirties," Gabe said, not following.

Trevor spread his hands. "She'd have been ten when Helena died."

"She didn't have to be there," Gabe said. "People talk. What did the woman who was blackmailing you really accuse you of?"

"I told you," Trevor said, his voice sharpening. "Adultery. It was a prank. Whoever it was never called back. I don't understand you, Gabriel. You keep trying to make this personal, about your family and your business. It wasn't. It was my family."

"But my family took the hit for it, too. This is why my mother left, isn't it?"

"Your mother," Trevor said, his voice quelling, "left regularly. Why your father always took her back is beyond me."

"He loved her," Gabe said. "And she loved him, that's why she kept coming back, even though he pulled stuff like this."

"Don't judge your father harshly," Trevor said as Gabe turned to go. "He was a good friend. You'd do the same for your cousin."

"No, I wouldn't," Gabe said. "I wouldn't have to. He'd never do anything like this."

"I didn't do anything," Trevor said.

"Exactly," Gabe said and drove home in his father's car, knowing for the first time how expensive it really had been.

"What do you think?" Riley said that evening in the office.

"I'll buy that Stewart didn't plan it," Gabe said. "Too many people say he's rash and stupid."

"Rash is taking the diamonds."

"That part I believe. Trevor was truly disgusted by that. But I will bet you that Trevor or Jack planned it. And my dad covered it up."

"Moving past that," Riley said. "Lynnie shows up twenty-two years later looking for diamonds. Who told her they were here? It'd have to be Trevor, wouldn't it?"

"He might have told Stewart or Jack," Gabe said. "But Trevor is still front and center."

"So why did he tell her?" Riley said. "If it was Jack or Stewart, I'd say pillow talk, she was not a difficult date, but I don't see Trevor cuddling up to Lynnie and saying, 'The McKennas have diamonds.' "

"I don't see that as pillow talk ever," Gabe said. "Even if money did turn her on. Somebody sent her in here after them and then killed her because she knew too much."

"Why look now?" Riley said. "It's been twenty-two years. The only person who'd wait that long for diamonds is Trevor, and he would just keep waiting."

"Maybe somebody just found out about them."

"Jack."

"Why Jack?"

"Because he's a son of a bitch," Riley said.

"As long as we're keeping an open mind," Gabe said.

"So what's this I hear about you and Suze having sex?" Margie said when she was sitting in the Sycamore with Nell and Suze the next Sunday for brunch, and Suze choked on her orange juice and thought, *Who talked?*

"Where'd you get that?" Nell asked.

"Tim told Budge," Margie said, picking up her mimosa. "We had dinner at Mother Dysart's." She sighed. "It was awful. I had to talk to Whitney and Olivia. I felt bad for you both, but now that I know you're having sex . . ."

"Okay, you know that was a joke, right?" Suze said, never sure about Margie.

Margie cut into her eggs Benedict. "Uh-huh. Except I bet you did do something. Nell doesn't lie."

"We kissed," Nell said. "In the interests of science. In case a plague wiped out all the men."

"And if the plague hits," Suze said, picking up her egg quesadilla, "you are invited to a three-way."

"No, thank you," Margie said. "If the plague hits, I'm going to go find Janice."

Suze stopped, her mouth full of quesadilla, and thought, *Margie had a Janice?*

Nell said, "Janice? Janice who?"

"Janice was a friend I had in high school," Margie said,

frowning at her eggs Benedict. "She was the best sex I ever had until Budge."

"So much for Stewart," Suze said.

The waitress came and Margie asked for another mimosa. When she was gone, Margie said, "I *learned* things from Janice."

"But you ended up with Stewart," Nell said. "Why?"

"Because Janice dumped me," Margie said. "And Stewart was somebody I'd known for a while, and he worked for Daddy. And he kept asking." She shrugged.

"I can't believe this," Nell said. "You had this secret life—"

"No, I didn't," Margie said. "I never kept it secret. Nobody noticed. Nobody ever notices what I do." She didn't sound too concerned about that. "And when I did tell Stewart, he got so upset I just let the whole thing die." She shook her head. "If I'd never said anything, he'd never have known."

"He got upset?" Nell said. "Why?"

"Because it was *unnatural*." Margie sighed. "He wasn't much fun."

"I still feel awful about that," Nell said. "I should have known you were unhappy."

"Why?" Margie shoved the plate away and picked up her drink. "It wasn't that bad mostly. He wasn't around much. But then one day there was trouble at the firm and I didn't know what to do. We had this huge fight, it was so awful, I really lost my temper."

Suze looked at her in disbelief. "You have a temper?"

"—and I just hit him. Then I went to Daddy and said I wanted a divorce, but Stewart left and didn't come back, so the problem solved itself."

"And then there was Budge," Suze said. "Did you tell him about Janice?"

Margie dimpled. "Yes, I did. It had a *completely* different effect on him."

"Yeah, it had a completely different effect on Gabe,

too," Suze said, smiling at the memory. "I've never seen two people leave a restaurant so fast."

"What about Riley?" Nell asked and Suze stopped smiling.

"Yeah. It interested him, too."

"You and Riley?" Margie said. "That's nice."

"No," Suze said, feeling like hell. "He won't."

"Maybe he respects you too much," Margie said.

"No," Suze and Nell said together.

"I'm just not the woman I once was," Suze said lightly.

"He can't be that stupid," Nell said.

"He's not stupid at all," Suze said and turned to Margie. "So where is Janice now?"

"Some big law firm in New York," Margie said. "That's okay. I have Budge, and if the plague hits, I can take the bus to New York."

"I find that hard to believe," Suze said. "You, on a bus?"

"And I paid for half of your present," Margie said sadly.

"I get a present?" Suze said, cheering up a little.

Margie opened her bag and put a clear plastic box full of decorated cookies on the table. "It's a divorce party. We thought you should have one so you'd go ahead and get one. A divorce, I mean."

Ouch, Suze thought.

"We thought you needed cheering up," Nell said, with more tact.

"I couldn't figure out how to get a cake and candles in my bag," Margie said, "so I made cookies. None of them are broken."

"Unbroken cookies," Suze said, prying open the box as she tried to sound cheerful. "That's a *great* present."

"That's not your present," Margie said, picking up her mimosa, "that's your cake."

"Present," Nell said, handing over a pink foil–wrapped box.

"We spent hours in the store picking it out," Margie said, as Suze unwrapped the box.

"No, it just seemed like hours," Nell said.

"Thank you," Suze said, taking the last of the wrapping off. The box said, "Lady's Home Companion. Batteries Included," and Suze wasn't sure what to say.

"It's a vibrator," Margie said.

"It certainly is," Suze said.

"That's to keep you from making any mistakes in the pursuit of orgasm," Nell said. "Easy to do, as I know only too well."

"Riley was not a mistake," Margie said. "He was an adventure." She sighed at the thought.

"Masturbation," Suze said, still staring at the vibrator box.

"I prefer to think of it as having sex with somebody I trust," Nell said.

"Good point," Suze said.

"And no wet spot," Margie said, gesturing with her glass. "Plus you get the whole bed to yourself."

It's not enough, Suze thought, and when she got home that afternoon, she put the box on a shelf in the closet. Then she made herself a drink because Jack was coming by to pick up the last of his clothes. When he was late, she made herself another.

When he came in the front door, Suze felt her chest tighten. He looked the same as always, tall and gorgeous, those blue eyes melting at her as if they were still together, and she tried to remember what he'd tried to do to Nell with Tim and the business, what he was still doing to Olivia. They talked politely as he gathered the last of his shirts from their closet, and then she followed him downstairs and into the hall, trying hard to breathe normally, fighting back the urge to say, "Don't go, maybe we can try again." She didn't want to try again, he'd cheated, he'd been awful to Nell, he'd watched her kiss Riley in a dark street, but she wanted to say, "Don't go," because the future was terrifying and boundless and he was the past she knew.

"I can't believe we're over," she said instead, her throat almost closing.

"I can't believe it, either. We had it all." He stood by the front door with a handful of shirts on hangers, the light from the porch showing the sadness on his face. *My husband*, she thought and felt guilty that she couldn't keep him no matter what, that as much as she'd loved him, she couldn't love him enough to forgive him for Olivia, for cheating on her to save his pride.

"It's not going to be the same without you, Suze," he said, and his voice was so honest and so painful that she went to him and put her arms around him.

"I'll always love you," she said. "Whatever else—"

He dropped the hangers and kissed her, and she thought, *Wait, I didn't mean that*, and then she remembered what they'd been once and was afraid she'd never feel good again, and she didn't want to be alone, and she did want *somebody*, some human touch, not a damn pink vibrator no matter how liberated that was, so she kissed him back as he pulled at her clothing, sinking to the floor with him and letting him back inside in one last valediction for her marriage and the life she'd had with him.

Then I'll let go, she thought and clung to him and his kiss.

The next week, as Gabe obsessed over Lynnie's death, Nell obsessed over Suze's inability to let go of Jack and Margie's growing inability to hold onto reality without a mimosa in her hand. The only stable thing in her life was the agency. She bought a mission couch with leather cushions for the outer office, and Gabe flinched at the bill but didn't argue, so for St. Patrick's Day she went for broke and gave Gabe and Riley new business cards. They were pale gray and had "Answers" embossed at the top in gold, old-fashioned type like the window. She left the boxes on their desks and when they came in, she waited for them to find them and tell her she'd been right all along.

Gabe came out of his office with blood in his eye, and Nell said, "Wait a minute, I took the design straight off your window."

"You can take them straight off my desk, too," he said, slamming the box down in front of her. "Burn those damn things and get the old cards reprinted."

"Look, you didn't pay for them, I did," Nell said. "They were your St. Patrick's Day present."

"Wish I'd known," Gabe said. "I'd have given you a case of Glenlivet."

"Well, if I'd known you were going to act like this, I'd have drunk it," Nell said. "If you'd just give these a chance—"

"Not only will I not give these a chance," Gabe said, "I'm not going to give you another one. Get my goddamn business cards back or you're fired. And for the last time, *stop changing things*."

"You'd give up sleeping with me for business cards?" Nell said, trying to lighten the mood a little.

"No," Gabe said. "But I'll give up paying you to type for me if you don't act like a secretary and follow orders."

"Hey," Nell said. "I am not just a—"

Riley opened the door to his office and came out with one of his new cards in his hand. "When did I become a really expensive hairdresser?"

"That's not—"

"Or maybe a hooker," he said, looking at the card. " 'Answers'? That pretty much depends on the question, doesn't it?"

"She's getting rid of them," Gabe said and went back into his office and slammed the door.

"Just because it's something new," Nell said, glaring after him.

"It's not because it's new," Riley said, dropping the card on her desk. "It's because it's geeky. Don't do stuff like that without checking with him first. You know how he is."

"But he's wrong," Nell said. "He's such a control freak. Those old cards—"

"—are the ones he likes," Riley finished for her. "You're not paying attention."

"Does this place look a lot better than it did before I came?" Nell said and watched Riley look around the reception room.

"Very shiny."

"And the bathroom—"

"—is a work of art," he finished for her again. "Nell, you're missing the point. It's his business. And this is not the way he wants it to look."

"It's yours, too," Nell said.

"And I agree with him." Riley shook his head at her. "You know, the problem is not that he's a control freak. It's that you're both control freaks. And one of you has to give in. You, to be specific."

"He's wrong," Nell said.

"And on that, I'm going back to my office," Riley said. "Let me know when the dust settles, and I'll talk to whoever is still standing."

"Damn it," Nell said and picked up the phone to order the old cards again, determined to find a better way. Okay, he didn't want anything too different. But that didn't mean he had to keep butt-ugly cards.

"Cream card stock," she told the printer five minutes later. "Dark brown ink. A classy older serif typeface. Very plain. Bookman? Fine. McKenna Investigations in twelve point . . ."

There, she thought when she'd hung up. *Who says I can't compromise?*

She went in to see Gabe and said, "I reordered the cards."

"Exactly like the old ones?" he said dangerously.

"No. I compromised. I think—"

"No, you don't think. I don't want you thinking and I don't want you compromising. I want you listening. And I want the old cards back."

"Look, you can't just keep saying no," Nell said. "You have to listen to me."

"Actually, I don't. I'm the boss, you're the secretary."

"Technically, yes. But—"

"No." Gabe looked up at her, impatient and exasperated. "Not 'technically.' That's the way it is."

Nell stepped on her anger. "You don't think my opinion counts."

"It counts," Gabe said. "Just not very much."

"In spite of everything I've done—"

"Nell, sleeping with me does not make you a business partner. I told you, this isn't Tim and the insurance agency."

"I'm not talking about sleeping with you," Nell snapped. "I'm talking about everything I've done for this place in the past seven months."

"You're a genius at organization," Gabe said. "Now go away."

"Just like that," Nell said.

"Just like that. I have to think and I can't with you bitching at me." He rubbed his hand over his forehead. "Can we talk about this later? I'm tired of this fight."

"No," Nell said. "If I'm hired help, there's no reason to talk about it at all."

"Well, what the hell did you think you were?" Gabe said. "We hired you and we pay you. At what point did that sound like a partnership to you?"

When I started sleeping with you, Nell thought and realized he was right. She'd slipped right back into her old life, sleeping with the boss and running his business.

He leaned forward, fixing her with those eyes, and said, "For the last time, you are *just a secretary*."

"My mistake," she said faintly and went back to sit at her desk, nauseated by her discovery.

The office looked lovely, the walls in soft gold, the couch in gray, the gold-framed photos breaking up the expanse over the bookcases and filing cabinets. Really lovely. Like an expensive insurance agency.

She hadn't started a new life at all. She'd found the closest guy who looked like Tim and remade her old world. She looked around the beautiful office, trapped again. Even fixing the window wouldn't change things. She'd just sold herself into the same old slavery. If Gabe dumped her, she'd be back on the street because she was still serving men. She hadn't started anything for herself at all.

She should quit.

That was it, she should quit. Force herself to find a new life. That would fix him. No, that wasn't right, that would fix *her*. There must be something she could do. Maybe take over The Cup? Nope, she'd still be working for somebody else, for Gabe, actually, until Chloe came back.

No, if she wanted to be her own woman, she'd have to quit and start her own business. The thought hurt, she loved being part of Gabe and Riley, loved the working relationship and even the work, loved the community of them, but she had to go. It was the only way to save what she had with Gabe. She should have gone long ago, after the first fight, except that would have been before the first kiss. She had absolutely no idea of what kind of business she wanted to start, but she was definitely going to take what was left of her divorce settlement and whatever Budge could screw out of Tim for the agency and start something new. The hell with security in her old age. She could get hit by a truck tomorrow. She should start something new today. Something that would be hers. No men involved.

Gabe came out of the office, shrugging on his suit jacket. "I'll be back at five," he told her as he headed for the door. "You want dinner at the Sycamore or the Fire House?"

"Neither," Nell said. She had a new life to plan.

"You are not going to start skipping meals again," he said from the doorway. "Just pick a place."

"I'm going to eat at home tonight. I want to think."

Gabe closed his eyes. "Oh, come on, don't sulk. That's not like you."

"I'm not sulking. I want some time alone to think about things."

"What things? Your life isn't that complex."

"I know," Nell said. "That's the problem. I jumped from one tidy situation to another without ever really finding out what the possibilities were. I just moved right in here and thought I had the same thing with you that I had with Tim. I don't."

"Well, I'm not cheating on you. I assumed that would be a plus."

"You did the same thing," Nell said, trying not to sound accusing. "You thought you had the same thing you had with Chloe."

"I never thought you were Chloe," Gabe said.

"You were right when you said just because I was sleeping with you that didn't make me a partner. Especially here, where the boss always sleeps with the secretary."

"Wait a minute—"

"No," Nell said. "It's okay. You were right and I was wrong."

"Okay," Gabe said cautiously. "So if I'm right, why am I eating alone?"

"Because it was sleeping with you that made me make that mistake," Nell said. "You scramble my thoughts."

"Do not tell me you think we should sleep apart from now on. That's just payback because I won't let you order new cards."

"No," Nell said, getting exasperated because he wouldn't listen. "There's a reason sexual harassment cases are serious."

"I did not sexually harass you," Gabe said. "For Christ's sake—"

"I didn't say you did. I'm just saying Lynnie was right, it's a bad idea for bosses to sleep with secretaries. You of all people know that. It's your rule. Which is why—"

"Which I was more than pleased to break for you," Gabe said. "Can we have this discussion over dinner? I've got places to go and things to do."

"So go there and do them," Nell said, fed up. "And while you're out, get dinner for yourself. I'm going home."

"I'll stop by later." Gabe turned to go.

"No, you won't," Nell said. "I want to think this through."

He shook his head at her. "Don't even think about breaking this off."

"*Listen,*" she said. "*You do not tell me what to do.*"

"Yeah, I do," he said. "I'm the boss."

"No, you aren't," she said. "I quit."

"You do not." Gabe slammed the street door and stood in front of it while she put her coat on and picked up her purse. "Goddamn it, Nell, I have an appointment. I don't have time for this—"

"So go," Nell said, coming around the desk to face him. "I'm not stopping you. I've got everything here so organized that anybody could take over. Get Lu in here. Hire Suze. I don't care. As long as I work here, I'm going to keep trying to be a partner and you're going to keep telling me I'm not, and we're going to be at each other's throats."

"Fine," Gabe said tiredly. "Take the rest of the day off. We'll talk about this tomorrow."

Nell felt the fury rise and smacked him hard on the arm with her purse. "Will you for once just *listen to me*? I *quit*. I won't be here tomorrow. I quit your business, I'm gone. *I quit.*" She was so mad she was sputtering. "I don't want to have dinner with you, I don't want to see you, I don't want to talk to you, I don't want to pretend everything is all right, and *I don't want you!*"

"Why do I always fall for the insane women?" Gabe asked the ceiling.

"Why do you always drive women insane?" Nell said. "A smart guy would see a pattern here."

"Hey," Gabe said. "I'm not the one with emotional problems."

"Too true," Nell said. "You have to have emotions to have emotional problems. Now *get out of my way.*"

"Fine." Gabe stepped aside and gestured to the door. "When you're over this snit, you still have a job. And me."

"I hate you," Nell said. "Drop dead."

She pushed past him and opened the door, planting her feet down hard as she strode away, exhilarated to have walked out on at least one bastard instead of waiting for him to throw her out. Progress.

Now all she had to do was find a job.

Chapter Eighteen

Riley came in while Gabe was standing in the doorway in his coat, thinking unprintable things and clenching his jaw to keep from yelling down the street after Nell.

"I just passed Nell," Riley said as he closed the door behind him. "She looked mad as hell. What happened?"

"She quit."

"Sleeping with you or working for us?"

"I don't know. And I don't care."

"You're a real genius with women, you know that? What did you do?"

Gabe tried to get his temper back. "I just told her the truth, that she wasn't a partner, just a secretary."

"And you felt it was important to share that with her because . . . ?"

"She changed the cards again." Gabe felt his blood pressure rise as he said it. "Jesus, she never stopped until she got what she wanted. If I hadn't put my foot down, she'd have painted the window."

"Let me get this straight," Riley said. "You'd rather lose the best thing that's happened to your business since me, and the best thing that's happened to your bed since Chloe, just so you wouldn't have to paint the goddamned window?"

"It was the principle of the thing," Gabe said.

"That should keep you warm tonight," Riley said. "Of course, it won't answer the phone tomorrow, but I'm sure you've got a plan for that, too."

"She'll be back tomorrow," Gabe said. He opened the street door to go before he got into another argument.

"She will not be back tomorrow. She's the only person I know who's more stubborn than you are. Give her time to cool down and then go apologize."

"For *what*? Being right?"

"What makes you think you're right?" Riley said. "The damn window needs to be painted. And she's worked as hard for the agency as you and I have, maybe harder. She's put in weird hours and never asked for overtime or time off or anything that any sane salaried worker would do. You expect her to behave like a partner and then you don't treat her like one. Hell, I'd have walked, too."

"Feel free," Gabe said and went out, slamming the door behind him, sick of the whole damn agency.

"Riley says you left Gabe," Suze said after work that night when Nell answered the door of her duplex. "Are you out of your mind?"

"No." Nell stood back so she could come in. "He was never going to listen to me as long as I stayed and played his game. So we'll just see how he does without me."

"Oh, good." Suze flopped down on the daybed and annoyed Marlene. "And while we're at it, we'll see how you do without him."

"Not a problem," Nell said. "I've been alone before."

"Yeah, you were alone without Tim," Suze said. "That was a step up. Alone without Gabe is going to be hell."

"He'll come to his senses," Nell said. "He'll ask me back. He'll want me back."

"And if he doesn't?"

"Then I'll start a new life. What would you say to starting a new business with me?"

"Doing what?" Suze said, frowning at her.

"I thought that could be your call," Nell said, coming

to sit beside her. "You decide what you want to do, and I'll run the business side."

Suze closed her eyes and shook her head. "Nell, I don't even know who I am right now, let alone what I want to do. I can't even walk away from the man I'm divorcing. He keeps calling and I can't bring myself to hang up. I know you can run anything, but I'm not your answer." She took Nell's hand. "And this is ducking the problem anyway. You love Gabe. You love the agency. I've never seen you as happy as you've been these past months. Walking out on him was dumb."

Nell swallowed. "You're supposed to be on my side."

"I am," Suze said. "Go back there right now."

"What?" Nell said, taking her hand back, outraged. "I'm not going to apologize."

"I didn't say apologize. Go back there and do him on his desk and he'll forget it ever happened."

"No, he won't. He'll remember and know I caved. If I'm ever going to be anything but somebody he orders around, I have to stick this out."

"He's probably thinking the same thing about you." Suze crossed her arms, looking disgusted. "I have to tell you, you're not going to get a lot of sympathy from me on this one. You were *happy* with him."

"I can't sell myself into bondage because he makes me happy," Nell said, her bravado gone. "Because I'm going to resent it, and then I'm going to resent him, and that'll kill it. That's what happened with Tim. I had to pretend that he was the smart one, that I lived only to serve, and I started to hate it and then I hated him. No wonder he left."

Suze sat back. "I had no idea."

"I didn't, either," Nell said. "Until I was listening to Gabe tell me I was nothing but a secretary, and it was déjà vu all over again." She bit her lip. "I can see it coming for us, too, and I swear to God, I'd rather leave him loving him than lose him hating him. I can't do that again."

"Oh," Suze said. "Oh. You're right. My God. That's what happened with me and Jack. Not the manipulating part, but . . ." She thought about it a moment. "I just got so tired of being the child bride, and he wouldn't let me be what I needed to be."

"I know," Nell said. "And that makes it so much worse. If you can look at somebody and say, 'I never loved you, you were a mistake,' that's one thing. But if you look at him and say, 'You were everything and I poisoned it because I wouldn't stand up for myself,' that's hard. That's too hard. I can't do that with Gabe."

"You're right," Suze said. "Okay, you win. How can I help? Besides starting a new business with you," she added hastily. "That's out until I get my life together."

"Go be Gabe's secretary on Monday," Nell said. "Call Margie to take back The Cup for a while, and go help him and Riley. You know how to keep the place running. I don't want the business to suffer. And God knows, Margie needs to get out of that house. She's getting stranger by the day."

"You sure you want to leave him?" Suze said.

"I'm sure," Nell lied.

On Monday, Gabe smelled coffee as he came down the stairs from his apartment and felt unaccountably relieved. Of course Nell hadn't really left him. She was a sensible woman. She loved him. She—

He stopped in the doorway to the office.

She was Suze, looking like a Hitchcock blonde in a well-cut gray suit a lot like the one Nell had been wearing when she'd put her shoulder into his window that first day.

"Hi," Suze said, pouring his cup of coffee. "Nell sent me to fill in until you find somebody else. I'm hoping it's just until you come to your senses and beg her to come back."

"Do you have any idea how to run this office?" Gabe said.

"Like Nell did?" Suze nodded. "She's been showing me things right along. I can't solve any problems, but I can keep the place going."

"Who's running The Cup?"

"Margie. Since it was an emergency, she told Budge she had to come back."

"You're hired," Gabe said. "As long as you don't mess with my business cards, you can stay."

"Your business cards are butt-ugly," Suze said.

He took his coffee cup from her, said "Thank you," went into his office, and sat down at his desk.

His father's pinstriped jacket sneered at him from the coatrack, reminding him of Nell and those long, long legs.

"Suze," he yelled and she came in. "Get rid of that coat. And take the hat while you're at it."

"Okay," Suze said, collecting them. "Anything else?"

She stood in a shaft of sunlight from the window, possibly the most beautiful woman he'd ever seen in real life, and he wished she were Nell.

"No," he said. "Thanks anyway."

Suze took the hat and coat out to the reception room and stowed them in the closet there. Until Gabe got out of this mood, she wasn't getting rid of anything. She sat down at the desk and called up the appointment log as Riley walked in and stopped dead in the doorway.

"No," he said.

"What?" she said. "I'm just filling in until they get over this."

"No, you are not," he said, looking like a maddened bull. He pointed to the doorway. "Out."

"Gabe said I have the job," Suze said. "What's the matter with you?"

He walked past her and went into Gabe's office without

knocking, and she heard him say, "No, no, no," before he slammed the door.

What the hell was wrong with him? She got up and pressed her ear to the door, but she couldn't hear anything, so she turned the doorknob slowly and pushed the door open just enough to hear Gabe say, "Get over it. We need her until Nell comes to her senses."

"Nell is not going to come to her senses," Riley said. "Nell is right. You are wrong. Go apologize and get that blonde out of here."

Good for you, Suze thought, ignoring the blonde part.

"You know, there's a distinct possibility she doesn't want to sleep with you," Gabe said. "It's not inevitable."

"Yes, it is," Riley said. "She goes."

Me? Suze thought.

"She stays," Gabe said. "Grow up."

"Let me ask you this," Riley said. "Has there ever been, in the sixty-year history of this firm, a secretary one of the partners didn't sleep with?"

"No," Gabe said. "But we're coming up on a brand-new century. Anything is possible."

"That's why I want her out of here," Riley said, and his voice was closer, so Suze scrambled back to her desk and was typing gibberish as he came out the door and glared at her.

"What *is* your problem?" she said to him, as innocently as possible. "I'm a terrific worker."

"I have no doubt," Riley said. "It's not you. Exactly."

"Well, then?"

"We have a tradition here. You don't fit it."

"Oh, please," Suze said. "I do, too. I'm perfect for it."

"What?" He look startled, and she pointed at the black bird on the filing cabinet.

"The Maltese Falcon," she said. "Sam Spade. I make a great Effie Perine. You can even call me 'Precious.' I'll gag, but I'll handle it."

"You know *The Maltese Falcon*?"

"Of course, I know *The Maltese Falcon*," Suze said, annoyed that he thought she was stupid. "It's not my favorite but—"

"What's wrong with it?" Riley said, looking belligerent again.

"Sam Spade, for one thing," Suze said. "That 'I won't play the sap for you, sweetheart' bit. What a crock."

"Hey," Riley said. "Do not criticize Sam—"

"He spent the whole story playing the sap for her," Suze went on. "She fed him one line after another and he bought them all because he wanted to sleep with her, and then she slept with him and he bought some more because he wanted to continue sleeping with her. If they'd stuck a spigot in him, they'd have had maple syrup."

"You clearly do not understand the code," Riley said.

"What code?" Suze snorted. "He was sleeping with his partner's wife. That's a code?"

"Women are treacherous—" Riley said.

"You're pathetic," Suze said. "I have work to do. You can go."

"—but I'm on to you," Riley went on. "I won't play the sap for you, sweetheart."

"Oh, sure you will," Suze said and turned back to the computer.

"Probably," Riley said and went into his office.

Suze sat and stared at the computer screen for a minute and then she got up and went into Riley's office. "Since you hate me anyway," she began.

"I don't hate you," he said, looking annoyed.

"—I slept with Jack Sunday night."

He was still for a moment, and then he leaned back in his chair. "Congratulations."

"I feel really stupid," Suze said. "I was really getting over him and—"

"Suze, you were married to him for fourteen years. You don't just walk away from that. At least women like you don't."

"What do you mean, women like me?"

"You loved him for a long time. It takes a while to get over a long marriage."

"Two years."

"What?"

"You said two years. When we were talking about Nell."

"Right," Riley said. "Most people are pretty much back on track after two years."

"I'll be thirty-four," Suze said.

"And still a babe," Riley said. "Relax and give yourself some time."

"You are being awfully nice about this," Suze said. "What's wrong with you?"

"I don't hit people when they're down. However, you seem to be recovering nicely, so watch it from now on."

Suze nodded and turned back to the doorway.

"So you came in here so I'd be lousy to you?" Riley said. "Thanks a lot."

"No. I had to talk about it with somebody, and for some reason I picked you."

"Okay," Riley said. "You all right?"

"Yes," Suze said and took a deep breath. "I certainly am."

Nell was sitting at her dining room table, drinking her third cup of coffee and trying to think of a plan, any plan, when the phone rang. Gabe, she thought, but when she picked it up, it was Jack.

"Hello, Nell," he said with his usual I-hate-you-because-you-broke-up-my-marriage chill. "Is Suze there? She's not at home or at The Cup."

"No," Nell said. "Can I take a message?" *You adulterous weasel.*

"Do you know where she is?" Jack said, and then as an afterthought, "Why are you home?"

"I quit," Nell said, figuring it was the easiest way to get rid of him.

"You quit." Jack was quiet for a few moments, long enough for Nell to wonder what the hell he was doing. Gloating didn't take that long, at least not for something as minor to Jack's existence as her employment. "I got the impression you were pretty much running the place," he said finally.

"Gabe got that impression, too," Nell said. "Don't worry, I'll find something."

"Of course you will," he said automatically, and she frowned at the phone. He wasn't gloating at all. "Well, best of luck," he said finally and hung up, and Nell thought, *What was that all about?*

Half an hour later, he called her back.

"She's still not here, Jack," Nell said.

"I know," Jack said. "I was just talking to Trevor, and he suggested you come work for us. And I think it's a good idea."

"What?" Nell said. "Jack, you hate me."

"That's a little strong," Jack said. "I don't think you helped my marriage any, but you are my sister-in-law. You're family. I want to help."

Sure you do. He was up to something. Seven months earlier, Nell would have told him to stuff his lunch, but working with Gabe and Riley had taught her the benefits of finding out why people did things.

"That's so sweet of you, Jack," she said, making her voice as mellow as possible. "Really, I'm touched."

"Family is family, Nell," Jack said, equally mellow. "Why don't we have lunch at the Sycamore at twelve and talk about it?"

"The Sycamore," Nell said. "All right. Thank you."

"Anything for family," he said.

Nell hung up and thought, *The lack of sincerity in that conversation was frightening.* What could he possibly want with her? And why the Sycamore?

It must be Suze. He couldn't possibly be hoping she was going to talk Suze into going back to him. Not even Jack was that delusional. But the Sycamore? Maybe he was hoping it would get back to Suze? Make her jealous? "This should be interesting," she told Marlene.

She picked up the phone and called the agency, praying Suze would answer instead of Gabe. She did.

"I just got an invitation to lunch from your husband," Nell said. "At the Sycamore. I'm going."

"From Jack?" Suze sounded dumbfounded.

"He's up to something," Nell said. "And I don't have anything to do today."

"Well, take notes," Suze said. "We'll discuss it later."

"Any tips?"

"When he's charming, he can be really tricky. If he's knocking himself out for you, he's going to be hard to resist."

"This is me," Nell said. "He's a weasel."

"I don't care," Suze said. "He's good."

"Not as good as I am," Nell said. "I'll drop Marlene off on my way."

While Suze was on the phone, Gabe was trying to concentrate on a report. He gave it up gladly when Lu knocked on his door and came in.

"Nell isn't out there," she said, sniffing.

"I know Nell's not there," Gabe said, and then he got a good look at Lu's swollen eyes and quivering mouth. "What's wrong?"

"Jase and I are over." Lu swallowed hard before she sat down. "Explain men to me." She was trying so hard not to cry that her whole face wavered.

"They're all after one thing," Gabe said automatically, horrified at how destroyed she was. "What happened?"

"It can't be that," Lu said. "He *got* that."

"Okay, I'll kill him," Gabe said.

"No, you can't, I love him." Lu sniffed. "I know that's dumb, but I can't help it."

"What happened?" Gabe said again, holding on to his anger with everything he had. "I thought this was forever."

"I thought so, too," Lu said and sobbed again. "But he won't marry me."

"Oh, Christ," Gabe said, going cold. "You're pregnant."

"I am not!" Indignation cleared Lu's face. "What do you think I am, *stupid?*"

"No," Gabe said, taken aback. "I got confused on the marriage part."

"I love him," Lu said. "I want to marry him."

"You're too young," Gabe said automatically.

"That's what he said." Lu sniffed one more time and then straightened in her chair. "He said we had to wait until we'd both graduated. That's more than *three years.*"

Gabe silently apologized to Jason Dysart. "Okay, calm down. You proposed to him?"

"Well, he wasn't," Lu said, looking annoyed. "I mean he's been telling me he loved me for months, and he does, you know. He really does. He's wonderful. We're wonderful together. Like you and Nell."

"Bad comparison," Gabe said, grimly. "Nell left me."

"Did you ask her to marry you?"

"No," Gabe said, taken aback. "My God, no. What are you talking about?"

"I thought maybe it was a family thing," Lu said, miserable. "You know, you start talking marriage and they bolt."

"Lu, Jase is right on this one. Although I don't see why he dumped you," Gabe said, thinking, *Like mother, like son.* Why anybody ever got involved with a Dysart—

"That was me," Lu said, looking miserable again. "I told him if he didn't marry me, it was over."

"That was stupid," Gabe said, and Lu burst into tears. "Well, I'm sorry, but it was. If you really love him, you don't give him an ultimatum and walk out the door, you

stick around and fix things." He thought of Nell, her chin
stuck out, walking past him. Quitter.

"Are you going to fix things with Nell?" Lu said, glaring
at him through her tears.

"No," Gabe said. "I'm going to wait until she comes to
her senses and comes back on her own. I don't like emotional blackmail."

"You and Jase," Lu said. "You're both willing to lose
the women you love rather than do the right thing. You're
willing to be alone *forever*."

She burst into tears, and Gabe went around the desk
and hauled her up out of her chair. She leaned against him
and he put his arms around her. "Look, if you're unhappy,
go get him back."

"How?" Lu said wetly into his suit jacket.

"Unless he's an idiot, if you start with an apology and
take back the ultimatum, I'd say you've got it made."

"I'm not going to apologize," Lu said. "I'm right."

"And *alone*," Gabe said, steering her toward the door.
"Being right is cold comfort, honey. And to tell you the
truth, you're not that right. Let me explain the art of compromise over lunch."

"You?" Lu said, blinking at him as she let him guide
her out. "This should be good."

On the way out, he said to Suze, "We're going to lunch.
Back in an hour."

"Lunch?" Suze said brightly. "You know, the Fire
House does a nice lunch."

"I want a Reuben at the Sycamore," Lu said, bending
to pat Marlene who was stretched out on the couch in her
trenchcoat.

"Excellent Reubens at the Fire House," Suze said. "And
it's quieter."

Gabe watched her smile encouragingly at Lu. "Since
when are you a fan of the Fire House?"

"Oh, I've always been a fan of the Fire House," Suze

said. "It's right around the corner from me. They do an almond-encrusted trout that—"

"What's going on?" Gabe said.

"Nothing," Suze said.

Gabe leaned on the desk, looming over her. "You are the worst liar I have ever met."

"Don't get out much, do you?" Suze said and turned her back on him to work on the computer.

"Is there something wrong?" Lu said.

"We'll find out when we get to the Sycamore," Gabe said and watched Suze's shoulders slump in defeat.

When they were gone, Suze buzzed Riley and said, "Is Gabe the jealous type?"

"In general, no."

"Because he's going to the Sycamore with Lu, and he's going to see Jack having lunch with Nell."

"Wonderful," Riley said. "If you mean is he going to go kick sand in Jack's face, no. If you mean is he going to come back in a lousy mood, yes. Why the hell is Nell having lunch with Jack?"

"Because he asked her to. Also it's a free lunch."

"There is no free lunch," Riley said. "You hungry?"

"Yeah, you and I having lunch at the Sycamore is exactly what this mess needs," Suze said. "I'm staying here. Somebody has to call 911 when the shouting starts."

"I was thinking more about Chinese takeout," Riley said. "You couldn't pay me to have lunch at the Sycamore today."

"Extra potstickers, please," Suze said.

"Vinegar with the fries, please," Nell said when the waitress had taken their order.

Jack laughed, and the waitress smiled her appreciation of Jack laughing. He really was a good-looking man, Nell thought, that rugged face, that silver hair, and those blue, blue eyes. It was so unfair. Men got better as they aged and women looked worse. How did that happen? It had to be perception, the idea that older men were richer and smarter, maybe. Of course, older women were usually richer and smarter, too, but those weren't selling points for women. High and tight were selling points for women.

"I'm glad you could join me," Jack said, and Nell refocused on him. "I know things have been strained between us, and that's not good for anybody. So how about coming to work for Ogilvie and Dysart?"

Nell thought, *Me and the O&D files.* "I'd love to."

"I can't believe Gabe let you go," Jack said, picking up his wineglass. "You revitalized his place."

"Well, my work there was done," Nell said. "Onward and upward."

"You revitalized yourself while you were at it," Jack said, smiling at her over his wine. "I've never seen you look this beautiful."

Oh, please. "Thank you," Nell said. "I did a little remodeling."

"That color's great on you, too," Jack said, gesturing to her purple sweater.

"It's Suze's," Nell said and watched his smile fade for a moment. "We traded wardrobes. She got enough gray suits to do a *Vertigo* remake."

He sat back and surveyed her for a moment, and Nell told herself not to fidget. What the hell was he doing?

"It looks better on you," he said finally. "It really does." He sounded faintly surprised, which added a veneer of honesty to the compliment. "You look great."

"Thank you," Nell said, taken aback.

"You're fun to look at," he said and grinned at her as he lifted his wineglass. "Thank you for brightening my day."

He drank, and Nell thought, *He's still a weasel.*

"So nine at my office tomorrow, then," Jack said, putting his glass down. "And that's it for business."

The waitress brought their food, and Nell sprinkled vinegar on her fries and waited for Jack's next move.

"I would never have pegged you as the Reuben type," Jack said, starting on his Caesar salad.

"I'm not a type," Nell said and bit into her corned beef.

"I'm beginning to see that," Jack said, his voice warm. "You know, I've been dumb."

No kidding.

"I have to stop chasing these younger women. Start concentrating on the smart, sassy women my own age." He smiled at her over his wine again, and Nell thought, *I'm twelve years younger than you are, you asshole*, but she smiled back at him to keep him going.

"Yeah, there's a lot to be said for seasoning," she said, popping a vinegar-soaked fry in her mouth.

"And you do look spicy today," he said. "You sure you don't want wine with your lunch?"

Yeah, what wine goes with a Reuben and fries? "Diet Coke's my drink," she said. *And Glenlivet.*

The waitress had cleared off a table next to the wall and now she motioned two people to it. *That looks like Lu*, Nell thought and then choked on her fry.

"Are you all right?" Jack said.

Nell nodded, grabbing her Diet Coke to wash down the rest of the fry as Gabe stopped at their table.

"Jack," Gabe said, and Jack jerked a little and then turned around. "We don't see you down this way much."

Jack stood up to shake his hand. "I just came down to steal Nell from you. She's working for us now."

"Is she?" Gabe said, and Nell braced herself for the storm, but there wasn't one. "She's a terrific secretary." Gabe said, and nodded at Nell. "Best of luck," he said and went over and sat down across from Lu, which put him right in her sight line.

"He took that pretty well," Jack said, sitting down again.

"I don't think he wants me back," Nell said, feeling sick. "We had some conflicts."

"I heard that wasn't all you had," Jack said. "Suze said you and Gabe were an item."

"Well, we got deleted," Nell said, and then, since Gabe was watching, she forced a smile and said, "So that's *two* positions in my life I have to fill, boss and lover."

"Only one," Jack said, meeting her eyes. "I'm your new boss."

"Then I'm halfway there."

Across the room, Gabe shook his head and turned his attention back to Lu.

"I have a court date this afternoon," Jack was saying, "or I'd take the time to show you around the firm myself."

"We'll have plenty of time," Nell said, still smiling like a maniac. "I'm sure there are *lots* of things for me to do at O&D."

"And I'll make sure you enjoy all of them," Jack said.

I'm going to throw up now. Nell looked over at Gabe, talking seriously with Lu, and thought, *I should be over there*. She leaned forward and flirted with Jack for the rest of lunch and didn't look at Gabe again.

Chapter Nineteen

Suze braced herself when Gabe got back, praying he'd keep right on going into his office, but Riley, the big schmuck, said, "How was lunch?" from the couch he was sharing with Marlene. Suze glared at him over her mu shu pork, and he stared calmly back at her over his General Tso.

"Interesting," Gabe said. "Jack and Nell were there."

"Really?" Riley said, and Suze thought, *I'm going to put vinegar in your coffee tomorrow*.

"He hired her," Gabe said, watching Suze.

Riley sat up, not kidding around anymore, annoying Marlene, who'd been doing her abused dog routine in hopes of some chicken. "To work at O&D? And you had to go and piss her off. You couldn't be nice so she'd tell us things."

Gabe looked at him with contempt. "Of course she's going to tell us things. Why do you think she took the job? What I want to know is why did they hire her? Trevor said he'd tried to get her out of here before because of the diamonds. What if there's something else here?"

Riley shook his head. "You know, your faith in yourself as the center of her universe is touching. She took the job because she needed the money. I just hope to hell she doesn't decide she needs the boss, too."

Gabe's face darkened and Suze said, fast, "You have a phone message. Somebody named Gina Taggart wants you to meet her at the Long Shot at eight tonight. I told her you'd call her back."

She held the message slip out to him and he took it. He started to say something to Riley, and then he shook his head and went into his office.

"*Are you out of your mind?*" Suze said.

"No." Riley sat back and gave Marlene a piece of chicken. "He's too damn sure of her."

"You know, she probably did take that job to look around," Suze said.

"I know," Riley said.

"Then why—"

"Because he needs to worry about her," Riley said. "Otherwise he'll just sit in that damn office and wait for her to come back, the way his dad always did with his mom. He's following a *tradition* here. Remember how long they both waited to move on each other?"

Suze nodded.

"You want to watch that mess again?"

Suze shook her head.

"Well?" Riley said and stabbed his fork into the garlic chicken. Marlene moved closer and fluttered her eyelashes.

"I don't want him yelling at me the way he yelled at Nell," Suze said. "I want him happy."

"He's not going to yell at you," Riley said. "You're not screwing up his life."

"No, he's doing that," Suze said and Riley grinned at her.

"I see you're developing a keen understanding of the McKennas," he said.

"Only one of them. You are still a mystery to me."

"Part of my charm."

"A seventeen-year-old mind in a thirty-five-year-old body. How do you keep that working for you?"

"Thirty-four," Riley said. "And I'm good, sweetheart, I'm very, very good." Marlene moaned, and he added, "See?"

"Yeah, you're hell with dachshunds," Suze said. "But will she still want you when the chicken's gone?"

"So young to be so bitter," Riley said and went back to his office, Marlene trailing him in her trenchcoat.

Jack had, not surprisingly, overstated O&D's recognition of Nell's skills. He'd also evidently not tipped his assistant, Elizabeth, that he had ulterior motives in hiring her, because once he'd introduced them, smiled warmly at Nell, kissed her on the cheek with an extensive grasp on the shoulder, and then left, Elizabeth looked at her with loathing and said, "We've found the perfect job for you."

Whoops, Nell thought and considered clueing Elizabeth in to the fact that Jack's interest was part of some plan. The fanatical light in Elizabeth's eyes stopped her. Elizabeth would tell Jack immediately. So all Nell said was, "Wonderful," and followed Elizabeth to a windowless room filled with mismatched filing cabinets and overflowing cardboard boxes and a battered desk with a computer on it from the early nineties.

"This is the newsletter room," Elizabeth said triumphantly under the one working fluorescent light. "We need it organized. I understand you're wonderful at organization. So we'd like you to file these and then index them."

"Index them," Nell said.

"Go through and make a list of names with issues and page numbers," Elizabeth said. "Not difficult."

A reasonably bright third grader could do this, Nell thought, but she smiled and said, "Wonderful. I love to organize. Uh, could we get these lights fixed?"

"I'll get right on it," Elizabeth said.

An hour later, Nell had scoped out the situation. Nobody wanted the newsletters indexed because nobody in his or her right mind would ever want to read anything *in* the newsletters. They were full of badly written puff pieces and badly lit photos of people standing stiffly with smiles pasted on their faces. All her dreams of tiptoeing through O&D files to find good stuff were buried under sixty years of good service award announcements and retirement dinner pictures. Given the futility of her task, there was only one reason Trevor had hired her: to make sure she didn't go back to the McKennas.

And the light still flickered.

"About the light," Nell said, when she found Elizabeth again.

Elizabeth stopped making whatever highly important decision she was making and looked at Nell with impatient contempt. "I've called them, Nell," she said. "Now I have work to do."

I'm going to be here two weeks, tops, Nell thought, *I don't need her.* "I need the light fixed before I can do any kind of real work."

Elizabeth drew herself up. "I *said* I called it in."

"And I appreciate it," Nell said. "But they're obviously not listening to you."

Elizabeth's eyes flared open, and Nell walked around her and knocked on Jack's door.

"You can't go in there," Elizabeth said, but Nell opened it and stuck her head in anyway.

"Jack, I don't have a light in my office," she said, as Jack looked up startled from his conversation with somebody in a suit. "Could you—"

"Elizabeth handles that," Jack said, clearly trying to keep his temper.

"Yes, but she's not," Nell said. "I'm going blind. They had light at the McKennas."

"*Elizabeth,*" Jack said, and fifteen minutes later Nell had light and Elizabeth's undying hatred.

And for the rest of the week, she also had the newsletters, sorting them, filing them, setting up the indexing system, and typing in one meaningless name after another. She had found the files from 1978 immediately, but the only thing of semi-interest was a full-page obituary of Helena that must have taxed the writer's imagination: Helena really hadn't lived enough to fill a full page. Nell looked in 1993, too, to see if Stewart Dysart had gotten a mention for lifting company funds and deserting the senior partner's daughter, but there was nothing. Only the good news got into the *O&D News & Notes*. And she was going to get to read all of them.

Maybe Gabe could learn to compromise, she thought as she started with the latest newsletter, prepared to work her way back through to the beginning of time. *Maybe I'll go surrender to Gabe and live with the old business cards.* The surrendering part sounded wonderful, right there on his desk would be good, but she kept typing anyway.

The Monday after Nell went to work for O&D, the new business cards came. Suze opened one of the boxes and looked at them, and then she took both boxes into Gabe's office where he was conferring with Riley.

"Okay," she said. "Your new business cards are here and they're good. Very quiet, very classy, and frankly, a huge improvement on your old cards, which looked amateurish."

"Look," Gabe said. "We don't need—"

"You haven't even seen them," Suze said. "Nell is gone, so this isn't about who's in charge. It's about the business cards, period, and these are better than your old ones. So keep an open mind."

"Let's see 'em," Riley said, and she handed him the box with his name on it. He opened it, took out a card, looked at it for a minute, and said, "She's right."

Suze put the other box on Gabe's desk and left, figuring Riley could take it from there. When he came out, she said, "Well?"

"He's coping," Riley said. "It helps that they're not geeky, and it helps a lot more that they really are better."

"But mostly it helps that Nell's not here," Suze said. "He was just blocking her."

"No," Riley said. "The last cards were a nightmare. This

is the first thing she's done that's shown any indication that she understands what this place is about."

"She means well."

"Which is about the worst thing you can say about anybody," Riley said and went into his office.

An hour later, Suze was finishing a phone check on a reference when Jack walked in. Every nerve in her body froze, but she nodded to him and held up a finger to say, *Just a minute*, and he sat down on the couch and waited, looking inscrutable.

Which meant he wasn't. The calmer Jack looked, the more intense he was about something. That couldn't be good, but then the fact that he was sitting in front of her wasn't good, either.

She finished with the check, thanked the guy she'd been talking to, hung up, and made a notation on the file. Then she looked at Jack and said, "Hi."

"You sound just like a professional," he said, smiling at her.

"I am a professional," she said. "What's up?"

He didn't say anything for a minute, just gazed into her eyes, and she thought, *Fat chance, buddy*, and wondered why that had always worked before. Probably because she'd loved him. *I don't love him anymore*, she thought and wondered when that had happened. Not when she'd found out about Olivia. Before. Everything after that had been letting go of illusions. Like Nell had said, she should have left while she loved him.

"I've been expecting a call from your divorce lawyer," he said, finally.

"Jean?" Suze blinked at him. He was right. She still hadn't told Jean to file.

"Suze," he said, leaning forward. "You don't want this divorce any more than I do."

"Well, yes, actually, I do," Suze said. "You slept with another woman. That pretty much did it for me." *That and fourteen years of being a child bride.*

"Suze, that's not fair," Jack said. "We were having problems, admit it."

"Jack," Suze said. "I stopped letting you tell me what was fair weeks ago. You knew I was unhappy and you had sex with another woman so you wouldn't have to admit that I had a right to a life, too. So fine, now I have the life I wanted and you have the other woman. I'm sure you'll learn to enjoy 'N Sync as much as the Righteous Brothers, you've always been good at adapting to new wives."

"This is the life you want?" Jack said, looking around the office. "Honey, this life won't get you diamonds."

"Jack, I don't like diamonds. I like this."

"This?" Jack said incredulous. "Oh, that's great. And what are you going to do if Nell comes back? I can't keep her on forever. It's been a week and she's already driving Elizabeth crazy."

"Nell says Elizabeth thinks she owns you when you're in the office," Suze said. "Elizabeth's just jealous."

"You always did listen to Nell before you'd listen to me," Jack said, an edge to his voice. "Maybe if you'd listened to me—"

"—you'd still have me entombed in that house," Suze finished for him.

"I notice you haven't left that house," Jack said.

"Put it on the market," Suze said. "I'll be out by the weekend."

Jack shook his head. "I don't want you out. Look, I was trying to be nice, but I've had it with Nell. She's not only bothering Elizabeth, she keeps coming on to me." Suze tried not to let her skepticism show on her face, but it must have because he added, "Yeah, I knew you wouldn't believe it, but she's not much of a friend, Suze, putting the make on your husband. I'm going to let her go, and then she'll come back here and take this job away from you and then where'll you be? Stay in the house and let's give this another chance."

"I have plans for when Nell comes back," Suze said.

"Really?" Jack said. "But none of those plans involves filing for divorce."

Suze got her Palm V out of her purse. She keyed in Jean's name and got her number, while Jack said, "Cute. A Palm Pilot just like the big girls."

She dialed Jean's office, and when she got the secretary she said, "Hi, this is Susannah Campbell," and watched Jack jerk back a little at the sound of her maiden name. "Right. Would you tell Jean to go ahead and file my divorce papers? I should have called sooner but I forgot. Thanks."

She hung up and looked at Jack. "Anything else?"

"You had it all," Jack said. "I gave you *everything*."

"Thank you," Suze said. "Now you can give it to Olivia. I'd send her my best, but I need it, so I'm just sending her you. Have a nice life."

Jack stood up, his face set and Suze thought, *I may have gone too far on that last one*. Then he left, and Suze flopped back in Nell's ergonomic desk chair and breathed again. Well, that was the past, this was the future. She was pretty sure she had a future. She definitely had plans, she was just afraid to get started on them.

It's time, she thought and stood up, straightening her skirt. Then she went to Riley's door, which was slightly ajar, knocked, went in, and sat down across from him.

"You know, most places, people wait for somebody to say, 'Come in,' before they come in," Riley said. He was leaning back in his desk chair with a stapled report in his hand, and he appeared to be on about the third page. "Appeared," Suze thought, was probably the right word. There was no way he'd missed anything in the outer office. The guy had ears like a bat.

"Maybe they wait most places," Suze said, "but not here."

"Picked that up, did you?" Riley tossed the papers on his desk.

Suze took a deep breath, opened her eyes wide, and smiled at him. "Riley, I—"

He sat up and pointed his finger at her. "Don't do that."

"What?" she said, mystified.

"That little-old-me look. I'm not Jack. Just tell me what you want and we'll talk about it."

"Okay. I want to work here."

Riley looked cautious. "You do."

"No," Suze said. "I'm filling in for Nell, and I can't wait until she comes back. This office stuff bores me to tears. But I like what you do. I like researching and talking to people and figuring out things. And you have a lot of work here, too much, you're turning down some people. You could train me to do this and I'd be good at it. I want to work here as an investigator when Nell comes back."

Riley sat back again and didn't say anything, so she waited. She'd once thought he was a Neanderthal, but not anymore. Now she had a great deal of respect for Riley's thought processes, or for most of them, anyway.

"Okay," he said and sat up again. He picked up the file he'd been holding and handed it to her. "Do this one."

Suze took the file and looked at the heading: Check-Out Girl. "This is Becca Johnson, right? She was in yesterday."

"What's she look like?" Riley said. "Give me a description. Detailed."

Suze called up the best of her memory of Becca. "She's about five six, a hundred and thirty pounds, early thirties, African American, brown eyes, brown hair, pretty, nervous, wearing a brown cotton turtleneck and a brown suede jacket from last year's Bloomingdale's catalog—maybe the year before, it's one of their standards—Levi's jeans, brown Aigner loafers. Her earrings were plain gold loops, but they were real gold. I'd say she has a middle-class income and uses it well. She had a mustard seed necklace, which was very old, so I'd also guess she's sentimental, romantic, and has a strong religious background although she may not be practicing anymore. She's not stupid, but that romantic streak could make her vulnerable. Also, she parked in front of the window and she was driving a good-condition Saturn, so she's practical, and there was an OSU parking tag hanging from her mirror, an A tag, so she's with the university." She stopped. "Those A tags run close to four hundred bucks; she must really care about parking."

"Anything else?" Riley said, looking a little taken aback.

"Yes," Suze said. "Her bag was Coach."

"Which means what?"

"Quality," Suze said. "Becca and I would get along fine. Why are you looking at me like that?"

"The Bloomingdale's thing," Riley said. "You know what *year* the jacket was?"

"Well, yes, but I couldn't tell you what year the Saturn was." Suze gestured with the folder. "So I just read this and then what?"

"She came in yesterday because she finally confronted her boyfriend and he told her his name is Egon Kennedy and he's from Massachusetts, a distant cousin of *the* Kennedys. She believes him. We're skeptical. So we're checking it out even though she just stopped by to tell Gabe everything is fine."   .

"Okay," Suze said. "Any advice on how to do this?"

Riley picked up a yellow legal pad and tossed it to her. "Take notes."

She leaned forward and took a pen from his Wile E. Coyote mug, her pulse picking up. "Go ahead," she said, and he started to talk, and she wrote down everything, stopping him only to ask a question when something wasn't clear. When he was finished, she said, "My God. You can find out anything about anybody."

"And it's so much easier with the Internet," he said. "Now go and find out about our boy Randy."

Suze nodded and stood up. "Thank you."

"Effie, if you can do this, we'll be thanking you," Riley said.

"I can do this," Suze said.

"So you don't like diamonds?" Riley said.

"No, but I like gold and Armani," Suze said. "I'm not cheap, I'm discriminating."

"Good for you," Riley said. "Get to work." She turned to go and he said, "One more thing."

"Yes," she said, turning back, waiting for whatever slam he had ready for her.

"That little-old-me thing?"

She nodded.

"You may use it on other people."

"Thank you," she said and escaped into the outer office before she grinned.

She was free. She had a chance at a real job. She was going to move, could move tonight if she wanted to, Nell would take her. She picked up the phone directory and looked under "Moving Companies." "Yes," she said when somebody answered. "I'd like to arrange for someone to pack a lot of very valuable china. Spode."

And then she told them to deliver it to Olivia.

Nell opened the door that night to find Suze standing on her doorstep with three suitcases and a large box full of egg cups.

"You know that extra bedroom you have?" she said. "Can I have it? I filed for divorce today."

Nell opened the door wider. "Come on in. It's about time you experienced how the other half lives."

She put Suze in her bed for the night and curled up on the daybed in the living room with Marlene and her chenille throw since she couldn't sleep anyway. She missed Gabe, and it wasn't getting better, and she didn't know how to fix it. She couldn't go back to the way—

Somebody hammered on the door, and for one moment she hoped it was Gabe. She patted a cranky Marlene and put her on the floor in case Gabe was in one of his sweeping moods, knowing that with her luck it was probably Farnsworth, demanding his SugarPie back. Which was only his right, she thought guiltily.

But when she turned on the porch light and looked through the curtain on the door, it was Jase.

"What's wrong?" she said, letting him in. "It must be midnight."

"This is me, cracking," Jase said grimly. "I need jewelry."

"What?"

"Do you still have the engagement ring Dad gave you?"

Nell blinked at him. "Probably. I think I stuck it in my jewelry box. Why? Oh, no, you're not—"

"It's that or she'll leave me," Jase said. "We fought a week ago. She's not backing down. I'm thinking I can talk her into being engaged until I can graduate and get a job."

"Jase, you're too young—"

"Mom, I've been over this. She wants it now, and she's serious." He looked more miserable than Nell had ever seen him. "Don't give me grief on this. You don't want the ring anymore anyway."

"Neither does she," Nell said. "It's a lousy ring. Your dad was really poor when he bought it. Plus, we got divorced. She's Chloe's kid, she's going to believe in karma."

"Oh, hell," Jase said. "Maybe I can get the stone reset."

"Jase, a jeweler would have a hard time finding that stone, it's that tiny." Nell leaned against the wall and tried to think.

"Uncle Jack buys Aunt Suze diamonds she never wears," Jase said, thinking out loud. "Maybe she'd let me buy one from her on time."

"More bad karma," Nell said. "Your Aunt Suze is asleep upstairs. She filed for divorce today."

"Great," Jase said.

"Okay, okay." Nell thought faster. "You don't want Aunt Margie's diamond from Uncle Stewart, that goes beyond bad. I'm running out of diamonds here."

"I'll sell my car," Jase said.

"Jase, you couldn't get a zirconium for what that car would bring. Are you sure this is a good idea? Because I don't like it that Lu's holding you up for jewelry."

"She's not. She doesn't care about the ring. She wants to get married."

"*Now?*" Nell said, finally comprehending.

"At last," Jase said, casting his eyes to the ceiling. "Yes, *now*. She wants to be Mrs. Jason Dysart."

"You're an *infant*," Nell said, really alarmed. "Is she insane?"

"I'm not an infant, and I want that, too," Jase said. "Just not right away. I think I should be able to support a wife before I take one."

"My God." Nell pulled out a dining room chair and sank into it. "*Married?*"

"Get used to it," Jase said, following her. "It's going to happen. We were going to move in together this summer anyway."

Nell jerked her head up. "Are you *nuts*? Do you know what her father would do to you?"

"Boy, does this guy have you snowed. Lu's nineteen. He can't do anything to me."

"That's what you think. And he's in a lousy mood right now, too. You guys sure know how to pick your moment."

"Great." Jase looked frazzled. "You know, I have enough problems without this. I have *finals*, for Christ's sake."

Nell laughed. "Finals. Yeah, you're old enough to get married."

"If I don't pass my finals, I won't graduate," Jase said grimly. "And if I don't graduate, I won't find a job. And if I don't have a job, I can't get married, and I'll lose the woman I love. So yes, *finals*."

"Sorry," Nell said. "You're right. I'm wrong."

"The least you could do is go over there and jolly him out of it," Jase said.

"I can't," Nell said. "I left."

"You what?"

"I quit. I quit the job and him. It's over."

"I am a dead man." Jase sat down on the chair next to hers and put his head on the table.

Nell smoothed his hair. "It'll be okay. We'll think of something. There's my divorce settlement. I can give you—"

"No," Jase said, sitting up. "I'm not that big a mooch. You're living on nothing now. Forget it."

"There must be something," Nell said and then she focused on her china cabinet. "Clarice Cliff."

"Who?"

"My china," Nell said. "There's a teaset in there worth some money. I could sell it."

"Grandma Barnard gave you that stuff," Jase said. "From England."

Nell looked at him. "So it's my turn to give it to you."

Jase swallowed. "You don't even want me to do this."

"I'd like you to think about it," Nell said. "I'd like you to do it without her threatening you. But if this is what you really want, then I want it for you."

"I want it," Jase said. "But don't sell the china yet. Let me talk to Grandma Dysart."

"Clarice would approve," Nell said. "And so would Grandma Barnard. I'll call the dealer in the morning."

"Just *wait*," Jase said.

"No," Nell said. "I've spent too many damn years waiting. This is the right thing to do."

The next day on her lunch hour, Nell sold the teaset— thirty-four pieces of pristine Clarice Cliff Secrets—to the antique dealer in Clintonville who had appraised it. Then she took the check to Jase, who was impressed and apologetic, and then she went back to O&D.

"You're late," Elizabeth said.

"Actually, I'm not," Nell said. "I left for lunch late because I was finishing up a section."

"We need to know where you are, Nell," Elizabeth said, and Nell thought, *Why? In case there's a newsletter emergency?*

"It'll never happen again," Nell said and went back to the newsletter room, thinking, *I give her until the end of the week before she fires me.* She'd seen assistants who were possessive before, but Elizabeth was raising it to a new level. It didn't help that during the past week Jack had made it clear that he found Nell charming, enchanting, colorful, funny, sweet, and indispensable. Nell knew that because he'd told her all those adjectives, dropping them on her one at a time for the cumulative effect. She hadn't bought it, but Elizabeth had, and as Jack had grown warmer, Elizabeth had grown positively frigid. When she'd taken to criticizing Nell's clothing—"The proper attire for women at O&D is the suit"—Nell had almost felt sorry for her. It was pathetic to fall hopelessly in love with your boss. For one thing, it played hell with your job security.

Get a grip, Elizabeth, Nell thought now, and then thought, *Was that me with Gabe?*

No, it wasn't. She hadn't been possessive of Gabe, she'd just wanted the right to run the office her way. He didn't want to run the damn office, he just wanted it run well. And she'd done that.

Maybe if I'd said that to him instead of ordering business cards and slapping them on his desk . . .

Well, that would be something they could talk about later. If they ever talked again. She went back to the newsletter files and picked up a stack from 1992, missing Gabe and thinking, *I hate this job.*

So fine, maybe she wouldn't wait for Elizabeth to toss her, maybe this weekend she'd get her plans together and figure out what she wanted to do, and then she'd go do that. She began to scan the old newsletters automatically, keying in the names she found, as she planned. She wanted to run an office, she liked running offices, keeping appointments straight, keeping other people organized. She really didn't want to sell anything or leave the office to work with others, she wanted to maintain a small perfect world for others to live in. "Cartouche life," Suze had called it, and she was right.

So all she had to do was find somebody she liked and respected who was doing work she liked and respected, and organize that person's business life. Of course, she'd already found that person in Gabe but . . .

She went on indexing newsletters until, close to five o'clock, she flipped over a newsletter and read "Stewart Dysart." It wasn't the first time she typed a page number after his name, but it was the first time there'd been a picture. It was Stewart all right, blond and running to fat and arrogant as hell, his arm around a pretty blonde, his secretary, according to the caption. Kitty Moran.

Nell looked closer. Kitty Moran looked familiar. Extremely familiar. Nell put her thumb over Kitty's blonde upsweep and imagined her brunette. Lynnie Mason.

"I will be damned," she said out loud and took the newsletter out to the copy machine. When she was done, she put the copy back in the files and stuffed the original in her purse, and then she went out to the hall—"Bathroom break," she said to Elizabeth, who frowned at her—and around a corner to another secretary's desk. "Can I use your phone?" she said. "Elizabeth is—"

The man pushed the phone toward her. "You don't need to tell me about Elizabeth," he said, and she grinned at him and dialed Riley's number.

"It's me," she said when he answered.

"Tell me you're coming back," Riley said.

"No. Listen, I have something you'd like to see."

"Never say that to me in front of Gabe," Riley said. "I gather this is something I haven't already seen?"

"Yes," Nell said. "But I could meet you in an hour and go into great detail."

"I also gather you are not alone," Riley said.

"I'm in the belly of the beast. How about the Sycamore? Say, six?"

"How about the Long Shot at eight? It's a bar on Front Street in the Brewery District. I have to be there anyway."

"Okay," Nell said, thinking it was probably just as well since Gabe was likely to show up at the Sycamore and feeling treacherously disappointed about that.

"I hate to sound melodramatic," Riley said, "but this isn't putting you in any danger, is it?"

Nell smiled at the secretary who was blatantly listening. "Yes," she said. "Elizabeth is going to kill me and hide my body in the newsletter room, and let me tell you, it'll be decades before anybody goes in there again." The secretary grinned at her.

"Eight, then," Riley said. "Look hot. I only hang out in bars with hot women."

"Like that's news," Nell said, and hung up, smiling at the secretary. "Thank you so much."

"My pleasure," he said. "I'm good for anything that bugs Elizabeth."

Nell went back to the newsletter room and found Jack waiting for her. "Taking a break?" he said, smiling tightly at her, and she thought, *Uh-oh. Something happened while he was out.*

"A small break," she said.

"Do you know the boss well enough to do that?" he said and took a step closer.

"Probably not," Nell said, trying not to overreact. "I'll just get back to work."

"No hurry." Jack loomed over her, looking mad as hell behind his smile.

Okay, is he going to hit me or kiss me? Nell thought, and when Jack grabbed her and kissed her, she was so relieved she didn't stop him. He was a pretty good kisser, even when she knew he was doing it so she'd tell Suze. Nell heard a bleating sound and pulled back to see Elizabeth, standing in the door to the newsletter room. Nell looked up at Jack and said, "Busted." Jack jerked back, glaring at Elizabeth, but before he could say anything, Nell said, "You know, I am absolutely *ruining* the working environment here. I quit."

She ducked away from Jack and grabbed her purse and escaped into the parking lot, neither knowing nor caring what was happening behind her, heading back to the Village where she belonged.

Gabe had just gotten back to the office when Riley came in and sat down across from him.

"We're missing a secretary again," Gabe said. "Spinal Tap didn't have this much trouble with drummers."

"She's out on a job," Riley said. "I gave her Becca's Randy."

"You did."

"She wants to be an investigator. I think she'd be good at it, and we're turning down work. So I'm trying her out, and if she's good, she can move into that when Nell gets back."

"And where would we put her?" Gabe said, trying to ignore the way his pulse picked up when he thought about Nell coming back.

"Chloe's storeroom," Riley said. "We get rid of the freezer and put a window in the street wall."

"Chloe might have something to say about that," Gabe said. "And then there's the question of where we'd put the freezer files."

"The basement," Riley said.

"Okay." Gabe turned on his computer, not really caring. "It's your call."

"She's going to be good," Riley said. "She has skills we don't."

"I never doubted it." He opened his notebook and flipped through until he found the notes for his report.

"By the way, I stopped by O&D on a background check and offered Trevor and Jack a reference for Nell. I told them she'd organized everything in the place except for the Porsche. We all got a laugh out of that."

"Very subtle. If the Porsche gets stolen it's nobody's fault but your own."

"We can only hope they're that dumb. I have it locked in the garage so they'll have to make an effort to get to it."

"You are sure there's nothing in it?"

"Positive," Gabe said. "I'm not that dumb."

"Jury's still out on that," Riley said, "considering your fine performance with Nell."

"Was there anything else, or are you leaving?" Gabe said.

"Something else. Chloe called from London."

"Did she?" Gabe squinted at his notes. "Did you ask about the earrings?"

"Yes. Your father gave them to her in a red box with a devil on it when Lu was born. He told her to save them for Lu when she got married. She wore them for the picture, and then she put them away and forgot about them until I asked."

"I knew she wasn't a diamond kind of woman," Gabe said. "He gave them to her in that box? The box with the car title?"

"Yep. But she put the box on the shelf in the bathroom because of the picture on top of it. The devil. Bad karma."

"*Chloe* put it up on the shelf? Did it have the title in it then?"

"She didn't notice. But I don't think anybody moved it since she put it up there, so my guess is yes."

"Then Lynnie never had it. So what was she looking for?"

"The diamonds," Riley said. "She was a diamond kind of woman. Back to Chloe. She talked to Lu, and Lu's upset, so Chloe's upset."

Gabe shrugged. "Lu and Jase are having some problems. They'll work it out. I still don't get how Lynnie knew Trevor or Jack or why they'd tell her about the diamonds."

"Pay attention to the present for a minute," Riley said. "Chloe's worried about Lu. She's coming home."

"When?"

"Should be here tomorrow. She was at Heathrow when she called."

"Okay," Gabe said and went back to the computer.

"And Nell called."

Gabe swung away from the computer. "Really."

"She found something at O&D. There were people listening, so she told me she'd tell me the rest tonight at the Long Shot. I'm meeting her at eight."

"There's a coincidence," Gabe said. "I'm meeting Gina Taggart there at eight."

Riley looked innocent. "I told Suze I'd take her there tonight, show her the ropes, so I'm meeting Nell there, too. Convenience. Not a coincidence."

"What ropes are there in a bar?"

"I have my reasons," Riley said.

"I'm sure you do," Gabe said. "And you did not tell Suze you'd take her to the Long Shot. You'll tell her that when she gets back. You set this whole thing up so I'd see Nell."

"You're a very suspicious man," Riley said.

"Am I right?"

"Yes."

"Thank you," Gabe said.

When Riley was gone, Gabe sat back and thought about Nell and Suze and Chloe and then Nell again. He wanted Nell back. "Compromise," he'd told Lu. Maybe he could corner her tonight and suggest a compromise. At this point, she could present a list of demands and he'd give her all of them. Except the window. But anything else, she could have.

Oh, hell, she could have that, too, as long as she came back.

He put Dean on and listened to "Everybody Loves Somebody Sometime," while he keyed in the report and felt happier than he had since Nell had left.

When Nell got home that night at six, she showed Suze the picture in the newsletter.

"We should take this to Margie," Suze said. "We have time. We don't have to be at the bar for two hours. And she'll know about Kitty, I bet." She put the newsletter down. "We should talk to her anyway. She's been a little . . . strange at work this week."

"Work does that to some women," Nell said, thinking of Elizabeth.

Half an hour later, sitting at her kitchen table over a glass of soy milk, Margie squinted at the picture and said, "Yep, that's Kitty. I always thought Stewart was sleeping with her."

"You don't sound too upset," Suze said.

"Well, it was Stewart," Margie said. "She could have him. In fact, I always thought she got him in the end."

"You think he left with her?" Nell said.

"Well, I did. But if she came back, where is he?" Margie said, and then she put her glass down, horrified. "Oh, no. What if he's back? What if he came back with her? What if they ran out of money and came back here for more? *What'll I do?*"

"You'll get a divorce," Suze said. "He's the embezzler. He can't make any trouble for you."

"Yes, he can," Margie said, staring stricken at her soy milk. "I tried to kill him."

Chapter Twenty

"Stop showing off, Marge," Suze said.

"I'm not showing off," Margie said. "I hit him hard and he went down, blood all over the place. It was the only part of my marriage I really enjoyed."

She smiled wistfully, and Nell and Suze looked at each other. Then Suze picked up Margie's milk and tasted it. "Amaretto," she said. "Lots of it."

"Margie," Nell said. "You've had enough calcium."

"It is impossible for women in our age group to have enough calcium," Margie said, her voice tight with panic. "As you stand there, calcium is just dripping out of your bones. Budge says so."

"What's he say about the Amaretto?" Suze said.

"He doesn't know about the Amaretto," Margie said. "And he's never gonna. What am I going to do about Stewart?"

"Nothing," Nell said, keeping her voice upbeat. "You did not try to kill him."

"Yeah, I did," Margie said, sniffing and sipping at the same time so that she choked a little. "He was leaving on a business trip and Budge came by and told me he'd taken money from Daddy. So I told him he had to give it back or I'd leave, and he laughed and said that I didn't have the backbone to leave, and even if I did, I wouldn't be much of a loss because I was boring."

"Uh-oh," Suze said.

"And then he turned his back on me and I hit him with my Franciscan Desert Rose milk pitcher."

"Oh," Nell said, believing her now.

"It was on the buffet, full of Queen Anne's lace." She nodded into the distance. "That pitcher was a big sucker, and I caught him right across the back of the head with it. He went down like a rock. Queen Anne *everywhere*."

"Okay," Nell said, regrouping as fast as she could. "Well—"

"Then Budge came in, and I called Daddy, and Daddy called Jack, and I went upstairs, and they got him to the airport. And he never got on the plane." She shook her head as if this were just one more example of Stewart's perfidy. "So I figured he was with Kitty and the money."

"Budge was there when you hit him?" Suze said.

"He was in the next room," Margie said. "When Stewart came home, I made Budge go hide."

"Stewart didn't see Budge's car?"

"He always parked over on the side street," Margie said.

"Always?" Suze said, straightening. "Margie?"

"Well, Stewart was really awful," Margie said. "In bed and out. And Budge is really good."

Nell got up and poured herself a milk and Amaretto. "Okay. You were sleeping with Budge while Stewart was alive?"

"It seemed like a good idea," Margie said. "Daddy doesn't believe in divorce. He thinks Jack is a scandal."

"So do I," Suze said and poured herself a glass, too.

"So I was stuck. And then Stewart left, and there was Budge. I owe him, so I have to stay with him. Most of the time it's all right, but sometimes he makes me crazy. Like he hates me working at The Cup. And the vegetarian thing. I mean, I do think being a vegetarian is important, but everybody needs to cheat a little. I haven't had a hamburger since he moved in. Sometimes I'd kill for a steak."

"That shattering sound you just heard was our illusions," Suze said to Nell.

"So then what happened? After Stewart left." Nell nodded at Margie to encourage her.

"Budge came back the next day and told me not to worry, that Daddy would see I'd have to divorce Stewart once he found out about the missing money." Margie looked mutinous. "Except he didn't. Daddy said he didn't want any more scandal. He said he'd fix it so Stewart never bothered me again."

"Hello," Suze said.

"I think he was going to make him be a good husband," Margie said. "Where Daddy got the idea he knew anything about being a good husband is beyond me."

"So you hit Stewart with the Desert Rose pitcher," Suze said, the wonder still in her voice.

"Keep up," Nell said to her. "We don't have time to stop and review."

"And he left and now I have Budge. Sex isn't everything. And he really wants to get married now." Margie put her nose back in her glass.

"You know, you're going to have to hit Budge with the milk pitcher, too," Suze said.

"Suze." Nell smacked her with her foot.

"Hey, if I could beat Jack to death with that damn Spode, I would," Suze said, and Nell took her glass of milk away from her.

"I really thought that if I just didn't tell anybody, maybe nobody would ever know," Margie said sadly. "But that never works."

"It's okay, honey," Nell said, pretty sure it wasn't.

"I have to go to the bathroom," Margie said to nobody in particular and wandered off toward her powder room.

"So Stewart's come back annoyed because Margie pasted him with her Franciscanware seven years ago?" Suze said. "That doesn't make sense."

"You're forgetting the two million in insurance Budge wants her to collect," Nell said. "That would bring a lot of people back from the dead."

"Margie better keep that pitcher handy," Suze said. "Give me back my milk."

"Gabe and Riley are not going to believe this."

Suze took her milk back. "You think we should tell them?"

"Of course we should tell them. Margie's off the hook. Stewart got up and walked away."

"Okay. But maybe you should leave out the part about her clocking him with the pitcher. And sleeping with Budge."

"Which means I tell them what? That Stewart fell down on his way to the airport?"

Suze looked conflicted. "She's our friend and she was married to a son of a bitch."

"She did not kill him with earthenware," Nell said. "She's clear even if he's dead. And he doesn't appear to be dead. Although Lynnie didn't sound like she was working with anybody. She wanted me to work with her, so he couldn't be with her."

"She was also the queen of the cons," Suze said. "Maybe it was a come-on."

"No," Nell said. "I trust her."

"You trusted Tim, too," Suze said, and Nell drank some more milk.

Margie came back. "I feel kind of sick."

"Soy poisoning," Suze said. "Lay off the milk for a while."

"Okay," Nell said, pushing the rest of her own milk away. "We need to concentrate on the important stuff here. Margie, Stewart cannot hurt you, so stop worrying about him. And you don't need to marry Budge if you don't want to."

"Nell," Suze said, warning in her voice.

"Stop doing whatever he says," Nell said.

"*Nell*," Suze said, and Nell looked up to see Budge standing in the living room doorway, looking like the Sta-

Puf Marshmallow Man at the end of *Ghostbusters*, ready to take out a city.

"Budge, she doesn't want to get married," Nell said.

"Yes, she does," Budge said. "She just thinks she doesn't because you're not. She thinks she wants everything you do, like an apartment in the Village, but she'd be miserable if she moved." He came up to the table and put his arm around Margie, and his voice rose as he went on. "You've upset her. You're always upsetting her. Every woman doesn't have to be like you. Every woman doesn't want a job and an apartment. Apartments are dangerous. Terrible things happen to women in apartments, rapes and burglaries and murders. Margie needs to stay here with me where she's safe."

Suze said, "Margie?" but Nell knew it wouldn't do any good. Margie would fight back about the time she threw out her dinnerware.

"I think you'd better go," Budge said.

The last thing they heard as they went out the door was Budge saying, "You know your daddy doesn't want you talking to them, especially Nell. You should have told them you couldn't see them," and Margie saying, "I need some more milk."

On the way back down High Street, Suze said, "He makes me ill."

"That might be the soy and Amaretto," Nell said.

"That might have been me," Suze said. "I used to listen to Jack like that."

"I let Tim pretend I was just the office help," Nell said. "We do it because we want to keep the marriage going."

"I don't think I'm doing that anymore," Suze said. "Of course, I'm pretty gullible. I believe anything I think."

"I'm lying to myself about one thing," Nell said.

"Gabe?"

"Marlene," Nell said, staring at the dog on her lap, and

Marlene picked up her head and looked at Nell to see if anything good was about to happen.

Suze frowned at her, incredulous. "*Marlene?* Come on—" Then she broke off. "You're not back on that I-stole-a-dog-from-its-loving-master thing, are you? He called her SugarPie, for heaven's sake. For that alone the ASPCA should have tagged him."

"I love her," Nell said. "I cannot tell you how much I love this neurotic dog. But she is neurotic. I adore her and she looks like I beat her daily. And if somebody took her from me—"

"I don't believe this," Suze said.

"It's been nagging at the back of my mind," Nell said, holding the dog closer.

"I know," Suze said. "I just don't know why."

"We've been carrying guilt for so long," Nell said. "You resented Jack, and Margie hated Stewart, and you both felt guilty about it. You faced Jack and you're free. Margie won't face Budge so she's stuck."

"So you're going to face Farnsworth?" Suze said. "Good luck on that one."

"I was thinking more of taking Marlene back to the yard," Nell said, "and letting her go. And then if she trotted off toward the house and was happy, I'd know I'd done the right thing. And if she stayed with me, then I could keep her without guilt."

"And if she rolls over on her back and moans pathetically?"

"Same thing," Nell said. "That's what she was doing when I dognapped her. It'll be getting dark soon. We could do it now before I lose my nerve."

"Now?" Suze said. "Listen, I'm against this. I love this damn dog, too. Plus, she has that wardrobe. Will Farnsworth get her a leather bomber jacket for the chilly nights?"

"Budge is holding on to Margie because he loves her," Nell said. "He really does. I thought he was awful back there, but he wasn't being mean. He was really tender with her. He thinks its okay because he loves her. I can't condemn him for that and keep Marlene for the same reason."

"I think it's different," Suze said, but her voice wasn't sure.

"Margie's going crazy from the frustration and the guilt. I always thought it was funny the way she solved everything with 'maybe he'll never know,' but that's how I am with Marlene. I want a clean slate, no guilt." She took a deep breath. "I have to do it. And then we have to tell Gabe about Margie."

"Great," Suze said flatly. "Nothing like ethics to ruin a perfectly good evening."

A little after eight, when the sun had given up for the day, Nell walked a naked Marlene down the lot line to her old backyard. When they got there, she crouched down and undid Marlene's leash and collar, and looked deeply into her eyes. "I love you, Marlene," she said. "I'll always love you. But this is your home. So if you want to go, it's okay." Marlene didn't move, and Nell said, "Of course, if you want to come back with me, that's okay, too."

Marlene yawned and looked around and then, evidently spotting something of interest, she trotted into the yard.

So much for the old *if you love something, set it free* bit, Nell thought as she stood and watched her. Of course, the depth of Marlene's feeling had always been a mystery. Nell wanted to yell after her, "You're losing the chenille throw here, did you think about that?" but the only word that Marlene really knew well was "biscuit," and it didn't seem appropriate under the circumstances.

Marlene examined the yard for a while and then sat down, bored, and Nell realized the flaw in her plan. Farnsworth was going to have to let Marlene in, but there was no way Nell was going to knock on the door and say, "Hi,

I stole your dog seven months ago and the guilt finally got to me. Here she is. Bye."

Marlene continued to sit in the middle of the yard, looking disgruntled. Whatever had piqued her interest was over.

Okay. Nell picked up a rock from the back of the lot and threw it at the back door. It hit low and made a good, solid thunking sound. She faded back into the trees, but nothing happened. Fine. She picked up another rock and threw it. *Thunk.* Nothing.

Marlene observed the proceedings with interest, moving her head from Nell's pitch to the impact on the back door twice without showing the slightest interest in chasing anything.

"One more," Nell said and threw the third rock, and this time, a woman opened the door, and the biggest German shepherd Nell had ever seen bounded out, barking like the Hound of the Baskervilles.

Marlene turned on her butt and raced for the lot line, zapping past Nell before she could catch her, and Nell followed her almost as fast, praying that Farnsworth still put those electronic collars on his dogs and that the shepherd wasn't moving too fast to stop. She saw Marlene streak into the street and Suze open the door of the Beetle. Marlene scrabbled into the car and then up and across Suze just as Nell opened the passenger door and slid in, grabbing Marlene and pulling her on her lap.

"*Drive,*" she said.

Suze took off without question, and Nell caught her breath. "I am so sorry about that," she said to Marlene, who was heaving in her lap. "I had no idea."

Marlene looked up at her with blood in her eye. Then she barked once, a short, sharp, furious *aaarp* sound that could have cut glass.

"My God," Suze said. "Garbo speaks. What happened?"

"Farnsworth got a new dog," Nell said. "A German shepherd the size of a horse."

Suze laughed, and then as she thought about it, laughed harder. "Oh, God," she said finally. "That is so perfect." Marlene moaned her anger and Suze said, "I can relate, Marlene. I was replaced, too."

Marlene barked at her, including her in the night of infamy.

"Hey, it wasn't my idea," Suze said, keeping her eyes on the road. "I bought the chenille and the bomber jacket. It was Mother Teresa here who wanted to do the right thing."

Marlene looked at Nell again, who said, "I'm sorry," and then she curled up grumbling in Nell's lap.

"You know, once you lose their trust, you never get it back," Suze said.

"Oh, please," Nell said. "One biscuit and she's mine for life."

Marlene looked up at her and barked again, a bark that spoke volumes about her contempt for and distrust of the woman she'd once moaned at daily.

"Can we stop and get some dog biscuits?" Nell said. "I think I'd better do something fast here."

"It'll have to be plain old grocery store biscuits," Suze said. "We're very late."

"One more betrayal," Nell told Marlene, but later, when Suze had run into Big Bear to get the biscuits, Nell gathered the dog up to her and hugged her and said, "Marlene, I'm so sorry. And I'm so glad we get to keep you. You didn't really want to go back there, did you? You were just curious about the yard, right?"

Marlene regarded her malevolently and barked.

"As long as we're still communicating," Nell said.

Marlene was grumpy about being left in the car with the windows rolled down the prescribed inch, and once Nell got into the Long Shot, she was willing to trade places. The bar was pretty much the norm in yuppie drinking holes—great beer, good wings, and mediocre music—and Nell couldn't think of a place she wanted to be less.

"You know," Suze said, "this is the kind of place I always wanted to go to and Jack would never take me. Now I see his point."

"Whose idea was this place, anyway?" Nell said.

"I'll get the drinks," Suze said brightly. "You grab a table."

Nell found a table near the door and sat down to watch Suze thread her way through the crowd to the bar, gathering second glances from men as she went and not noticing any of them. Nell looked around, hoping to spot Riley, and stopped cold when she got to the bar. A man there who looked a lot like Gabe was talking to a very attractive brunette who looked a lot like the Hot Lunch. She squinted through the smoke. Yep, Gabe and Gina. She felt sick for a moment, as if she'd been punched in the stomach, and then she turned away. If Riley had set this up so she'd get jealous and go back, she was going to hurt him. And if he hadn't. . . . *Gina Taggart*, she thought. What was Gabe, stupid? He, of all people, knew what she was like.

Of course, if he wasn't looking for a permanent relationship, what Gina was like was probably just what he wanted.

Men.

Nell sat back defeated and let the darkness and the music wash over her. The music was fairly lousy but the dark was good. It hid the fact that she didn't care where Riley was and that she cared desperately what Gabe was doing with Gina. She looked over at the bar, and they were gone. That hurt a lot more than it should have. She looked at her watch. It was only quarter to nine. Gabe moved fast. But then she knew that.

"So what've you got to show me, kid?" Riley said, pulling out the chair beside her and making her jump.

"What? Oh. Nice to see you, too." Nell fumbled with

her purse, trying to forget Gabe and Gina. "This." She handed him the newsletter and pointed to the picture. "That's Stewart and his secretary."

Riley squinted at the picture. "And if there was light in here, I could probably see them."

"His secretary was Lynnie Mason," Nell said, and Riley stopped looking superior.

"Jesus. Lynnie and Stewart?"

Nell nodded. "If you were wondering who figured out the embezzling thing, that would be Lynnie. She said she was good with money, and she certainly did a nice job on your place."

"Gabe would like to see this," Riley said, looking around.

"He left with Gina Taggart," Nell said, trying not to sound pathetic.

"He's not that dumb." Riley peered at her through the gloom. "You okay?"

"Yes. You don't need to save me from my broken love life again."

"I didn't save you the first time. You did. I just provided some distraction."

"Well, thank you for that," Nell said, and on an impulse, she leaned forward and kissed his cheek. "You are something special, you know?"

"Me? Nah," Riley said, but he looked flustered and pleased. Then he looked past her and frowned. "Oh, fuck." He handed her the newsletter. "Stay here."

Nell looked where he had been looking and saw Suze backed against the bar by some tall guy. "She can take care of herself," she began and then the guy leaned forward and she realized who he was. "*Go*," she said, and Riley went.

Suze had gone to the bar and ordered two Diet Cokes, scanning the room for Riley while she waited. The place was packed, but Riley was nowhere. The Cokes were a long time coming, and when she paid for them and turned to go back to Nell, she found a tall, scowling man in her way.

"Excuse me," she said as he peered closer at her. *Terrific, just what I need, a pickup.* "Look, I'm not interested, okay? No offense, but—"

"I thought so," the man said, slurring his words a little. "It was hard to tell from across the room, but I *thought so.*"

"Did you?" Suze said, trying to move past him. "Good for you. Now if you'll excuse me—"

"You stole my dog," the man said and took a step closer, and Suze thought, *Farnsworth*, and took a step back, bumping into the bar.

"I don't know what you're talking about," she said, looking around for the bartender. The place must have bouncers. The guy was drunk.

"I'm going to have you arrested," he said. *"You stole my dog."*

Men on both sides of them turned to stare appreciatively at her, but nobody seemed inclined to interfere. *Great,* Suze thought, trying to slide away down the bar. *Nobody wants to be a hero anymore.*

Farnsworth slapped his hand down on the bar, blocking her slide, stepping even closer, almost touching her, and said, "You're not going anywhere—"

"Oh, sure she is," Riley said from behind him, and he swung around scowling, while Suze slid the other direction and away from the bar.

"Who are you?" Farnsworth said.

"I'm with her," Riley said easily. "Stop putting the moves on my woman."

Suze lost her interest in Farnsworth completely.

"Moves?" Farnsworth laughed. "She stole my dog."

"No, she didn't," Riley said, putting his shoulder between her and Farnsworth. He had great shoulders.

"Yes, she—"

"No," Riley said. "She didn't."

Yeah, Suze thought from behind him. *Don't push us around.*

Farnsworth snorted. "Tough guy."

"Not really," Riley said. "But I do get tense when people bother the blonde. Go away."

"She stole—" Farnsworth began again, and this time Riley stepped closer, backing him into the bar.

"Let me put this another way," Riley said, his voice even. "You don't know her, you never saw her, and you're never going to see her again."

Farnsworth opened his mouth again and then looked at Riley's face. Suze couldn't see what he saw because she was behind Riley, but she saw Farnsworth's scowl disappear.

"I'm sure if you look at her closely," Riley said in a reasonable tone, "you'll realize you've never seen her before. There are a lot of thirtysomething blondes in this city."

"Not like her," Farnsworth said, looking at Suze over his shoulder.

"Dime a dozen," Riley said, with unmistakable menace in his voice this time. "You just made a mistake, that's all."

Farnsworth looked from Riley to Suze and back again. "I didn't like the damn dog anyway," he said and shoved himself away from the bar, and Suze let out her breath.

"Don't even start with me on the dime-a-dozen thing," Riley said, turning to her.

"I think you're wonderful," Suze said.

"Oh." He looked taken aback, but he also looked solid and sane and honest and on her side.

"And not just for him," Suze said. "Thank you for giving me the Becca thing."

"Well, you're going to be good," Riley said, still thrown. "We need you."

"And for treating me like an adult." She took a chance. "A partner."

Riley frowned at her. "Well, hell, Suze—"

"And for looking at me the way I am now and not thinking of me in that cheerleader uniform and saying 'You're not young anymore, babe.' "

"What?" Riley said.

"I saw the pictures you took," she said, not looking at him because it was so embarrassing. "I saw what Jack married and why he left."

"Oh," Riley said. "Yeah, you were pretty."

Suze winced.

"But nothing like you are now," he said, and the certainty in his voice made her lift her head. "And nothing like you're going to be tomorrow. You've got one of those faces that get sharper and brighter every day. When you're eighty, people are going to have to wear sunglasses to look at you."

Suze gaped at him.

"What?" he said. "Don't give me that. You have a mirror. You know you're beautiful. Stop fishing for compliments."

"Why do you spend time with me?" she said.

He frowned at her. "What is this?"

"Why?"

He shrugged. "It feels good."

She nodded. "It does, doesn't it?" No stress, no worry, no tension, no fear. She looked up at him and thought, *I could look at that face for the rest of my life. I could live with that face.*

"What?" he said, still wary.

"I think I just got it," she said, and smiled at him, feeling her heart lift.

He looked at her for a long moment, and then he bent and kissed her.

It was a soft kiss, the way first kisses are supposed to be—the one on the porch didn't count, Suze thought, it hadn't been real, she hadn't known then—and she put her hand on his cheek and kissed him back, loving and wanting him this time without any motive at all. His mouth fit hers so perfectly that when he pulled back, she said, breathless with discovery, "That's why Jack was so jealous all those years. It was supposed to be you all the time."

"I don't want to hear about Jack," Riley said and kissed her again, and Suze fell into her future.

Back at the table, Nell watched them and thought, *Well, something's working out the way it's supposed to. Maybe I'll hunt Gabe down and pull Gina's hair.* That was her fault. It had taken her twenty-two years to blow her first relationship and only three months to destroy her second. If she decided to let Jack have his way with her, it'd be over in a week.

She put her chin in her hand and contemplated a Gabeless future. It was too bleak to face, she'd just have to get him back, and she'd begun to plan when somebody sat down next to her. She turned to see Gabe sliding a drink her way. "You look like you need this," he said, and her heart lurched a little as she faced him.

"Thank you," she said, ignoring the drink, while she tried to breathe normally. "Where's Gina?"

"I just put her in a cab. Where's Riley?"

"Chasing Suze," Nell said. He leaned toward her and made her breath go away. "What are you doing?"

"Chasing you," Gabe said and kissed her, taking her back to the beginning, and she thought, *Yes, thank you*, and kissed him back. When he pulled away, he said, "I just wanted to make sure I still had a chance."

"I *love* you," she said, holding on to him.

"I love you, too," he said. "If you want to talk, I'll listen." He looked wonderful, dangerous and hot and sweet and solid and good and everything she'd ever wanted in a man. Then she remembered that "just a secretary" crack, and for a minute, he looked like Tim.

"Okay." She took a sip of her drink—Glenlivit and ice, like old times—and then centered her glass in front of her, choosing her words carefully. "You have to understand this. Tim and I had a good marriage. We really did. I met him my first year in college and fell in love right there, at nineteen. We got married, and I dropped out of school to help him at his uncle's insurance agency, and he told me every day how he couldn't live without me. He was a great guy, Gabe. I really loved him. He really loved me. It wasn't a mistake."

Gabe nodded, and Nell took a deep breath.

"His uncle died and left us the business, and we started to get ahead, started winning an Icicle every other year or so, and Tim didn't change at all."

"But you did," Gabe said, and Nell sighed with relief.

"Yes," she said. "I made all the office decisions and Tim made all the sales and insurance decisions, but he still thought of me as that freshman he'd married." She leaned forward. "I don't want to tell this wrong. He was good to me, he just wouldn't admit I was a partner. So I manipulated him so he'd think he was making the decisions, and the agency really took off. For nine years after that, we won the Icicle every year. Tim was a legend in the company."

"But you weren't," Gabe said.

Nell sat back. "I don't know if I really cared that I wasn't for other people. But I cared that Tim didn't see it. I started to get sloppier about manipulating him, I think because I'd been so mad for so long. We started to argue, and during one of those arguments, I told him he couldn't run the place without me." She shifted in her chair. "He told me that I did a good job, but not to get ideas about who was the boss. He patronized me. So I went back to manipulating, but I was so angry, and that kind of anger just poisoned us. And then one Christmas, he stood up and said, 'I don't love you anymore,' and walked out."

"And you think we were getting there, too," Gabe said.

"I think we might have," Nell said. "I don't know, we're so different from what Tim and I had. I need you in ways I never needed him. Not to do anything for me or be anything for me, just to be you. And I don't want to destroy us. Because the thing is, Gabe, when I see Tim now, I *hate* him. I mean acid, seething hate. And it's not because of Whitney. It's because he took me for granted for twenty-two years and I let him. It's twenty-two years of frustration and resentment and manipulation and denial. And I don't think he deserves it, he's not a bad guy at all. But I still really hate him and I hope the agency goes downhill and his life corrodes and he's left empty and wanting." She sat back. "I never want to look at you the way I look at Tim now."

Gabe rubbed his forehead. "I was sort of hoping you were going to give me a list of demands. This is harder."

"Yes," Nell said. "Because I'm not exactly sure how to do this. You're like Tim, you haven't changed. You'll say what you have to say so I'll come back, you'll humor me, but you won't really believe I'm important."

"You're important," Gabe said. "I know you're more than a secretary, I was just trying to slow you down."

"I don't want to slow down," Nell said. "Which doesn't mean I think it's my way or the highway. There's got to be a way we can make this work, I want to come back, but if I do, I'll start manipulating and you'll start yelling and—"

"You're right," Gabe said. "Look, we don't have to solve this tonight. Suze is doing a great job for us, so we're not in trouble, and when you're ready to come back, she'll be ready to work on other things."

"Okay," Nell said, trying not to feel jealous.

Gabe let out his breath. "We can do this."

"We have to," Nell said. "I can't live without you, but I can't stand the way we were." She stood up. "And now I'm really tired. Marlene has been sulking in the car for an hour now, and I've had a rough day, and this place stinks on ice."

"Riley said you found something," he said.

"Oh, God yes," Nell said, remembering. "A newsletter."

She dug it out of her purse, and he squinted at it in the dim light. "It's a picture of Stewart and his secretary. Lynnie."

"Jesus," Gabe said. "*Lynnie?*" He stood up. "Let's go find Riley."

"So what have we got?" Gabe said an hour later at the Sycamore as he pushed his empty plate away. "We've got Stewart killing Helena in 1978, probably following a plan by Trevor or Jack, and then stealing the diamonds."

"And embezzling from O&D fifteen years later with Lynnie," Nell said, over her vinegar and fries.

"And then Margie hits him with her pitcher and he disappears," Suze said.

"Unbelievable," Riley said, looking at the newsletter again.

"And Lynnie hits the road because she thinks Stewart will call her to join him and because she doesn't want to take the heat for the embezzling," Gabe said. "Then seven years later, she shows up on our doorstep and convinces Riley's mother to take a vacation. And she begins to blackmail Trevor and Jack and Budge and Margie for Stewart's disappearance."

"She got Budge for embezzling," Nell said, frowning. "That doesn't fit."

"Budge is the one who busted Stewart and Lynnie for embezzling," Riley said. "He always tattles. It fits."

"Why'd she come back now?" Nell said.

"Seven years," Riley said. "They were going to declare Stewart dead and collect the insurance. Except Margie kept stonewalling." He grinned. "Like father, like daughter."

"So she blackmails Margie and Trevor goes to meet her?" Nell said. "Is that it?"

"Or Budge," Suze said. "Or Budge might have told Jack. Budge tells Jack everything."

"And whoever it is tells her that there's been a snag in

the insurance and to back off from Margie, but there are diamonds at our place," Riley said. "There is a way this makes sense."

"Why does Trevor care about the diamonds?" Suze said. "He has plenty of money."

"Because they were the last loose end," Gabe said. "My dad died without telling him where they were. And he couldn't come to me to look for them without telling me everything. So he—"

"Waited," Nell finished for him. "Did he kill Lynnie?"

"It could have been Jack," Suze said, her voice small. "He could have met her and done the same thing. He'd do anything to protect that law firm."

"We have to give this to the police," Gabe said. "Let them track it down."

Riley nodded. "Couldn't agree with you more."

"So is there a chance that Stewart's back?" Suze said. "Is Margie in trouble?"

"No," Nell said. "Lynnie said she was working alone. She didn't lie to me."

"Your faith in her is touching," Gabe said. "She lied to everybody."

Not me, Nell thought, and stood up. "I'm tired. I'm calling it a night. Suze?"

"I think I'll stay a little longer," Suze said, not looking at Riley.

Good for you, Nell thought.

"I'll give you a ride," Gabe said to Nell, and her pulse kicked up when he smiled.

His hand felt good under her arm again as he walked her out to the car, and when he was sitting beside her in the dark, she said, "I missed you." He leaned over and kissed her, and she said, "I missed the car, too. Do you think—"

"Fat chance," he said and started the car.

When they pulled up in front of the duplex, Nell said, "Are you ever going to let me drive this car?" and he leaned over and kissed her again, a long slow kiss this time, and then he said, "No."

"This relationship needs work," she said, but she kissed him again before she went inside.

She was asleep when she first heard the yelling, like part of a dream. Then Marlene barked, and she woke up and heard Suze screaming her name, and she sat up and inhaled smoke and heard muted crackling outside her door that could only be flames. She rolled out of bed and the floor was warm, and she grabbed Marlene, who yelped and tried to squirm out of her arms, and went to the door, her heart pounding.

The only way out was the stairs, so she opened the door slowly when she saw smoke and then all the way when she didn't see fire. She dropped to the floor, Marlene under one arm, and began to crawl, one-handed, toward the head of the stairs, trying to stay under the worst of the smoke. She could hear Suze outside screaming, *"Nell,"* but she was afraid to yell back, she needed all the oxygen she could get. At the top of the stairs, she could see an orange glow from below, and Marlene squirmed harder and fishtailed out of her arms to run back into the bedroom. Nell scrambled after her and found her back on the bed, pushing her nose under the chenille throw, and she gathered the dog up so that the throw wrapped around her and covered her eyes, and this time she made a dash for the stairs. She stumbled down through the orange light, afraid to look behind her until she got to the door. Then she turned around just for a second and stopped, horror-stricken.

The center of the apartment was an inferno, her grandmother's dining set glowing orange before her eyes. The glass cracked in the hutch, the Susie Cooper figurine fell forward, almost in slow motion, as the Clarice figure followed, looking over her shoulder as she slid down the glass door and the glass shelf collapsed under her. The kestral teapot fell down onto the Stroud tureen and cracked the cartouche, and the Secrets plates pitched forward and crashed onto fragile bone china, which shattered on impact, bubble trees and houses and crescents and swirls, shattering in front of her—

Then Riley was there, frantic, yelling, "Come *on*," and she said, "*My china,*" and he pulled her out into the spring night, across the street to Suze who was crying and Doris who was swearing. The fire trucks were there, and she realized she'd heard the sirens all along. She looked over Riley's shoulder to the apartment, to the furnace that had been her living room, and thought of Clarice and Susie, melting and cracking, all those memories, all that beauty, murdered and gone.

"Somebody did this," she said to Riley when she was standing barefoot in the cold grass. "Somebody—"

Suze pushed Riley out of the way and hugged her. "Oh, thank God you got Marlene, I thought you were dead, I thought you were both dead."

"I think you saved me," Nell said, keeping her back to the house as a car fishtailed to a stop beyond them. "I woke up when I heard you scream, I—"

She heard a car door slam, and then Gabe said, "What the *fuck* is going on?" and she turned and went to him, letting him wrap his arms around her and Marlene both, and only then did she realize that Marlene was struggling to get out of the chenille. She leaned back a little and pulled the blanket off Marlene's head, and Marlene barked, three times, sharp high barks on the edge of hysteria, but she didn't try to get down.

"This is what I saved from the fire," she told Gabe. "Marlene and a blanket. Everything else is gone. All my china. My grandmother's dining room set. The rest of it I don't care about, but, Gabe, all my china. My grandma's china is gone."

Even as she said it, she knew she was being frivolous, she was safe and Marlene was safe and so was Suze, they weren't losing anything really important, but she knew when she closed her eyes again, she'd see Clarice, flirting back over her china shoulder, falling into the perfect world of the Stroud cartouche, everything shattering.

Two hours later, Nell sat exhausted at Gabe's kitchen table in one of Lu's nightgowns, still overwhelmed, while Marlene dozed in her lap.

"You need sleep," Gabe said.

"I'll never get the smoke out of those blue pajamas."

"No," Gabe said. "I wouldn't even try."

"You used to like them."

"I liked what was in them. If you remember, I got rid of them as soon as possible every time."

"Right," Nell said and tried to smile.

An hour later, she was in bed staring at the ceiling, listening to the comforting sound of Marlene's snores, hearing that crackle again, and the crash of the china. Susie's crescent bowls and kestral teapots, Clarice's Stroud and Secrets. The china had rung with her mother's and her grandmother's voices. Tim had bought her the pieces to the Secrets teaset one by one when he still loved her. Jase had given her the sugar bowl when he was ten, his face lit with excitement. Her throat grew tight. The son of a bitch who'd torched her apartment had dissolved her past, melted it down into slag. It was almost more than she could bear, and she rolled over and buried her face in the pillow and wept until she gasped.

Eventually she realized there was something cold on her neck, and she pulled back from the pillow to find Marlene, poking at her with her nose, probably telling her to keep it down. "Sorry, puppy," she said, and Marlene licked the tears from her cheek, and then Nell broke down again, cuddling the dog to her while Marlene licked her face. When she finally stopped crying, Marlene flopped down on the bed, exhausted, and Nell kissed her furry little head and went into the bathroom to wash off the tears and the dog spit.

She scrubbed her face hard and then looked in the mirror. Her face was full, her cheeks ruddy from the towel, her eyes tired but bright. She'd survived divorce and depression and arson and life in general, and now she was going to survive the loss of her china, too.

She was suddenly so tired, she wanted to sleep on the bathroom floor. She plodded back to Lu's bedroom and saw into Gabe's room. He'd left his door open so he could hear her if she called, and in the moonlight from the skylight, she could see him asleep in his bed, his dark hair a slash against the white pillows.

She went in and crawled under the covers with him, and he woke and made room for her, circling her with his arm as she sank into his bed.

"I almost died tonight," she said.

"I know." He tightened his arm around her.

"I lost everything."

"You've still got me."

"Thank God," she said and buried her face in his shoulder.

"I think we should get married," Gabe said after a minute, and she pulled away from him.

"*What?*"

"After I dropped you off, I thought about what you said, about me not changing, that I'd tell you you're a partner just to get you back. And you're right. I would. I'd tell you damn near anything to get you back."

"I know," she said. "I'd believe damn near anything to get you back."

"So let's make it legal and binding," he said. "Let's get married for the reason marriage was invented, to make sure we take each other seriously and stick with each other through the bad times and don't quit because that's easier than making it work. I sign over half of my half of the agency to you. You put the money from the insurance agency into the business. We divide up the responsibilities three ways with Riley, and we make the big decisions together. No wishy-washy feel-good promises. We put it down on paper and sign it."

Nell felt dizzy. "Riley will have fifty percent. That's a controlling share. Can you stand that?"

"Against you and me? In his dreams. He wouldn't want control anyway. And besides, two years from now, he's going to give half of his half away, too."

"You'd give me half of your share," Nell said, her heart pounding. "Even though you don't—"

"If I don't, you'll take all of it," Gabe said. "And then we'll both be miserable. Look, I can't create an epiphany here. You're right, I still don't see how you can demand an equal voice in an agency you've worked at for seven months and I've run for twenty years. But you've sure as hell got an equal voice in my personal life, so I'm willing to take the rest on trust."

This is it, Nell thought. Whatever she decided, he'd take her seriously. If she married him, she'd be a partner, but she'd be answerable to him forever. He swore now it was what he wanted, but now he was shaken and desperate. She'd have to trust that when the apartment fire was just a memory, when passion cooled, when he was tired and they disagreed about work and he regretted giving up what he'd had, that then he'd still honor his promise, that he'd be faithful to it even though he didn't want to be, that he'd pay the price for the deal he made tonight.

That was a lot to take on trust.

"Will you marry me?" Gabe said.

"Maybe," she said.

"Not the answer I was looking for," he said, "but it's a start," and she curled against him in the circle of his arm, her arm across his chest, and felt safe as she finally fell asleep.

Chapter Twenty-One

Nell met the fire marshal at eight the next morning and told him everything she knew.

"It looked like somebody set out to burn your china cabinet," he said. "Shoved a lot of paper on the bottom shelf and lit it. What I can't figure out is why anybody would want to burn a bunch of dishes."

"Symbolism," Nell said. "It's personal. I don't know who did it, but it was somebody who knew I loved that china."

"The police found a vandalized car a couple blocks from your place with kerosene cans in the backseat. Looks like somebody stole it, and then somebody else slashed the tires while the first guy was at your place. It belongs to a Jack Dysart. Ring any bells?"

"A few," Nell said and explained the situation to him. When he was gone, she went back upstairs and thought about Jack, about how much he hated her. Would he torch her hutch just for revenge on the same day he'd tried to kiss her? And then leave his car sitting around with kerosene cans in it? That made no sense.

But Budge might. He hated her that much for Margie. Would he frame Jack for it?

That was such a ridiculous thought—Budge was a lot of things, but he wasn't devious—that she knew she was tired. She took off Lu's sweats and crawled back into Gabe's bed, and Marlene jumped up beside her. She was going to have to call Tim and say, "You know that renter's insurance I bought from you? Pay up." Nell lay back and tried to imagine Tim's face when he read the itemization of Marlene's wardrobe: one dachshund angel costume, one dachshund cashmere sweater with heart, one dachshund trenchcoat . . . that stuff hadn't been cheap.

She heard Gabe come in the apartment and forgot Marlene's trenchcoat.

"Nell?" he called, and she called back, "In here," and waited for him with her heart beating faster.

"Tired?" he said sympathetically, and she said, "Not exactly."

"I ran into Suze on the stairs and told her you were moving in here," he said. "In fact, you're in since you've got nothing left to move."

Nell nodded. "I didn't even ask, where did Suze spend last night?"

"Riley's bed," Gabe said. "He was on the couch. Don't ask me what they're doing, I don't know. I don't care as long as you're in here with me."

There was something in his certainty that hummed in her veins. It was like a tuning fork; when you heard the right note from the right person, it vibrated inside you.

She smiled at him. "Do you know how long its been since anybody made love to me?"

"To the minute," he said, coming toward her.

"I think I'm going to be better soon," she said, and then he crawled into bed with her and put his arms around her and she was.

When she woke up, Gabe was gone, and Suze was shaking her. "Come on, Sleeping Beauty. It's four. Margie didn't show up to run The Cup today, and she sounded funny when I called her. I think Budge is pushing her over the edge. I quit work early so we could go get her out of there. We have to go up there to get our old clothes anyway."

"What?" Nell sat up and yawned, squinting at Suze who was lost in a gray T-shirt that said "FBI" on it in big black letters and a pair of black sweats that pooled around her ankles. "Cute."

"One of the many reasons we're going to Margie's," Suze said.

"Right," Nell said and got out of bed. "She sounded funny when you called her?"

"Very," Suze said.

"So we'll hurry," Nell said.

"The boxes of your clothes are all down in the base-ment," Margie said, after she'd been horrified about the fire and wept for Nell's china, all in the space of about five minutes.

"Great," Nell said cautiously. "You know, Margie, you should come back to the Village with us. It'll be like a slumber party."

"Oh, I can't possibly. I'm selling my Franciscan Desert Rose on eBay. If I sell it all this week, I can start buying the Fiestaware without filing for Stewart's insurance. Isn't that a good idea?" Margie's cheeks had two bright circles on them, and her eyes glowed, and her milk glass was full.

"Super," Suze said, casting a doubtful look at Nell.

"And you can help!"

"Okay," Nell said. "What do you need?"

"You bring up the extra pieces from the basement," Margie said. "I've done all the pieces up here, but I got tired running up and down those stairs." She stopped and smiled at them. "And dizzy."

"Stay off the stairs, Marge," Suze said, and they went to the basement. "We have to do something about her," she said when they reached the bottom. "She hasn't stopped drinking since we left her yesterday. It's that damn Budge, pressuring her about the insurance, not letting her move out of here. She has to get out of here and start over again. Without him."

"For right now, we get our clothes back and take her the Franciscanware." Nell pulled the chain on the light and Margie's basement sprang into view: an old bicycle, a lopsided plastic Christmas tree, a chest freezer with the boxes of their clothes stacked on it next to an ugly golf trophy, and floor-to-ceiling shelves with box after box after box labeled "Desert Rose." It was a sad comment on the extent of Margie's existence: her ex-husband's freezer, her in-laws' clothes, and her stockpile against an earthenware shortage.

My basement used to look like this, full of china and other people's things, Nell thought. Of course, now she didn't have a basement. Or china.

"How much of this stuff does she have?" Suze said, appalled.

"More than God." Nell squinted at the boxes that filled the shelves on the far wall. One was labeled "sandwich sets," another "cake plate," another "pitcher," and another one just said "cups." There must have been twenty boxes there, all with "Franciscan Desert Rose" printed at the top in Margie's neat little script.

"Did you find the boxes?" Margie called from upstairs.

Nell looked at the wall of Franciscanware. "Yes."

An hour later, they had their clothes in Suze's Beetle and most of the Franciscanware upstairs, and Margie was much calmer, typing in descriptions and posting to the auction site.

"It's like therapy," Suze said when they went down for the last of the boxes.

"It's mindless," Nell said. "Maybe if we let her go for a while longer on the computer, we can get her out of here without a fight, and she'll be okay." She looked around the now almost barren basement and added, "We just have to get her out of here."

Suze picked up a box and read the side. "An entire box

of cups?" She put it down, pushed the golf trophy out of the way on the freezer, and boosted herself up on the dust-smeared top. "I'm exhausted. No sleep last night, I worked all day, and now I'm schlepping two thousand pieces of this stuff. How long ago did she lose her grip?"

"Oh, please, how many running egg cups did you own?" Nell said. "You don't even eat eggs in cups. Come on. Let's get the last of this upstairs before she changes her mind and decides to keep it."

"She can't," Suze said, sliding off the freezer. "She needs the room for her incoming two thousand pieces of Fiestaware." Suze dusted off the seat of Riley's sweats. "You know, while she's at it, she should get rid of Stewart's golf trophy and Stewart's freezer. After all, she got rid of Stewart."

"Let's just get her out of the house." Nell slid a box labeled "breakfast set" off the shelf and then, as she turned, caught sight of the freezer chest with the golf trophy sitting on top like a tombstone.

Don't be ridiculous, she told herself.

"What?" Suze said.

You're just sensitive about freezers, Nell told herself. Lynnie would make anybody morbid about ice cubes.

"Why are you looking at the freezer like that?" Suze said.

Nell put her box down on the concrete floor, her heart pounding like mad.

"You're breathing funny," Suze said, breathing a little funny herself.

Nell swallowed and walked over to the freezer. She picked up the trophy carefully and set it on the floor, and then she took a deep breath and tried to lift the lid.

It was locked.

"We need a key," she told Suze.

"I'll get it," Suze said and came back a minute later with the key, saying, "Margie didn't even ask me why."

The lid stuck at first, and then gave way with a creak,

as if it hadn't been opened in years, like a casket in a Vincent Price movie. But when Nell looked inside, it was full to the brim with everyday white packages labeled in black marker "porterhouse, 6/93" and "sirloin, 5/93."

"Thank God." Nell leaned on the side of the freezer in relief. "Talk about a morbid imagination."

"They're all from 1993," Suze said, her voice sounding odd. "They haven't used this freezer since Stewart left."

They looked at each other, and then they began to unload the top layer of white packages.

"This stuff should be thrown out anyway," Nell said, stacking beef. "It can't be any good anymore."

"If it was, Margie wouldn't eat it," Suze said. "It's not—"

Her breath went out on a whoosh, and Nell forced herself to look at Suze's end of the freezer.

There, wrapped in green plastic, one cheek against a package labeled "grilled hamburgers 6/93" and the other next to a package labeled "grilled porkchops 5/93," was something the size of a man's head.

Nell swallowed and took a deep breath and then she tore the brittle plastic away. Beneath it was an unpleasantly blue, pudgy face topped by blond hair with a lot of brown stuff crusted in it.

"Stewart," Nell said.

Chapter Twenty-Two

Suze said, "Oh, God," and turned her back and slid down the side of the freezer case, and Nell shifted enough of the packages to see that the rest of Stewart's body was there, that nobody had decapitated him or otherwise chopped him into steaks. "He's all here."

"Oh, good," Suze said faintly from the floor.

"So," Nell said, trying to keep her voice calm. She began to repack the freezer, taking pains to replace the meat as neatly as before.

"Uh, Nell?" Suze said, her voice still unnaturally high.

"We have to think," Nell said, still stowing meat. "So we'll just put this all back and think."

When she had the last of the packages back in place and the lid closed again, Nell sat down beside Suze, who had put her head between her knees.

"He's been in there since 1993." Suze lifted her head. "That's Margie for you. 'Maybe they'll never know.' *My God.*"

"Margie didn't know," Nell said. "She's a vegetarian. You know how she feels about fresh food. She'd never look in here."

"It has to be Margie who put him there. Anybody else would have done something with the body in the last seven years."

"Like what?" Nell said. "Look, Margie couldn't have put him in the freezer. Stewart outweighed her by a hundred pounds."

"She could have dragged him down here. By his feet."

Nell winced at the picture of Margie dragging Stewart down into the basement, his head bouncing on the stair treads. "Could you have kept Jack in the basement that long?"

Suze tilted her head. "Yes. But then I'm really mad at him."

Nell tried to picture Tim wrapped in plastic in the basement in their old house. It wasn't entirely impossible. There had been a time not too long ago that she would have positively enjoyed it. A little payback for freezing her out. "Maybe. But I think I might have trouble sleeping at night."

"Soy milk and Amaretto," Suze said.

"We have to call Gabe," Nell said, and then she stopped, hearing voices upstairs.

"What is it?" Suze said.

"Budge," Nell said.

An hour later, Gabe was scowling over the fire marshal's report when Chloe knocked on the door, marched in, and plopped herself down in the chair across from him.

"Our daughter is getting married," she announced. She was tan and healthy and happy in spite of the concern on her face.

"Welcome back," he said. "Lu's not getting married. He turned her down."

"What?" Chloe was, if anything, more upset. "How could anybody turn her down?"

"He's sane," Gabe said. "Also he's a good kid, and he loves her. He's not going to screw up her life, although she's doing her damnedest to screw up his."

"You like him," Chloe said.

"I like him," Gabe said. "I'd like him better if he wasn't sleeping with my daughter, but somebody's going to do it, so it might as well be him."

"He's a Pisces."

"Is that good?" Gabe said. "You're a Pisces, right?"

"For you, it was awful. You're a Taurus. For Lu, it's excellent. She's a Capricorn. What do we know about him?"

"He's Nell's kid."

"Really?" Chloe sat back, calm again. "Have you realized Nell is your soul mate?"

"Yes. Try not to gloat."

"I'm not gloating, I'm happy. Even with the stars behind you, you could have screwed that up." She stood up. "I'm going to go home and call around until I find Lu. I want to meet this Jason."

"You'll like him," Gabe said. She turned to go and he said, "Hey. It's good to see you again."

"It's good to see you, too," she said. "I'm going to Tibet next. You know anybody who'd like to buy The Cup?"

"Possibly," Gabe said. "Put Nell on it."

She nodded and left, and he thought, *Tibet?* and then dismissed her from his mind. Half an hour later, there was another knock on his door and this time Lu stuck her head in. "Can we come in?"

"We who?" he said, and she pushed the door open farther and came in, pulling Jason Dysart behind her. "Oh." He felt suddenly guilty because he hadn't called Jason the night before. If he'd gone to see his mother and found that burned-out apartment—

"We're engaged," Lu said, her eyes bright, daring him to make a scene, making him forget the fire for a moment. "See?"

She held out her hand, and Gabe was taken aback at the size of the ring.

"You knock over a jewelry store?" he said to Jase, wanting to smack the kid for tying Lu down so young.

"My mother's china cabinet," Jase said, looking fairly miserable for a newly engaged man.

"Do you want this?" Gabe said to him, ignoring Lu.

"Or are you just caving in because she cut you off?"

"I want this," Jase said, his face darkening at Gabe's tone. "We're going to wait to get married until I graduate, but not until Lu graduates. Compromise."

"And we're moving in together," Lu said, holding on to him tighter. "Next quarter. Jase has an apartment right on High Street. It's so cool, with a sun porch and everything."

"And you're expecting me to help pay for it," Gabe said.

"No," Jase said before Lu could say anything. "I've got it covered."

"You've got a job," Gabe said, leaning back in his chair.

"I've always had a job," Jase said. "I'll just work some extra hours. Not to mention what I'll save by not dating." He looked down at Lu. "I do have to give up dating, right?"

She grinned back at him. "Only if you want to live."

Jase shrugged. "See? Plenty of money."

Gabe shook his head at Lu. "You should be spanked for what you're doing to this kid."

"I didn't do anything," Lu said, her smile dwindling.

"You held your breath and turned blue until he gave you what you wanted," Gabe said. "And now he's going to work extra hours to make sure you have everything you need. I'm ashamed of you."

Lu's smile disappeared completely.

"Wait a minute," Jase said.

"And for the rest of your life," Gabe said, staring his daughter down, "you're going to remember that this is how he asked you to marry him. Not because he wanted to, but because he didn't want to lose you." He stopped, caught by the realization that he was doing the same thing with Nell.

"I wanted to," Jase was saying, but Lu was looking up at him, horror-struck.

"That's not what I wanted," she said.

"Then why did you do it that way?" Gabe said. "So what if he said no, he didn't want to get married right away.

Obviously, he loves you. That wasn't enough?" It wasn't enough for Nell. He chilled a little bit at the resentment that came with the thought.

"I just—"

"If love isn't enough, Lu," Gabe said, "you don't deserve him." *Love should always be enough.*

"Hey, you're supposed to be yelling at me," Jase said, stepping in front of Lu. "I'm sleeping with your daughter, remember?"

"Don't push your luck, kid," Gabe said, watching Lu.

Lu tugged Jase back beside her. "He's right."

"Oh, great," Jase said, glaring at Gabe. "I knew we should have just sent you an e-mail. Do you have any idea of the hell I went through to get this?"

"Because I blackmailed you," Lu said. "That's wrong. Daddy's right, I don't want to spend the rest of my life feeling like I made you propose."

Gabe nodded at him. "And trust me, kid, you don't want to spend the rest of your life trying to convince her you would have proposed anyway." *Like I did. Like I'm going to.*

Lu looked at him, startled. "Mom did that?"

Gabe shook his head. "Your mom was great, always. But we had to get married. So I had to work a little harder to convince her I'd have married her anyway. It wasn't always fun."

"But you would have," Lu said, and Gabe shook his head.

"No. I wouldn't have. I wasn't ready."

Lu swallowed. "Are you sorry?"

"Nope. Your mom and I had a good marriage for a while. We had you. It was never bad. But she never bought it that I married her because I wanted to. And right now you don't believe Jase proposed because he wanted to."

"I wanted to," Jase said. "I honest to God did."

"Just not right now," Lu said.

"Well," Jase said. "No. Although now that we did it, I

like it. We're good."

"No, we're not." Lu took off the ring and handed it back.

"Oh, that's just fine," Jase said, and he sounded so much like his mother that Gabe flinched. "Now look what you've done," he said to Gabe. "Do you have any idea how hard it's going to be to talk her into this again?"

"Yes," Gabe said. "That was my plan." He looked at Lu. "I'll pay your half of the rent and expenses. He does not work extra hours for you. Not yet, anyway."

"Thank you, Daddy," Lu said, and blinked back tears. "I think."

"I want to talk to Jase alone," he said. "Go next door and say hello to your mother. She's home."

"Mama?" Lu sniffed and left, and Gabe watched Jase watch her go. The poor bastard was really in love with her. That meant he was the one who was going to have to cope with her from now on. There was always a silver lining.

Jase turned back to him. "I really do—"

"I know, I know," Gabe said. "And you promise to take good care of her. I got it. Good luck, kid, you're going to need it."

"Okay," Jase said warily. "So?"

"Tell me what that ring has to do with your mother's china."

"That's between my mother and me," Jase said stiffly.

"She sold her china to get the ring," Gabe said.

Jase sat down in the client chair, looking even more miserable. "I told her not to, but she came over the next day and told me she'd sold it—"

"I know," Gabe said. "Believe me, I know how your mother works. Who did she sell it to?"

"You don't—" Jase began, and then his face cleared as he began to catch Gabe's drift. "Oh. This dealer in Clintonville." He began to search his pockets. "I've got the card right here. I thought maybe I could ask him to hold onto it until I could . . . Here it is." He held up a business card.

"Good," Gabe said, taking it. "There was a fire last night. Your mom lost everything."

Jase froze. "Is she—"

"She's fine," Gabe said. "Go next door and meet Lu's mother and then later we'll all have dinner."

"Lu's mother," Jase said and took a deep breath. "Any advice?"

"You're in, kid," Gabe said. "You're a Pisces."

Jase looked mystified. "Okay."

"One more thing," Gabe said. "If you hurt my little girl, I'll have you killed."

"Right." Jase stood up. "If you make my mother cry again, I'll kick your ass."

Gabe nodded, and Jase nodded back, still wary but looking much happier

"Don't tell anybody about this," Gabe said.

"Who'd believe it?" Jase said and went out to meet Chloe.

Gabe sat back and thought about Nell. He wanted her, he'd do anything to keep her, but she was right: the resentment could poison them. He shook his head and picked up the phone and dialed the dealer in Clintonville, who was delighted to hear from him. He traded his Visa number for the promise of next-day delivery and thought, *Well, that's one thing I've done right.* Then he hung up the phone and it rang again right away. When he answered, it was Nell.

"We have a problem," she said.

No kidding. "What now?"

"We found Stewart," Nell said. "He was in Margie's freezer. Then Budge came by and threw us out. We're at a pay phone at the Marathon station on Henderson, and Margie's back at her house with her dumb boyfriend and her husband's corpse. We're okay, but we've been better. He really looked awful." Her voice was high and much too flippant to be normal, but she sounded like she was coping. Nell always coped.

Gabe exhaled. "Okay. Does Budge know you found the body?" He looked up to see Riley standing in the open doorway, his eyebrows raised at "body."

"I don't know," Nell said. "But he wasn't happy to see us. He thinks we upset Margie. Margie's drunk and selling Franciscanware on eBay."

"Stay there," Gabe said. "We're coming." He hung up and said to Riley, "They found Stewart in Margie's freezer."

"Of course they did," Riley said. "Jesus."

"More company," Margie said, when she answered the door, not pleased. "Budge was here and so was Daddy. I told them you were coming back to help me clean the basement, but they didn't get the hint so I had to throw them out." She looked severely at Gabe and Riley. "If you're staying, you have to help. I'm very busy." Then she went back to typing, Suze beside her, while Gabe and Riley went down to the basement with Nell and opened up the freezer.

It was half full of protein from 1993, but no Stewart.

"Budge," Gabe said.

"Budge is a wuss," Riley said. "You think he got a frozen corpse out of a chest freezer by himself without throwing up or fainting? And Trevor is old."

"Well, forget Margie helping," Nell said. "She wouldn't be typing if she'd just seen Stewart."

"Jack," Riley said.

"What are they going to do with him?" Gabe said. "Look for another freezer?"

"Jack has a freezer like this in his basement," Nell said.

"There's a freezer at our place, too," Riley said. "The town's full of them."

Gabe closed the freezer lid. "If Stewart's been in here since 1993, he didn't kill Lynnie."

"Margie hit him and went upstairs," Nell said. "Jack and

Trevor and Budge handled it from there." Her eyes went to the freezer and then slid away. "Do you think they all knew he was in here?"

"No," Gabe said. "I'm finding it hard to believe one of them left him here, let alone all of them. And at this point, I don't care. I just want to know where that body is, and who killed him and Lynnie. We can fill in the details later."

By midnight, the police had come and gone, less skeptical about the missing-body-from-the-freezer story than they had been before Gabe filled them in on the background. By then, Margie had posted all her Franciscanware and was working on the rest of the house, oblivious to the fact that her husband had been living with her longer than she'd thought. "I think she's discovered a way to get out of the house," Suze told Nell. "She's going to sell it out from under Budge on eBay." When they'd convinced Margie that she could check her auctions on the agency computer and that Gabe would watch the house for her, she went to pack a bag so she could spend the night at Chloe's. Gabe handed Nell his keys as they left.

"I get to drive your car?" she said.

"You get to close the office," he said. "Check all the locks, please. You may also let yourself into my apartment so you can sleep in my bed. I will be driving my car."

"How, if I have the keys?"

"I have a spare key. Do not touch my car."

"Right," Nell said. "You know, if we got married, you'd be endowing me with all your worldly goods."

"All of them except my car."

"And I thought you were incapable of change," she said and went to help Suze pour Margie into the Beetle.

"She's going to be okay," Suze said to Nell when they were hauling a sleepy Margie up Chloe's stairs, Chloe fluttering behind them in concern. "We just had to get her out of that house."

"And off the soy milk," Nell said.

When Margie was asleep, Nell went back to the agency

with Marlene to close the offices. Gabe was probably staked out at Margie's for the night, but she left her desk light on for him, just in case, and then headed for his office to lock it, only to turn back when she heard a weird purring snarl.

Marlene was growling.

Nell went cold. *Get out*, she thought and took a step toward the door, and then she heard somebody say, "Nell," from the storeroom behind her. She turned back and saw Trevor standing in the doorway, smiling at her as benevolently as ever. "I was hoping you could help me," he said.

"Gee," Nell said. "I was just on my way to bed."

"I need the freezer key," Trevor said. "It doesn't seem to be on Margie's key ring."

"Oh, well, Gabe pretty much holds on to that," Nell said. "But I'm sure tomorrow he'll be glad to—"

"Those are his keys," Trevor said. "In your hand."

"These?" Nell said brightly, shoving them in her jacket pocket. "No. Those are mine. I—"

"Nell, I gave Patrick that key ring," Trevor said tiredly. "I know those are Gabe's keys. I've had a very long day, and I want to go home. Open the freezer for me."

Nell took a step back. "I really don't have the authority—"

Trevor took a gun out of his coat pocket, and he was clumsy enough that Nell gave up any thought of making a run for it. She didn't want to be the one who finally prodded Trevor into an impetuous streak, especially if he was armed and awkward. "You're the one who runs this place," Trevor said, all the geniality gone from his voice. "You know where everything is. I want the files from 1982."

"What?" Nell said, incredulous. "That's all?" He wasn't looking for a place to stash Stewart? Maybe she'd misjudged him. She looked at the gun wavering in his hand. On the other hand, he was pretty serious about those files. "What's in the files?"

"You didn't find it then," Trevor said. "I thought you could find anything."

"I didn't look in 1982," Nell said, indignant. "Nothing happened in 1982."

"Oh," Trevor said sadly, "something happened in 1982." He waved the gun at her, nodding toward the freezer, and Nell nodded back, eager to please.

"Sure." She edged around him carefully, and he pivoted as she moved, keeping the gun on her. She went into the storeroom with him close behind—too close—and unlocked the freezer. "There you go," she said, opening the door. "Have at it. All yours."

"Find the files from '82 and bring them out." Trevor held out his hand. "I'll take the keys."

"Uh, these are Gabe's."

"But I need them," Trevor said gently and raised the gun a little.

"Okay." Nell handed them over, fairly sure that was a mistake but not seeing an alternative. Gabe would have seen an alternative. If she took his offer to divide up the agency work, he was going to get everything involving people with guns. "Listen, there are going to be two or three boxes from 1982. You want to help?"

"No," Trevor said, and waved the gun toward the door.

"You want to give me a hint of what we're looking for?"

"No."

"Is this what Lynnie was looking for?"

"Nell—"

"Because I was just wondering what it was. We thought it was the diamonds, you know." She edged away from the freezer a little, babbling to distract him. "We had no idea there was anything in the 1982 files. Is that what you were looking for when you broke into my apartment that night? Boy, that must have given you a start, to find me in there. You probably thought the place was empty. So what were you—"

"Nell," Trevor said. "Shut up and get the files."

Nell took a deep breath. "Okay, look, you're not going to shoot me. That's probably the gun Stewart shot Helena with. You meant to get rid of it, and then put it off, right? I think that's wise. People make mistakes when they hurry. We should think this over. Because, you know, if you shoot"—*me*—"the gun, the police will get the bullets"—*from my body*—"and trace the gun right back to you. So let's just put the gun down—

"Calm down," Trevor said. "I don't want to have to get rid of another body. They're too damn heavy. At least, human bodies are." He moved the gun from her to Marlene, who sat on her haunches and looked up at him with her usual contempt as he took aim between her eyes.

"*No,*" Nell said, going cold.

"A dog body," Trevor said, "would be easy to get rid of."

"*Wait,*" Nell said again and stepped into the freezer.

"Much better," Trevor said, keeping the gun on Marlene. "Now get me the files."

"Just *give me a minute.*" Nell shoved the boxes from the nineties out of the way to get to the eighties, determined to not panic. "Definitely two boxes at least," she called back to Trevor. She brought the first box out, thinking fast. As long as she brought him the boxes, he wouldn't shoot Marlene. And of course he wasn't going to shoot her, either. Stewart shot people but Trevor didn't.

Trevor put them in freezers.

She went back in and got the second box. "That's it," she said as she brought it out and put it on the floor in front of him. She reached for the freezer door to close it, but he was standing in the way. "If you'd just back up, I'll close this up and help you go through the files," she said, trying to edge her way around him. "They'll be a mess—"

Trevor shoved her hard and she tripped back, falling flat through the freezer door as Marlene went crazy behind him. She tried to roll to her feet, but he kicked at her and, when she rolled away from him, he slammed the freezer door, cutting off Marlene in mid-bark, leaving Nell entombed in the darkness.

"*Trevor, you son of a bitch,*" Nell screamed and stumbled to her feet to open the door as the darkness settled around her like a shroud, impenetrable.

He'd locked the door. He'd locked her inside and he was outside with Marlene. He wouldn't kill Marlene now. There was no reason to. Marlene was safe, she was sure of it.

But she could die.

Trevor was going to freeze her like he'd frozen Lynnie, so he could keep his life the same once he'd found whatever he was looking for in 1982.

"*Trevor, you dumbass,*" she yelled at the door. "*You'll never find anything in those files.*" She couldn't remember if the freezer was soundproof, and she didn't care. It felt good to yell at him. It felt better to remember that Riley's mother had been doing the filing in 1982 while Chloe was on maternity leave. Trevor didn't have a hope in hell of finding anything in those files unless he went through them page by page.

Of course, he was going to have a lot of time to look if he took the files with him. And in the meantime, she was freezing.

She wrapped her arms around herself to ward off the cold. Okay, the way not to freeze to death would be to keep moving until Gabe showed up and let her out. She had one moment of doubt—that was putting a lot of faith in Gabe's powers of deduction—and then realized that she didn't have to rely on deduction. When Gabe got home and she wasn't in his bed, he'd tear the city apart until he found her.

So all she had to do was not freeze to death until then.

Movement, that was the key. She began to pace up and down the freezer in the blackness, stumbling over file boxes, flailing her arms, trying to think hot thoughts, anything to keep her blood from freezing in her veins, checking the door periodically to see if Trevor had unlocked it yet. *Heavy breathing*, she thought and began to jump up and down. *Hurry up, Gabe.* She switched to walking again when the jumping got painful, thinking that it must be midnight, that Gabe would give up watching Margie's when the sun came up, that she'd only have to walk for six hours—could she walk for six hours?—and then she'd be out.

Or she could break out. That's what Gabe would do. How did you break out of a locked freezer? There should have been a safety latch on the damn door, but you couldn't accidentally lock yourself into this freezer, somebody had to deliberately lock you in with a key, so there was no safety latch because that dumbass Patrick hadn't realized that his best friend would be turning his future daughter-in-law into a Popsicle thirty years later.

Think, she told herself. *Be like Gabe. Stop whining and think.* What did she have to work with? Twenty years of files. If she had a match, she could set them on fire. Then at least there'd be some light. Of course, then she'd be trapped in a freezer full of flames. And carbon dioxide, since fire tended to use up oxygen.

Oxygen.

Freezers were airtight.

How long did she have? Six hours until Gabe got home, how much longer after that until he found her, how much air did she breathe an hour, how much air had she already breathed in, walking fast?

If she slowed down, she'd freeze to death. If she speeded up, she'd suffocate. Why wasn't there ever a middle ground?

Goddamn Trevor. He was going to kill her, the same way he'd killed Lynnie. Lynnie. There was a role model. Lynnie hadn't given in to him, hadn't let him run her. She'd been a tough woman, hadn't compromised, hadn't let men get her down.

Of course, Lynnie was dead. Maybe "What would Lynnie do?" wasn't the inspiration she needed at the moment.

I need help, she thought. *I cannot get out of here alone. I need backup. I need Gabe.*

She felt sick at the thought. She shouldn't need anybody, she should be able to save herself, a strong woman would save herself and not rely on any man. For the next half hour, she fumbled through the blackness for any opening, any possibility, stacking boxes to get to the ceiling, growing colder and more desperate, and with the cold sicker and sleepier.

I am not going to give Trevor Ogilvie the satisfaction of my death, she thought and repeated it in her head, like an affirmation while she searched for something, anything, a switch, maybe she could turn the freezer off, there was a thought. She'd still suffocate but—

The door opened and the light came on, and Marlene barked hysterically as Gabe said, *"Nell?"*

"Oh, thank God," Nell said and stumbled across the freezer into his arms.

"What the hell?" Gabe said but he caught her at the door and pulled her out, slamming the door behind them.

"Take the door off of that damn thing," Nell said, shivering uncontrollably against him. "Take the whole thing out. It's horrible."

Gabe tightened his arms around her. "God, you're like ice. Who—"

"Trevor," Nell said. "Get me out of this storeroom."

"He locked you in? *Where is he?*"

"I don't know." She realized she was shaking, the cold, she thought, and the adrenaline and the exhaustion and the fear. "He wanted the '82 files. He must have taken them. He took your keys, too. I don't know what—"

Outside, a motor erupted, and Gabe said, *"That's my car."* He let go of her and ran for the reception room, and Nell followed in time to see him go out the door.

"Hey, it's all right, I'm fine," she said, still shuddering

from the freezer, and then she heard tires squeal and a crash that sounded like an explosion, short and sharp and hard and loud.

"If there's a God," she told Marlene, "that was that bastard, Trevor."

"That was my car," Gabe said, when they'd all gathered in the office two hours later, after the paramedics had taken Trevor off to the hospital and the police had arranged to tow the remains of the Porsche.

"Yeah, it was selfish of him to try to commit suicide in your car," Nell said, cuddling a toasty-warm Marlene to her.

"He didn't try to commit suicide," Riley said. "He was taking the car to search it. Gabe's bright idea."

"Don't remind me," Gabe said.

"Your idea?" Nell said.

"It was the last place you hadn't looked," Gabe said. "I told him that last week, thinking he'd try to get into it. And of course, being Trevor, he *waited*."

"So what happened?" Suze said. "Why'd he crash into the park?"

"A Porsche 911 is not your average car," Riley said. "The turbo lag is insane."

"He lost control," Gabe said. "It was just his bad luck he was headed for the park and those stone pillars."

"Turbo lag?" Suze said to Riley.

"It hesitates," Riley said. "And for once, Trevor didn't. He must have stomped on that accelerator. Which meant after the hesitation, he was airborne."

"I don't care about Trevor or turbo lag," Nell said, holding Marlene closer. "What the hell happened in 1982 anyway?"

"My dad died," Gabe said.

"Oh," Nell said.

"I don't want to think any more tonight." Riley stood

up. "You can all stay up and look for Stewart and the '82 files if you want, but I'm going to bed."

Suze stood up, too. "I'm going to go next door to stay with Margie. I don't even want to think about explaining all of this to her tomorrow."

Riley held the door open for her, and Suze stood close to him for a moment and then left. When Riley had gone upstairs, Gabe said to Nell, "You sure you're okay?"

"No," Nell said, cuddling Marlene closer. "What would you have done if Trevor had locked you in there?"

"Haven't a clue," Gabe said. "Why?"

"I kept thinking you'd have known what to do," Nell said. "I felt stupid, freezing to death in the dark. You'd never have let him put you in there in the first place."

"Maybe. Depends on the circumstances."

"He threatened to shoot Marlene."

Gabe was quiet for a moment, and then he said, "He has a concussion and multiple fractures."

"Good," Nell said. "How did you know I was in there?"

"I called to make sure you'd closed the office, and Suze said you'd come over here, and when there was no answer here, I came back and found Marlene throwing a fit at the freezer door. So I got the spare key out of my desk and—"

"*Marlene?*" Nell kissed the top of Marlene's furry little head. "Marlene, you heroine, you saved me."

"Well, I helped," Gabe said.

"Yeah, you did." Nell looked at him in the lamplight, the hero who'd saved her. That kind of guy was dangerous, she thought. A woman could start depending on that kind of guy.

He smiled at her, his concern for her plain, and she thought, *The hell with it.* For tonight, she was that kind of woman. "You get a reward, too," she said and pulled him upstairs, determined to be warm again, one way or another.

*   *   *

The next morning, Nell and Suze helped a shocked and sober Margie pack the things she hadn't managed to sell on eBay and move into Chloe's. As they'd carried the last of her things out, Budge had put his foot down, forbidding her to go, and Margie had stared at him for a moment and then said, "I'm sorry, Budge, I think you just wasted seven years," and left while he'd sputtered behind her. That afternoon, Suze took Margie to the hospital to see Trevor, and Nell came down to the office wrapped in Gabe's thickest sweater. She wasn't cold anymore, but it was still good to have something warm wrapped around her, especially something warm that was Gabe's. It was all of a piece with being rescued, she thought. At least Gabe didn't rescue like Budge did, expecting a lifetime of grateful service in return. With Gabe, it was more all in a day's work. She could live with that.

She went into his office and said, "Okay, I've been thinking."

He was sitting behind his desk, looking tired, staring into space as if in deep thought, and she took the seat across from him while Marlene found a sunny spot on the rug and stretched out.

"You were right," she said. "About me being here seven months and you being here a lifetime. I didn't contribute one thing last night, didn't even leave a trail of bread crumbs—"

"What the hell are you talking about?" he said, frowning as he focused on her. "You were locked in a freezer."

"That equality thing," Nell said. "I want it so I won't get left with nothing again. But I haven't earned it. My seven months is a drop in the bucket compared with what you know. It's okay. We don't need to get married to work together. I can wait until I've learned more."

"You think too damn much," Gabe said. "I saw Trevor this morning."

"I do not think too damn much," Nell said, annoyed at being dismissed. "I'm *capitulating* here, you dumbass."

"My dad wrote a letter in 1982," Gabe went on as if she hadn't said anything. "One of those in-the-event-of-my-death things. He confessed to helping Trevor cover up Helena's murder."

"Oh," Nell said, momentarily sidetracked. "In 1982."

"Yeah. The same year my mom died, and Lu was born, and his heart started giving him trouble. I think he . . ." Gabe shook his head. "Oh, hell, I don't have a clue what he was thinking. I want to believe he was finally trying to do the right thing. In the letter, he said he was going to the police, but first he was going to tell Trevor and Stewart what he was going to do, so they'd be prepared. He also said he was going to tell them that he'd written the letter, to protect himself."

"And then he died of a heart attack," Nell said.

"And then Stewart locked him in the freezer," Gabe said, "and waited until he was dead, and put him in his bed upstairs, and we never knew the difference. The doctor signed the death certificate without an autopsy."

Nell felt her breath go. "How—"

"Trevor told me," Gabe said. "About an hour ago. The police found the letter in the files and took it to him this morning. They also found Stewart thawing in the trunk of his Mercedes. He's trying to explain everything away by blaming it on everybody else: Stewart killed my dad, Margie killed Stewart, Jack killed Lynnie and burned your apartment, and Trevor's just trying to keep the scandal quiet so the family won't suffer."

All that death, Nell thought, all because Trevor didn't want to be married anymore. Helena, getting ready to kill herself because she didn't know who she was if she wasn't married. Margie, hating Stewart but sticking because they were married, and fifteen years later, smacking him with a pitcher because she couldn't stand being married. Lynnie, marinating in resentment because Stewart hadn't kept his promise to come back so they could get married. She and Tim, mutilating each other because they were stuck together, married. Jack imprisoning Suze and Suze not even trying to escape for fourteen years because they were married. *It should be harder to get married*, she thought. You should have to take tests, get a learner's permit, you should need more than a pulse and twenty bucks to get a license.

"You wouldn't believe some of the explanations he's been giving," Gabe said.

"How much do you believe?"

"I believe Stewart killed my dad. Margie didn't kill Stewart, though. When the coroner unwrapped him, his fingernails were torn. Trevor put him in the freezer alive and then went back and wrapped him up and buried him under his own grilled porterhouse when he was dead. I think he did it on purpose. I think it was payback for my dad."

"Eleven years later," Nell said. "Trevor waited a long time for that revenge."

"It's what he's good at," Gabe said. "I think he killed Lynnie, too. I think she pushed him too far and he hit her and put her in the freezer and then waited to see if anybody would find her. I think he tried to frame Jack for the fire in your apartment. And I know he tried to kill you."

Nell thought of being helpless in that freezer again. "How's he explaining that one?"

"Accident. He didn't realize you were still in the freezer when he shut the door."

"You are kidding me."

"Well, he has a concussion. Also, nobody ever crosses him. He's been getting away with murder for years. Nobody's ever made him accountable." Gabe met her eyes. "He didn't have anybody like you."

"I missed a step there," Nell said.

"I've been thinking," Gabe said. "That letter got lost because my aunt was such a lousy secretary. If my mom had been here, she'd have turned the letter over to the cops as soon as my dad died. There'd have been an autopsy. Stewart would have gone to jail, so Margie wouldn't have stayed married to him for fifteen years and then hit him with a pitcher, and Trevor wouldn't have frozen him to death. Or Lynnie. Or burned your place and tried to kill you. Or wrecked my car." He sounded most bitter about the last one.

"Not just a secretary," Nell said.

"And the reason she wasn't here," Gabe said, "is because she and my dad had fought over what he was doing, over the car, over his not telling her what was going on. If he'd come clean to her in 1978 when Helena died, if he'd listened to her, Stewart wouldn't have been around to kill him four years later."

"If you weren't so controlling," Nell said, "you wouldn't have called to make sure I'd locked everything up. You wouldn't have rescued me. I'd be dead. You can play the 'if' game forever. It's the past. Let it go."

"You're not listening." Gabe got up and came around to face her, bending over her to put his face close to hers, his hands on the arms of her chair. "It doesn't matter, seven months or twenty years, that doesn't mean a damn thing. We're not equal partners. We're never going to be. We balance each other. We keep each other in check. We're *necessary to each other's survival*."

"Oh," Nell said.

"We can get married," Gabe said. "I get it now. No resentment. I need this, too. I don't want to be my dad."

"You're not your dad," Nell said, outraged that he'd think he was.

"Good." Gabe straightened. "We need an office manager. Riley's out on a background check, and Suze went to give Becca the good news. If you want the job, it's yours."

"I want the job," Nell said, and remembered the last time she'd said it, in a gloomy office with the blinds pulled down, thinking he was the devil. She looked around the spotless office at the restored leather furniture and gleaming wood, at Marlene basking trenchcoat-less in the sun, at Gabe, looking as tired as he had then but different now.

Happier, she thought. *Because of me.* "What good news?"

"Oh. Becca's guy was telling the truth. Suze ran the check yesterday. Becca will be vacationing at Hyannis Port."

"You're kidding," Nell said. "Well, good. Somebody deserves a happy ending."

"*Hey*," Gabe said.

"Besides me," Nell said. "And you. And Suze and Riley."

"That one remains to be seen."

"You're such a cynic." Nell looked around the room again and thought, *The rest of my life.* "I, on the other hand, am an optimist. I've decided it's a good thing Trevor burned my china."

Gabe looked taken aback. "You have. And that would be because . . ."

"It was my past," Nell said. "And you have to let go of your past to make a future. Same way with your car. Trevor did you a favor by destroying it, it was a bad memory. Now you can forget it and go on."

"I *liked* that car," Gabe said, sounding a lot more exasperated than the situation deserved.

"I liked my china, too," Nell said, equally exasperated since once again he wasn't getting the point. "But it's good that it's gone." She frowned at Gabe. "You have to stop mourning that car."

"I'm over the car," he said, "but I just dropped seven grand on a wedding present you don't want. You have to keep me in the loop on this stuff."

"Wedding present?" Nell said, and Gabe sighed and pointed to a large cardboard box next to his desk.

"UPS just delivered it. Welcome to the past."

She sat on the floor and opened it to see a lot of bubble-wrapped china, and when she unwrapped the first piece, it was her Secrets sugar bowl. "You bought it back," she said and her breath went. "You bought my china back."

He sat on the edge of the desk beside her. "So the past is okay?"

She ran her fingers over the flat side of the bowl, over the two houses sitting close together, looking down over the hill at the river running blue and free. "This isn't the past," she said, knowing that every time she looked at it, she'd remember Gabe had rescued it for her, had been there when she'd needed him. "This is you." She looked at the houses again, balancing each other at the top of the hill, the smoke streaming from their chimneys side by side toward the sky. "This is us."

"Good," Gabe said. "Because I don't think the guy is going to take it back." His voice was light, but when she looked up at him, his eyes were dark and sure.

"I love you," she said.

"I love you, too," he said. "Let's make it legal."

He sat there in the sunlight, the devil made flesh, tempting her into an eternity of heat and light. *Marriage is a gamble and a snare and an invitation to pain*, she thought. *It's compromise and sacrifice, and I'll be stuck forever with this man and his damn ugly window.*

Gabe smiled at her and made her heart clutch. "Chicken."

"Not me," Nell said. "I'm getting married."

Bet Me

Once upon a time, Minerva Dobbs thought as she stood in the middle of a loud yuppie bar, *the world was full of good men*. She looked into the handsome face of the man she'd planned on taking to her sister's wedding and thought, *Those days are gone*.

"This relationship is not working for me," David said.

I could shove this swizzle stick through his heart, Min thought. She wouldn't do it, of course. The stick was plastic and not nearly pointed enough on the end. Also, people didn't do things like that in southern Ohio. A sawed-off shotgun, that was the ticket.

"And we both know why," David went on.

He probably didn't even know he was mad; he probably thought he was being calm and adult. *At least I know I'm furious*, Min thought. She let her anger settle around her, and it made her warm all over, which was more than David had ever done.

Across the room, somebody at the big roulette wheel–shaped bar rang a bell. Another point against David: He was dumping her in a theme bar. The Long Shot. The name alone should have tipped her off.

"I'm sorry, Min," David said, clearly not.

Min crossed her arms over her gray-checked suit jacket so she couldn't smack him. "This is because I won't go home with you tonight? It's Wednesday. I have to work tomorrow. You have to work tomorrow. I paid for my own drink."

"It's not that." David looked noble and wounded as only the tall, dark, and self-righteous could. "You're not making any effort to make our relationship work, which means . . ."

Which means we've been dating for two months and I still won't sleep with you. Min tuned him out and looked around at the babbling crowd. *If I had an untraceable poison, I could drop it in his drink now and not one of these suits would notice.*

". . . and I do think, if we have any future, that you should contribute, too," David said.

Oh, I don't, Min thought, which meant that David had a point. Still, lack of sex was no excuse for dumping her three weeks before she had to wear a maid-of-honor dress that made her look like a fat, demented shepherdess. "Of course we have a future, David," she said, trying to put her anger on ice. "We have *plans.* Diana is getting married in three weeks. You're invited to the wedding. To the rehearsal dinner. To the *bachelor party.* You're going to miss the *stripper,* David."

"Is that all you think of me?" David's voice went up. "I'm just a date to your sister's wedding?"

"Of course not," Min said. "Just as I'm sure I'm more to you than somebody to sleep with."

David opened his mouth and closed it again. "Well, of course. I don't want you to think this is a reflection on you. You're intelligent, you're successful, you're mature. . . ."

Min listened, knowing that *You're beautiful, you're thin* were not coming. If only he'd have a heart attack. Only four percent of heart attacks in men happened before forty, but it could happen. And if he died, not even her mother could expect her to bring him to the wedding.

". . . and you'd make a wonderful mother," David finished up.

"Thank you," Min said. "That's so not romantic."

"I thought we were going places, Min," David said.

"Yeah," Min said, looking around the gaudy bar. "Like here."

David sighed and took her hand. "I wish you the best, Min. Let's keep in touch."

Min took her hand back. "You're not feeling any pain in your left arm, are you?"

"No," David said, frowning at her.

"Pity," Min said, and went back to her friends, who were watching them from the far end of the room.

"He was looking even more uptight than usual," Liza said, looking even taller and hotter than usual as she leaned on the jukebox, her hair flaming under the lights.

David wouldn't have treated Liza so callously. He'd have been afraid to; she'd have dismembered him. *Gotta be more like Liza*, Min thought and started to flip through the song cards on the box.

"Are you upset with him?" Bonnie said from Min's other side, her blond head tilted up in concern. David wouldn't have left Bonnie, either. Nobody was mean to sweet, little Bonnie.

"Yes. He dumped me." Min stopped flipping. Wonder of wonders, the box had Elvis. Immediately, the bar seemed a better place. She fed in coins and then punched the keys for "Hound Dog." Too bad Elvis had never recorded one called "Dickhead."

"I knew I didn't like him," Bonnie said.

Min went over to the roulette bar and smiled tightly at the slender bartender dressed like a croupier. She had beautiful long, soft, kinky brown hair, and Min thought, *That's another reason I couldn't have slept with David*. Her hair always frizzed when she let it down, and he was the type who would have noticed.

"Rum and Coke, please," she told the bartender.

Maybe that was why Liza and Bonnie never had man trouble: great hair. She looked at Liza, racehorse-thin in purple zippered leather, shaking her head at David with naked contempt. Okay, it wasn't just the hair. If she jammed herself into Liza's dress, she'd look like Barney's slut cousin. "*Diet* Coke," she told the bartender.

"He wasn't the one," Bonnie said from below Min's shoulder, her hands on her tiny hips.

"Diet rum, too," Min told the bartender, who smiled at her and went to get her drink.

Liza frowned. "Why were you dating him anyway?"

"Because I thought he might be the one," Min said, exasperated. "He was intelligent and successful and very nice at first. He seemed like a sensible choice. And then all of a sudden he went snotty on me."

Bonnie patted Min's arm. "It's a good thing he broke up with you because now you're free for when the right man finds you. Your prince is on his way."

"Right," Min said. "I'm sure he was on his way but a truck hit him."

"That's not how it works." Bonnie leaned on the bar, looking like an R-rated pixie. "If it's meant to be, he'll make it. No matter how many things go wrong, he'll come to you and you'll be together forever."

"What is this?" Liza said, looking at her in disbelief. "Barbie's Field of Dreams?"

"That's sweet, Bonnie," Min said. "But as far as I'm concerned, the last good man died when Elvis went."

"Maybe we should rethink keeping Bon as our broker," Liza said to Min. "We could be major stockholders in the Magic Kingdom by now."

Min tapped her fingers on the bar, trying to vent some tension. "I should have known David was a mistake when I couldn't bring myself to sleep with him. We were on our third date, and the waiter brought the dessert menu, and David said, 'No, thank you, we're on a diet,' and of course, he isn't because there's not an ounce of fat on him, and I thought, 'I'm not taking off my clothes with you' and I paid my half of the check and went home early. And after that, whenever he made his move, I thought of the waiter and crossed my legs."

"He wasn't the one," Bonnie said with conviction.

"You *think?*" Min said, and Bonnie looked wounded. Min closed her eyes. "Sorry. Sorry. *Really* sorry. It's just not a good time for that stuff, Bon. I'm mad. I want to savage somebody, not look to the horizon for the next jerk who's coming my way."

"Sure," Bonnie said. "I understand."

Liza shook her head at Min. "Look, you didn't care

about David, so you haven't lost anything except a date to Di's wedding. And I vote we skip the wedding. It has 'disaster' written all over it, even without the fact that she's marrying her best friend's boyfriend."

"Her best friend's *ex*-boyfriend. And I *can't* skip it. I'm the maid of honor." Min gritted her teeth. "It's going to be hell. It's not just that I'm dateless, which fulfills every prophecy my mother has ever made, it's that she's crazy about David."

"We *know*," Bonnie said.

"She tells everybody about David," Min said, thinking of her mother's avid little face. "Dating David is the only thing I've done that she's liked about me since I got the flu freshman year and lost ten pounds. And now I have no David." She took her diet rum from the bartender, said, "Thank you," and tipped her lavishly. There wasn't enough gratitude in the world for a server who kept the drinks coming at a time like this. "Most of the time it doesn't matter what my mother thinks of me because I can avoid her, but for the wedding? No."

"So you'll find another date," Bonnie said.

"No, she won't," Liza said.

"Oh, *thank you*," Min said, turning away from the overdesigned bar. The roulette pattern was making her dizzy. Or maybe that was the rage.

"Well, it's your own fault," Liza said. "If you'd quit assigning statistical probability to the fate of a union with every guy you meet and just go out with somebody who turns you on, you might have a good time now and then."

"I'd be a puddle of damaged ego," Min said. "There's nothing wrong with dating sensibly. That's how I found David." Too late, she realized that wasn't evidence in her favor and knocked back some of her drink to ward off comments.

Liza wasn't listening. "We'll have to find a guy for you." She began to scan the bar, which was only fair since most of the bar had been scanning her. "Not him. Not him. Not him. Nope. Nope. Nope. All these guys would try to sell you mutual funds." Then she straightened. "Hello. We have a winner."

Bonnie followed her eyes. "Who? Where?"

"The dark-haired guy in the navy blue suit. In the middle on the landing up by the door."

"Middle?" Min squinted at the raised landing at the entry to the bar. It was wide enough for a row of faux poker tables, and four men were at one talking to a brunette in red. One of the four was David, now surveying his domain over the dice-studded wrought-iron rail. The landing was only about five feet higher than the rest of the room, but David contrived to make it look like a balcony. It was probably requiring all his self-control to keep from doing the Queen Elizabeth Wave. "That's David," Min said, turning away. "And some brunette. Good Lord, he's dating somebody else already." *Get out now*, she told the brunette silently.

"Forget the brunette," Liza said. "Look at the guy in the middle. Wait a minute, he'll turn back this way again. He doesn't seem to be finding David that interesting."

Min squinted back at the entry again. The navy suit was taller than David, and his hair was darker and thicker, but otherwise, from behind, he was pretty much David II. "I did that movie," Min said, and then he turned.

Dark eyes, strong cheekbones, classic chin, broad shoulders, chiseled everything, and all of it at ease as he stared out over the bar, ignoring David, who suddenly looked a little inbred.

Min sucked in her breath as every cell she had came alive and whispered, *This one*.

Then she turned away before anybody caught her slackjawed with admiration. He was not the one, that was her DNA talking, looking for a high-class sperm donor. Every woman in the room with a working ovary probably looked at him and thought, *This one*. Well, biology was not destiny. The amount of damage somebody that beautiful could do to a woman like her was too much to contemplate. She took another drink to cushion the thought, and said, "He's pretty."

"No," Liza said. "That's the point. He's *not* pretty. David is pretty. That guy looks like an adult."

"Okay, he's full of testosterone," Min said.

"No, that's the guy on his right," Liza said. "The one with the head like a bullet. I bet that one talks sports and slaps people on the back. The navy suit looks civilized with edge. Tell her, Bonnie."

"I don't think so," Bonnie said, her pixie face looking grim. "I know him."

"In the biblical sense?" Liza said.

"No. He dated my cousin Wendy. But—"

"Then he's fair game," Liza said.

"—he's a hit and run player," Bonnie finished. "From what Wendy said, he dazzles whoever he's with for a couple of months and then drops her and moves on. And she never sees it coming."

"The beast," Liza said without heat. "You know, men are allowed to leave women they're dating."

"Well, he makes them love him and then he leaves them," Bonnie said. "That is beastly."

"Like David," Min said, her instinctive distrust of the navy suit confirmed.

Liza snorted. "Oh, like you ever loved David."

"*I was trying to,*" Min snapped.

Liza shook her head. "Okay, none of this matters. All you want is a date to the wedding. If it takes the beast a couple of months to dump you, you're covered. So just go over there—"

"No." Min turned her back on everybody to concentrate on the black and white posters over the bar: Paul Newman shooting pool in *The Hustler*, Marlon Brando throwing dice in *Guys and Dolls*, W. C. Fields scowling over his cards in *My Little Chickadee*. Where were all the women gamblers? It wasn't as if being a woman wasn't a huge risk all by itself. Twenty-eight percent of female homicide victims were killed by husbands or lovers.

Which, come to think of it, was probably why there weren't any women gamblers. Living with men was enough of a gamble. She fought the urge to turn around and look

at the beast on the landing again. Really, the smart thing
to do was stop dating and get a cat.

"You know she won't go talk to him," Bonnie was saying
to Liza. "Statistically speaking, the probable outcome is not
favorable."

"Screw that." Liza nudged Min and sloshed the Coke in
her glass. "Imagine your mother if you brought that to the
wedding. She might even let you eat carbs." She looked at
Bonnie. "What's his name?"

"Calvin Morrisey," Bonnie said. "Wendy was buying
wedding magazines when he left her. She was writing
'Wendy Sue Morrisey' on scrap paper."

Liza looked appalled. "That's probably why he left."

"Calvin Morrisey." Against her better judgment, Min
turned back to watch him again.

"Go over there," Liza said, prodding her with one long
fingernail, "and tell David you hope his rash clears up soon.
Then introduce yourself to the beast, smile, and don't talk
statistics."

"That would be shallow," Min said. "I'm thirty-three.
I'm mature. I don't care if I have a date to my sister's wedding. I'm a better person than that." She thought about her
mother's face when she got the news that David was history. *No, I'm not.*

"No, you're not," Liza said. "You're just too chicken to
cross the room."

"I suppose it might work." Bonnie frowned across the
room. "And you can dump him after the wedding and give
him a taste of his own medicine."

"Yeah, that's the ticket." Liza rolled her eyes. "Do it for
Wendy and the rest of the girls."

He was in profile now, talking to David. *The man should
be on coins*, Min thought. Of course, looking that beautiful,
he probably never dated the terminally chubby. At least,
not without sneering. And she'd been sneered at enough
for one night.

"No," Min said and turned back to the bar. Really, a cat
was a good idea.

"Look, Stats," Liza said, exasperated, "I know you're

conservative, but you're damn near solidifying lately. Dating David must have been like dating concrete. And then there's your apartment. Even your furniture is stagnant."

"My furniture is my grandmother's," Min said stiffly.

"Exactly. Your butt's been on it since you were born. You need a change. And if you don't make that change on your own, *I will have to help you.*"

Min's blood ran cold. *"No."*

"Don't threaten her," Bonnie said to Liza. "She'll change, she'll grow. Won't you, Min?"

Min looked back at the landing, and suddenly going over there seemed like a good idea. She could stand under that ugly wrought-iron railing and eavesdrop, and then if Calvin Morrisey sounded even remotely nice—ha, what were the chances?—she could go up and say something sweet to David and get an intro, and Liza would not have movers come in while she was at work and throw out her furniture.

"Don't make me do this for you," Liza said.

Standing at a roulette wheel bar sulking wasn't doing anything for her. And with all she knew ahead of time, it wasn't likely that he could inflict much damage. Min squared her shoulders and took a deep breath. "I'm going in, coach."

"Do not say 'percent' at any time for the rest of the night," Liza said, and Min straightened her gray-checked jacket and said a short prayer that she'd think of a great pick-up line before she got to the landing and made a fool of herself. In which case, she'd just spit on the beast, push David over the railing, and go get that cat.

"Just so there's a plan," she said to herself and started across the floor.

Up on the landing, Cal Morrisey was thinking seriously about pushing David Fisk over the railing. *I should have moved faster when I saw them coming,* he thought. It was Tony's fault.

"You know, that redhead has great legs," Tony had said.

"See her? At the bar, in the purple with the zippers? You suppose she likes football players?"

"You haven't played football in fifteen years." Cal had sipped his drink, easing into an alcohol-tinged peace that was broken only slightly when somebody with no taste in music played "Hound Dog." As far as he was concerned the only two drawbacks to the place were the stupid décor and the fact that Elvis Presley was on the jukebox.

"All right, it's been a while since I played, but she doesn't know that." Tony looked back at the redhead. "I got ten bucks says she'll leave with me. I'll use my chaos theory line."

"No bet," Cal said. "Although that is a terrible line, so that would shorten the odds." He squinted across the room to the roulette wheel bar. The redhead was flashy, which meant she was Tony's type. There was a little blonde there, too, the perky kind, their friend Roger's dream date. Behind the bar, Shanna saw him watching and waved, but she didn't smile, and Cal wondered what was up as he nodded to her.

Tony put his arm around Cal. "Help me out here, she's in a group. You go over and pick up her chubby friend in the gray-checked suit, and Roger can hit on the short blonde. I'd give you the short blonde, but you know Roger and midget women."

Roger jerked to attention at Cal's elbow. "What? What short blonde?" He peered across the room at the bar. "Oh. *Oh.*"

"Suit?" Cal looked back at the bar.

"The one in gray." Tony nodded toward the bar. "Between the redhead and the mini-blonde. She's hard to see because the redhead sort of dazzles you. I bet you—"

"Oh." Cal squinted to see the medium-height woman between the redhead and the blonde. She was dressed in a dull, boxy, gray-checked suit, and her round face scowled under brown hair yanked back into a knot on the top of her head. "Nope," he said and took another drink.

Tony smacked him on the back and made him choke. "Come on, live a little. Don't tell me you're still pining for Cynthie."

"I never pined for Cynthie." Cal glanced around the crowd. "Keep an eye out for her, will you? She's in that red thing she wears when she's trying to get something."

"She can get it from me," Tony said.

"Great." Cal's voice was fervent. "I'll even go pick up that suit if you'll marry Cyn."

Tony choked on his drink. "Marry?"

"Yes," Cal said. "She wants to get married. Surprised the hell out of me." He thought for a moment of Cynthie, a sweetheart with a spine of steel. "I don't know where she got the idea we were that close."

"There she is." Roger was looking over Cal's shoulder. "She's coming up the stairs now."

Cal got up and tried to move past Tony to the door. "Out of my way."

Tony stayed in his chair. "You can't leave, I want the redhead."

"So go get her," Cal said, trying to get around him.

"Cynthie's got David with her," Roger said, and there was great sympathy in his voice.

"Cal!" David's voice grated over Cal's shoulder. "Just who we were looking for." He sounded mad as hell, but when Cal turned, David was smiling.

Trouble, Cal thought and smiled back with equal insincerity. "David. Cynthie. Great to see you."

"Hello, Cal." Cynthie smiled up at him, her heart-shaped face lethally lovely. "How've you been?"

"Great. Couldn't be better. You, too, looking great." Cal looked past her to David, and thought, *Take her, please.* "You're a lucky man, David."

"I am?"

"Dating Cynthie," Cal said, putting all the encouragement he could into his voice.

Cynthie took David's arm. "We just ran into each other." She turned her shoulder to Cal and glowed up at David. "But it is nice seeing him again." Her eyes slid back to Cal's face, and he smiled past her ear again, radiating no jealousy at all as hard as he could.

David looked down into her beautiful face and blinked,

and Cal felt a stab of sympathy for him. Cynthie was enchanting up close. And from far away. From everywhere, really, which was how he'd ended up saying yes to her all the time. Cal glanced at her impeccably tight little body in her impeccably tight little red dress and then took a step back as he jerked his eyes away, reminding himself of how peaceful life was without her. Distance, that was the key. Maybe a cross and some garlic, too.

"Of course," David was saying. "Maybe we can do dinner later." He glanced at Cal, looking triumphant.

"Well, don't let us keep you." Cal took another step back and bumped into the railing.

Cynthie let go of David's arm, her glow diminished. "I'll just freshen up before we go." Tony and David watched as her perfect rear end swung away from them, while Roger ignored her to peer across the room at the pixie blonde, and Cal took another healthy swallow of his drink and wished he were somewhere else. Anywhere else. Dinner, for example. Maybe he'd stop by Emilio's and eat in the kitchen. There were no women in Emilio's kitchen.

"So, David," Tony was saying. "How'd our seminar work out for you?"

"It was terrific," David said. "I didn't think anybody could teach some of those morons that new program, but everybody at the firm is now up to speed. We've even . . ."

He went on and Cal nodded, thinking that one of the many reasons he didn't like David was his tendency to refer to his employees as morons. Still, David paid his bills on time and gave credit where it was due; there were much worse clients. And if he took over Cynthie, Cal was prepared to feel downright warm toward him.

David wound down on whatever it was he'd been saying and looked toward the stairs. "About Cynthie. I thought that you and she—"

"No." Cal shook his head with enthusiasm. "She left me a couple of months ago."

"Isn't it usually the other way around?"

David arched an eyebrow and looked ridiculous. And still

women went out with him. Life was a mystery. So were women.

"Aren't you supposed to be the guy who never strikes out?" David said.

"No," Cal said.

"He's losing his edge," Tony said. "I found an easy pickup for him, and he said no."

"Which one?" David said.

"The gray-checked suit at the bar." Tony motioned with his glass, and David looked at the bar and then turned back to Cal, smooth as ever.

"Maybe you *are* losing it." David smiled at him. "She shouldn't be that hard to get. It's not like she's a Cynthie."

"She's all right," Cal said, cautiously.

David leaned in. "After all, nobody says no to you, right?"

"What?" Cal said.

"I'm willing to bet you that you can't get her," David said. "A hundred bucks says you can't nail her."

Cal pulled back. "*What?*"

David laughed, but there was an edge to his voice when he spoke. "It's just a bet, Cal. You guys love risk, I've seen you bet on damn near everything. This isn't even that big a bet. We should make it two hundred."

That was when Cal had contemplated giving David a healthy push. Tony turned his back to David and mouthed, *Humor him,* and Cal sighed. There must be something he could ask for that would make David back down. "That baseball in your office," he said. "The one in the case."

"My Pete Rose baseball?" David's voice went up an octave.

"Yeah, that one. That's my price." Cal slugged back the rest of his scotch and looked around for a waitress.

David shook his head. "Not a chance. My dad caught that pop-up for me in seventy-five. But I like your style, upping the stakes like that." He leaned in closer. "Tell you what. The last refresher seminar you ran for us set me back ten grand. I'll bet you ten thousand in cash against a free seminar—"

Cal forced a smile. "David, I was kidding—"

"But for ten thou, you have to get her into bed. I'll play fair. I'll give you a month to get her out of that gray-checked suit."

"Piece of cake," Tony said.

Cal glared at Tony. "David, this isn't my kind of bet."

"It's *my* kind," David said, drawing his brows together, and Cal thought, *Hell, he's going to push this, and we need his business.*

Okay, clearly booze had shut down David's brain. But once it was back up and working again, David would back down on the ten thousand, that was insane, and David was never insane about money. So all he had to do was stall until David sobered up and then pretend the whole thing never happened. He stole a glance across the room to the bar and was delighted to see that the gray suit had disappeared sometime during their conversation.

Cal turned back to David and said, "Well, I would, David, but she's gone." *And God bless you, gray suit, for leaving,* he thought and picked up his drink again.

Things were finally going his way.

Min had walked across the room, telling herself that it was a real toss-up as to which would be worse, trying to talk to this guy or enduring Di's wedding unescorted. When she neared the landing, she edged her way under the rail, catching faint snatches of conversations as she went, not stopping until she heard David's voice faintly above her, saying, "But for ten, though, you have to get her into bed."

What? Min thought. It was noisy up there by the door, maybe she hadn't heard him—

"I'll play fair," David went on. "I'll give you a month to get her out of that gray-checked suit."

Min looked down at her gray-checked suit.

"Piece of cake," somebody said to David, and Min thought, *Son of a* bitch, *the world is full of sex-crazed bastards,* and forced herself to move on before she climbed the railing and killed them both.

She headed back to Liza and Bonnie, fuming. She knew exactly what David was up to. He assumed she wouldn't sleep with anybody because she'd turned him down. She'd warned him about that, about the rash assumptions he made, but instead of taking her advice, he'd kept asking her out.

Because he thought I was a sure thing, she realized. Because he'd looked at her and thought, *Overweight smart woman who'll never cheat on me and will be grateful I sleep with her.* "Bastard," she said out loud. She should have sex with Calvin Morrisey just to pay David back. But then she'd have no way of getting even with Calvin Morrisey. God, she was dumb. Fat and dumb, there was a winning combo.

"What's wrong?" Liza said when she was back at the bar. "Did you ask him?"

"No. As soon as you finish your drinks, I'm ready to go." Min turned back to the balcony and caught sight of them, just as they caught sight of her.

David's face was smug, but Calvin Morrisey clutched his drink and looked like he'd just seen Death.

"There she is," David crowed. "I told you she'd be back. Go get her, champ."

"Uh, David," Cal began, consigning the gray-checked suit to the lowest circle of hell.

"A bet's a bet."

Cal put his empty glass down on the rail and thought fast. The suit did not look happy, so the odds weren't impossible that she'd go for a chance to get out of the bar if he offered dinner. "Look, David, sex is not in the cards. I'm cheap, but I'm not slimy. You want to bet ten bucks on a pickup, fine, but that's it. Nothing with a future."

David shook his head. "Oh, no, I'll bet on the pickup, too, ten bucks if you leave with her. But the ten thousand is still on. If you *lose* . . ." He smiled at Cal, drawing out the 'lose,' "you do a seminar for me for free."

"David, I can't make that bet," Cal said, trying another tack. "I have two partners who—"

"I'm good for it," Tony said. "Cal never misses."

Cal glared at him. "Well, *Roger* isn't good for it."

"Hey, Roger, you in?" Tony said, and Roger said, "Sure," without looking away from the blonde at the bar.

"*Roger*," Cal said.

"She's the prettiest little thing I've ever seen," Roger said.

"Roger, you just bet that I could get a woman into bed," Cal said with great patience. "Now tell David you don't want to bet a ten-thousand-dollar refresher seminar on sex."

"What?" Roger said, finally looking away from the blonde.

"I said—" Cal began.

"Why would you bet on something like that?" Roger said.

"That's not the question," Tony said. "The question is, can he do it?"

"Sure," Roger said. "But—"

"Then we have a bet," David said.

"No, we do not," Cal said.

"You don't think you can do it," David said. "You're losing it."

"This is not about me," Cal said, and then Cynthie slid back into the group and put her hand on his arm. She leaned into him, and he felt his blood heat right on cue.

"She's over there waiting for you," David said, an edge in his voice.

"She?" Cynthie's glow dimmed. "Are you seeing somebody?"

Oh, hell, Cal thought.

"Cal?" David said.

"Cal?" Cynthie said.

"I *love* this," Tony said.

"What?" Roger said.

Cal sighed. It was the suit or Cynthie, the rock or the soft place who wanted to get married. He detached her hand from his arm. "Yes, I'm seeing somebody. Excuse me."

He pushed past Cynthie and David and headed for the bar, wishing them both the worst fate he could think of, that they'd end up together.

Min watched Calvin Morrisey move toward the stairs. The beast. He thought that he could get her in a month, that she was so pathetic she'd just—

Her brain caught up with her train of thought, and she straightened.

"Will you tell us what's wrong?" Liza said.

"A month," Min said.

He walked down the steps and made his way through the crowd, ignoring the come-hither looks of the women he passed.

He was coming to pick her up.

Suppose she let him.

Suppose for the next three weeks she made him pay by stringing him along and then took him to Di's wedding. He wouldn't leave her; he had to stick for a month to win his damn bet. All she had to do was say no to sex for three weeks, drag him to her sister's wedding, and then leave his ass cold.

Min settled back against the bar and examined the idea from all sides. He more than deserved to be tortured for three weeks. And in that three weeks she could figure out a way to make David suffer, too. And her mother would have somebody beautiful to point out to people at the wedding as her date. It was a plan, and as far as she could see, it was all good.

The bartender came back and Min said, "Rum and Diet Coke, please. A double."

"That's your third," Liza said. "And fourth. The aspartame alone will make you insane. What are you doing?"

"Was he mean to you?" Bonnie said. "What happened?"

"I didn't talk to him." Min waved them away. "Move down the bar a couple of feet, will you? I'm about to get hit on and you're cramping my style."

"We missed something," Liza said to Bonnie.

"Move," Bonnie said, and pushed Liza down the bar.

Min turned away when the bartender brought her drink, so when The Beast spoke from beside her, she jerked her head up and caught the full force of him unprepared: hot dark eyes, perfect cheekbones, and a mouth a woman would betray her moral fiber to bite into. Her heart kicked up into her throat, and she swallowed hard to get it back where it belonged.

"I have a problem," he said, and his voice was low and smooth, warm enough to be charming, rich enough to clog arteries.

Dark chocolate, Min thought and looked at him blankly, keeping her breathing slow. "Problem?"

"Well, usually my line is 'Can I buy you a drink?' but you have one." He smiled at her, radiating testosterone through his expensive suit.

"Well, that is a problem." She started to turn away.

"So what I thought," he said, his voice dropping even lower as he leaned closer to her and made her heart pound, "was that we could go somewhere else, and I could buy you dinner."

The closer he got, the better he looked. He was the used car salesman of seducers, Min decided, trying to get her distance back. You could never get a good deal from a used car salesman; they sold cars all the time and you only bought a couple in a lifetime so they always won. Statistically speaking, you were toast before you walked on the lot. She could only imagine how many women this guy had mutilated in his lifetime. The mind boggled.

His smile had disappeared while he waited for her answer, and he looked vulnerable now, taking a chance on asking her out. He faked vulnerable very well. *Remember*, she told herself, *the son of a bitch is doing this for ten bucks*. Actually, he was trying to do *her* for ten bucks. Cheapskate. Suddenly, breathing normally was not a problem.

"Dinner?" she said.

"Yes." He bent still closer. "Somewhere quiet where we can talk. You look like someone with interesting things to say. And I'm somebody who'd like to hear them."

Min smiled at him. "That's a terrible line. Does it usually work for you?"

He froze for a second, and then he segued from sincere to boyish again. "Well, it has up till now."

"It must be your voice," Min said. "You deliver it beautifully."

"Thank you." He straightened. "Let's try this again." He held out his hand. "I'm Calvin Morrisey, but my friends call me Cal."

"Min Dobbs." She shook his hand and dropped it before it could feel warm in her grasp. "And my friends would call me foolhardy if I left this bar with a stranger."

"Wait." He got out his wallet and pulled out a twenty. "This is cab fare. If I get fresh, you get a cab."

Liza would take the twenty and then dump him. There was a plan, but Liza didn't need a wedding date. What else would Liza do? Min plucked the twenty from his fingers. "If you get fresh, I'll break your nose." She folded the twenty, unbuttoned her top two blouse buttons, and tucked the bill into the V of her sensible cotton bra so that only a thin green edge showed. That was one good thing about packing extra pounds, you got cleavage to burn.

She looked up and caught his eyes looking down, and she waited for him to make some comment, but he smiled again. "Fair enough," he said, "let's go eat," and she reminded herself to ignore what a beautiful mouth he had since it was full of forked tongue.

"First, promise me no more lame lines," she said, and watched his jaw clench.

"Anything you want," he said.

Min shook her head. "Another line. I suppose you can't help it. And free food is always good." She picked up her purse from the bar. "Let's go."

She walked away before he could say anything else, and he followed her, past a dumbfounded Liza and a delighted Bonnie, across the floor and up onto the landing by the door, and the last thing she saw as they left was David looking outraged.

The evening was turning out *much* better than she'd expected.